Taxi to Siberia

KATHERINE KELLY-BRUSS

This is a work of fiction. Names, characters, places and incidents are the product of the author's imagination or are used fictitiously, and any resemblance to actual persons, living or dead, business establishments, events or locales, is entirely coincidental.

DEDICATION

To my dad,
who was by my side
when I caught my first brook trout,
found my first morel mushroom,
wrote my first poem and
hit my first home run.

And to my mom,
who has always supported me,
always forgiven me,
and always welcomed me home.

Part 1
Near Pittsburgh, 1995 - 1997

ONE

I follow the Moskva
Down to Gorky Park
Listening to the wind of change...

The future's in the air
I can feel it everywhere
Blowing with the wind of change...
                    Scorpions, 1991

Naked except for stockings, garter belt, and three-inch heels, I stand before a full-length mirror, sipping California burgundy. Mentally transforming my reflection into a man, I imagine him looking at my body. Letting my hands become his hands, I run them over my stomach and cup my pointed breasts, massaging each nipple between smooth fingers. My nipples harden in response to this imaginary foreplay.

I dab Opium perfume on my neck, between my breasts, and around my mound of pubic hair.

Actually, my tits are too small to really cup—small tits are the price of a lean body—my hips as slim as an adolescent boy in a growth spurt, my waist small but undefined, my stomach only slightly rounded, and my legs as slim and muscular as a dancer's.

One of my beefy co-workers with a butt like two watermelons and a headful of henna is always accusing me of being too skinny. 'You ain't got no ass,' she says. Although she means it as playful criticism, I'm not the least offended. Her comments definitely don't inspire me to go eat a whole gallon of chocolate chip cookie dough ice cream to acquire a butt like hers and mammary glands destined to go south in later years. In truth, I love my body. I don't have a trace of fat anywhere that I don't want it, and my tits will never be able to sag.

I check my stockings, attached with small clips to a garter belt, for runs. They are delicate as a spider web, much thinner than the pantyhose I usually wear to work. Thinking I'll probably snag them on the car door after we arrive, I cram an extra stocking into a small leather clutch purse. I pull on ivory lace panties over the matching garter belt. With their back a mere strip fitting neatly into the crease of my butt, the panties are really meant to be worn underneath, but I can remove them more easily this way. Otherwise I would have to unhook the stockings, causing them to bunch up at my knees, and then struggle to pull my panties over them, which doesn't present a very alluring picture. Besides, according to an article in Cosmopolitan, men enjoy making love to a woman dressed in nothing but stockings, garter belt and high-heeled shoes.

Over my head, I slip a smooth silk dress, its color matching my wine. Its loose bodice disguises my small breasts, and being sleeveless, draws attention to the rippling muscles of my upper arms. Falling just below mid-thigh, it barely conceals the tops of my stockings. I loosely tie a hip sash, subtly disguising my high waist.

After applying lipstick in a color called Red Maple, I rub rouge into my cheeks and then use a small brush to sweep translucent powder onto my nose and forehead. I run a comb through shoulder-length blonde hair and fluff my bangs, fine and feathery as the tail feathers of a chickadee. I'm glad that I bleached it recently—the dark roots have yet to appear. Before leaving the mirror, I stare at my face for a long time, looking for flaws.

I have dark Irish circles under my eyes. My hair is too thin, my jaw too square, my nose like a pygmy, and my cheeks like small apples. But are these really flaws? I convince myself I am gorgeous. Then I take a bottle of Prozac out of the medicine cabinet and pop two pills into my mouth before taking a last swig of wine. If a little serotonin is good, more can only be better.

Although I act like a woman planning to seduce a married oil baron, I am only preparing for a business dinner, not as a paid escort, but as a bilingual sales engineer. I work for a small company near Pittsburgh called Ampere Power Dead Tank. Since I speak the country's language, my job is to travel all over Russia, giving presentations about our equipment and trying to convince the Russian utilities, called Energos, to buy it.

Ampere Power Dead Tank (APDT) produces high voltage circuit breakers. There are two primary types of circuit breakers—live tank, which are under voltage and extremely popular in Europe, and dead tank, which are grounded and preferred in the United States and in Russia. My task is to promote the dead tank design in Russia. These are extremely large pieces of equipment which transport electricity at voltages of up to 550 kV and are used to break the circuit in an emergency. Such massive amounts of current can't be stopped easily. After contact separation, the current is carried through a powerful arc and is interrupted only when this arc is cooled by a gas blast of sufficient intensity. For this reason the heavy metal contacts are pressurized inside of a tank with sulphur hexafluoride, an inert, heavy gas having good dielectric and arc extinguishing properties. I'm not really an expert here—I'm just quoting directly out of the technical manual.

APDT belongs to Ampere Power International, a global leader in power and automation technologies, targeting power utilities and industrial customers. Ampere Power International consists of numerous semi-independent companies operating all over the world with its corporate headquarters in Switzerland. With just 150 employees, APDT is a very small fish—a minnow really—and limits its production to circuit breakers ranging from 38 to 550 Kilovolts, which we ship internationally. That was straight from the marketing manual.

Ampere Power International also has a division in Sweden producing the live tank design. Since they cost less (very important for Russia) and don't have to be shipped as far, the live tank breakers could be a major source of competition for me. During my training, I learned a great deal about both designs, namely the pros of dead tank and the cons of live tank. Of course, if I go into Russia and start badmouthing live tank breakers, I risk angering the Swedes, who are also trying to promote their product in Russia, although up to now without success.

Since the Russians already use the dead tank design, I have the advantage of the status quo. Since live tank breakers are cheaper, the Swedes have a price advantage. Treading carefully, I'll somehow have to convince my customers that live tank circuit breakers are a risk to national security (or something equally serious) and do it in a way that makes the customer believe he has reached the conclusion himself.

Another factory in Switzerland produces gas-insulated substations (GIS), the avant-garde of high voltage technology, but much too expensive for Russia. I doubt they will even try to enter the market.

Even though I have a degree in mechanical engineering, I have the mechanical skills of a basset hound.

It is actually more of a mental block than a real lack of talent. Whenever I start to assemble something, I become incredibly bored. So I debated between graduate school (those who can't do, teach) and going to work in sales (if you can't build it, sell it.). Excelling in theoretical subjects, even taking advanced calculus as an elective, I was tempted to enter a PhD program. It seemed like an easy way to escape from the real world for a few more years, and possibly for a lifetime.

Then this incredible job announcement appeared—mechanical engineer, fluent in Russian—as if somebody had created the position just for me. Although it probably wasn't necessary—it's not like Russian-speaking mechanical engineers are jumping out of the bushes in Wisconsin—I tore the paper off the wall of the career center so that nobody else would see it and stuck it in my pocket. I hadn't been to Russia in eight years and was beginning to think I'd never go back. Until seeing the job announcement, I didn't even want to.

But I've always heard that once you've experienced the great bear called Russia, she will capture your soul forever. I imagine myself dressed in fox fur, trudging through a Siberian snowstorm, surrounded by white birch trees, on the arm of Dr. Zhivago, stopping at a dacha to warm ourselves with shots of vodka and tea from a samovar in front of a blazing fire tended by a wrinkled woman with a flowered shawl on her head and heavy felt boots on her feet, an icon of Jesus hanging in the corner where a single candle burns. And suddenly I wanted this job more than I wanted to breathe.

Not surprisingly, I get the job easily—I'm the only candidate. I almost blow the interview, though, when my checked baggage gets lost on the way to Pittsburgh. Dressed only in leggings and a ragged T-shirt with my Pendleton business suit possibly on its way to Mexico, I wait nervously in my hotel room, chain-smoking, raiding the mini-bar, and trying not to chew my nails, until the garment bag finally arrives at my door shortly before midnight.

I started my job three months ago and have just finished my training, including two weeks of drudgery on the factory floor. Our marketing manager, a portly man in his sixties with no formal education, believes the only way to learn about the equipment is to build it. Until he inflicted this cockamamie notion on me, I had been quite content to study the brochures, memorizing every technical detail of the equipment without ever actually touching it.

So I endure the two weeks assembling current-interrupting units and attaching bushings. I even try to wire a control cabinet. Feigning interest, I ask questions, then ignore the answers—I'd forget them anyway. Ironically I learn the most from a younger woman who drives a Harley. She has hair the color of a midnight sky and a unicorn tattoo on her shoulder. As we assemble a 145 kilovolt interrupter, she explains every detail, not just knowing how the parts fit together, but also knowing why. I almost find it interesting. Almost.

Feeling like a soldier who's just completed basic training, I return two weeks later to the comfort of my office and reading materials, assuring everyone that the experience in the factory has been valuable.

Before I started working for Ampere Power, Vladimir Kashirnikov, the director of Ampere Power Russia, a Moscow sales office opened the previous year by Ampere Power International, arranged a deal with MosEnergieExport, translated as Moscow Energy Export, a major Russian player in the field of power projects construction and the export of electrical power, also headquartered in Moscow. The plan is to install our equipment in a substation in St. Petersburg. Kashirnikov arrived from Moscow two days ago with three of the company representatives to inspect the plant and sign a contract for four 362-kilovolt dead tank circuit breakers, massive machines, each selling for almost $330,000. Transport and installation costs have brought the contract to well over 1.4 million dollars.

Until yesterday, I was acquainted with Dr. Vladimir Kashirnikov only through telephone conversations concerning contract changes and technical requirements. With his deep husky voice and an academic title as my only clues, I pictured a stocky man with greasy hair, rough features, thick-rimmed glasses, mismatched clothing, and who was definitely a chain smoker.

But entering the meeting room yesterday morning, I come face to face with Al Capone. Okay, it isn't really Al Capone. This man is much more attractive—tall with broad shoulders and a domineering posture, a John F. Kennedy haircut, perfect teeth, a double-breasted pinstripe, baggy pleated pants. And an expression that looks like he is perpetually mocking someone. *Catch me if you can. You can't.* Although bearing no real resemblance to Al Capone, he captures the essence of the man and the era of 1920's gangsters. In any case, I wouldn't have minded if he put a gun to my head and took me hostage.

Eyes the color of a summer sky stare straight into mine before wandering over my body. I wonder if he is imagining me naked and wish I had worn something more alluring than a conservative blue suit which makes me look like I belong at a job interview for librarian.

'Katey,' my boss says. 'This is Vladimir Kashirnikov. Vladimir, Katey O'Hara.'

Don't laugh. Please don't laugh. Please don't have seen the movie.

The simple touch of his hand sends currents of desire through my body, causing my knees to quiver and blood to rush to my pelvis. Almost feeling his hands caressing me, I desperately want to press my body against him. Suddenly I have an idea.

'Vladimir, is it you?' I ask, feigning surprise. 'Oh my God, I can't believe it!' I throw myself into his arms, kissing both of his cheeks, as is customary in European countries. His leg pushes against my crotch, just hard enough for me to know it is intentional, and I feel his cock bulging against my thigh. Raising my head to his ear, fighting off an urge to kiss his neck, I whisper in Russian, 'Just play along.'

Quickly aware of my ruse, Vladimir hugs me back, his hand discreetly caressing my butt. Since nobody is behind me, the gesture goes unnoticed. I long to kiss his pale lips, but instead we part, Vladimir turning to my boss.

'We met once in Moscow,' he lies in perfect English, 'It really is a small world.'

My boss, a tall rubbery vegetarian from Pakistan in his late fifties named Anis Nanji, looks at me as if I'm forcing him to eat meat. He is obviously trying to decide whether or not to believe his foreign guest. True, I had spent time in Moscow as a student, but with nine million people, the chances of our having met are remote. At the same time, Anis can't accuse Vladimir of lying. He asks for no further explanation and neither I nor Vladimir offers one. We embraced like lovers. Perhaps Anis will think we are. I don't know if this will be advantageous or not.

It is more than sexual desire that attracts me to Vladimir. Upon seeing him, I instantly recognize a savvy businessman radiating confidence and charisma. I sense that by making him my personal ally, by whatever means necessary, I can ensure my success in the Russian market. And I am going to enjoy the seduction.

We all sit down at a long conference table, Vladimir and the other Russians huddled on one side, with Anis, who is the head of international sales, and I seated on the opposite side like opponents in a group chess match. Although Anis has planned the meeting as a formality to sign a contract, the Russians have other intentions. They have come to negotiate a discount, a request which makes

Anis shrivel up his face like an old man with constipation.

'We've already agreed on a price,' he insists, stuttering slightly. 'It's in the contract. We can't go changing it.'

'We came to negotiate the contract,' says a small man with a mustache, staring at my boss like a cobra preparing to spit. 'That's why we're here.'

My boss can only stare blankly until Vladimir translates the Russian.

'But we've already done that,' Anis insists. 'Everything was decided—'

'We'll give you a 5% discount,' Vladimir says like a referee making a call. I can tell that Anis's ignorance of Russian business practices has prompted Vladimir to resolve an awkward situation quickly. But my main thought is how his lips would feel against mine.

Anis stares at Vladimir like a child who has found nothing but coal in his Christmas stocking. Even though Anis had no intention whatsoever of giving a discount, Vladimir has granted one without consulting him.

'Well now that you've offered this discount,' Anis says, looking away from Vladimir, 'I guess we have to accept it.' He smacks his lips in annoyance.

If the Russians notice my boss's displeasure, they don't let on. They wouldn't have cared anyway—they've gotten their discount. I note that Vladimir and Anis avoid looking at one another.

Later, Vladimir explains to Anis that the Russians expected to negotiate, just for the sake of bargaining. If he had set the initial price higher, he could still have given the same discount, gotten the price he wanted, and both sides would have been happy. He could even have set it 10% higher, still given just a 5% discount, and actually could have come out ahead. This announcement, however, coming much too late, doesn't make Anis particularly happy.

Anis, Vladimir, and the cobra sign the contract, the latter being the vice president of MosEnergieExport.

Since it is Russian custom to christen a new contract with vodka, one of the Russians, a bull of a man with bushy hair and eyes like sapphires, pulls a bottle out of a briefcase. Obviously shocked, but trying not to show it (as I try to hide my pleasure), Anis calls his secretary and asks her to bring shot glasses. Finding none in the office, she brings water glasses which are large enough for the bullish man to slosh a good four ounces into each of them.

Trying to prove that I can hold my ground with the men, I empty my glass in one solid gulp. At first I think I've swallowed kerosene and almost gag before a warmth and calmness fill my throat and face, radiating through my body. My mouth relaxes, and I can't suppress a smile. I enjoy it much more than Anis, a somewhat reformed follower of the Hindu religion and not normally a drinker, who sips his vodka as if it were hot.

Before I can set down my glass, the Russian with the bottle is tilting it again. Partly because I don't want to offend, but more because I'm enjoying the effects of the vodka, I accept a refill. So does Vladimir, clearly faking enthusiasm but still doing a decent job. Anis, however, whose glass is still half full, refuses like a teenager in a Nancy Reagan ad to 'Just say no.' Since he is still sulking about the 5% discount, another drink would have relaxed him. As it is, he's not scoring any points with the Russians, who are completely ignoring him and recognizing Vladimir as the man in charge.

The second shot tastes better than the first. Feeling pleasantly inebriated, I find myself gawking at Vladimir, wanting to touch him again. He keeps glancing my way, smiling subtly enough to remain unnoticed.

The contract signing is the first formality of the delegation's visit, the second being a plant inspection. Showing them a completed specimen of the 362 kV breakers they have just purchased, I can tell they are impressed by the compact design and neat construction. I wonder how it compares to their outdated Soviet models, which are probably products of one of Stalin's five-year-plans. Although it is difficult after so much vodka, I try to memorize every word as Vladimir translates technical details into Russian. It won't be long before I am doing the translating myself and giving technical presentations.

Anis is waiting in his office to take us to lunch. He has thoughtlessly chosen a steakhouse without a liquor license, which must have reminded the Russians of Gorbachev's anti-alcohol campaigns of the 1980's. Although my customers can survive without a drink, they are much happier when they have one, and the lunch is a solemn affair.

'Not even a beer?' one of them asks in Russian.

'Why did we come here?' asks another.

'My boss doesn't drink,' I say. 'He probably didn't even think of it.'

'And why do they put ice cubes in the water? It's so cold I can barely drink it. It hurts my teeth.'

'It tastes like tap water. Is it okay to drink tap water?'

I keep glancing at Vladimir, seated across from me with Anis at his side. They are engaged in conversation. On impulse I slip out of my high-heeled shoe and stretch my stockinged foot under the table until my toes brush against Vladimir's leg. Pretending to read the menu, I sneak my toes under the cuff of his pants and extend them upward until I am touching bare skin. Vladimir doesn't react, but Anis does. He glares at me as if wanting to say something but trying desperately not to.

Oh My God. It's Anis's leg. I quickly snap my foot back under my chair and slide it into my shoe. Not looking at either man, I pick up my fork and spear a cucumber.

After lunch, Anis announces that he will be taking the group to Pittsburgh on a sight-seeing trip before returning them to their hotel. Although our factory is fifty miles from the city, Anis has chosen a hotel near Pittsburgh, located on the premises of a large shopping mall and a short distance from his own home. He doesn't suggest I come along and I don't openly object to staying at the office, figuring Anis has his reasons and wondering if he is deliberately trying to exclude me or even to keep me away from Vladimir. I suspect he caught on to my boggled attempt at flirtation during lunch. I'll have to be more careful next time.

Since I will be traveling to Russia in the near future, I spend the afternoon translating a marketing presentation into Russian, my thoughts constantly returning to Vladimir's blue eyes, his erotic smile, his strong hands and sturdy wrists. Had I known I would be meeting Eros, the primordial god of lust, love, and sex, I certainly would have dressed appropriately. Since I have spent the past ten years dressed mainly in Levis and tank tops, I'm not sure how to transform myself into a sex object, but am determined to find a way.

With this goal in mind, I leave work early bothered by a nagging thought; Vladimir Kashirnikov wears a wedding ring.

TWO

What Turns Men On. Grabbing the book from a shelf in Barnes and Noble, I leaf through the pages, stopping at a chapter titled 'Keeping a Man Through the Power of Sex.'

History has proven many times
That the power of sex is strong enough
To make empires tumble,
To alter the course of lives and nations drastically—
Just think of Anthony and Cleopatra.

If this book could help me tumble an empire, it can certainly break up a marriage. Putting the selection under my arm, I scan the shelf. *What Men Really Want—Straight Talk From Men about Sex.* Turning to a random page, I read, 'Most men complain that they do not get enough fellatio.'

Deciding to buy both books, I take them home and read in bed until long past midnight. I learn how to dress—high heels ('No man ever misses a pair of legs with high-heeled shoes'), skimpy lace undergarments, short skirts, silky dresses that move with the body, ankle bracelets. I learn the importance of perfume—'Perfume is always a turn on.' The alluring effects of makeup—men

13

especially appreciate eye makeup. No pantyhose—men much prefer stockings. Surprisingly big boobs aren't considered particularly important. Men seem to like all boobs, regardless of their size or shape.

By the time I go to bed, I am ready to defend a dissertation on seductiveness. Katey O'Hara, Ph.D. Sex.

The next afternoon following another nonalcoholic lunch in the company cafeteria, Anis suggests I take our visitors to the local mall. Even my boss seems to know that shopping is a favorite activity of Russians visiting the United States. I drive them in a rental minivan which I will later be using to take Vladimir and the customers to Washington DC for a few days of sightseeing and more shopping.

Since Vladimir has stayed at the office with Anis, I am alone with the Russian customers but know exactly where we need to go first. Finding a poorly-lit bar directly in the mall, I lead the three men to a table in the back and order four beers and four shots of vodka.

'Let's drink to our pretty young guide,' toasts the same man who had requested the discount. We clink our vodka glasses together before downing them, followed immediately by a swig of beer.

In this relaxed atmosphere they bombard me with questions about where to buy specific items. All over fifty, these men haven't abandoned the shopping mentality of Soviet Russia when shortages and low quality goods were a way of life. Although the shopping scene in Russia has improved in the past decade, the prices are still much higher than in the West and nothing ever goes on sale. And since American imports are still scarce in Russia, receiving a gift from the United States remains a novelty.

They all have detailed shopping lists, probably dictated by relatives, specifying brand, size and color. Noting a woman's size 50 on one of the lists, I wonder if the mall has a specialty store for obese women.

14

I find a store appropriately called 'More to Love' which carries sizes *for the voluptuous woman* and the three men began boldly sorting through the racks. Assuming they are looking for presents for their wives, I explain the situation to the petite salesgirl, who tries to hide her amusement. The little mustached man, Valentine Andreevich, pulls out and inspects an enormous pair of jeans. I approach him to offer assistance.

'She wears a size 52,' he reads from his shopping list. After a quick mental conversion I determine she needs a size 22. He is holding a size 26.

'They're a bit too large. You need a size 22.' I find the correct size and try to visualize this small man walking hand in hand with a woman of such proportions.

I help the others select garments in the appropriate sizes. The oldest of the three, Roman Ivanovich, is a taciturn gentleman wearing coke-bottle glasses with thick black frames. He needs size 18, and chooses a basic suit in an elegant shade of aqua. The third man, Evgeni Davidovich, who provided the vodka after yesterday's contract signing, is the most attractive of the three, or rather the least unattractive, and doesn't buy anything. I wonder if his wife is skinny.

All interested in undergarments, they follow me like three slobbering bloodhounds into a sexy boutique. Valentine Andreevich begins sorting through negligees and quickly selects a skimpy black silk teddy in size small. I assume it is for a different woman than the recipient of the size 22 jeans. Roman Ivanovich is reading his shopping list through his thick glasses and buying queen-sized pantyhose. Evgenii Davidovich fondles the skimpy silk underwear as if they contain a woman, finally choosing several pair. I wonder if they are for his wife.

After two hours at the mall, I take the Russians back to the office to meet up with Vladimir and Anis, who will be taking them back to their hotel in Pittsburgh until

15

dinnertime. Anis has planned an expensive dinner at a ritzy restaurant in Pittsburgh for the Russians, to be joined by our chief engineer and our general manager. Working as interpreter, I will be the only woman to attend, a fact which I find shamelessly exciting.

Leaving work early, I return to the mall with my own agenda. I have three hours to prepare myself for tonight's event. Three hours to transform myself into a seductive temptress.

Remembering everything I read the night before, I go into a ritzy dress boutique, my eyes immediately spotting a delicate silk dress in a dark burgundy fabric which is expensive enough not to shimmer. Although the dress isn't really appropriate for an engineer at a business dinner, I imagine Vladimir's eyes when he sees it and the feel of his hands through the silk.

After finding pumps in a color similar to that of the dress and with heels much higher than I usually wear, I return to the same boutique where I had been with the Russians and notice a display of garter belts. Although I have seen them only on the cover of Playboy, I find one in a size small made of ivory silk with a lace front and four hooks to hold the stockings. Deciding to buy it, I then select three pair of sheer stockings. Up to now, I have never worn anything but pantyhose and even then, only when it was absolutely necessary. But my book insists that men detest them.

Silk panties are the last item on my list. I find some flimsy, silk thongs in shades of ivory, burgundy, black, navy, and pink. I choose one in every color except pink. By six o'clock, I am speeding down the expressway towards home.

THREE

Shortly before seven, I stand in front of the Colonial Inn, a quaint hotel not far from my apartment. A warm breeze plasters my flimsy skirt against my thighs, outlining my crotch. I'm waiting for Dave, our chief engineer, to drive me to the restaurant in Pittsburgh. Since I hate big city traffic, especially at night, I am happy to accept his offer. Notorious for his tardiness, Dave pulls up at 7:20 in a flaming red Volkswagen sports car.

Dave Richardson isn't really an engineer—he has a PhD in physics. Considered the brains of Ampere Power Dead Tank, he designs most of the equipment. Dave looks a bit like Clark Kent—tall, glasses, dark hair, a goofy grin.

'I don't know how to handle the vodka,' he says. 'I don't want to offend the Russians, but I don't want to get shit-faced either.'

'Just don't mix your drinks,' I say. 'If you drink vodka, chase it with water. Don't even think about mixing it with wine.' *Is it really a good idea for me to sound like such an expert here?*

'When I was in Siberia with Anis, I got really sick,' Dave explains.

I want to ask him if Anis got sick as well. Instead I say, 'Maybe we can ask Vladimir to drive us home. He can sleep on my couch.' *Why on earth did I just say that?*

'I don't think he'd stay on the couch,' Dave says, glancing briefly at my legs.

God! Was I that obvious?

I don't respond, hoping he's right. I've said too much already.

After a short pause, Dave launches a new topic.

'So...do you like my car? It can go 150 mph.'

'Just don't try it when you've been drinking vodka.'

Dave laughs. 'Have you ever done curves?' he asks.

I assume he's referring to sharp turns taken so fast that the outer wheels come off the ground. 'I've never even ridden in a car that is capable of such feats,' I say, and we both laugh. I wonder if he's going to demonstrate, but I don't ask.

Upholding Dave's reputation for late arrivals, we're the last ones to reach the restaurant. The only empty seats are at the end of the table next to Anis and Vladimir. The three Russians are at the other end, drinking beer and looking bored. Jack, the general manager, as well as our Chief Accountant and our Human Resources Director (*What the Hell is he doing here?*), are seated across from the Russians, talking among themselves. Engaged in their own conversation, Vladimir and Anis are ignoring the rest of the group.

Instead of grabbing the empty seat next to Vladimir, I should suggest a seat change and place myself among the company VIPs and the Russians. Without the help of an interpreter, the two nationalities can only grin awkwardly at one another. Instead of seducing Vladimir with my appearance, I should be trying to impress Anis and Jack with my communication skills. I should be translating the menu for our guests of honor. I should be doing just about anything else besides drooling over Vladimir, but....

'That's a dangerous dress,' Vladimir whispers in

Russian, his eyes drifting over my body.
'It's pure silk and I'm not wearing anything under it,' I say. I consider going to the bathroom and removing my panties. I wouldn't want to be accused of lying.
'What should we order?' Vladimir asks me. 'You'll have to help our customers.'
'Look at the prices,' I say. 'If it's over thirty dollars, it's probably pretty good. I'm getting filet mignon, extra rare, with a crabmeat-Provolone topping. It's the best cut of steak you can get.'
'It sounds like a winner,' Vladimir says. 'Why don't you order it for everyone? But get theirs cooked through. Russians generally have a distrust of meat.'
I have a vision of my student days in Soviet Russia, of outdoor meat counters in bright sunlight, cuts of pork with 3-inch rims of fat and much smaller strips of meat in dubious colors and quickly understand what he is saying.
'It's a shame to cook the hell out of a good steak,' I say. 'At least try yours rare. I promise you won't be sorry.'
I order the steaks and a second round of drinks, chardonnay for myself and beer for the three customers. Although red wine is the best choice for steak, I'm afraid it will turn my tongue purple. Having tried it somewhere and liked it, Vladimir asks for white zinfandel. Sticking to his vegetarian diet, Anis orders a pizza and a coke. Since there's no pizza on the menu, I can't help wondering if it will be delivered from Pizza Hut.
Noticing the Russians sitting quietly as if in church, I suggest to Vladimir that we get some vodka. When Vladimir agrees, I order shots for everyone, not bothering to ask Anis. When the waiter brings the drinks, I say, 'These are Russian customers. We'll probably be drinking a lot of vodka. How about if we buy an entire bottle?' Not only do I not ask my boss, I consciously avoid looking at him.
'I suppose that would be okay,' he says after a moment's hesitation. 'But I can't give you a discount. I'll

have to calculate the total number of shots.'

From the corner of my eye, I see Anis staring at me, his mouth hung open as if wanting to object but not knowing quite what to say. I don't know if he is bothered by the potential cost or the prospect of drinking so much vodka. I'm about to ask his permission when Vladimir speaks up.

'That's fine,' he says in accented English. 'Bring the bottle. The biggest one you have.'

The waiter brings a 1.5-liter bottle and pours the first round of shots, not leaving anyone out and much too quickly for anyone to object. When he's finished, he sets the bottle between Vladimir and me. Recognizing the label, I'm surprised that such a ritzy restaurant stocks third rate American vodka and wonder—only briefly—what it will do to my head in the morning.

'Jack should make the first toast,' Vladimir says in English, loud enough for our General Manager to hear. 'Katey, you translate.'

Not needing further encouragement, Jack raises his glass and looks directly at the three Russians. As the man at the top, he knows his role. 'In the name of Ampere Power, I'd like to welcome you all to the United States. We are honored to have you both as our customers and as our guests.'

As soon as I translate, Valentine Andreevich replies, 'And we are honored to be your customers.'

Standing, the Russians lean across the table, determined to clink glasses with everyone. I have to lean over really far to reach them and can feel the top of my dress revealing my tits directly in front of Vladimir's eyes. Satisfied that every glass has touched every other, Evgenii Davidovich slugs his vodka down with one quick jerk of his wrist. Everyone but Anis follows his lead. Anis takes a small sip, barely wetting his lips, and then, trying to be discreet, uses his vodka to water the cactus in the middle of the table. If he plans to do that all evening, he'll probably kill the poor plant.

As soon as we set down our glasses, Vladimir picks up the bottle and refills all of them he can reach, including Anis's, and then passes the bottle across the table to Evgenii Davidovich. This time, Valentine Andreevich stands to make the second toast.

'To the success of our contract,' he says. 'May it be flawlessly carried out from both sides.'

'I'll drink double to that,' Jack says after I translate. Then he says to Anis, 'Don't kill the bloody plant. They might charge us for it.'

Looking embarrassed, Anis immediately stops watering the cactus and after staring at it for a moment, sips at his glass.

We drink one more shot before the meal arrives. I notice that Anis's glass has disappeared from the table. He has probably hidden it in his pocket. I also see that after the second round Vladimir has only been sipping his vodka, leaving the glass almost full. It occurs to me that I should follow his lead but instead I slug down the third and fourth rounds and, ignoring the advice I gave Dave earlier about not mixing his drinks, order another glass of wine.

The filet mignon is exquisite, so tender you can almost cut it with a fork. Slicing into it with a knife, I am pleased by the brilliant shade of red.

'This is delicious,' Vladimir says softly, leaning over and speaking into my ear. 'As soon as we get out of here, I'm going to kiss you.'

This announcement sends me off into my own world of euphoria. Suddenly the room is empty except for me and Vladimir. In a vodka haze, I caress his leg. Laughing at one of his remarks, I lean over and rest my head on his shoulder, ignoring the shocked expression on Anis's face. I completely forget about Anis, Jack, Dave, and the Russians. I can't care less that I am supposed to be the translator at an official business dinner, that I am representing Ampere Power, that Anis will probably fire me—Vladimir is going to kiss me!

I don't notice that the dinner has ended until we are all standing. In my drunken oblivion, the hours have raced by as if in a time warp and it is suddenly midnight. Wobbling on high heels, I grab Vladimir's arm as we walk to the door. Outside he leaves me with Dave and follows Anis and the Russians across the parking lot.

I should come to my senses. I should get quietly into the car with Dave and go home. Okay, I have already made a spectacle of myself, but it wasn't extreme. I can still save the situation. But I'm not in the mood to be sensible. I am desperately worried that I am not going to get the promised kiss. So instead, I blurt out in Russian, 'Do you want to come with us?'

I don't really expect him to come. In my present condition I feel like someone else is doing the talking and I am watching my own actions on a movie screen. But suddenly and much to Dave's surprise, Vladimir is climbing into the backseat of the sports car. I'm not sure but I think I hear Jack chuckle and the Russians are watching as if each one of them would like to take Vladimir's place. As we drive away, I catch a glimpse of Anis, who looks like he is trying to catch a tennis ball in his mouth. I'm glad we are leaving the next day. I won't be back until Saturday and not be returning to work until Monday. Hopefully I will still have a job.

Anis planned this trip to Washington as a little incentive for the upper management of the Russian company. The cost of the trip, of course, is secretly included in the price of the circuit breakers so the customers are actually paying for it themselves. Although we plan to see the traditional sights, we will primarily shop, eat, and drink—activities the Russians like best. In any case, Anis didn't intend it as a romantic getaway for his junior sales engineer.

Trying to appear innocent, I explain to Dave that I

need Vladimir to drive the car home for me since I am above the legal driving limit—I don't admit that I am totally shit-faced—and especially since the car is a rental minivan, brand new, and I've only driven it twice. Having never owned a car less than ten years old, I am not used to the new gismos and don't want to tinker with them at midnight in my present condition. I'll quickly pack my bag, I explain, and then we'll drive back to the hotel in Pittsburgh where I can get a room for myself as well. Of course, this is all just a ruse. We both know I won't be getting a hotel room.

Anis has rented me the minivan for the purpose of driving Vladimir and the customers to Washington DC the following morning. My own car is rusted, dirty (I've never been to a carwash), and full of empty coffee cups and other junk.

If Dave disapproves of my actions, he doesn't let on. On the way home, I start a discussion about the advantages of dead tank breakers over live tank. Although not sober either, once Dave, the author of the dead tank design, gets started on the topic, there is no stopping him. When he starts using mathematical formulas to describe transient recovery voltage, I tune him out, uttering an occasional 'uh huh' to make him think I am listening.

I reach behind me between the seat and the door to find Vladimir's hand, large and solid and not the least bit sweaty. Letting go again, I find his leg, and straining my arm until it hurts, I reach to his crotch. He is hard as a steel pipe. Because Dave is concentrating on both the road and his physics lecture, he doesn't notice my bodily contortions.

When we arrive at the hotel where my car is parked, Dave surprises me by inviting us in for a drink. I expected him to be angry about my tactless seduction of Vladimir and eager to get away. Instead we roam around in the dark lobby before realizing that the bar is already closed and since there are no other bars in this remote location, we watch Dave zoom away in his little sports car. There will be talk in the office tomorrow, but fortunately I won't be there.

We stand in the cool breeze for a minute, as if trying to accept that we are alone. I resist a desire to press my goose-bumped flesh against his body, wanting him to make the first move. Instead, I show him the van and give him the keys.

'It's not locked,' he says, opening the door.

'I never lock my car,' I say. 'If anyone steals my car, he will have only himself to blame.'

I expect him to laugh, but instead he says, 'This isn't your car.'

'It's insured,' I say, drunk enough to be nonchalant.

'I don't think you can collect if you don't lock it.'

'Who's going to prove I didn't lock it if it's gone?'

'Good point,' he says. 'Get in.'

I go around to the passenger's side and slither into the seat, fondly remembering the cars of my youth with a middle seat instead of the gearshift that has replaced it. As a teenager, I used to snuggle against my dates, never wearing a seatbelt—the immortality of youth.

I sit stiffly and stare straight ahead, almost afraid to look at Vladimir. Hearing him stick the keys in the ignition, I worry for a moment that he is simply going to drive off. I want him to kiss me more than I want to breathe.

As if reading my thoughts, Vladimir puts his arm around my shoulder, leans over and rests his other hand on my thigh, just below the edge of my stocking. Before kissing me, he whispers, 'This is to thank you for that delicious steak.'

His lips bulldoze mine with unexpected urgency, his tongue tasting every corner of my mouth. I tremble as his hand inches under my dress; and as he touches bare skin between stocking and garter belt, I wince like a jellyfish.

I am floating. I keep my eyes closed. Sinking into a

black hole. Black as death. No smell but the scent of a man. Nothing to touch but his skin, nothing to feel but the electric tingle of his hand and the moist sweetness of his mouth. Nothing to hear but a scream of ecstasy fighting to escape from my throat if he would only release my mouth. There is no yesterday, no tomorrow, just this moment, and if I don't peek, it will last forever.

Suddenly he pulls away, leaving me like a compressed spring. A tall light in the parking lot hurts my eyes. Without a word he turns the key in the ignition, starts the engine, and drives away.

FOUR

I'm only slightly embarrassed by the mess as we enter my apartment. I haven't had any visitors since moving here. The blue lace camisole I slept in is lying on the floor beside the couch where I took it off this morning. My exercise videos are scattered in front of the television beside my gym shoes, sports bra and shorts. This morning I did an upper body workout called 'Firm Parts.' There's a half empty coffee cup on the table and the last bite of a donut without a plate. The suit I wore to work hangs carelessly on the back of a chair, panty hose bunched up on the floor beside it. One shoe lies near the chair, the other several feet away where I kicked it off.

Vladimir slouches on the sofa and watches me scurry around, picking up the mess like a squirrel gathering nuts. He takes the camisole from my hands and fingers the lace. 'I'd like to see you in this,' he says, 'for about two seconds before I tear it off of you.'

'I'll take it with me,' I say quickly, grabbing it from his hands.

'Squeak, squeak…squeeeeeak.'

'What the hell was that?' Vladimir asks, sitting upright in his seat as if expecting to be attacked by some wild animal.

'That's just my guinea pig,' I say, heading for a small cage near the window.

Homer, who is larger than most and always hungry, continues his serenade. I pick him up, scratch him under the chin and plop him onto Vladimir's lap like a bean bag.

'What if he shits on me?' Vladimir asks.

'He only poops after he eats,' I assure him.

I got Homer four years ago while a student in Wisconsin. I found him in a pet store, looking lonely and unloved. Bigger than the other guinea pigs, even then he had his mouth full. I took him home that same day and let him crawl around on my bed until he sneaked under the covers and pooped. And since I often let him run loose, there are pee stains on the carpet which I haven't bothered to clean. I normally take him to a kennel when I'm away, but since I'll only be gone for two nights, the neighbor is going to look in on him.

I go to the refrigerator and pull out a stalk of celery.

'Holy bloody Hell!' Vladimir shouts, standing up and letting Homer bounce onto the floor. 'He just shit on me.'

'Damn,' I say, 'He's under the couch. Don't worry about the poop. They're just like little dry beans. They don't hurt anything.'

Crawling on all fours, I peek under the couch, arching my back and sticking my ass in the air. Vladimir, who has shed the poop and sat back down, reaches behind me, lifts my dress and smacks my butt. Hard.

'That's for letting your bloody hog shit on me.'

Then his hand returns to my behind, rubbing and caressing as I lure Homer out of hiding with the celery stick.

With Homer back in his cage, I offer Vladimir a glass of California wine which he gladly accepts.

Since I haven't yet packed for the trip, not even thought about what I need to take, I get down to business, going into the bedroom where I start sorting through clothes piled carelessly on shelves in the walk-in closet. Several dresses have fallen off the hangers and are lying like old rags on the floor. After debating about changing into a more comfortable outfit, I decide to leave the dress on. I feel so seductive in the garter belt and stockings that I want to preserve the sensation as long as possible.

I pack a dark green velvet miniskirt, brown patterned stockings, short leather boots, a brown denim jacket and an olive green top which reaches to just above my navel. I also toss in a pair of brown jeans, a few t-shirts, a sweater, and a pair of leather shoes. I choose several pair of the sexiest panties I can find. I don't pack any bras. Lastly I head to the bathroom and quickly pack all the essentials: shampoo, hairdryer, toothbrush, cologne, and loads of make-up.

It's after midnight when I'm finally ready to go. Approaching Vladimir on the couch, I lean into him, putting my face close to his. I take a sip of his wine and kiss him. He starts reaching his hands up the sides of my dress, and almost has it over my head when I gently pull away.

'Let's drive to your hotel first,' I say, pulling the dress back down around my body. 'It's late.'

We drive for a while along the deserted street without talking, my hand resting on his leg. Suddenly Vladimir chuckles. 'I bet Anis is having a cow,' he says in Russian.

'I hope I still have a job on Monday,' I say.

'I wouldn't worry about that,' he says.

'How can you be so sure?'

'Anis will do anything I tell him to.' Then grinning, he adds, 'He only hired you because I demanded it.'

'What exactly did you tell him?'

'I told him to find a real American who speaks Russian. I couldn't have a vegetarian who looks like he should be wearing a turban traveling around Siberia. Of course, I thought he would hire a man.'

'Are you disappointed?'

'No, I think you may have some definite skills which could prove useful to me.'

'And they are?'

'I intend to find out as soon as we get to the hotel.'

He drives silently, not asking directions. Although he's only driven the route twice, once with Anis that morning and once with Dave an hour earlier, he seems to know where he's going, even in the darkness. After about an hour we arrive at the hotel where the other Russians are staying.

Vladimir grabs my small suitcase and I follow him into the lobby. As we wait for the elevator, he doesn't look at me, as if afraid someone will see us together. It is 1:00 A.M and the lobby is deserted except for a chubby desk clerk with pink cow lips. When the elevator door opens I follow Vladimir in.

We stand side by side like two strangers, not touching, eyes focused on the door. After we exit on the fourth floor and enter an empty hallway, I follow him to his room, where he uses a code card to open the door. When he switches on the light, I see a single suitcase open on the dresser with socks and underwear neatly folded, a sharp contrast to the disarray he encountered in my living room. The bed has been turned down by the maid. A mini-bar stands in the corner as if beckoning to me.

After tossing my bag on a chair, Vladimir removes his blazer, puts it on a hanger and packs it into a leather garment bag, carefully smoothing out the creases. He takes off his tie, folds it, and puts it into the small suitcase before sitting down on the bed and reaching out his arm towards me. When I approach, he grabs my legs and pulls me to him. Falling against his body, I kiss him once before pulling away again, my eyes drifting to the mini-bar.

'I wonder what's in the mini-bar,' I say, tearing open the small door. The fridge is full of tiny airplane bottles of liquor and soft drinks. Ignoring the price list posted on the door, I select a small bottle of white wine and a glass from a tray on top of the refrigerator. The wine is much too sweet for my liking, tasting like it came from a third world country.

Vladimir gestures to me and when I approach, he takes my wine, sips it, and sets the glass on the nightstand.

'Tastes like baboon piss,' he says.

Before I can ask him where he ever tasted baboon piss, he clutches my waist and pulls me towards him. As he kisses me, his hands slide down and reach under my dress, his fingers hooking around the top of my panties. He slides them down easily, his mouth pressed against mine, and as I try to step out of them without removing my shoes—men enjoy making love to a woman wearing nothing but high heels, stockings and a garter belt—my heel gets caught in the waistband and I trip, falling into Vladimir's arms. As our lips separate he reaches under my dress again and pulls it over my head, leaving me naked except for the garter belt, stockings and pumps with my panties still caught on the heel.

I kiss each of his eyes. Then I move my lips across his face, softly caressing every inch of skin, teasing him. His hands find my bare breasts—they're bigger when I'm leaning over—and cups them a bit roughly, rubbing the erect nipples between his fingers.

I reach down, unbutton his shirt, and spread it open with both hands. Sinking lower, I taste his chest, the hairs tickling my chin. My hands reach for his belt, unfastening it, and I yank his pants over his hips, finding his penis like a hidden treasure. The largeness of it doesn't surprise me as I hold it eagerly in my hand before taking the tip into my mouth. As I slide him deep into my throat, he whispers 'malenkaya Chueda', which means 'little wonder' and grasps my head with both hands.

After a few minutes, he pulls me up, kicking off his shoes and pants while I kiss every inch of his face. Then with our mouths locked together and our tongues exploring, he lies back onto the bed. We end our kiss and I straddle him, resting my palms on his shoulders. I am so hungry for his touch that I almost climax the moment he enters me, feeling the tension build even higher as he thrusts deeply, holding tightly to my hips and controlling every move. His eyes are closed and he is smiling as if he knows a secret. I want to lie down and press myself against him, savor every inch of his body, but before I get there myself, he pushes me aside and turns me over so that I am lying on my stomach. He lays on top of me, his face close to mine, his feet touching my own, his stomach pressed against the arch of my back. He enters me from behind, causing a pleasant pressure against the front of my pelvis. He kisses my neck as he thrusts, his body tight against my own. His breathing accelerates as he climaxes and I feel his muscles tighten as he grips my shoulders and wedges himself even deeper inside of me. At the same time I feel my body tighten and explode in flames of ecstasy. Although I want to cry out, I experience the pleasure in silence. I've never been a screamer.

Then he lies still, covering me like a blanket, his penis still inside of me, breathing steadily as if asleep. We remain that way for a long time before he rolls off of me and onto his back.

Like a typical man, Vladimir falls asleep minutes after our lovemaking. I lie in the gap between his arm and torso like a puppy, nuzzling his underarm, which smells faintly of sweat. Unable to sleep, I listen to his snoring, taking great pleasure in the smell and feel of a man against my body. Instead of the tranquilizing effects one would expect from sex and alcohol, I am so wired I can blow a fuse. I fight off an urge to wake him. I want so desperately to talk to him—women always want to talk. I want to know if he feels the same way I do. I want to look deep into his eyes and see what I find there.

Damn that wedding ring! I will just have to be the best lover he's ever had. I will make him want me so much that he always thinks of me when he's with her. I will study the

Kama Sutra, The Story of O, and The Joy of Sex. I'll wear nothing but silk, lace, and high heels. I'll become Aphrodite. I will make him desire me so strongly that he will always come back to me. I will make him love me.

I press my naked body tighter against his chest, entwining my legs with his, letting my thigh rub against his crotch. It works. I feel a subtle movement, and then hardness. Arms wrapping around me, he pulls me onto his chest. In the moonlight, I notice his eyes are closed and wonder if he is making love to me in a dream.

Cupping my buttocks, he maneuvers me back and forth in steady rhythm. It takes him several minutes to climax. Then he lies still, holding me tight against him.

Thinking he is still asleep, I whisper directly into his ear, 'I love you.'

He turns his head and kisses my cheek before returning to the steady rhythm of sleep. I drift off in the early morning hours, only to be awakened by the sun hitting the window.

Since we're both naked, I can't imagine getting up before another round—men always claim the morning erection is the best. I climb gently onto his hips, lean over, and plant a soft kiss on his mouth, my hair brushing his cheeks. I wonder what kind of a dream has caused his erection. When I lift my head again, his eyes are open. He reaches down and circles my waist with his hands. We make love without speaking and after we climax he looks into my eyes and says, 'Good morning.'

When I come out of the bathroom, my hair blown dry and my face made up like a supermodel, he is on the telephone. He showered before me and is dressed casually in slacks and a sweater—it is the first time I have seen him without a suit. He is speaking in Russian, and after a few sentences I realize he is talking to a child. Wrapped in a towel, I walk over to my suitcase, pretending not to listen.

'Make sure you do what Mommy tells you,' he says in a mock serious tone.

During a pause, he smiles like a little boy at Christmas. I wonder what the child is saying and if his mother is nearby. It is one thing to know that Vladimir is married, and quite another to stand naked, intruding on a Kodak moment. Feeling awkward and almost ashamed, I rummage through the clothes in my suitcase.

'Did you do your homework?'

Another pause. More smiles. He looks at me, winks, and beckons me to him. Half dressed, I approach him where he is sitting on the bed and let him wrap his arms around my legs. He talks for another five minutes, but only to his son. I am pleased that he doesn't speak to his wife.

Suddenly he stands up and releases me. 'Let's go,' he says.

'I'm not ready,' I say. I am still dressed only in a tank top and panties.

'You look fine to me.'

I toss him a smile before pulling on brown jeans, which mold my ass like a second skin, throwing a dark green sweater over my head and slipping into my shoes—short leather boots with three inch heels.

He already has the door open and is standing in the hall. I hear voices in Russian and realize the others are waiting outside. I hesitate, unsure if Vladimir will want them to know I am here. But he beckons me to come out and I oblige, where they all greet me as if I am Vladimir's wife. We eat a quick breakfast in the hotel restaurant and head for the van. Nobody mentions the previous night. Considering the Russians' reputation for drinking, it was probably a comparably dull evening. There were no fist fights, no orgies, no dancing on tables, and nobody passing out in the street. I only wish my boss would see it that way.

Before we enter the van, Vladimir holds out his hand for the keys. I don't know if he should be driving since I rented the van in my name, but I hand them over without protest.

'I don't like it when dames drive me around,' he says.

I can't help laughing. I am truly a terrible driver. I can't parallel park, get nervous in heavy traffic, and avoid big cities. Although I've never caused an accident, I have had some close calls.

Valentine Andreevich, Roman Ivanovich, and Evgeni Davidovich sit in the back. I put on some Russian folk music to entertain them, songs by Vladimir Vysotsky, a Russian bard who was extremely popular in the Soviet Union during the sixties and seventies.

He sings about Sergey Fomich, a boy nobody liked as a child. When World War II starts, all the boys are drafted into the army. The narrator himself volunteers. Sergey's father, a professor in the Communist Party, uses his influence to keep his son away from the front lines. The others go to fight, some of them are killed, others lose arms or legs. After the war Sergey, who did nothing, is given a medal as a Hero of the Soviet Union.

Vysotsky sings a ballad called 'Song of Friendship.' Friendship has a much deeper meaning to a Russian than to an American. He sings in Russian:

If your friend suddenly seems
To not be a real friend
If you aren't really sure of his trust
Take him with you into the mountains
Tied together on one rope.

If he gets scared on the slope,
Slips on a patch of snow
And wants to go home,
Don't get angry, but send him away.
You don't need this sort as a friend.

If the guy doesn't complain,
If he hides his fear and goes forth
When you slip from the cliff,

He heaves, holds you safe in his grip;
When you stand side by side on the peak,
You will know
You can count on him!

How does a Russian recognize a true friend? If he tells him he killed a man, the friend will ask just one question: Where is the body?

Another song is called 'Katerina, Katya, Katerina.' They toast me with whisky from the back seats. Valentine Andreevich offers me a paper cup. I hesitate, feeling funny about drinking whisky in a moving vehicle, especially at eleven o'clock.

'The customer is always right, *Katerina*', Vladimir says in English, not wanting the other passengers to understand.

'Now I know why you wanted to drive,' I say, accepting the whisky from Valentine Andreevich. They make a toast to *Katerina* and we drink it down. It tastes awful, and I fight back nausea. I've always considered whisky a sipping drink, not something to slug down like medicine. But the second one tastes better. There's always a second one. The first rule of drinking with Russians is don't drain your glass unless you want a refill, because you'll always get one. You may be sprawled on the table with your face in your stroganoff, but you'll still get that refill.

We pull into a McDonalds where I purchase five large coffees.

'Americans drink buckets of weak coffee,' jokes Valentine Andreevich. I can't help remembering my student days in Moscow where I was often served coffee that had been brewed three times using the same grounds. After the third round, it resembled weak tea. But I keep my thoughts to myself.

We are all drunk except Vladimir by the time we reach Washington.

FIVE

It turns out that Anis has chosen a plush hotel in an upscale part of the city. After checking into our rooms, all with king-size beds and balconies, we go for lunch in the hotel restaurant.

'We'd like to eat something typically American,' Valentine Andreevich says. 'What do you suggest?'

I don't need to think about it very long. 'I would suggest filet mignon cooked rare, topped with mushrooms and served with onion rings or a baked potato and a Caesar salad,' I say.

'Then that's what we'll have,' Valentine Andreevich says.

"Onion rings or baked potato?" I ask.

"Both," Vladimir says without hesitation. "They want to try everything."

'I always eat my steak extra rare,' I say. 'It brings out the flavor. Should I order them that way?'

'No, no, we like them cooked through,' Evgenii Davidovich says.

This is exactly what Valdimir told me the night before, but I still wanted to give it a try. To me, a well-done steak, even filet mignon, is just a step up from hamburger. I like mine so rare that it's almost breathing. But when I again remember the unrefrigerated meat counters in Russia, sometimes even outdoors in sunlight, I can understand why they want to cook the hell out of it.

Vladimir orders his rare like the real man he is.

I order five beers, not even suggesting that we get vodka. I'm still working the whiskey out of my system.

The quiet older man, Roman, has become more talkative since our morning drinking binge. 'To Katey,' he says, raising his glass. And then, 'Do you know where I can buy a camcorder?' He says camcorder in English with a heavy Russian accent. *Kahmkoorrrderrr*.

'My daughter wants American CDs,' says Evgeni Davidovich. 'The most popular.'

'Can't you get those in Russia?' I ask.

'Yes, but my daughter is convinced that the CDs here are even more recent and more popular.'

Not sure how to answer and also knowing that most of the CDs are probably produced in China, I say, 'I'm sure we can find what you're looking for.' Then I say to Vladimir, 'I think we'll have to delay the trip to Arlington Cemetery.'

'Yes, but we should go to the White House,' Valentine Andreevich insists.

'First I need my camcorder,' Roman Ivanovich says. 'I want to film everything.'

'Why didn't you say something earlier?' Valentine Andreevich chides. 'Our last hotel was right next to a shopping mall.'

'The White House tours are only in the mornings, anyway,' I say, not knowing or caring if this is the truth. 'We can go to the mall today and to the White House tomorrow.'

'I want to get a laptop computer,' Evgenii Davidovich says. 'They're so much more expensive in Russia and we usually only get the European models.'

They aren't exactly cheap here, I think, wondering how

much money they have. They don't have credit cards or traveler's checks in Russia, so they must be carrying one hell of a lot of cash.

Roman Ivanovich examines every camcorder in the store, almost acting like he invented the things. He asks all kinds of complex technical questions, which I have difficulty translating for the tall black salesman. Trying to hide his boredom, Vladimir helps me with some of the words, although he seems to prefer letting me struggle. Roman Ivanovich finally buys a compact, pricey Japanese model, paying with eight crisp one hundred dollar bills.

The salesman laughs. 'What bank did you rob?' Something tells me this joke is going to get old really fast. I am glad that Roman Ivanovich doesn't understand English.

Evgenii Davidovich's computer is next on the list. Since he wants an American brand, I lead him to the IBMs. When he begins examining one for $2999, I wonder if he is going to produce thirty bills, actually thirty-two with tax.

The laptop is multi-voltage, functioning with 220 volts as well as 110. Evgenii Davidovich examines it for a long time, turning it over and caressing it like a woman. He stares in puzzlement at the English lettering on the back. I ask if they have a user's manual in Russian. They don't. Strangely enough, he doesn't ask the standard questions, like how much storage and memory. Since he doesn't care that the software is in English, I suspect he has his own pirated software at home.

Evgenii counts out the 32 one hundred dollar bills as if he were counting pennies. I wait for the salesman's inevitable question.

'Did you rob a bank?' he asks. Again I am glad that Evgenii Davidovich doesn't understand English.

'Yeah,' I say without smiling. 'The First National.'

He stares blankly for a few seconds before laughing nervously. He counts the money twice before putting it into the cash register, placing it carefully under the tray like a child hiding a tooth beneath his pillow.

Evgenii Davidovich tucks the large box under his arm, and we head for the music store. Immediately all three men start sifting through the titles, much too quickly to be reading them. Remembering Evgenii Davidovich, I approach the salesgirl, who looks to be about fourteen with an IQ not much higher. *Okay, I never could stand the cheerleader types.*

'They're from Russia,' I explain. 'They want to buy top hits for their kids.'

'We don't have any Russian music,' she says.

Oh my God. I was right about the IQ. 'They want top American hits.' At my ripe age of 29, I don't have a clue what the kids are listening to in 1995.

'Celine Dion, Mariah Carey, Coolio...the top 20 CDs are over here,' the girl says, pointing toward a rack unsurprisingly labeled 'Top 20'.

I grab the top three CDs and bring them to Evgenii. 'Are they any good?' he asks.

'Probably not,' I say, my own tastes in music being stuck in the 70s and 80s. 'But they are the most popular.' He laughs, understanding my attempt at humor, and decides to buy them.

As we enter the men's department of a moderately priced clothing store, I'm curious about what kinds of clothes they will buy. They are all dressed in their own unique styles. Evgenii Davidovich resembles an unpopular teenager trying to look cool. He's wearing unfaded blue jeans, a tad too tight for his ample behind, a matching jeans jacket, a tad too small for his expanding girth, and white Puma gym shoes.

Roman Ivanovich is wearing Russian-made clothing, probably not due to lack of money, but rather a lack of fashion sense. His attire includes a grey suit of questionable quality, a shirt with vertical stripes, and a diagonally striped polyester tie which clashes with his shirt.

His Russian-made loafers with thick soles are a putrid shade of brown.

Only Valentine Andreevich seems to possess a decent amount of fashion sense, his clothes not only fitting properly, but also matching. He's wearing a red polo shirt, a blue Ralph Lauren jacket, spiffy dark slacks and soft black loafers, which probably cost more than the other two's entire outfits. The only thing missing is the Rolex.

As if reading my thoughts, Valentine approaches me. 'I'd like to buy a new watch,' he says. *Too bad we're not in Switzerland.*

'What kind of watch?' I assume it isn't Timex.

'A Rolex.'

I'm glad it isn't Patek Phillipe. They cost $25,000. I try to imagine what the jeweler would say if he pulled out 250 crisp hundreds.

We head to an expensive jewelry store in the center of the mall, Vladimir hanging back.

'I'll wait for you here,' he says, perusing a row of designer suits. I suspect he's getting tired of the Russian shopping spree.

The salesman approaches as soon as we reach the counter. 'May I help you?'

'We want to buy a Rolex.'

He makes a face as though he just ate a raw lizard. Considering the way we're dressed, I don't expect him to take us seriously, so I add, 'They are businessmen from Russia.'

'Oh I see,' he says, lighting up like a Christmas tree. He must know that Russians like expensive watches. 'We have several models. All solid gold and stainless steel.'

He reaches under the counter and pulls out one which has the price tag hidden. 'Here we have a Men's Rolex Perpetual Oyster DateJust in two-tone with 18 carat gold & Stainless Steel. It features an 18-carat yellow fluted gold bezel, a stainless steel case, and diamond dials and numbers. It has a flawless sapphire crystal and quickset date, with the much more sought-after 3035 Automatic Chronometer Movement and a signed fold over clasp and locking crown. The watch comes complete with box, booklet, hang tag & certificate.' He sounds like a robot spewing out data or rather to me at least, like a pompous ass. *What more could we want?* I stumble with the translation, leaving out the phrases I don't understand or don't know how to translate. I've never spent more than twenty dollars on a watch and have no idea what a fluted gold bezel is, much less how to translate it.

'How much does it cost?' I ask.

'3995 plus tax.'

Forty one-hundred dollar bills, plus tax. I translate the price to Valentine who picks up the watch and examines it, rubbing his skinny fingers over every crevice and curve. 'Okay,' he says in English.

This time when Valentine Andreevich produces his wad of hundreds, the salesman counts them silently, not asking if we robbed a bank. Perhaps he is afraid we did and doesn't want to risk losing his commission by spooking us. I wonder how much more money the Russians have hidden away and am waiting nervously for one of them to tell me he'd like to buy a Jeep Grand Cherokee and ship it to Russia with the circuit breakers.

When we return to the clothing store, Vladimir is beaming beside a coat rack as he shows us a stylish khaki-colored trench coat that looks like something Columbo would wear. 'Look,' he says in Russian. And then in English: 'Made in Russia.'

The other three understand this single phrase and charge over to look at the coat. After trying it on and posing in front of the mirror, Evgenii Davidovich decides to buy it. Although he looks like Porky Pig playing detective, I don't say a word.

It's four o'clock when we leave the mall. The sky is as

blue as Vladimir's eyes, and the sun comfortably warm. Now we decide to head for Arlington Cemetery. As we drive along, the trio huddles together in the back, examining Roman Ivanovich's camcorder. It doesn't take long before he is pointing it at me and filming. I've never liked being filmed, but once again, I don't say anything.

The tombstones of Arlington Cemetery stand like rows of white dominoes, waiting to be toppled. The rows extend so far into the distance that they also appear as white ropes stretching across the perfect green grass. The Russians are respectful, but unimpressed. They lost 20 million people in World War II, a tragedy that the Americans, despite their own ample losses, can't begin to understand. Roman Ivanovich is trying out his camcorder. I don't see the point of filming tombstones—it's not like he's capturing any motion—but I keep my opinion to myself. The others, especially Vladimir, look bored. It's almost six o'clock, four hours since our last drink. I don't expect to find a bar near a cemetery, especially a cemetery as dignified as Arlington.

I walk over to Vladimir and say, 'I think they're bored.'

'They're probably hungry,' he replies.

'So am I,' I say, rubbing my hand over his crotch. Nobody is looking.

'That's blasphemous,' says Vladimir with mock seriousness. He grabs my ass and slides his hand between my legs.

'I'll be sure to go to church on Sunday.'

We drive back to the hotel and decide to meet in the lobby in half an hour. Just enough time for a quickie. We head straight for Vladimir's room—I haven't bothered to use mine—and he lies down on his back. I go to the end of the bed, slither between his legs and pull at his belt buckle. He doesn't resist as I pull his slacks down to his knees and slip his penis into my mouth, letting it slide deep into my throat. He reaches down and rubs his fingers through my hair. Then he grabs my head and starts moving it up and down in rhythm. I almost choke as he approaches my vocal cords, but then relax, tightening my lips on his shaft. He starts to withdraw as he reaches climax but I hold him in, and he comes deep into my mouth, so deep that I don't even taste it.

'I'm going to haunt your dreams,' I tell him silently.

I'm still holding him in my mouth as he relaxes, gently stroking my hair. I release him slowly and crawl up to him. We kiss long and passionately, our tongues exploring every corner of our mouths.

Instead of whispering romanticisms into my ear, he pushes me away gently, stands up and buckles his pants. 'Let's go,' he says. 'They're waiting for us and they're hungry.' Men are so practical.

'Are you still hungry?' I ask.

'I'm always hungry.' As he says this I notice a bulge forming in his crotch.

We go down to the lobby where all three are waiting. Roman Ivanovich is holding his camcorder, probably planning to film every minute of our trip. Evgenii Davidovich is carrying a small paper bag which I am sure contains a bottle of Russian vodka. Russians like to have their own bottle of vodka when they're eating. I hope the waiter understands.

Before heading out onto the streets of Washington, I ask the concierge for the name of a good seafood restaurant. I am assuming my guests will want more typical American food. He gives me directions to a place called the Lobster Claw, but once we are outside, his list of street names, blocks, and left and right turns becomes a muddle. I'm not familiar with the city and feel like we are wandering aimlessly, but Vladimir takes off like a soldier with a mission, and I hurry to walk beside him. He has been to Washington only once before, so he either has a photographic memory or is trying to give that impression.

A trio of black teenagers approaches us from the subway. One is balancing a boom box on his shoulder. It is playing a rap tune. They are all wearing Bermudas, the crotch hanging almost to their knees, and baseball caps on backwards.

'I don't give a flyin' fuck!'

'What the fuck you saying to me, bro?'

'You can fuckin' go fuck yourself, Jamal!'

'Hey, what the fuck are you fuckin' lookin' at?' I suddenly realize he is talking to me.

'We ain't fucking looking at fucking nothing,' I say, and Vladimir chuckles.

The kid who addressed me smiles. 'Hey, not bad. Keep cool, babe.' He punches my shoulder lightly as they continue past. 'Nice fuckin' ass,' he says, glancing over his shoulder.

'Thanks,' I call after him.

Letting the others walk ahead, Vladimir reaches out and caresses my butt. 'Nice fucking ass,' he says.

When we reach a section of the city packed with restaurants, the Lobster Claw pops out in front of us. It isn't crowded and the hostess seats us at a large round table in the back. This time I sit between Vladimir and Valentine Andreevich.

'So Katey, you're the expert,' says Vladimir. 'What do you recommend?'

'The most expensive meal is lobster,' I say, thinking that might impress them.

'Then order five lobsters.'

I order five lobsters, five beers, and five shots of vodka. When the waiter brings the drinks, I lean over to him. 'These are my customers from Russia. They brought their own bottle of Russian vodka. Is it okay if they drink it here?'

'I'll have to ask the manager,' he replies.

'They'll be offended if you don't let them. Tell him that,' I say. As he's walking away, I add, 'Don't forget to tell him we all ordered lobster.'

Valentine Andreevich lifts his shot glass. 'Let's drink to American hospitality.' I wonder if he'll still like that toast if the manager doesn't let him drink his Russian vodka.

'And to our pretty guide,' adds Roman Ivanovich.

We all slug it down. It tastes like diesel fuel, at least the way I would imagine diesel fuel to taste. It must be Popov's, the cheapest vodka on the market. I take a deep swig of beer.

The waiter returns and grants his permission to put our bottle on the table.

'I've got two bottles,' says Evgenii Davidovich, winking.

Oh joy!

He opens the first bottle and refills the five glasses.

'To our host company, which is paying for this dinner.' This toast comes from Evgenii Davidovich.

His vodka is a brand from St. Petersburg, tasting much smoother than the restaurant vodka. If the other was diesel fuel, this is liquid gold. Evgenii pours another refill.

'To the American soldiers who died in World War II.' Refill.

'To all the pretty women in the world.' Vladimir winks at me.

The salads arrive, each buried in ranch dressing. Refill.

'To Bill Clinton,' Valentine Andreevich says. Refill.

'To Boris Yeltsin,' I say.

The lobster arrives, accompanied by little bowls of melted butter. I don't know how to eat a lobster properly, but the vodka has made me incredibly hungry and four equally hungry men are staring at my plate, ready to follow my lead. Not sure what to do with the lobster's body, I pick it up in my hands and crack it in two, splattering juice on my sweater. Now I know what the lobster bibs are for, still lying untouched on the table.

'I think I did that wrong,' I say. And they laugh.

Refill.

Then I break one of the claws, pull out the flesh with my little fork, and dip it in butter. I notice the others watching me eat. Then they each break off a claw, following my lead.

'You better use these,' I say, passing the bibs around.

They tie them on before attacking the lobster. For a while they are so busy pulling out chunks of meat and dipping them in butter that they forget the vodka. But not for long.

Refill.

Evgenii Davidovich empties the first bottle and produces the second.

'To the enchanting Katey.'

'To my charming guests,' I say.

Evgenii Davidovich finishes his meal before the others. He pushes his plate aside and grabs the bottle.

'One more for digestion,' he says.

We drink to digestion.

'Would anyone like dessert?' I ask. I don't expect them to say yes, but they do. They all order hot fudge sundaes.

'If you offer it, they'll take it,' says Vladimir softly in English.

The same is true for the coffee. I order five double espressos. There's nothing like a bunch of wide-awake drunks.

When the waiter brings the bill he hands it to Vladimir, who promptly passes it on to me, with the waiter first looking surprised and then amused to see a young woman picking up the dinner tab for four older men.

'Women's lib,' Vladimir says to the waiter and they both laugh. I wonder where he learned that phrase, certainly not from Russian women. At least not from the ones I'd encountered and heard of – overworked, underpaid, dressed up like hussies with cheap makeup, struggling alone with children in tiny apartments, enduring multiple abortions, tolerating the abuse of alcoholic husbands. Maybe the influx of western culture will change their lot, but I doubt it will happen quickly. I figure the waiter has saved me at least a hundred dollars by letting us drink our own vodka. So when I pay with my Corporate American Express card, I write in $80 on the line asking for 'tip.' I'll have to explain that to Anis by saying I probably saved him $400 in vodka costs.

We come out of the restaurant and onto the dark streets. If I were sober, I'd be really nervous about wandering around Washington at night. I wonder how many hundred-dollar bills my guests are carrying, hoping they have a few in case we need them. I don't remember the way back to the hotel, but Vladimir knows exactly how to get there. Walking past the subway entrance, I expect someone to jump out with a knife and am only slightly wrong. This mugger has a gun. Before I realize what is happening, a gangly man in jeans and a hooded sweatshirt plants the point of a revolver on Vladimir's chest. Everyone stands paralyzed like statues, as if the pause button has been pushed on a video.

'I ain't be wanting to hurt nobody,' our mugger says in a drawl. 'Just give me your Goddamn fucking money.'

Although I've only heard it once, I recognize the voice. 'Jamal?' I say. He must have changed his clothes for the night shift.

Upon hearing his name, Jamal drops the gun to his side and looks towards me. 'Who that be?'

Although I should be paralyzed with fear, the vodka has made me bold. 'I'm that fucking white bitch with the nice fucking ass and these are fucking KGB agents from Russia and they're all carrying Makarov PMs.' Then I say in Russian. 'Say something in Russian. Sound mean.'

Vladimir, who has understood my game, begins ranting like a sheriff interrogating a suspect, explaining the situation to the others, who promptly join in the cussing match.

I don't know how I expect Jamal to react. Perhaps he won't believe us, perhaps he'll shoot us all, perhaps he'll run. Instead he does the last thing I would have expected. He laughs.

'Oh yeah, now I remember you all. I ain't never met no Russkies,' he says, 'KGB. They be bad fucking asses.'

'Give him some money,' I say in Russian.

Valentine Andreevich pulls out a wad of rubles—thousands and hundreds. I am surprised he brought them with him from Russia, but glad he did. With the exchange rate at 6000 to one, the entire value, although appearing impressive, doesn't exceed $10.

'Cool,' says Jamal.

Evgeni Davidovich pulls out a hundred dollar bill and hands it to the boy. 'That's for not shooting us,' he says and I translate.

Taking the money, Jamal says, 'I sure ain't gonna shoot no fuckin' bad ass Russkies. They might come back and nuke me.' And with that he vanishes into the subway.

'Typical American,' Valentine Andreevich says as we hurry along, now more aware of our surroundings. I can't argue with him, although I also can't help thinking that Jamal must have a good heart for not robbing us of every last penny.

A streetlight illuminates the face of a woman, but it's too dark to guess her age. Even though it's summer, she's wearing a stocking cap, a heavy coat, and oversize boots. She's sitting on an old blanket on the grass next to the sidewalk and drinking from a bottle in a paper bag. There's a shopping cart parked beside her loaded with grocery sacks and some ragged clothes and blankets.

'I wonder who she is,' I say solemnly in Russian. 'Or was,' I add. The sight of the woman has sobered me.

Roman Ivanovich walks over to her and drops 5 twenty-dollar bills in her lap, obviously smart enough to realize that she might have trouble exchanging a single hundred. 'We don't have homeless people in Russia,' he explains.

I don't mention the countless old women I encountered begging on the streets of Moscow, shriveled up like old potatoes and dressed in rags. Or the drunks tottering through the parks, pissing on themselves and on monuments. I am too touched by his generosity, and I also can't forget that '...the customer is always right.'

SIX

Heading down 14th Avenue, we turn left in the direction of the White House. As we pull into a narrow street, a black Sedan practically bulldozes us from the front, causing Vladimir to swerve and blast his horn. Thinking it is some idiot, I flip him the bird. As we turn into a plaza, an armed security guard, dressed in black, races towards our car.

'How the hell did you get in here?' he wants to know.

'We're looking for the White House,' I explain innocently.

'This area is off limits today. You could be shot for coming in here.'

What would he think if he knew the car was full of Russians?

'I'm so sorry,' I say. 'We'll turn around and get the hell out.'

He waves us away, but watches as we turn around and head back into the alley. Since we have to pass the guy in the Sedan again, I hope he has a sense of humor.

'I could have shot you,' he says as I roll down the window.

'So I've been told,' I say.

'What are you doing here?' he demands to know.

'We got lost,' I say. 'I'm really sorry. Aren't there any White House tours today?'

'No. The president is hosting a Russian delegation.'

I fight back the urge to laugh. I want to tell him the delegation has arrived, but keep my mouth shut and smile. I wait for him to smile back, but his glare remains as cold as January in Michigan.

As we drive away, I explain why we can't tour the White House. 'A Russian delegation is visiting the president.'

'It's good to know our fellow countrymen are nearby,' Valentine Andreevich says.

'So should we visit the Smithsonian?' I ask.

'What is that?' they all want to know.

'It's a bunch of museums.'

'Well, you know Katey, we have so many museums in Russia,' Valentine Andreevich says.

'I'm sure the museums are nice, but we have so little time,' adds Roman Ivanovich.

'So what do we do now?' I ask Vladimir.

'Shopping. What else? Let's park and find the downtown area.'

He returns to the hotel and parks the car in the underground garage. We walk back to the same area where we ate the night before. There are many quaint boutiques, book stores and souvenir shops, loaded with American paraphernalia. Since they can't read anything in the bookstores, I take them into a souvenir shop. 'Washington DC' T-shirts in various colors line the walls. Counters are crammed with figurines of The White House, The Capitol, and The Washington Monument. A little glass ball with The White House inside snows when you shake it. There are necklaces with White House pendants and dangly earrings with The Washington Monument. Like children at Christmas, the men rush from counter to counter, picking out one figurine after another.

They need twenty minutes to make their selections. Loaded down to the max with T-shirts, pennants, figurines, and jewelry, they approach the check-out counter.

'They're from Russia,' I tell the clerk, a portly black woman dressed in a flaming red blouse and matching cap.

She smiles. 'Yeah, we sell a lot to the Russians.'

We go back out into the late morning sun of a beautiful September day and decide to roam a bit before stopping for lunch. We enter a small shoe store, where they try on Nike running shoes. We visit a sexy boutique where they buy even more black lace lingerie. We go into a spiffy men's store, and I notice Vladimir sifting through the designer neckties. He pulls out a Versace, a light grey color with little yellow suns and buys it for $138, more than I paid for most of my suits.

'I need to find an antique shop,' Vladimir says as we return to the street.

'Why?' I ask.

'I asked my son what I should bring him, and you won't believe what he said. An antique pocket watch.'

'How old is he?'

'Igor is ten. He already knows he wants to be a lawyer.' His face lights up when he talks about his son, his eyes looking into another world.

Realizing I better show more interest, I say, 'He must be very smart.' Then I add, 'My grandfather was a lawyer and I remember he carried a pocket watch.'

'I'll have to tell him that.'

So we find an antique shop, carpeted, poorly lit, and crammed with expensive junk. We find a display counter in the back.

'May I help you?' asks a tall thin salesman in his sixties. I immediately think of Leland Gaunt in Stephen King's Needful Things.

'I'm looking for a present for my ten-year-old son,' Vladimir says.

'We have some very nice antique model airplanes.'

'He wants a pocket watch.'

If the proprietor is surprised, he doesn't let on. He says, 'That's an interesting desire for such a young chap. We have some nice pieces right here in front of you.'

I spot a gold watch with a turquoise face and large roman numerals. 'I bet he'd like that one,' I say, pointing. Then I add, 'It looks like something a lawyer would carry.'

The proprietor whips the watch out onto the counter. Picking it up, Vladimir asks, 'How much does it cost?'

'The model is old. Circa 1900. And the color is rare.'

'How much does it cost?' I repeat.

'Six hundred and that's a bargain.'

I'm sure it's not a bargain.

'How about four hundred?' asks Vladimir, as if reading my thoughts.

'Five-fifty,' he says. 'I can't go any lower.'

'Let's go,' I say to Vladimir.

'Wait,' Leland Gaunt says quickly.

'Four hundred?' I ask.

Leland sighs. Then he says, 'Yeah, four hundred.'

Vladimir takes out his wallet and produces four one-hundred dollar bills.

Leland Gaunt accepts the money without protest.

'Thanks,' Vladimir says as we're leaving. 'I think it's going to be very interesting working with you. You're a tough negotiator.' He grins.

'Your son must be really special,' I say.

'He's the most important person in the world to me.'

I'll have to remember that.

We visit a few more shops before lunch time. At 1:30, when rush hour is past, I take them into a fancy hamburger café, serving massive rounds of chopped steak in hot homemade buns, where you can choose your own toppings from a wide selection. Although Anis wouldn't approve of such a tacky eating establishment, I am determined to expose them to all kinds of American foods.

I'm not surprised when Evgenii Davidovich pulls a bottle of vodka from his backpack. I order five beers and five empty juice glasses. The waiter is an attractive black man who appears to also be the owner and looks a bit like Isiah Thomas from the Bad Boys Detroit Pistons team. He only smiles at our request. Suspecting there might even be a second bottle stashed away, I slip two twenty-dollar bills into the waiter's hand as Evgenii fills the empty glasses almost to the brim.

'To Katey,' says Evgenii Davidovich.

I have a feeling we won't be visiting The Lincoln Memorial.

SEVEN

'So how was the trip to Washington?' Anis asks me on Monday morning.

'Everyone had a great time,' I say.

'Vladimir called me on Thursday, but I missed a call from you. I really would have liked to have heard your thoughts.'

No, you really wouldn't have. 'He called you?'

'Yes. He told me that everything was fine.' He looks like he's about to spit. 'But I would have liked to have heard it from you.'

'Sorry,' I say. *I'm not really.*

'I hope you paid attention to the other customers, and not just to Vladimir.'

Okay. Here it comes. Keep a poker face. 'They had a wonderful time,' I say again.

Anis links his hands, then releases them. He picks up a pencil, twiddles it between his fingers. 'I saw your expense report,' he says. 'There were only four rooms on the bill.'

'I didn't notice that until later,' I say. 'Must have been a mistake.'

Anis still looks like he is about to spit. 'I'm not going to tell you how to manage your personal life, but when the company's involved, you need to be more discreet.'

Although trying to keep my expression sober, I can't prevent a smile scurrying across my face.

'Dave was really upset,' Anis says.

'He didn't seem upset.'

'What do you mean?'

'He wanted to have another drink in the hotel, but the bar was already closed.'

'The others were upset as well,' he says. 'They said you spent all your time with Vladimir instead of doing your job as translator.'

'I should have been sitting next to Jack, but we got there late and I took the only remaining seat.'

'I know. I defended you on that point.' I don't believe him.

'They said you were drunk,' he continues. 'You had your hands all over Vladimir. If you had been a man and done that to a woman, we'd have to worry about a lawsuit.'

'I don't think that's an issue here,' I say, trying to be diplomatic. 'There was a lot of vodka and things got a little wild. It's always that way with Russians. I had to drink the vodka. I didn't want to offend them.'

'I understand. Like I said, I defended you.' After a brief pause he continues, 'I already talked to Vladimir.'

I'm sure Vladimir got a kick out of that.

'It won't happen again,' I promise. But I know it's a promise I won't be able to keep.

The first thing I do after talking to Anis is call Vladimir. Fortunately he is still in his Moscow office.

'Is everything okay?' he asks.

'Dave and Jack complained about me,' I say. 'I don't think Anis was too thrilled either.'

'Yeah, so I've heard. He called me. I think he's afraid I might file a sexual harassment suit.'

'Are you going to?' I ask.

'Of course,' he says. 'Then I can retire early.' Then he says, 'I wouldn't worry too much about it. I explained everything to Anis. I told him you did a terrific job with the customers in Washington.'

'Did he say anything to you about going home with me that night?'

'He tried to, but I pretended not to understand. I think he knew I was pretending.'

'Was it worth it?' I ask flirtatiously.

'Definitely. And I've never cared what other people think. Especially Americans. They're much too uptight.'

'They sure are,' I say, almost forgetting that I am one.

'And Katey,' he says. 'I really don't think Dave and Jack complained. And I am quite sure Bob did not defend you. I suspect it was the other way around. Bob was forced to hire you, but I think he wants you gone.'

'I'll have to be careful who I trust,' I say.

'Don't trust anyone.' Vladimir hangs up the phone.

EIGHT

I am sitting in an aisle seat on an airplane to Moscow
with a transfer in Frankfurt. The man beside me looks like
Abe Lincoln would have if he had lived to an old age, tall
as if his bones have been stretched, a slight paunch and
hair, beard and mustache as white as snow. Rosy cheeks
peeking out from the top of his beard like tiny suns setting
on a winter landscape make me suspect he's a drinker.
Turning his head, he catches me looking at him and
although his mouth is hidden by whiskers, I can tell by the
wrinkles around his eyes that he is smiling.

'Are you going to Germany?' he asks with an accent
once we are in the air. I'm not surprised he speaks English.
Most Europeans know at least a little.

'No,' I say. 'To Russia.'

'Russia?' I hear a definite '*What on earth for?*' in his tone.

'Yes. I sell high-voltage electrical equipment.'

'It's a strange job for a woman.'

'Actually it's a perfect job for a woman.'

'Why's that?'

'All of my customers are men. Men are more willing to
talk to an attractive woman than some aging bald man with
a pot belly. Why do you think men make the best door-to-

door salesmen? All of their customers are women. It's the same idea.'

'Do you have to drink a lot of vodka?' I've heard this question from just about everyone I've told about my new job.

I decide not to tell him this is my first business trip. 'Yeah, you can't do business without drinking vodka.'

'Should we drink some now?'

The question catches me off guard. His eyes are twinkling like two sapphires. I had been planning to stay sober and read my book.

'Sure, why not,' I say. 'It's a long flight.'

When the stewardess returns, my seatmate requests two little bottles of vodka. The stewardess gives us four.

'My mother is from Leningrad,' he says, as if to explain his fondness for vodka. I don't remind him that the name has been changed to St. Petersburg.

'A toast to pretty ladies,' he says.

'Thank you.'

We slug it down.

'Would you like another?'

Even though I should say no and read my book, I say, 'Sure.'

'To German men with beards,' I say for lack of anything better. I hold out my second shot of vodka.

'Thank you. How sweet.'

The second shot tastes better than the first. I feel my inhibitions fading and hope he'll suggest a third. He does. But it takes a while for the stewardess to appear.

'Ever try a Bloody Mary?' I ask. A Bloody Mary is one of my favorite drinks.

'What's that?'

'Vodka with spicy tomato juice.'

He makes a face as if I'd asked him to eat a worm. 'You should never mix vodka.'

His Russian mother taught him well.

When a different stewardess rushes past without the

drink cart, my seat mate reaches across me and grabs her arm.

'You might as well give us four again,' I add after he requests the vodka, 'and save yourself time.'

The stewardess wrinkles her nose. 'If you want more after you've finished the first ones, I'll bring them then.'

'Bitch,' I whisper as she leaves. My German friend laughs.

'The American stewardesses are stingy with drinks,' he says. 'The Europeans will give you anything you want.'

Somehow I believe him. 'Do you fly a lot?' I ask.

'I used to,' he answers. 'Before I had my stroke.'

'You had a stroke?' He seems so healthy.

'Yes. Two years ago. That's why my voice sounds so terrible.'

His voice does sound raspy. 'It sounds fine to me,' I say.

'It used to be much better.'

'How do you speak English so well?' I ask, no longer wanting to discuss his health.

'I worked for three years in a German company in Atlanta when I was young and handsome. I had an American lover.' He leans back in his seat and smiles. 'She looked a bit like you.'

The same stewardess returns, pushing a dinner cart.

'I'd like chicken, please,' I say, glancing at the cart. There is no menu, but they always have chicken and it is usually the most popular choice.

'We're all out,' she says. *Surprise, surprise.* And there are also no drinks on the cart.

We both choose beef—although choose isn't really the right word—little chunks of meat, stewed in gravy, with synthetic mashed potatoes. The salad is so small I can barely find it; an apple pastry with one slice of apple looks like it is preserved in formaldehyde. *Why do they even bother offering a second main course when everyone wants chicken anyways?*

After dinner a black steward, just fat enough to look

like he enjoys life, walks past our row of seats on his way to the back of the plane.

'Sir,' says my neighbor, reaching past me again. His arm grazes my breast as he stretches to touch the man's arm. The steward stops and turns around. Unlike the bitchy stewardess, he actually smiles.

'Some vodka for me and the lovely lady,' my travel companion says.

'Anything else?' he asks before going to get the drinks.

Well, since you're asking. 'A beer, please,' I say. All that vodka has made me thirsty.

'Make that two,' says my companion.

In a few minutes, the steward returns with four little bottles of vodka and four beers. Arranging them on our trays, he says, 'I'm gonna fix you guys up real good.'

I thank him and turn to my new friend. 'Are you married?'

'For 42 years,' he says. 'What about you?'

'I got divorced last year.' But I have a wonderful new lover, I want to say. 'Do you have children?' I ask instead.

'No.' He frowns, wrinkles appearing in the center of his forehead, so I let the subject drop. He doesn't ask me if I have children.

'What were you doing in the states?' I ask.

'I was visiting my lover.'

'You're kidding.'

'Yes, I am kidding,' he says. 'I was visiting my brother.'

'How long has he lived there?' I ask.

'I would have liked to visit my lover,' he says, ignoring my last question.

'So, why didn't you?' I ask.

'She's dead.'

I seem to keep asking the wrong questions. As I am trying to decide what kind of question would be the right one, he raises his shot glass. I raise mine and we clink them together, not bothering to propose a toast.

'What happened to her?'

'To whom?'

'Your lover.'

'What about her?'

'You said she was dead.'

'Hell, I don't know if she's dead. I can't screw her. That's all I know.'

'Why not?'

'It's those damned beta blockers,' he says. 'I can't get it up.'

I don't respond.

'Haven't slept with a woman since I had my stroke.'

'Does it bother your wife?'

'My wife?' He chuckles. 'She hasn't let me touch her in ten years.'

'So you haven't slept with a woman in ten years?'

'I didn't say that.'

I swig my beer. He continues staring at me, which suddenly makes me uncomfortable. I turn my head toward the front, stretch my legs as far as possible in the tiny foot space, and put back my seat. I close my eyes and pretend to sleep. Otherwise, he is going to tell me whom he slept with and I don't want to know. *A young woman who looks just like you*, I imagine him saying.

I keep my eyes shut ten minutes. When I open them, the old man is snoring softly, his hands crossed in his lap, his tray still down with the half-finished beer. It is almost ten o'clock and we'll reach Frankfurt in about three hours. I turn on my reading lamp and take out my book, a Sidney Sheldon novel. Even though it is fast-paced and easy to read, the vodka in my head makes the words swim on the page like black minnows. Giving up, I close my eyes, the book in my lap, my finger marking page one. Even though I never sleep on airplanes, when I open my eyes again, the lights are on and we are approaching Frankfurt.

NINE

The Moscow airport, Sheremetevo, looks like a giant tomb. As if part of an official funeral procession, we exit the plane without talking and proceed down a grey corridor leading to a poorly lit windowless room with a row of booths for passport and visa checks. *You are now entering the Twilight Zone.* Only two of the booths are occupied, and we form two sloppy lines behind them. Several Russian women in skirted military uniforms and heavy makeup are running around looking busy.

Reaching my turn, I stand before a baby-faced boy in a green uniform with eyes as pale as a summer sky. Without smiling, he examines my passport and visa. Since the pictures were taken before I started bleaching my hair, he stares at them for a long time. I stand stiff as a statue, forgetting to breathe. Finally the boy hammers the passport and visa with several large stamps and hands them back to me. Even though Communism has become a relic, I am as relieved as I was the last time I entered the 'Evil Empire' eight years earlier during my student days.

The rest of the airport has changed only slightly since the last time I saw it, still lacking luxury and brightness, the baggage-claim area smoky and dingy. Men dressed in dark colors, either undercover cops or gangsters, are hanging around with no clear purpose. Some westerners keep looking nervously at the baggage chute.

Fifteen minutes later, the track rumbles into action, but it still takes several minutes for the first bags to emerge. At a little stand, I rent a cart for two dollars. Returning to the luggage track, I spot my first bag and heave it onto the cart. When ten minutes later, my second suitcase still hasn't appeared, I start to worry. It would be just my luck to lose another bag on my very first business trip.

Finally, after most of the luggage has been collected, my coveted suitcase appears like a lost child. I wonder if somebody had been searching it. Greatly relieved, I push my cart towards the exit.

When I get outside, a cold wind slaps my face. It is already becoming dark and although it is only October, I sense impending snow. Taxis are racing by and people are running around trying to catch them. A heavyset man with a row of metal teeth approaches me.

'You need taxi?' he asks in English.

'I don't know yet,' I answer in perfect Russian. Although I haven't seen Vladimir since Washington, we've had enough telephone conversations to cause Anis to complain about my phone bill. I asked Vladimir to meet my flight and he said he would try. I'm hoping he is only late.

I stand on the sidewalk for another ten minutes while several men approach me about a taxi. I finally tell the fourth yes and get into the back of the car.

'Aerostar Hotel,' I say.

His tires squeal as he takes off. He's driving too fast and I see pedestrians rush out of the way. We race from the airport and are soon cruising along a busy highway. The emergence of capitalism in Russia is evident by the increased number of cars since the last time I was here. Although it's dark, I can tell many of them are western imports.

It doesn't take long until we're cruising down Leningrad Prospect, although it's probably been renamed to St. Petersburg Prospect or something else entirely. We pass metro stations every few miles—*Rechnoi Bokzal, Vodnii Stadion, Sokol, Aeroport, Dynamo.* Since my ex-husband lived near *Vodnii Stadion,* I recognize all the landmarks. At every metro station, I notice rush hour mobs coming up from underground into the streetlights.

Before long we reach my hotel, a modern building set back from the road. The long driveway is lined with leafless trees decorated with Christmas lights, a strange sight for October. Although the forty-five minute taxi ride costs me ninety dollars, I give the driver a hundred-dollar bill, and request a receipt for the same amount. It would have been cheaper and more reliable to arrange airport pickup from Aerostar, but I had been hoping Vladimir would meet me.

Although already costing $220 a night, my room is loaded with ways to spend even more money, starting with a five-dollar tip for the bellboy. Tiny bottles of liquor from the mini bar cost six dollars, in-room movies, mainly porno, are offered for eighteen dollars a showing, and a menu on the bed lists entrées starting at twenty-five dollars for a bowl of borsch, a traditional Russian soup made from red beets. The Russians are obviously not timid about embracing capitalism.

Even though I've barely slept in over 24 hours, I am now too excited to sleep. I have a phone number from an old friend of my ex-husband's who is probably still living in Moscow. It's been eight years, and he may have moved, but I dial the number anyway.

'Kulinov,' says a voice. Russians always sound so cold when they answer the telephone. None of this smiley *Johnson residence, Gloria speaking* that you hear in the states.

'Andrei?' I say shyly. Every time I talk on the telephone to a Russian, I'm afraid they're going to cuss me out.

'Yeah.'

'This is Katey,' I say. I'm pretty sure he'll remember me. It's not like there are a lot of Russians running around named Katey. All the same, I hold my breath until he answers.

'Alexander's Katey?'

'I was, yeah. I'm in Moscow.'

'Where?' he asks. *Don't you want to know why? Don't you want to ask where Alexander is?*

'At the Aerostar Hotel, room 342,' I say. 'I'm alone.' *Why am I telling him that? He'll probably think I'm looking for a quickie.*

This time he doesn't hesitate. 'Give me 40 minutes.' He hangs up without saying good-bye. I wonder why he is so eager. Maybe he's always had the hots for me.

I have time to shower and change my clothes. I can't decide if I want to look seductive or casual. It's really hard to look sexy after being awake 24 hours. Even my hair looks tired. All the same, I've never been able to meet a man without at least trying to look my best.

So instead of slipping into sloppy jeans and a T-shirt which would really correspond to my mood, I take a hot shower and wash my hair. After I blow dry it to the best of my ability, my hair still looks drowsy. I put on a brown suede miniskirt with matching patterned tights, a baggy olive sweater, and high-heeled boots. I apply green eye shadow in two shades, followed by coral rouge and lipstick. Although my eyeballs still look like they've been dipped in glycerin, I'm fairly satisfied with my appearance.

I open the door to Andrei's knock. With pale blue eyes and hair like a wheat field, he looks just like James Dean. I remember the words of an old song,

If you can't be with the one you love,
Love the one you're with.

Dressed smartly in slacks and a blazer—definitely not Russian made—he could easily pose for 'Gentlemen's Quarterly'.

After all these years, I have no idea what to say. We

embrace silently, kissing the air beside our cheeks. I detect a scent which smells much more expensive than the Soviet-made au de cologne that Russians used to drink during Gorbachev's war on alcohol.

'Should we go to the bar?' he asks, glancing at the bed.

'It costs a fortune here,' I reply. 'Why don't we get a bottle and drink it in the room?' In the back of my mind, I am still hoping Vladimir will call. On the other hand, I don't want Andrei to think I'm ready to hop in the sack with him. I definitely shouldn't have called him. I wish I could reel the camera backwards.

'I can afford the bar,' he says, sounding slightly offended.

The last time I saw him he was living with his mother and sewing fake designer clothes for a living. I wonder what he is doing now to earn so much money.

We take the elevator to a bar on the seventh floor. Only one other table is occupied. A pot-bellied man in a spiffy suit is sitting knee-to-knee with a woman in a red miniskirt, knee-high black patent leather boots with spike heels, heavy makeup in vibrant colors, and a plunging neckline. She is probably one of the hotel 'escorts'.

When a skinny waiter approaches our table, dressed in a black dinner jacket, white shirt and bowtie, Andrei asks for their best cognac. Remembering the expensive soup on my room-service menu, I'm afraid to imagine the price. Although cognac is one of my least favorite drinks, I don't want to disappoint Andrei.

The cognac, served in snifters, is mild and warms my throat. Andrei leans back thoughtfully and stares at me.

'So, how's Alexander?' he asks.

'He divorced me,' I answer, not offering an explanation. I don't really want to talk about him.

'What's he doing now?'

'The last I heard he was spending his time in casinos.'

'Losing?'

'Yeah, but at least he's not losing my money anymore.'

Andrei takes a sip of his cognac. 'So, what are you doing in Russia?'

I tell him about my new job and don't know if he's impressed or not.

'You can make a lot of money in Russia now,' he says.

'How?' I ask.

'Speculating, simply buying and selling at the right time.'

When I was in Russia eight years earlier, the penalty for speculating in foreign currency was at least seven years in prison, even execution if the amounts were great enough.

'Isn't it dangerous?'

He brushes my question off with his hand. 'Nah, everyone's doing it.'

He orders another round of cognac. This one tastes better than the first.

'So why did Alexander leave you?' he asks, lighting a cigarette.

'I didn't say he left me.'

'Did you leave him?'

'Not exactly. He wanted to marry a Ukrainian chick for two years so that she could get a green card. Then he planned to divorce her and marry me again.'

'So you didn't go for it?'

'Would you have?'

'I guess not,' Andrei says hesitantly. I'm not sure he liked my decision. Alexander had been one of his closest friends.

Although I hadn't planned to trash my ex-husband, the cognac has loosened my tongue. 'Anyway, I called his bluff. I told him if he divorced me, it was over.'

'How did he react?'

'He started divorce proceedings.'

'Was the girl paying him to marry her?'

'I think her family was, but I'm not sure. He wouldn't tell me. Actually, I don't think he ever did marry her.'

The waiter comes back and Andrei orders a third

round. I hope he has enough money because I don't want to get stuck with the bill.

In a few minutes a man in a red blazer approaches the table. 'Excuse me, sir,' he says.

Andrei turns toward him but doesn't speak.

'May I talk to you privately?' the man asks.

Still without a word, Andrei gets up and follows the man a few steps. Although I can't hear what they're saying, I see Andrei pull out a wad of bills as thick as three decks of cards and peel off a half inch. The other man takes the money, looking embarrassed. I hear him apologize for the inconvenience before Andrei returns to the table.

In less than two minutes, the third round of cognac is before us on the table.

'Do you still sew leather jackets?' I ask. When I was in Russia as a student, Andrei had earned a decent black market salary buying low-quality Soviet leather coats, cutting them up, and restyling them into trendy jackets. It hadn't mattered that they were low-quality leather. He made them flashy, and flashy in Russia was not only in, but hard to find in those days. At one point he was also buying material from some man who was siphoning off supplies from a factory making artificial limbs. In other words, some of those Afghanistan war veterans hopping around Moscow on one leg would have had a prosthetic had it not been for Andrei's little sideline.

'No, I gave that up. It wasn't very much money.'

By the way he is buying cognac, I know he is getting his money somewhere.

'So what do you speculate in?' I ask.

'Everything. Just buying and selling.' He's being purposely vague.

Just when I decide he doesn't want to tell me, he continues, 'I'm also trying to get involved in barter with foreign companies.'

'What kind of barter?'

'The Russians want foreign products, but they don't have any dollars,' he explains. 'But they have a lot of other things to trade—wood, metals, grain, vodka.'

This conversation is becoming interesting. I suspect that my customers have the same monetary problems. 'Maybe we can work together,' I suggest.

'Yeah, the power companies tend to have a lot of resources.'

'That's good to hear,' I say.

'But you have to offer them something.'

'What do you mean?'

He empties his cognac and looks around for the waiter, who appears as if on cue. 'Do you want anything to eat?' he asks.

'No,' I say. 'I don't like to eat when I'm drinking.'

'Another round,' he says to the waiter. It arrives almost immediately.

'Are you going to tell me what you meant?' I ask.

'You give them something, they give you something,' he says as we clink our glasses together and drink.

His vagueness is starting to irritate me. Does he mean I have to bribe them or sleep with them?

The waiter places still another round before us. I don't remember Andrei ordering it, but he doesn't object.

'That could be tricky,' I say. *And illegal..*

Andrei only shrugs. I imagine telling Anis I need $10,000 for a bribe.

The combination of jetlag and cognac is making me dizzy. I don't know if I should drink the cognac, order coffee, or say goodnight. Andrei leans back in his chair and stares at me with glistening eyes. For the first time, it occurs to me that he probably expects me to sleep with him. Suddenly I can only think of Vladimir and wonder if he has tried to call my room.

I choose to drink the cognac. I can never sleep anyway when I have jetlag and don't feel like being alone. Maybe I shouldn't wait by the phone like a lovesick teenager.

'So, whatever happened to Natasha?' I ask.

'We broke up,' he says. 'I didn't have enough money for her then.'

Natasha had been Andrei's girlfriend when I was a student in Russia. We were having a party at Andrei's one evening when she almost literally ripped the stockings off an Irish friend of mine. Wobbling on high heels, with black fishnet stockings, hair like fire and tits like a pair of late-October Uzbek melons, Ingrid was barely five feet tall.

At first Natasha only admired Ingrid's stockings. But as the evening progressed, Natasha began to moan about the scarcity of such items in Russia. Finally, after several glasses of champagne, she demanded that Ingrid give them to her. Although it was the middle of winter, Ingrid peeled off the stockings and presented them to Natasha as if the idea had been her own. Ingrid went home that night barelegged in the winter cold.

Ingrid's boyfriend Max, who has a face like Rambo, was furious, Andrei embarrassed, and I too drunk to notice. Alexander, who didn't drink, had been a neutral observer and told me about the incident afterwards.

'Where is Natasha now?' I ask.

'She married some director and has a kid.'

I wonder if she still has the black stockings.

By the time we finish our cognac and drink a fifth one, Andrei is slumped in his chair, looking like he could drink the entire night. Although I'd like another, I stand up and tell him I am tired. I'm not wearing a watch, but the time must be around 11:00, probably too late for Vladimir to call.

Andrei pays for the last three rounds and we head back to my room. I stop at the door, not intending to invite him in.

'It was really nice to see you,' I say.

'Should we have a nightcap from the mini-bar?'

Although the idea sounds tempting, what's left of my better judgment tells me to say goodnight. 'It's really late and I need to sleep…'

His mouth pressing against mine cuts off my words. Before I can protest, his hands creep under my sweater, finding my bare breasts. Knowing I'll regret it, I reach behind me and open the door. It seems like too much effort to fight him off and I've never been good at saying no. Maybe I need the constant reassurance that men find me attractive. Maybe I'm a nymphomaniac and don't realize it. Maybe I'm angry at Vladimir for not picking me up at the airport and want to get revenge. Maybe I'm just too drunk to know what the hell I'm doing.

Once inside, he releases me long enough to remove his jacket and toss it on a chair. Then he pulls my sweater over my head, kisses each of my nipples, and unzips my skirt before pushing me backwards onto the bed. After removing my boots, he peels off my tights and panties.

Lying naked on the bed, I watch him undress, tossing his clothes onto the floor. In less than a minute, he's on top of me. Just as he enters me and is starting to thrust, the phone rings.

'Don't answer it,' Andrei whispers.

'I have to,' I say, pushing him off me. 'It could be my boss.'

Picking up the phone, I murmur, 'Hello.'

'Where have you been?' I immediately recognize Vladimir's husky voice, and although he can't possibly see me, I feel ashamed.

'I waited for you at the airport,' I say.

'I was busy,' he says.

'I was with an old friend,' I say. *Keep him guessing.*

'What old friend?'

'Nobody you know,' I say.

'I'll pick you up tomorrow,' he says. 'Shortly before nine.'

I'm disappointed that he doesn't ask more about my friend. If he's jealous, he's not showing it. 'Okay,' I say. 'I'll see you tomorrow.'

After I hang up, I remember Andrei lying beside me, and suddenly want to be alone. Standing up, I go into the bathroom and slip into the white terrycloth bathrobe provided by the hotel. Andrei is still waiting on the bed when I return. I notice he's lost his erection.

'Listen,' I say, not approaching him. 'It really is late, and I'm tired.'

'Do you want me to leave?' he asks, still not moving.

'It's not that I want you to leave,' I say. 'But, yeah, I think you should.'

As Andrei dresses, I go to the mini bar and pour myself a glass of wine. All I want is a hot bath and a cool pillow.

After he leaves, I sink into a lavish bubble bath, my wine glass on the rim of the tub. But the water is so hot I am quickly forced to get out. After drying my red skin, I slip on an undershirt. Then I set my unfinished wine on the nightstand and sit on the bed. Before getting under the covers, I fill out the breakfast card, ordering only coffee, and hang it on the outside doorknob.

I wish I had waited for Vladimir's call instead of calling Andrei. Perhaps he would have stopped by. Although tempted to drink another glass of wine from the mini-bar, I turn out the light and crawl under the heavy down comforter. I lie awake for a long time before drifting off into a restless sleep.

TEN

I'm lying naked on top of Vladimir, his tongue exploring my mouth, his hands caressing my buttocks. I raise my head and look into his eyes, glistening in the moonlight, and kiss each of them. 'I love you,' he says.

Before I can tell him the same, the phone rings. At first I don't understand who could be calling in the middle of the night, but when the ringing persists, I awaken from my dream to the morning sun, see that I am alone, and pick up the receiver.

'Good morning. It is eight o'clock,' says a heavily accented voice in English.

Dropping the receiver onto the phone, I let my head sink into the feather pillow. Awake most of the night because of jetlag, I had drifted off shortly before dawn. Even though it's morning, my body tells me it's midnight and my head feels so heavy I can barely lift it. All I want to do is return to my dream.

Lifting my cannonball head, I roll out of bed and head for the bathroom. After peeing as if I'd been holding it for weeks, I get into the shower and let hot water flow over my body, almost putting me back to sleep. After washing my hair I turn the water so cold that the shock makes me jump around like a scared chicken. But at least I'm awake. I leave the shower just in time to hear a knock on the door and quickly slip on my bathrobe.

Then, thinking it must be Vladimir arriving early and hoping to catch me naked, I toss the bathrobe onto a chair and open the door.

'Oh fuck!' I say, standing face-to-face with the bellboy. He looks like a high school kid, who has probably just seen his first naked woman besides his mother. He stands frozen, face and ears reddening, eyes focused on my vagina. I'm surprised he doesn't drop the tray with the coffee pot.

I jump back and grab the bathrobe, awkwardly stuffing my arms into the sleeves. Then I return to the door, trying to ignore the incident. For several seconds, neither of us says a word.

'Your coffee,' he finally says without looking at my face. He's dressed in a red suit which looks like a circus uniform. He enters the room cautiously, as if expecting, perhaps even hoping, to intrude on an orgy, and sets the tray on the table.

I take a ten dollar bill out of my purse and press it into his palm. Although the tip is much too large for a pot of coffee, it's my way of thanking him for his tact. When he looks up at me, a smile escaping from his lips, I wink.

Sitting on the bed, I sip my first cup of coffee, black without sugar. My parents let me start drinking coffee at the age of 12, but they said only if I drink it without sugar and milk. They didn't want it to taste too good, I guess, for the fear that I would become too easily addicted. Their strategy didn't work. I'm as addicted as hell. The Russians brew their coffee stronger than the Americans, drinking it with loads of sugar and milk. No wonder so many of them have a mouth full of metal teeth, I think, my thoughts wandering to Vladimir's perfect white pearls, and I remember that he also drank his coffee black in

Washington. Blood rushes to my pelvic region when I realize I'll be seeing him in half an hour.

Although tempted to wait for Vladimir naked, I pull on silk panties and thigh-high stockings. Standing before the mirror with a blow-dryer, I notice I've lost weight, and my breasts have gotten smaller. My triceps ripple as I maneuver the dryer around my head. Using a round brush, I attempt to curl the ends neatly under, but the brush keeps getting tangled in my hair and I have to yank it out. Already damaged by numerous bleach jobs, my hair looks slightly better than straw when I'm finished.

After applying a combination of brown and teal eye shadows and neatly tracing my eyes with liner, I brush poppy-colored rouge onto my cheeks, followed by a matching lipstick. I skip the mascara. Regardless of what the commercials promise, it always smudges, making me look like a raccoon. Finally, I use powder to dull the sheen of my nose.

A sleeveless silk top covers my shrinking tits. Then I don a periwinkle suit with a short narrow skirt, finally stepping into matching pumps with heels too high for serious walking. Even though I'll freeze and have sore feet, I still want to look sexy.

At five minutes to nine I pace around the room, looking repeatedly into the full-length mirror at various angles. Turning sideways I suck my stomach in so hard that my skirt slides down to my hips. With the mirror from my powder compact, I inspect myself from behind. I return to the bathroom and comb my hair again, the strands so fine that the slightest breeze will turn them into a rat's nest. I start to bite my thumb nail but stop by picking up a file and manicuring each finger.

At ten after nine, I'm tempted to call Vladimir on his cell phone, but decide to give him ten more minutes. I don't want to appear desperate. Perhaps he's just stuck in rush hour traffic. After pouring the last of the lukewarm coffee into my cup, I realize I'll need to brush my teeth again and decide not to drink it.

A fleeting thought that he's late because he's been making love to his wife unnerves me. I reach for the phone and start to dial his number, but return the receiver to its cradle before it starts to ring. Just as I realize he might be waiting in the lobby, there is a knock on the door.

I look in the mirror one more time and rehearse a toothy smile, mentally thanking my parents for forcing me to have dental checkups every six months. Then I go to the door, breathe deeply, and open it, my heart beating so strongly I'm sure Vladimir will hear it.

Instead of the relaxed and good-natured character I remember from Pittsburgh and Washington, I am suddenly facing an agitated businessman in a dark suit with a familiar Versace necktie, a wool coat, and a black leather briefcase. Before looking at me, he looks at his watch.

On impulse I put my arms on his shoulders and plant several kisses on his cheeks and forehead, smelling familiar cologne. But when I try to pull him into the room, he sets down his briefcase and returns my arms to my sides.

'The others are waiting downstairs,' he says, picking up his briefcase. 'And we're already late.'

Without kissing me he heads for the elevator. I stiletto back into the room to grab my coat, purse and bag of souvenirs for the visitors: Swiss army knives, corkscrews, travel alarms, and pens, all with the company logo.

When I enter the hallway Vladimir is already in the elevator holding the door open. Walking as fast as my shoes allow, I join him. Then the doors close and we are alone.

'Hello, Katey,' he says, elongating the 'a' sound and looking into my eyes. He sets down his briefcase and pulls me to him. As he kisses me, I feel his hand reach under my skirt and wander up my thigh. Reaching under the crotch of my panties, he caresses me, and I shudder. In less than a minute, however, the elevator stops at the ground floor. Vladimir pulls away as if he's just been caught by his grandmother, straightens his tie, and turns to face the door. I smooth my skirt and resist an urge to press against him.

As we enter the hotel lobby, Vladimir charges towards two men who are waiting near the front door. One is husky and bearded with cheeks like tennis balls, obviously a German. The other is tall and fair, probably Swedish. Both are over forty and wearing wedding rings.

'Katey, this is Hermann Mathias and Bjorn Anderson,' Vladimir says in English.

Mr. Mathias squeezes my hand so hard I'm afraid he'll break my fingers. Mr. Anderson's grip is more pleasant. I hold his hand longer than I should, staring briefly into his hazel eyes. He looks a bit like Robert Redford.

'So this is the pretty American,' Bjorn says as he releases my grip. 'Vladimir has done nothing but talk about you.'

'Of course,' Vladimir says, winking. 'You can't keep such a pretty lady a secret.'

It thrills me to know Vladimir has been talking about me. Perhaps I should be offended by their blatant sexism, but like all women, I am flattered by their references to my appearance. Even the most ardent feminists with their doctoral degrees and Wall Street jobs still want to be considered beautiful. And those who insist they don't are simply unwilling to admit it.

Although Hermann hasn't said anything, I notice him grinning and undressing me with his eyes.

'Vladimir says you speak his language very well,' he says in Russian.

'So do you,' I say, also switching to Russian.

'I was born in Kazakhstan.'

'I was born in Michigan.' Although I expect him to bombard me with questions about my background, he lets the subject drop. Maybe he's never heard of Michigan.

We follow Vladimir out of the hotel to a large blue

Volvo. The two men climb into the back, letting me have the seat beside Vladimir. As we drive through Moscow traffic, I spread my legs slightly, letting my skirt ride up towards my crouch.

We race down Tverskaya Street, previously called Gorky Street, and turn off in a direction unfamiliar to me. We seem to be heading out of town. After ten minutes we pull into a crowded parking lot where Vladimir finds the last empty spot as if it had been waiting for him.

We walk toward a brown pavilion with people congregated outside. Entering, I notice an array of partitioned cubicles with posters displaying electrical equipment from international companies. I quickly see Ampere Power Dead Tank and follow Vladimir to our section. One corner contains posters of our circuit breakers and several piles of brochures which had been shipped the previous month. Placing my bag on the table I begin to arrange the souvenirs. I don't hear Vladimir approaching me from behind.

'Don't do that,' he says, startling me.

'Why not?'

'They'll take everything at once,' he says. 'You have to distribute them carefully.'

'I should have thought of that,' I say, returning the items to my bag.

'Most people show up just to collect trinkets,' he says. 'They're not real customers.'

'How can I tell who the real customers are?'

'I'll let you know.'

'What if you're not around?' I say. 'What if you're over talking to Bjorn, and a real customer shows up. How will I recognize him?'

'I'll keep an eye on you,' Vladimir says. 'If I see anyone important, I'll come over and join you.'

'How do you recognize them?'

'By the way they're dressed, by the expressions on their faces, some of them I've already met. I just do. It's not an exact science.'

'So what do I do now?' I ask, glancing at the table, the brochures, and the posters.

'Just stand there and look pretty. If anyone asks a really technical question, you can come and get me.' He grins and winks.

'Thanks a lot,' I say, feeling like a Barbie doll. But because I know he is right, I can't really be offended. My experience with the technical aspects of the equipment is still limited; I can barely discuss SF6 gas properties and interruption times in English, much less in Russian.

'So how much does one of those cost?'

I look up and face a man in an ill-fitted grey suit and flakes of dandruff in his greasy hair.

More than you can afford, I want to say, looking at his pea-green polyester tie. 'The 145-kilovolt breakers cost around $150,000, including transport and installation. We send our own service engineer.'

'Expensive,' he says. 'Ours aren't so expensive.'

I'm sure they aren't.

'I'm the chief engineer from Kostromenergo,' he says, extending his hand. 'Boris Ivanovich Bashkov.' He pronounces it 'Bash-KOHF.'

I take his hand. It's clammy. 'Katey O'Hara. Is Kostromenergo planning to replace some circuit breakers?'

'We'd replace them all if we had the money,' he says. 'Nobody has any money in Russia.'

Not knowing how to respond, I reach into my bag and pull out a Swiss army knife with our company logo. I also hand him two brochures.

'I'll be happy to make a trip to Kostroma and give a presentation about our products,' I say.

'You'd certainly be welcome, but we still don't have any money.'

He wanders on to the next booth.

As soon as he's gone, Vladimir is at my side. 'Who was that?' he asks.

'The chief engineer from Kostromenergo. Weren't you supposed to help me out when real customers show up?'

'What did he say?' he asks, ignoring my accusation.

'When I told him how much they cost, he said they don't have any money.'

'They all say that.'

'Well, if nobody has any money, how am I going to sell anything?'

'Next time, don't talk about prices,' he says. 'You don't want to scare them off before sparking their interest.'

'What do I say if they ask?'

'Tell them you have to see their specifications first. Then tell them they will need to come to America to inspect the factory. They always like that.'

'What good will that do if they don't have any money?'

'They'll find the money if they want the product badly enough. Here comes somebody else.'

This time a stocky man in an expensive blue suit with an elegant silk tie approaches me. He has bushy grey hair and kind eyes which wander over my body, pausing at my breasts and finally stopping at my face.

'Hello,' he says, taking my hand. 'Dmitri Sergeevich Miasnikov.'

'Nice to meet you,' I say. 'Katey O'Hara. I'm representing Ampere Power Dead Tank.'

'We may have a mutual interest,' he says, his eyes fixed on my own. 'We need to replace some circuit breakers.'

I notice he hasn't asked about the cost.

'I could come to your company and make a presentation,' I offer.

'That would be very nice,' he says. 'Have you ever been to Tula?'

'No.'

'We have the best vodka in all of Russia.'

'Then I'll have to come,' I say, smiling.

'Katey appreciates good vodka,' Vladimir says, extending his hand. He has been standing behind me, silently observing my performance. He says, 'Kashirnikov. Vladimir Aleksandrovich. I run the Moscow office. I'm sure we can arrange a trip for Katey to Tula.'

'Now is a bad time,' Miasnikov says. 'We have a lot going on. How about early December?'

Vladimir whips out a business card. 'Would you like to call me or should I call you?'

Miasnikov also produces a card. 'Why don't you call me in the middle of November?'

'I'll do that.'

Miasnikov takes my hand once more and brings it to his lips. 'It's been a great pleasure, Katey.'

I press a Swiss army knife into his palm. 'Something to remind you of us.'

'A present for my grandson. Thank you.'

After he's gone I ask Vladimir, 'Who exactly was that?'

Looking at the business card, Vladimir says, 'The chief engineer of Tulenergo. We might have something here.'

'So they have money?'

'I'll explain that at the proper time.'

'Explain it now,' I say.

'I can't talk about that here, Katey.'

His tone tells me not to push it.

The day progresses slowly. I stand around the table talking to various men in polyester suits and although I try to avoid the subject, they always try to get me to reveal the price.

'How much does one of those cost?'

'I would have to see your specifications'

'Well, approximately?'

'And if you place an order, you will need to send a team to inspect our plant in America. It's also included in the contract price.'

'How much do they cost?'

'They start at 140,000 US dollars,' I say, giving up.

'Expensive.'

Around lunch time Vladimir takes us to a buffet. Bjorn

and Hermann have been hearing similar stories of impoverished Russian power companies. They both seem to think the trip was a waste of time and money. I don't tell them about Miasnikov. I have one advantage over them, remembering how the chief engineer had looked at my legs.

Bottles of wine, vodka and beer decorate the counter. Not wanting to be the only drinker, I am relieved when Hermann selects a beer. When I ask for a glass of wine, a plump woman tells me I have to buy the whole bottle. Vladimir also brings four shots of vodka to our table. Bjorn opens my wine bottle and pours me a glass.

'Are you going to drink it all?' he asks.

'I need to do something to add some excitement to this afternoon,' I say.

Vladimir returns to the counter and collects various dishes: hard boiled eggs smeared with red caviar, open-faced sandwiches with slices of dark red salami speckled with chunks of fat, a tray of pickles, rye bread, and a metal dish of black caviar with butter.

Taking an egg spread with caviar in one hand, he raises his vodka. 'The Russians always say there is no such thing as too much vodka,' he says. 'Just not enough food. You will hear this expression again and again here. You can't enjoy good food without vodka, and you shouldn't drink vodka without good food.'

I spread butter and black caviar on a slice of bread. Bjorn and Hermann follow my lead.

'To our success in Russia,' Vladimir says, once the glasses have all been raised.

The caviar melts on my tongue, a delightfully mild flavor I haven't tasted in years, not too salty like the cheap caviar sold in the states. I remember seeing a tin of it in the duty-free shop in Moscow years ago for forty dollars and wonder what it costs today.

Vladimir brings another round of vodka to drink with

the remaining snacks. He then recommends that we try the borsch, a Russian beet soup. The others take it but I decline, preferring to finish the caviar and wine.

After eating, we disperse to our various stations. Tipsy from wine and vodka, I lose my balance and fly onto my ass. So much for high heels! As the afternoon drags on, my alcohol high starts to plummet and I yearn for sleep. I don't meet any more potential customers, just a steady stream of poorly dressed engineers and technicians hoping to take home a few souvenirs.

By late afternoon I've developed a sore throat and scratchy chest, and by six o'clock, when the exhibit ends, I am shivering with chills and fever. All I want is a heavy blanket and a bowl of hot soup.

Vladimir drives us back to the hotel. We say our goodbyes in the lobby and I head for my room. Shivering, I remove my clothes. Even though an unwise choice with a high fever, I take a hot shower to generate warmth into my body. Then I put on pajamas and crawl under the down comforter.

Scanning the menu I find a bowl of expensive cabbage soup with bread. Although I could probably buy cheaper food elsewhere, I'm too sick to move from the bed.

After the soup arrives I balance it on my lap in bed, feeling almost too weak to lift the spoon. Although I don't have a thermometer, I'm guessing my fever at 104 degrees. All I want is to burrow under the blanket, but I need medication (I've hear that the flu in Russia is nothing to joke about). After finishing the soup, I dress in jeans and a sweater, put on my winter jacket, and set out.

The late October wind makes me shiver like a dachshund in a snowstorm. I follow the driveway to the main sidewalk, which runs parallel to Leningrad Prospect. Finding a kiosk with medicinal supplies, I approach a middle-age woman.

'I need something for the flu,' I say. 'I'm burning up with fever.'

'You need a doctor,' she says.

'No, I just need something for this fever.'

She quickly produces a small box. 'Take this. It's 3000 rubles.' Since the exchange rate is 6000 to one, this is actually quite cheap.

'I also have a sore throat and bronchitis,' I say.

'Mustard packs,' she says, whipping out several sheets which look like sandpaper. She wraps them in brown paper. 'Wet them and put them on your chest when you go to sleep. 1800 rubles.'

Although I'm skeptical, I buy the mustard packs. When in Rome...

Back in the hotel I open the little box of fever medication to find individual packets of white powder. Not knowing how much to take, I dissolve an entire packet in water and drink it down. After changing back into pajamas, I run hot water over the mustard paper and apply it to my chest before crawling under the heavy down comforter. I lie under the covers, shivering with fever as the mustard burns my skin and pleasantly warms my chest. As the powder sinks my fever, the jetlag kicks in and I fall into a dreamless sleep.

I awake several hours later, sweating and no longer feverish, remove the soaked pajamas, and let them drop to the floor. The mustard pack is still stuck to my chest and I pull it off. I go into the bathroom, flick on the light, and stand before the mirror. I am horrified by the rectangular red patch on my chest. My face is as pale as a China doll's, my hair matted with sweat.

After drinking another glass of powder solution, I turn the blanket over to the dry side and crawl back into the bed, naked. As I sink into sleep, I glance at the phone and suddenly realize that Vladimir hasn't bothered to call.

ELEVEN

By morning my fever and sore throat are gone, a miracle of Russian medicine. Even the ugly rectangle on my chest has faded to a subtle shade of pink. I'm leaving the shower when the phone rings.

'Are you ready?' Vladimir asks. 'I'm downstairs.'

Why didn't you call last night? I was practically dying of the flu. Weren't you worried? Why don't you come upstairs? Are you trying to avoid me?

'I'm standing here naked,' I say coquettishly.

'I'll be right up.'

It occurs to me that Hermann and Bjorn might also be in the lobby. Maybe that's why he didn't want to come up at first. What else could be the reason? 'What about the others?'

'They're having breakfast.' He hangs up the phone, and after unlocking the door, I scurry into the bathroom. My reflection in the mirror horrifies me; face as pale as newly fallen snow, towel-dried hair like an abandoned bird's nest, eyes like a bloodhound's. Maybe I shouldn't have asked him up. He'll probably take one look at me and run for the elevator.

I struggle to comb the tangles out of my hair, apply

rouge and lipstick, and step into high heels. They are all I am wearing when Vladimir opens the door.

'Don't kiss me,' I say. 'I have the flu.' *Please kiss me anyway. We can both have the flu together and spend the entire day in bed eating soup.*

'The red tattoo is a nice touch,' he says, tracing the patch on my chest with his finger.

'Do we have time for a quickie?'

'Not really. I just wanted to see you naked. Besides, I don't want to catch the flu.' He sits on the bed. 'I'm sending you a helper today.'

'I thought you were my helper.'

'I have a lot to do and can't stay at the tradeshow. But don't worry, you'll like him. His name's Sasha.'

I'll like him? I decide immediately to wear slacks.

'Dress warmly,' Vladimir says. 'It might snow.'

'It's only the end of October.'

'You're in Russia, my dear.'

After I'm dressed, we head down to the lobby without fooling around in the elevator. Although I desperately want him to touch me, Vladimir stands like a statue, holding his briefcase in front of him, conveniently keeping both hands occupied, and staring at the door. *Good God, it's not like I have the bubonic plague. Just the fucking flu.*

Bjorn and Hermann are waiting together with a lanky young man in a tweed blazer. With piercing brown eyes, a pronounced nose, and a narrow face, he reminds me of an eagle. Nice to look at, but much too young. A teenage dream date!

The three men crowd into the back of Vladimir's car, Sasha in the middle. Still feeling weak from the flu, I slouch silently against the door of the front passenger seat. It pisses me off that Vladimir and I are never in the car alone. He's making it impossible for us to talk.

As soon as we're at my cubicle, Vladimir leaves with a quick good-bye and Sasha begins chattering. 'I talked to your boss yesterday,' he says.

'To Anis?'

'Yes, he was asking all about you. Have you called him?'

Damn! Even with eight time zones between us, Anis keeps harassing me. 'Not yet,' I say. 'What did you tell him?'

'I told him you were working on a million-dollar contract.'

'Did he believe you?' I ask.

'I think he did,' Sasha replies.

Great. So now I have exactly five days to get a million-dollar contract signed! 'Where am I going to find a million dollar contract?' I ask.

'Did Anis ever tell you about his trip to Siberia?' Sasha asks. Apparently he doesn't know where I'll get the contract either.

'He mentioned it,' I say.

'Did he mention the bananas?' Sasha asks.

This could be interesting. 'Bananas?'

Sasha's entire face is like Pinocchio coming to life. 'He doesn't eat meat so they didn't have anything to give him to chase the vodka.'

'He drank vodka?' I ask.

'He drank a lot of vodka.'

'And he ate bananas?'

Sasha laughs. 'Yeah, everyone was eating salami and he was eating bananas. No wonder he's so skinny.'

Anis will be annoyed to find out I know his little secret. I wonder if he'll deny it. I am starting to like Sasha and feel that we will be friends.

'Vladimir told me about the contract negotiations with MosEnergieExport,' he says. 'Apparently Anis wasn't too happy.'

'He behaved like a child,' I say.

'A vegetarian from Pakistan who doesn't like to drink,' Sasha says. 'Just perfect for Russia.'

We both guffaw. I suppose I shouldn't make fun of my boss. But he's a joke waiting to be laughed at. A living punch line.

'He calls me every day,' Sasha says. 'He's always asking when the customers are going to pay.'

'When are they going to pay?' I ask.

'They're having trouble with the documents. There is something wrong with the wording in the letter of credit and the bank guarantee.'

'So they still don't have the money,' I say.

'Something like that,' he says. 'But I wouldn't worry too much about it. It's Anis's contract, not yours.'

I'm sure Anis will figure out a way to make it my contract if it fails. 'We've already manufactured the breakers,' I say.

'The contract specifies a delivery date of six weeks after receipt of payment,' Sasha explains. 'You wouldn't have had enough time to produce them afterwards.'

'Why did Anis allow such a contract?' I ask.

'The customer insisted,' Sasha says, 'although I'm not sure why.'

'Is anything being done to correct the documents?' I ask.

'Vladimir is meeting with the director today. That's why he isn't here.'

Nice of Vladimir to tell me. He should have taken me with him. Instead I'm stuck here at this silly tradeshow, passing out trinkets to people I'll never see again. How am I supposed to explain the situation to Anis if I don't have a clue myself?

As if reading my thoughts, Sasha says, 'Anis complained that you haven't called him.'

'I don't know what to say to him,' I say. 'I hate talking to him on the phone.' When I was in the home office and Anis was traveling in Saudi Arabia, he called me every day *just to chat*. He always asked a lot of questions and didn't listen to the answers.

'You better call him anyway.'

I'm glad I don't have a cell phone. It would probably

be ringing constantly. *Just to chat.*

Shortly before lunch, Vladimir returns to the tradeshow, looking relaxed. When we go to the buffet, Vladimir orders me soup without even asking.

'I don't want soup,' I say. I generally hate soup. It always makes me sweat. It's like eating a sauna. Last night I was very sick and it tasted good, but I am much better today.

'You need soup if you have the flu, Katey,' Vladimir says like a father instructing a child.

While we're eating, Vladimir looks up thoughtfully. 'Anis called last night. He wants you to call him.'

'He called you at home? He's been spending a lot of time on the telephone.'

'He phones constantly. He's quite upset that you haven't called.'

'So I've heard. What am I supposed to tell him? You haven't told me anything about the little meeting you had today.'

'After your presentation, we'll go back to the office. I'll fill you in on my meeting and you can call from there.'

'My presentation?'

'Yes. Every company is giving a short presentation this afternoon.'

I feel my face getting hot. 'I haven't prepared anything,' I say. 'I have the flu—'

'I wouldn't mention that in your presentation. Russians get nervous when they hear the word *flu*,' Sasha says.

'I can't give a presentation.' Actually I have no excuse. I've been speaking Russian for more than ten years. Obsessed with plans to become a diplomat behind The Iron Curtain, I enrolled in an intensive summer Russian course in Vermont right after my high school graduation.

In the summer of 1983, nobody had heard of Gorbachev, Ronald Reagan was president, Evil Empire was a household word, Americans were terrified of a nuclear strike by the Soviets, and the Russian language was becoming fashionable. As a result, my classmates included members of the FBI, CIA and National Security Agency.

That first evening everyone gathered on the lawn with cases of beer and bottles of wine. Having spent the past two years at a creative arts boarding school in Michigan, where I didn't dare drink alcohol for fear of expulsion and where most of the boys were obsessed with their art, in love with themselves, gay, or a combination of all three, I was thrilled to accept my very first beer from a tall blonde Floridian, at least ten years my senior, with a surfer's body. After three beers, I was having trouble walking, and took the surfer's arm as we made our way to a local bar.

That night I drank beer like water and mixed my drinks like a chemist, my last memory being of the surfer placing a drink in front of me, with vibrant layers of orange and red, called a Tequila sunrise.

The next thing I knew I was lying on my back naked in a strange bed, the surfer climbing on top of me. Still half drunk, I barely understood what was happening when he bore into me like a power drill. Although the sex was painful, I lost my virginity without a whimper, pleased to get the dreadful experience over with.

During the course of the summer, between grueling Russian classes, my surfer taught me the joy of sex, my favorite game being when he chased me through the woods and pretended to rape me. (This little game ended one day at dusk when we were attacked by bats). We also made love on the campus lawns under the moon. At the end of the summer, we kissed goodbye tearfully, and I left Vermont as an experienced woman who could even speak a little Russian. I never saw my surfer again.

The next summer, after studying second-year Russian at the University of Michigan, I returned to Vermont for the third-year course. Missing my surfer, I immediately seduced my professor, an American in his forties who spoke Russian better than the natives. On the pretense of going jogging, we rendezvoused in the woods, where he taught me many erotic Russian expressions and also a few maneuvers which I hadn't been familiar with.

The next few years I became so obsessed with speaking Russian that I latched onto a graduate student from Bangladesh, who had spent six years as a student in Moscow, where the Soviets had tried to indoctrinate him with Communism. Instead, he had somehow managed to escape from there to the United States where he entered a doctoral program in Russian literature.

We were both living in the 'Russian House', a small dormitory for Russian language students, with Khan being back in Ann Arbor after a summer vacation in his homeland. He had arrived a week late and we had all been wondering where he was. Although I had barely known him at all the year before and we had maybe spoken three words to each other tops, I found myself missing him and hoping nothing had happened. When he finally popped up in the kitchen, I actually ran up and hugged him like a long-lost lover.

A group of us were later sitting in the lobby speaking Russian and drinking wine. Actually it was only Khan and I who were speaking Russian. The others were just kind of listening and nodding, pretending to understand, or holding their own conversations in English.

In a manner that made me laugh hysterically, Khan recounted how the American Consulate had initially refused him a visa to return to the United States, making the argument that he would try to stay there illegally. Although he argued back that he had already been in the US for 3 years and wouldn't have returned to Bangladesh willingly if he was trying to stay in their *wonderful* country, the American representative seemed to be suffering from a learning disability. Khan then called the Russian department at the University of Michigan, calmly notified a highly respected Jewish professor that he would not be coming to teach his classes, and then returned home without further ado. The next day, Khan received a phone call from the American Consulate, instructing him to pick up his visa. No reason for this sudden change of heart was provided and Khan had no need to ask.

At some point in the midst of our private conversation, the others had gradually gone off to bed, leaving us alone. Feeling tired, I said goodnight at around midnight and headed up to my single room. I left the door ajar. Five minutes later, just as I was removing my shirt, Khan showed up as if on cue, holding the half empty bottle of wine and asking me if I wanted another glass. I was 19 years old, he was almost 30. We stayed together for almost two years, speaking only Russian and cooking Bangladeshi cuisine, which I still enjoy occasionally to this day.

Thanks to Khan, when I finally went to Moscow myself in the fall of 1988 for a ten-month Russian course, I was not only fluent in the language already, but also a highly experienced lover. I was sad to leave—Khan was my first real relationship—but I knew it was time to move on and to take my memories with me. We would always have the Russian House.

Although there were forty Americans in my group of students in Moscow, I preferred to explore the city alone, not wanting to speak English, and always hoping to meet some Russians.

Riding the subway one evening during rush hour, I became aware of a tall handsome man in a black overcoat staring at me. Allowing a smile to escape, I was pleased when he grinned back at me.

Following me out of the subway, the man invited me to a nearby restaurant where I drank a bottle of champagne and tasted my first caviar. He wrote down his phone number and told me to call him. After leaving the restaurant, he shoved me into the entrance of an apartment building and smashed his lips against mine, his hand reaching under my skirt.

When I tried to call him the next evening, a bitchy woman told me I had the wrong number. Either she was protecting her husband from strange women or he had purposely changed a few digits. I suspected the latter.

A friend who had studied in Moscow the semester before had given me a list of phone contacts, specifically telling me to call Alexander. I called him from a pay phone, and we agreed to meet at the metro station Lenin Prospect at two p.m. on Sunday. Not knowing how long it would take me to get there, I arrived a half hour late. Although I didn't think he would still be there, I looked around for a man in search of somebody. Just as I was about to leave, a hand grabbed my arm and I turned to face a young man in a black overcoat with hair even blacker, dark brown eyes and a chipped tooth. I immediately thought of Dostoevsky's Raskolnikov.

We spent the afternoon in Gorky Park, admiring the snow statues. By late afternoon, we were holding hands and by evening we were kissing. We spent every day together, finally getting married in the spring.

I took him back to the US where we lived together for six years, during which time I studied engineering and he economics. After getting his citizenship, he started gambling and playing around, finally hooking up with a Ukrainian student and deciding to marry her. I got drunk the night he told me, hunted the couple down in a bar, and approached the bitch, shaking her hand and introducing myself only as the wife, while she stood staring at me like a frightened fawn.

To top it off, he had used my credit cards to ring up over ten thousand dollars in gambling debts, even draining the last reserves from my checking account before I had time to close it. The following year I finished my engineering degree and applied for a job that would take me far away from my ex-husband.

In any case, I guess my Russian should be good enough by now for me to be able to manage the presentation, although certain phrases like hydraulic spring operating mechanism, transient voltage, and single self-blast interrupter per phase have never been part of my everyday vocabulary in either language.

'The presentations start a two-o'clock,' Vladimir says.

'I don't have any overheads.'

'We've got some for you.'

'Can't you give the talk for me?'

'It will be much more effective if given by a pretty lady,' Vladimir says. 'You don't have to say much.'

Despite what I said earlier, this *pretty lady* shit is starting to piss me off. I might as well have studied cosmetology instead of engineering. 'How about a good-looking man?' I say without thinking.

'Don't be absurd, Katey,' he replies. 'The customers are men. If they were women, I'd be the first one to jump up there.' He winks.

I know he has a point. I have to use every asset to my advantage if I want to be successful.

'I don't know all these words in Russian,' I protest.

'Which words don't you know?'

'Hydraulic spring mechanism, interrupter, SF6 gas, tank heaters.'

Vladimir rattles off the Russian translation for each term as easily as if he were reciting the alphabet and much too quickly for me to note them.

'I still can't do it,' I say.

'You have to, for at least five minutes.'

'But I have the flu.'

'I'm not asking you to kiss anybody,' he says. 'Just give the damned presentation.'

I'm wishing I'd worn a short skirt after all. At least then the audience would be watching my legs instead of listening to my words. In my three months with the company I have not given a single presentation in either language and hadn't been expecting to make my debut today. Vladimir has a set of overhead slides with pictures of each type of circuit breaker, as well as a diagram of the spring mechanism. There is also a list of SF6 gas data.

SF6 gas is used to break the current. Since all the words have been translated into Russian, I plan on just reciting the content and hoping they don't ask questions.

'This is our 145 kilovolt dead tank breaker,' I say, partially reading from the screen. I pause, letting the audience see the picture.

'How much does one cost?' someone blurts out.

'It depends on your specifications.' I see Vladimir chuckling from the back of the audience – either laughing with me or at me, probably the latter.

Before the questioner can pursue the issue, I switch to another slide. 'This is the 362 kilovolt dead tank breaker,' I say.

'Are they manufactured in Russia?' someone asks.

'No, in the United States. We ship them to you.'

'Why don't you manufacture them here?' he persists.

'We're trying to set up a joint venture,' I lie. I notice Vladimir nodding in approval.

Somebody asks a technical question in Russian which is so complicated I don't understand it. Hands trembling, I rifle through my slides, pretending to look for the information while hoping a member of the audience will answer the question for me, and carelessly knock all of them onto the floor. The men charge towards me, each trying to retrieve more slides than the other, and the technical question is forgotten.

I thank my audience and end the presentation.

TWELVE

The tradeshow ends the following evening with a lavish buffet, financed by the participation fees charged to the western companies. Bottles of vodka surrounded by shot glasses and rows of bubbling champagne goblets cover a separate table. A plump Russian woman with flat-soled shoes pours drinks while two skinny young men dressed like penguins distribute them on trays among the male-dominated guests. Although most are dressed in mismatched suits with drab polyester ties, I notice a few fashionable gentlemen who look wealthy.

I assume that the few women hovering around the buffet and sipping champagne are secretaries. They are dressed in tight skirts, low cut blouses and high heels and wearing heavy layers of make-up with too much rouge, especially the ones over thirty. Except for a few souvenir collectors during the last few hours of the tradeshow, I am not approached by a single woman. Not wanting to lug souvenirs back to Pittsburgh, I leave my remaining trinkets on the table and they quickly disappear.

Not sure how to behave, I mingle through the crowd, grabbing a glass of champagne from a passing waiter. Sipping my drink, I look for familiar faces and spot Sasha filling his plate with sandwiches. Before I can reach him, Bjorn from Sweden grabs his arm and pulls him aside. Since they seem to be discussing an important issue, I turn to the buffet table.

As I'm stuffing a caviar-covered egg into my mouth, Vladimir approaches with a jovial man in his late fifties who has the friendliest eyes I have ever seen. He's wearing a T-shirt with an imprinted collar, tie and vest under a wool blazer which looks like it shrunk in the washing machine.

Vladimir grabs three shots of vodka from a passing penguin and hands them to us.

'Katey, I'd like you to meet Sergey Davidovich Kushkov,' he says. 'He's a member of the electrical inspection team and a good friend of mine.'

'Inspection team?' I ask, taking his hand. He grasps mine gently as if afraid it will break.

'Before you can ship electrical equipment to Russia a committee has to certify your production facilities,' Vladimir says.

'You mean we aren't even allowed to ship yet?' I ask.

'Not until you're certified,' Vladimir explains. 'It's Russian law.'

'What if they don't certify us?' I ask. 'We already have a contract.' I can just imagine Anis's reaction when he hears this. Four massive circuit breakers sitting in our factory with no place to go.

'Don't you worry about that,' says Kushkov, winking. 'I'll take care of everything.' Even though I don't know him, I believe him. There is something sincere about his demeanor that I can't pinpoint, but my gut tells me I can trust him.

'I thought perhaps the two of you should get together and make arrangements for the visit,' says Vladimir. 'Sergey can tell you what documents you need to prepare.'

'My flight leaves on Sunday,' I say.

'How about Saturday night?' Vladimir suggests.

'Will you come too?' I ask, hoping.

Vladimir looks at me as if I deserve the award for the world's dumbest question. 'I'm busy on Saturday,' he says.

Although not pleased that Vladimir wants to send me on a date with a stranger, I realize the meeting could be important. But because I had been hoping to spend Saturday night with him, I can't help feeling hurt.

'Where would you like to go?' I ask Sergey.

'That depends on how much you want to spend,' he replies. *Okay. I appreciate his honesty.*

'It doesn't matter,' I say. 'As long as they take American Express and serve caviar.'

'Then I know a nice little place with violin music. You can have buckets of caviar and they take all major credit cards.'

We arrange to meet at seven p.m. in front of the Hotel National. It is centrally located on Tverskaya Street across from Red Square and easy to get to.

After the party, Hermann and Bjorn take a taxi directly to the airport and Sasha goes home on the subway, leaving me alone with Vladimir in his car.

'What are you doing on Saturday that is so important that you can't come with us?' I ask.

'I spend week-ends with my son,' he says.

'I could join you,' I say as we stop at a red light. 'Is he studying English? I could help him.' If I got the son to like me, I would earn points with his father.

'It's much too soon for that, Katey.'

'Can't you find a few hours for me,' I ask as we stop at a red light. Knowing his son ranks much higher on the priority list than I do, I try to hide my irritation.

Turning his head toward me and resting his hand on my thigh, Vladimir says, 'Katey, we're not in America. Life is hectic in Moscow. Every second of my life is organized.'

'Can't you come up to my room now?' I ask.

'You've been talking all day about having the flu,' he

says. 'You need to order some more soup and go to bed early. I want you healthy by Saturday night.'

'What about tomorrow?' I ask. Tomorrow is Friday.

'I have meetings all day,' he says. 'Why don't you stay at the hotel and relax. Order some movies. I bet they have some good porno films.' He winks. 'I'll try to stop by in the afternoon or evening.'

We ride silently the rest of the way to the hotel. Before I get out, he kisses my forehead, making me feel about as sexy as a puppy dog.

I stay in my room all day Friday waiting for Vladimir. He doesn't even call.

Since I need to take a hotel taxi at 5:00 AM to catch my Sunday morning flight, I pack my bags on Saturday afternoon before meeting Sergey. Not considering business attire necessary, I dress in a long wool skirt to keep my legs warm and short leather boots. I pull a shimmering brown tank top over my head and top it off with a low-cut baggy sweater. Without Vladimir, I have no interest in appearing sexy. But since I never appear in public without makeup except when I'm jogging, I still apply eye shadow, rouge and lipstick. *Who am I kidding? Even like this, I am still dressed to kill.*

With darkness falling, I trudge toward the subway, wearing a winter coat and a colorful Russian scarf. I could take a taxi, but the subway route is quicker and much cheaper. Even though I can put all costs on my expense report, I avoid letting them get excessive. I wouldn't want Anis to decide that my trips to Russia are too expensive. I get on at the station Dynamo and ride for twenty minutes to the center of town where I depart in front of the Hotel National not far from Red Square and the Kremlin.

Sergey is already waiting when I arrive. When he smiles, tiny creases form in the outside corners of his eyes. Tonight he's dressed like a trucker: jeans, cowboy boots—I wonder where he got them—black leather jacket and a

1920's style leather cap.

'I was afraid you wouldn't come,' he says shyly.

'Is there some reason I should stay away?'

'No, of course not. I just thought—well, you hardly know me.'

'I hardly know anyone in Russia,' I say. 'I have to start somewhere.'

'You seem to know Vladimir pretty well.'

'Not really. Are you two good friends?'

'Let's just say I've known him for a long time.' He tries to light a cigarette with a match but the wind keeps blowing it out. He finally gives up and puts it back in the pack. 'Do you mind if we walk?'

'I love to walk.' I'm glad not to be wearing such high heels.

As we go through the underpass I notice an old lady hunched over like a wilted flower, a tattered grey shawl draped over her shoulders, her face almost mummified. By appearance alone I would guess her to be at least 100. She weakly extends her hand, palm up.

Almost automatically, I press a twenty-dollar bill into her withered hand.

She nods and murmurs, 'God bless you' before making a weak fist around the money and stuffing it into her pocket.

'You shouldn't have done that,' Sergey says.

'Why not?' I ask. 'She looked like she was dying.'

'She's part of the granny mafia,' he says. 'She's very wealthy and earns enough to support her whole family.'

'Sending an old lady out to beg seems cruel,' I say.

'What else is she going to do with her time? Besides, she probably enjoys being the breadwinner. Her generation is used to hard work.'

'You call that hard work?'

'You try crouching for several hours with your hand extended. I think it would be grueling.'

'I see your point.'

'But there's probably five or six of them,' he says, 'and they change shifts every few hours. And did you notice? She is the only one there. A lot of western tourists pass by here. Somebody with a lot of clout is paying for that spot.'

'You're probably right,' I say.

We come out on the other side of Tverskaya Street and head north from the Kremlin. We continue for ten minutes until reaching the McDonald's on the other side of the street and the Pushkin Monument on our side. We turn right and head into a neighborhood with old style architecture, the houses built directly on the roadside, and the streets so narrow that when cars approach from opposite directions, one has to back up or pull into a driveway.

A scruffy man totters past us, carrying a brown paper bag. As he passes, the smell of liquor, tobacco, sweat and urine invades my nostrils. Other people are moving like pendulums, heavy cloth grocery sacks balanced in each arm. Everybody except the drunken man seems to be in a hurry.

We pass a Kiosk where men with missing teeth are drinking draft beer and smoking. I remember when I was a student and living with my now ex-husband in an apartment on the outskirts of Moscow, how his little brother Oleg cut to the front of the line and brought back an eight-liter jug of foamless diluted beer. The salesmen always add water to make the beer go further.

We pass several other Kiosks, selling newspapers, books, cosmetics, electrical appliances, souvenirs, pantyhose, candy and cigarettes. They also offer cans of imported beer, bottles of Russian champagne and vodka, and stay open now until nine pm, some of them until midnight.

Sergey stops in front of a yellow house on a corner. A small sign on the door reads Restaurant Golden Eagle. I also notice stickers for Visa, MasterCard, and American Express. When we enter the small dining room, I am surprised to find it empty. Two waiters, dressed in black pants, white shirts, and bow ties, are smoking at a table. Once inside, Sergey pulls out his cigarettes, and a waiter immediately offers him a flame from his silver lighter.

'Good evening,' Sergey says. 'Table for two.'

Without smiling or speaking, the waiter leads us to a corner table.

'May I bring you something to drink?' he asks.

Sergey looks at me. 'Vodka?' he asks. 'And maybe champagne?'

'Sure,' I say, fully aware that this is a deadly combination, especially with an early morning flight. But that's not for another ten hours.

Sergey orders a bottle of champagne, a bottle of vodka, and several bottles of mineral water.

'So what would you like to eat?' he asks.

'Black caviar to start with.'

'Have you ever eaten sturgeon?'

'I don't think so.'

'Then you must try the sturgeon kebab.'

Knowing how men enjoy ordering for women, I don't want to offend Sergey. 'Sounds good.' Maybe it will be.

The waiter sets the bottles on the table. First he opens the champagne and pours two glasses. Then he opens the vodka and fills our shot glasses. Lastly he pours the mineral water.

'We need *zakuska*,' says Sergey loud enough for the waiter to hear. *Zakuska* is the Russian word for appetizers. When Russians drink vodka, they like to have plenty of them.

'May I take your order now?' the waiter asks in a subservient tone.

'Black caviar, mushrooms, a plate of olives and pickles,' says Sergey.

'We also have very good ham,' says the waiter.

'Okay, bring the ham.'

'And what would you like as the main course?'

'Two portions of Sturgeon kebabs.'

'Would you like the house salad?' House salad is typically made with potatoes, ham, peas, hard-boiled egg, pickles and mayonnaise.

When Sergey looks at me, I shake my head. I'll be drinking so many calories that I don't need extra ones.

'Would you like rice or potatoes with the Sturgeon?'

Again Sergey looks at me.

'Neither,' I say directly to the waiter.

'I'll have potatoes,' Sergey says. 'You don't eat much,' he says to me.

'I don't like to eat a lot when I'm drinking,' I say.

'That's dangerous,' he says.

'I like to live on the edge.'

'Then let's get started,' Sergey says, raising his vodka. 'To new friends.'

We drink down the vodka and I immediately reach for my water glass. I take a swig and pick up my champagne, Sergey following my lead.

Soon the waiter reappears with a silver dish of black caviar. There is also a little plate of butter and a basket of white and dark bread. He refills our vodka glasses.

'May I fix you some caviar?' Sergey asks.

'Yes, please,' I tell him. I'd rather do it myself, but decide to be polite. 'But with dark bread.'

He smears butter over the bread and covers it with a thin layer of caviar.

'You can put more caviar on it,' I say.

He adds another layer before handing me the delicacy. After preparing one for himself with white bread, a generous serving of butter, and a thin layer of caviar, he raises his vodka glass. 'It's actually better not to smear the caviar too thickly,' he says.

'Because it's so expensive?' I ask. 'We can always order more.'

Sergey laughs. 'That's one reason. But mainly because it has such a strong flavor.'

'I love it,' I say. 'I could eat it with a spoon.'

'Are you sure you're not Russian?'

'I'm Irish. We love to drink.'

'Then a toast to the Irish,' he says, clinking his glass against mine.

'And to Russian caviar,' I add.

The combination of black caviar, sweet butter, and black bread following the smooth warmth of vodka tastes exquisite. I have no objection when the waiter, standing quietly in the shadows, emerges to refill our glasses. By the time the sturgeon arrives, the bottle is almost empty.

The fish is cut in chunks, marinated, and on a skewer, the plate decorated with a rainbow of canned carrots, peas, red pepper, and a beige-colored vegetable that I don't recognize.

Before we start on the main course, the waiter refills our vodka and champagne glasses again and Sergey orders another bottle of vodka. No longer thinking about the hangover I'll have at five in the morning, I boldly alternate shots of vodka with swigs of champagne occasionally eating a chunk of sturgeon.

'So how long have you been sleeping with Vladimir?' asks Sergey.

'What are you talking about?'

'I could tell by the way you looked at one another.' *God, was it that obvious?*

After so much vodka, I suddenly feel like Sergey is my closest friend. 'I think I'm in love with him,' I say.

'Be careful. Vladimir likes the women.'

His statement suddenly depresses me. I wonder if Vladimir is really with his son, and not in bed with some buxom Russian dame. Not wanting to let my mood show, I douse my champagne, the bubbles and alcohol causing me to giggle.

'I think he's going to get divorced,' I say.

'Never,' Sergey says. 'His wife is the daughter of a professor who has a lot of friends in high places. Vladimir needs her for his career.'

If I wasn't so drunk, the news would have upset me. As it is, I hear him speaking as if in a dream. I keep downing my vodka, and Sergey keeps refilling it as soon as the glass hits the table.

'Besides, he has a gorgeous wife,' Sergey says. 'And very intelligent. She's an economics professor.'

I bet she's a bitch, I think, picking up my champagne glass.

'Don't tell him we talked about him,' I say. As drunk as I am, I still regret having brought up the subject.

'You don't have to worry. I'm like a black body in physics. Information enters me but it never comes out.'

'I'm really starting to like you.' I tend to like everyone when I'm drunk.

'I think we're going to be really good friends,' Sergey says.

Our plates are empty and the second bottle of vodka is below the half-way point. I have to use the restroom, and upon standing, grab the table to keep my balance. I totter to the lady's room, my head floating near the ceiling.

When I return, my vodka glass has been refilled. There is a fresh tray of caviar, butter and bread.

'Would you like a photo?' asks the waiter, appearing with a Polaroid camera.

'Sure, why not?' I say.

We crouch together like lovers and smile for the camera. A few minutes later he produces a photograph of two drunks surrounded by vodka and caviar.

As we empty the last bottle of vodka, I have difficulty connecting my mouth to the glass and spill it several times on my chin and sweater. Afterwards we order strong coffee served with little Russian chocolates. When the waiter brings the bill, I grab it before he can hand it to Sergey. The paper slips out of my hand and as I lean over to pick it up I slide from the chair and crash my butt onto the floor.

When several people from the next table, the only other guests in the restaurant, look up curiously, Sergey says simply, 'She saw the bill.' Laughing, they continue eating.

Gripping the bill in one hand, I pull myself back onto the chair with my other. When I finally read it, I am too drunk to be shocked by the sum of $256. I pull out my American Express card and offer it to the waiter. My signature on the receipt is so sloppy it doesn't resemble the one on the card, but the waiter seems neither to notice nor care.

We stumble from the restaurant into the night air, cold enough for snow. I wrap my scarf around my head and, trying not to fall, snuggle against Sergey. He says we should walk back to Tverskaya Street and hail a taxi from there.

'What time is it?' I ask.

'Close to midnight.'

'What? We were there that long?'

'Time flies when you drink vodka.'

'I have to get up at five.'

'Good luck.'

Once on Tverskaya Street, we quickly find a taxi. As we huddle in the back, the driver zooms off toward my hotel. Paying the driver, I forget to ask for a receipt, which means I can't put it in my expense report. Quickly checking my purse, I'm relieved to find the restaurant bill. Otherwise I wouldn't be able to deduct that either.

I totter into the hotel, falling several times, Sergey at my heels. I look like a hooker taking a trick to her room. Once we're in the elevator I rest my head on his shoulder and close my eyes.

'I have to get up in less than five hours,' I murmur.

Once we enter my room I fall onto the bed like a rag doll, my head spinning like a carrousel. Sergey remains standing and lights a cigarette.

'Are you going to be okay?' he asks.

'Aren't you going to hit on me?'

'As much as I'd like to, I don't take advantage of drunken little girls. You need your sleep.' I pull myself off the bed and stagger towards him, falling into his arms. He extends his arm to avoid burning me with the cigarette. We kiss briefly like lovers and I feel his hardness against my leg, but he pushes me away.

I sit back onto the bed, grateful that Sergey is a gentleman.

'Make sure you get some sleep,' he says. 'Do you have a wake-up call and a taxi reserved?'

'I'll do that right away,' I say.

Sergey walks over to the bed, kisses me on the forehead and departs, reminding me to lock the door.

Forgetting to lock the door, I struggle out of my clothes and toss them onto the carpet. I turn off the light and crawl under the covers, dressed only in an undershirt. Without calling the wakeup service or ordering a taxi, I fall into a corpse-like sleep.

When I awake the sun is shining through my window. It must be another of Murphy's Laws: *the sun shines when you have a hangover.* My head feels like somebody filled it with rocks, my stomach like somebody dried it with a towel, and my mouth like I've been eating cotton. When I slide out of bed, keeping my head as steady as possible to thwart the throbbing pain, I notice a pile of vomit on the carpet.

Trembling like an old lady with Parkinson's disease, I fumble with the zipper on my cosmetic bag and pull out a bottle of pills. Cursing childproof lids, I struggle to open it and dump four tablets into my hand. I take a bottle of mineral water from the mini bar and swallow the pills all at once. After drinking the entire bottle too fast, I lie on my back, hold my head still, and close my eyes, waiting for the pain to subside.

In thirty minutes, the pills take effect. Once the pain

vanishes, I assess my situation. Checking my watch, I see that my plane left two hours ago which, of course, doesn't surprise me. Although the ticket is changeable for a fee of $150, I wonder what excuse I can use for missing a Sunday flight. I decide to call Vladimir at home.

Unprepared for a female voice, I hesitate awkwardly before speaking, imagining a beautiful woman dressed in a silk chemise, just having gotten up from sex with Vladimir. Even though she probably can't understand me, I speak English to make the call seem official.

'One moment,' she answers in Russian.

A few seconds later I hear Vladimir's voice. 'Shouldn't you be five miles in the air?'

'I missed my flight. What do I do now?'

I expect Vladimir to be surprised. Instead, he doesn't even ask for an explanation. He says, 'I'll call Anis on Monday and tell him you had a very important meeting with one of the inspection team members on Sunday.'

'And why was this meeting so important?'

'I'll explain that since these people can be difficult, it is a good idea to forge friendships.'

'Well, I certainly did that.'

'I'll also tell him we are meeting on Monday afternoon with one of the chief engineers from Mosenergo who is interested in a two million dollar contract.'

'Will I really meet with him?'

'No, but I will and I can tell you what to say.'

'Since I'll be here anyway,' I say, 'why can't you take me with you?' I don't know what bothers me more, missing an important meeting or not spending the day with Vladimir.

'Because I'm not really meeting with them until Wednesday,' he says.

'That's a good reason,' I say. 'Is it really true about a two million dollar contract?'

'Of course it's true,' he says. I don't know whether to believe him. He hasn't mentioned such a contract until now. He says, 'You can fly home on Tuesday.'

'What do I do until then?'

'Today you can recover from your hangover. Go in the sauna, eat some soup, get some fresh air. I'll pick you up Monday morning.' *Fucking soup again!*

'Don't you want to come by today?'

'I already talked to Sergey. He called early this morning and told me how much vodka you two drank. You probably smell like a distillery. I'll wait until Monday.'

'Did he say anything else?'

'He was worried about you.'

'What did you tell him?'

'I told him not to worry. You're just typical Irish.'

'How's that?'

'You can't hold your liquor.'

'I'll learn,' I promise.

'You'll have to if you want to play the game.'

I wonder what game I am playing and what the rules are.

THIRTEEN

I'm working on a bid for a company in Canada, typing options into a computer program which automatically calculates the price. This Canadian utility company is interested in buying twenty 72-kilovolt dead tank circuit breakers and have sent me a really boring forty-page technical specification. My job is to read through each page, comparing the details to our standard breaker and looking for any deviations which can increase the cost.

I notice they want tank heaters to keep the SF6 gas from liquefying when the air temperatures fall below -55° Celsius. And they want redundant tank heaters as well, essentially spare tires in case the primary heaters malfunction.

In other words, they're worried that the primary heater will malfunction on the one day in ten years when the temperature drops below -55°, causing the gas to liquefy and become ineffective at exactly the same moment when they need to shut down the electrical current.

Since the main reason for breaking the current is to perform maintenance, I wonder who would choose a day with temperatures below -50° to shut down the current anyway. Okay, emergency situations can occur, but precisely on such a cold day and precisely when the heaters malfunction? Then again, I'm just a sales engineer, not one to question the customer's motives, especially when they add to the price; I only determine the cost and make a proposal. Punching the options into the cost-calculation program, I watch the price increase nicely as I add the redundant heaters.

Since business is slow in Russia at the moment, Anis gave me the Canadian market after I returned from my first trip. And since the Canadians request so many bids, I have a great deal of paperwork, which is boring as hell but results in a modest number of sales. Their technical specifications are long and tedious. It takes hours to wade through them and I am constantly asking the project engineers for explanations. And constantly letting my thoughts drift to Vladimir. Maybe Anis gave me this market to punish me for all the fun I've been having with the Russians.

The various power companies in Russia are also constantly requesting bids, usually one-page without details, which Sasha routinely faxes to me, even though Vladimir is fairly certain nothing will come of them.

After receiving a request from Irkutsk for eight 242 kV breakers, I decide to call the local representative to arrange a trip.

'Ushikov.'

'Hello, this is Katey O'Hara from Ampere Power in the United States. I got your request for a bid.'

'Can you fax it to me urgently?' His voice is not friendly.

'I thought it might be better if I bring it,' I say. 'Then I can meet the customers personally.'

During a long pause, I wonder if the connection has broken. Then he says, 'I don't need any help from a woman.'

Who is this asshole? 'Vladimir Kashirnikov says it's a good idea for the customers to meet the American representative,' I say. 'It makes them feel important.'

'They need equipment. They don't need to feel important.'

My God, who hired this guy?

'Just fax the bid, please,' he continues. 'I need it urgently.'

What could possibly be so urgent? I am guessing he is just trying to make himself seem important. 'As you wish,' I say.

When the phone rings several minutes later, I grab it without turning my head from the computer screen. Expecting it to be our sales representative in Toronto—he calls at least five times a day—I'm surprised by a heavily accented *Hello*, spoken in a sleepy baritone.

'I was hoping you'd call,' I say. Since Anis likes to eavesdrop, I enjoy speaking to Vladimir and Sasha in Russian on the telephone.

'Do you remember Miasnikov from Tula?' Vladimir asks. 'I called him.'

'What did he say?'

'He wants to see you. I think he remembers your sexy legs.'

'What about you? Do you also remember my sexy legs?' I ask flirtatiously.

'Of course. I really miss your tight little ass. That's why I'm arranging your trip to Tula.'

'I thought we were trying to sell circuit breakers.'

'Well, that's part of it,' he says. 'I've made an appointment for December 20th. You'll need to fly to Moscow a few days earlier.'

'Consider it done,' I say as I end the call. I wish I could be so certain.

After I hang up I go into Anis's office. He is sitting at his empty desk, talking on the telephone. It's no secret that Anis never has papers on his desk, the theory being he delegates his work to others so quickly that nothing ever accumulates. He seems to spend the entire day on the telephone or admiring the shiny surface of his desk, while bragging to everyone about how organized he is.

'I just spoke to Vladimir,' I say after he hangs up the phone. 'He needs me to come to Tula.'

'Sit down,' Anis says, gesturing toward a chair across from him. 'Now why do you need to go to Tula?' He speaks to me as if I'm a teenager asking for permission to go to a drinking party. *Yeah, okay, the comparison isn't far off.*

'To negotiate a contract for six 145 kV breakers,' I say. 'I met the chief engineer at the exhibition in Moscow.'

'Why can't Vladimir take care of it?' he asks. 'Why do you need to go there?'

'The customer is expecting to see me,' I say. *He likes my legs.*

'Maybe I should go,' Anis says.

The customer wouldn't like your legs. They're much too skinny and hairy.

'Let me call Vladimir and find out what's going on,' he says.

I just told you what's going on. I've been telling you for the past six weeks. I told Anis about Tula as soon as I returned from Moscow.

'Hello, Vladimir! What's going on?'

During a lengthy pause, Anis's grin fades.

'Tula?' he says. Then he says, 'Katey?' I wish I could hear both sides of the conversation.

'Maybe I should come,' he says.

There's a long pause. A very long pause. I wonder if Vladimir is explaining how Miasnikov looked at my legs.

Sounding disappointed, Anis says, 'Okay, we'll send her on the eighteenth,' pronouncing *her* as if it were a dirty word.

'He says that Tulenergo is interested in six 145 kV circuit breakers,' Anis says after hanging up the phone.

Why am I not surprised? Isn't that exactly what I just told him?

'He's faxing the specification,' he says. 'We'll look at it together.'

'I don't think there will be much to look at,' I say. 'Tulenergo wants pretty basic equipment.'

'The meeting is on December 20th,' he says 'You'll need to ask Sally to get you a flight for the 18th. I'd make the trip myself, but I'm busy at that time.'

Even though Vladimir and I have both explained the situation, Anis refuses to acknowledge that Miasnikov is my customer and I can handle the negotiations better myself. I decide to butter his ego.

'Yes, it would be nice to have you along,' I say. Then I add, 'I have plans for Christmas. I hope I'm back by then.'

I have a nonrefundable plane ticket to Michigan.

'That shouldn't be a problem. You can fly home after the meeting.'

'I'll see if the fax has come,' I say, heading for the door.

'Bring it to me,' Anis says.

A fax in Russian is lying next to the machine. It's very simple: Six 145 kV dead tank circuit breakers. There are no other details in the specification. It is simply a standard design. We will have to add some other costs, including shipment, into the price estimate, and also send a service engineer for the installation. And we'll need an additional five thousand to pay for the company managers to visit our plant. I assume that Miasnikov will be among them.

I put the fax on Anis's desk. He picks it up and looks at it for a long time, as if trying to read something that isn't there.

'This is all?' he asks.

'Yeah, there weren't any more details.'

'Okay, you need to call our transport center to get an estimate on the shipping costs. Then you'll need to add $8000 for a factory visit and another $5000 for the service engineer. Use all the standard options and add a profit margin of thirty percent.'

'Thirty percent?' I've been adding ten percent to the Canadian bids.

'It's a high risk country,' he says. I assume he is

recalling the unpaid contract from St. Petersburg.

'Isn't $10,000 too much for a factory visit?'

'We have to pay for three plane tickets,' Anis says. 'Plus hotel and meal costs.'

'And we add a 30% profit margin to the cost of the visit as well?'

Anis winks. 'Of course. We get our highest profits from the international business.'

'And the Russians always say they don't have any money.'

'Everybody has money somewhere. Russia has more oil reserves than Saudi Arabia. We just have to know which pockets to rob.'

Anis understands the Russian market better than I thought. He has, after all, been in the business for over twenty years, traveling all over the world, including China and Saudi Arabia. He may have chased his vodka with bananas, but he still has a good grasp of the Russian mentality. And his sales to Asia and the Middle East topped ten million dollars last year.

'Let's hope Tula is the right pocket,' I say.

'I think Vladimir is our man,' Anis says.

He's certainly my man.

I enter the information into our cost program, arriving at a contract price of slightly more than $900,000. Anis skims my printout, focusing on the price.

'I like the price,' he says. 'We can always get more money with our international sales.'

'Except Canada,' I say.

'They're not really international. Have Sally type this up and fax it to Vladimir.'

'Don't I need to translate it into Russian?'

'Vladimir can have somebody do it,' he says, and then adds, 'I forgot to ask him about the St. Petersburg contract. Why don't you call him back and ask?'

'It's 9 pm in Moscow. I don't think I'll reach him.'

'Then call him tomorrow.'

I go back to my office and resume work on the Canadian bids. Vladimir doesn't call me and I assume he is at home with his family. What I'm really thinking about is driving into Pittsburgh to buy a new suit for my trip, something in a sexy color with a short skirt. I've always looked good in dark periwinkle. I imagine seducing Miasnikov into giving me a million-dollar contract and wonder if Vladimir would be jealous.

Bored, I exit the bid program and open my e-mail. Addressing the message to Vladimir, I begin to write:

Hello, you sex god!
Hearing your voice has gotten me all hot and wet. How can I do my work when all I want to do is press my naked body against yours? I want to be your sex slave. I want you to tie me up behind your desk and use me whenever and for whatever you want to.

I glance up briefly to see Anis walking into my office. Fortunately, I've arranged my furniture so that I'm facing the door, giving me time to exit the program before Anis can come around behind me and see the computer screen. I quickly reopen the Canadian bid.

It's too bad I didn't have time to send the e-mail. Vladimir would have enjoyed it.

FOURTEEN

We're on the road to Tula, driving 100 miles an hour in Vladimir's Volvo. At least it's a safe car. It's ten below zero, the ground covered with a fresh blanket of snow, and I'm grateful for the heat on my stockinged legs. Despite the weather, I am wearing my new periwinkle suit with a short slit skirt. I need every trick to get this contract.

In less than two hours we arrive in Tula, an old industrial city that still has a statue of Lenin in its center. Vladimir quickly finds the buildings of Tulenergo. My legs become numb with cold as we walk towards the entrance; and as the wind bites my ears, I wrap my Russian scarf, shades of blue with colorful flowers, more tightly around my head.

Entering an office, we are greeted by a middle-aged secretary with maroon-colored hair and orange lipstick. She smells faintly of bath powder. Vladimir pulls a package of Swiss chocolates from his briefcase and presents them to her.

'Dmitri Sergeevich is expecting you,' she says, her voice becoming friendly. 'Follow me.'

Miasnikov's office is directly behind her desk. We follow her in and see the chief engineer speaking on the telephone. Typical of Russian bureaucrats, he is shouting into the receiver.

'Then send out the men to take care of it! Roman Fomitch! Talk to Fomitch! Okay. Call me back! I have a meeting now!'

He slams the phone down, frowns at the receiver and then looks up smiling. 'Katey, Vladimir Igorovich, welcome to Tulenergo.' He comes around to the front of the desk, takes my hand, brings it to his lips, and plants a soft kiss between my middle finger and ring finger. Then he shakes hands with Vladimir.

'I'm always happy to come to Tula,' says Vladimir. 'Such a friendly city.'

'And,' Miasnikov begins, taking my coat, 'we have the best vodka in Russia.'

'We'll have to try some,' I say.

'Aha,' says Miasnikov, approaching a cabinet behind his desk. Opening the door, he produces a clear bottle and three long-stemmed shot glasses. Placing them on a low table, he returns to the cabinet for a dish of peanuts and pretzels.

After motioning us to sit on a couch near the table, he pours three shots, picks up two, and hands one to each of us.

'A welcome toast,' he says, raising his glass.

We clink the glasses together and drink them down. I'm getting used to imbibing before noon, actually starting to enjoy it. A morning aperitif seems to be the norm in Russia and I certainly can't offend the customer.

'This is our own vodka, made in Tula,' Miasnikov says proudly.

'It's very good,' I say, impressed by the smoothness.

Without another word he refills the glasses.

'To our pretty American lady,' he toasts.

I'm always flattered when the Russians compliment my appearance. American men are so intimidated by diehard feminists and sex-discrimination lawsuits that they're afraid to tell a woman she's attractive. Sexism is a foreign concept in Russia, and I'd be a fool to let it bother me when I can use it to my advantage. And it doesn't do any harm to my ego either.

'So, how many breakers do you want to buy?' I ask as the vodka releases my inhibitions.

'We'll get to business later,' he says, setting down his glass. 'Did you have a nice drive from Moscow?'

'We got here quickly,' Vladimir says, grabbing a handful of peanuts. 'The road is very good.'

'Yes, it's a straight drive from Moscow to Tula. I make the trip often. Of course, I have a driver.'

'I don't like other people driving me,' Vladimir says.

'Especially women,' I add, looking at the peanuts, but not taking any. 'He wouldn't let me drive in Washington.'

'When you reach my age, you'll be happy to let someone else drive,' Miasnikov says.

'When you visit our plant, I can drive you around,' I say.

Miasnikov sits back in his chair and smiles. 'I'd be delighted to have such a pretty chauffeur,' he says. 'The one I have now is kind of ugly.'

As he speaks, I cross my legs, letting my skirt ride up almost to my crotch, and flex my foot seductively.

'We always include a customer visit in the contract,' I say.

'I can see the pretty lady wants to talk business,' says Miasnikov, standing up, resigned. 'Well, we need to replace four 145 kilovolt dead tank breakers.'

I smile. 'Do you have a specification?' I ask. 'The fax I got didn't tell me much.'

'A specification? 145 kilovolts. What else do you need to know?'

'That's enough,' answers Vladimir. 'Katey also works for the Canadians and they require a lot of technical information.'

'We're a simple folk here in Tula,' Miasnikov says. 'We

just want basic equipment. Let's take a little walk and I'll show you where the old breakers are'. He goes back to the closet to get our coats. He hands Vladimir his and helps me into mine.

Miasnikov leads us behind the main building and we take a narrow snow-covered road to the switchyard. The high heels of my boots sink into the snow and a gust of wind blows snowflakes onto my bare legs. When I hit a patch of ice and almost go flying onto my ass, Miasnikov grabs my arm and tucks it under his own. Since he's not especially tall, his cheek touches mine.

'It's a pleasure to do business with such a pretty lady,' he says.

'It's an equal pleasure to do business with such a handsome man,' I reply. How many times has he called me *pretty lady*? At least fifteen. Even I have my limits, but I haven't reached them yet.

We come to the switchyard and he points out two monstrous circuit breakers, over twice the size of the ones we manufacture.

'They were built right after the war,' Miasnikov says, not specifying which war. Then he says, 'We should have replaced them years ago.'

Before I came on this trip, Dave had given me a lesson on Russian oil breakers. The huge oil-filled tanks are bulky, messy, ugly, and inefficient for arc interruption. They first started being manufactured in the 1920's and I wonder if these could be that old, a sobering thought since the operating life should not exceed thirty years.

After forty years, the risk of failure increases considerably. Gaskets, seals, O-rings, and wire insulation can become brittle and crack. Metal parts rust, and latches and bearing surfaces may have too much friction to even operate. Although many breakers around the world are in this condition, the utility company won't even know if an old breaker is in danger of failing until it is called on to operate and doesn't live up to its task.

Since breaker operation is infrequent, a malfunctioning circuit breaker can go unnoticed for years. With extensive maintenance, the life of a circuit breaker can be greatly extended, but considering the unproductiveness of the Communist work ethic, one can probably assume that rigorous maintenance programs have not been standard practice.

'Dmitri Sergeevich,' Vladimir says, interrupting my thoughts, 'we would like you to join us for lunch. But you need to recommend a spot.'

'Tula has some very nice restaurants,' he says, looking at me.

Is there anything in Tula that isn't nice?

He asks, 'Do you like sturgeon?'

Although I ate sturgeon with Sergey several months ago, I was too drunk to taste or remember it. 'No, I've never tried it,' I lie.

'Then you absolutely must,' says Miasnikov.

'Katey likes to try new things,' Vladimir says. I wonder if he's imagining new sex positions.

'My driver can take us,' Miasnikov says. 'It's much too cold for Katey's legs.'

He definitely has a point. I can barely feel them. Even my toes are starting to freeze inside my impractical boots.

We return to Miasnikov's office and remain standing in our coats as he picks up the telephone. I notice the vodka bottle and three shot glasses still on the table.

'Yuri!' he shouts into the phone. 'I need you to drive us to the Black Swan. Five minutes? Good!' He hangs up without saying goodbye.

'I got my driver a cell phone,' he says. 'It's very convenient. Katey, you must be freezing. You really need a long fox fur coat.'

'I'd love one,' I say as Miasnikov picks up the vodka bottle and refills the glasses. I imagine myself dressed from head to toe in luscious red fox, a real Tsarina. Maybe if I continue to flirt, and most importantly, continue to freeze,

Miasnikov will present me with one.

'Vodka's not as good as fox fur,' he says. 'But it can warm you up, too.'

And it's a hell of a lot cheaper. 'To warmth,' I toast as we slug down the vodka.

When we go outside again, a black Russian Volga, formerly the favorite car of Communist officials, is waiting in front of the door. The driver smiles at us, revealing several missing teeth. Miasnikov was right. This man really is ugly. He's wearing a tattered fur hat and dark clothing, eyes bloodshot—probably from a bottle of Tula vodka the night before. I wonder if he's sober now.

Miasnikov insists that I take the front seat—'You're closer to the heater'—and crawls into the back with Vladimir. It's a short drive to the Black Swan, not long enough for the heater to warm my legs.

The Black Swan is more like a tavern than a restaurant. Only one of the six tables is occupied. To avoid the draft, we take the one farthest from the door.

'Vodka and Sturgeon?' Miasnikov asks, looking at both of us.

'Sturgeon sounds great,' Vladimir replies, 'but I need to skip the vodka. I have to drive.'

'But Katey doesn't have to drive', Miasnikov says, winking at me.

When the waiter comes to the table, Miasnikov orders 300 grams of vodka and several bottles of water. He also orders three portions of sturgeon and three house salads.

'Katey is a good vodka drinker,' Vladimir says. 'You could almost think she is Russian.'

'You look Russian,' Miasnikov says to me.

'I'm Irish.'

'That's almost the same,' he says. 'The Irish drink like the Russians.'

'At least Katey does,' Vladimir says.

I kick Vladimir's leg under the table and he grins at me.

'Then let's drink to the Irish,' Miasnikov says, clinking

his glass against mine.

It's my fourth shot of vodka and I am feeling the effects. Miasnikov refills the glasses as soon as they hit the table. I'm guessing Vladimir has been talking about my drinking so that Miasnikov will get drunk. I feel like a pawn, but unsure of the game.

We drink several more shots before the meal comes. The salads are exquisitely cone-shaped on the plate. Inebriated, I discover a ravishing appetite and try not to eat too fast.

'There's nothing like Russian salad with vodka,' Miasnikov says, refilling my glass.

'What kind of meat is it?' I ask, spearing a brown chunk.

'I think it must be rabbit,' he says, sliding his chair around the arc of the round table until our legs touch. 'I want to whisper the toast into your ear.'

Miasnikov is so close that I smell his cologne. He is not unattractive; slightly stocky, but solid, with a handsome face. Unlike many Russians I've encountered, his hair looks freshly washed and I don't detect the slightest hint of body odor.

'To you, Katey. I want you, Katey,' he whispers, grabbing my thigh and squeezing.

I'm drunk enough not to mind his caress, at least not to hinder it. Although I can see the signed contract falling into my lap, I wonder what my success will cost me. As his hand slides under my skirt and presses against my crotch, I drink my vodka in one gulp, glad to be wearing pantyhose.

If Vladimir has noticed Miasnikov's advances, he doesn't let on. Hoping to spot jealousy, I see only pleasure.

The sturgeon arrives, batter-fried and served with French fries, different from the sturgeon kebab I ate in Moscow. Again, I'm too drunk to taste the food, but devour it like a hungry dog, even eating the French fries which I usually leave on the plate. Miasnikov remains close to me, his knee pressed against mine.

'One more for digestion,' Miasnikov says, picking up the almost empty vodka carafe. Even though I've often heard the Russians extol vodka as an aid to digesting fatty foods, I have always seen it as just an excuse for another drink.

'Now I think we really must talk business,' Miasnikov says after we return to his office. 'Katey needs to bring her boss some good news.'

'Should we prepare a proposal?' I ask. The winter air has sobered me enough to think clearly. 'I still could use a specification.'

'We'll draw up a contract,' Vladimir says. 'Can you come to Moscow next week?'

'I think I could manage.' He looks at a calendar on his desk. 'How about December 25th?'

'That sounds perfect. I think Katey can stay that long, can't you Katey?'

Wait! That's Christmas! My parents are expecting me. I reply, 'Sure, that sounds perfect. As long as you call Anis and explain.'

'Anis will be thrilled,' Vladimir says.

Or jealous of my success, I think.

'I suppose we should be heading back,' Vladimir says. 'I heard they're predicting snow.'

'It's already starting,' Miasnikov says, looking out the window. I see large flakes floating down like feathers. 'But it doesn't look too threatening.' He goes to the closet to get our coats.

'The snow's not bad yet,' Vladimir says. 'But you never can tell with a Russian storm.'

'May I have a moment alone with Katey before you go?' Miasnikov asks. 'I want to discuss a private matter.'

If Vladimir finds the request odd, he doesn't let on. 'Of, course. Why don't you have another drink? I'll warm up the car.' He winks at me before going out the door.

'Katey, Katey, my darling,' Miasnikov says after Vladimir is gone. 'How I would love to kiss you.'

I smile sweetly, wondering if he's really going to kiss me and if I am going to let him.

'I have some very good cognac,' he says instead.

'I love cognac.' I don't really like cognac but at the moment, I think I'd rather drink it than be kissed.

He brings a dark bottle and two brandy snifters from the cabinet and sloshes a double shot into each glass. Then he motions for me to sit on the couch. He sits next to me and pushes his body against mine, his pants tight enough so that I can see his erection.

'What should we drink to?' he asks.

'Let's drink to our future as business partners,' I suggest.

'How about to our future as friends?' he asks. 'I like friends much better.' Again he is resting his hand on my leg, and again I don't pull away.

'To friends,' I say as we clink our glasses together. We both sip the brandy and then Miasnikov takes my glass and sets it on the table.

'Now I am going to kiss you,' he says.

The contract, the contract, the contract, I think as he presses his lips against mine. Rubbing his hand over my breast, he drills his tongue into my mouth. *The contract, the contract, the contract.* I don't resist him and kiss him back, the vodka making me act like a floozy.

'Vladimir is waiting,' I say softly when he finally pulls away.

'Beautiful Katey,' he says, looking deep into my eyes. He takes both of my hands in his. 'I'm looking forward to seeing you next week.'

'So am I,' I say. 'But now I really must go.'

We stand up and he helps me into my coat. 'Maybe I can get you that fox fur coat, all the way down to your ankles,' he says.

'I'd like that,' I say, knowing he can't be serious. It

would probably cost him half a year's salary.

Vladimir has driven up to the entrance and is sitting in the car with the engine running. I am pleased by the warmth as I sit beside him.

'Did you have fun?' he asks, smirking.

'Just drive.'

We don't talk until we are out of Tula and speeding along on the highway. We must have been in the restaurant longer than it seemed because dusk is approaching. Moscow is so far north that there are only about six hours of complete daylight in December.

'So what's the plan for Christmas?' I ask.

'The Russians don't celebrate Christmas until January 6th.'

'Well, I'm missing my Christmas.'

'Here's the plan,' Vladimir begins, ignoring my complaint. 'I'll leave you two alone when he comes. Then you offer him some money.'

I should be shocked but suddenly the plan makes sense. Everything is clicking into place. Of course. 'And where am I supposed to get this money? Anis could never arrange that even if he wanted to.'

'Don't worry. I'll take care of it.'

'Then why do you want me to talk to him?'

'Russians get nervous when other Russians offer bribes. It's illegal in Russia. It's better coming from a foreigner.'

'It's just as illegal for us.'

'I know that and you know that, but the customer doesn't know that. A lot of Russians, especially the older ones, think that Westerners can offer bribes legally. It's another anti-capitalist myth.'

'So where are you going to get the money?' I ask again.

'We'll invent some added cost to your contract and manufacture some receipts,' he says. 'Then you can have your company pay them out in cash.'

Too drunk to worry about the feasibility of such a plan, I accept it at face value.

The dusk gradually becomes night. Bored, I reach my hand over to Vladimir's crotch. When he doesn't resist I pull down his zipper and pull out his penis. Unbuckling my seatbelt, I crawl onto the floor and take him into my mouth. *Most men complain that they don't get enough fellatio.* Maybe if he gets enough from me, he'll start to resent his wife, who probably spreads her legs once a week in the missionary position.

Vladimir quickly pulls to the side of the road, stops the car, and turns off the engine and the headlights. He remains wordless as I slide my mouth back and forth more and more quickly until he reaches his high point. When I crawl back onto the seat, he zips his pants silently, starts the engine and drives off.

After about ten minutes on the road, he asks, 'Did you do that for Miasnikov?'

'Go fuck yourself,' I tell him.

FIFTEEN

Vladimir chooses an engineer named Evgenii to draw up the contract for Miasnikov's circuit breakers. He has a face like a ventriloquist's dummy and talks nonstop. Always trying to be funny, he succeeds only at being annoying.

'Why can't Sasha do it?' I ask Vladimir when we are alone.

'Because Evgenii is very good at details, like an accountant. He's my contract man. What do you have against him?'

'I just don't like him,' I say.

'You don't have to like him,' he says. 'Just work with him.'

Evgenii uses the proposal which I put together with Anis back in Pennsylvania to write up a contract with a value of $924,000. The unit price of $154,000, which is much higher than the prices I give the Canadians, carries a profit margin of 30%. Anis explained that we need higher profits from the poorer countries because of the higher risks involved; but since we require payment 100% in advance and don't start manufacturing until we receive payment, I don't understand this risk. In truth, we are simply cashing in on the customer's ignorance of our market prices.

As requested by Miasnikov, we offer standard circuit breakers with no extras. We specify a delivery date of sixteen weeks after receipt of payment, which includes six weeks shipping time. A five-day trip, officially a plant inspection, but in reality a shopping and drinking vacation, is also written into the contract. Finally, a service engineer from our plant will travel to Tula for one week to install the equipment.

On Friday, Vladimir calls and tells me to take a day off. When I invite him to visit me in my hotel room, he claims to be busy all weekend. Bored by early afternoon, I buy a bottle of cherry brandy and a bottle of champagne and head for the office. I am really hoping to convince Vladimir to celebrate Christmas with me.

When I exit the bus and walk across the parking lot, I see Vladimir's blue Volvo pulling out of its reserved spot. He stops and rolls down the window.

'What are you doing here?' he asks.

'I missed you,' I said. 'I was hoping we could spend some time together.'

'I'm sorry, Katey. I have a meeting.'

'Can I come with you?'

'No, this doesn't have anything to do with dead tank circuit breakers.'

'What does it have to do with?'

'Something else,' he says in a tone which makes it clear he doesn't want to tell me any details.

'Will you be back?' I ask.

He looks straight into my eyes. 'No, my son is expecting me. I'll be going straight home.'

'What am I supposed to do all week-end?'

'Katey, you are in Moscow. There are museums all over the place.'

I've always hated museums and have no intention of going to one. 'I hate museums.'

'You sound like a child. Evgenii is in the office with the final draft of the contract. Why don't you take a look at it.'

'Then I guess I'll see you Monday,' I say, not hiding my disappointment.

'Monday is a very important day,' he says. 'You're about to get your first contract.'

'Do you really think Miasnikov will sign?'

'If you follow my directions, he'll sign.' Vladimir rolls up his window and waves before driving off.

When I enter the office, I find it empty except for Evgenii seated behind a computer, looking serious, his chin protruding like the toe of a woman's shoe. Seeing me, he smiles like a child receiving a present.

'Well, hello, Katey,' he says. 'I'm ready to print out the contract. What are you doing here?'

'I wanted to look at it,' I say.

We both listen to the hum of the printer, Evgenii checking each page as it slides out. When the printer becomes silent, he hands me the small stack.

Staring at the first page, I am quickly bored by the bureaucratic Russian. 'Monday is Christmas,' I say instead.

'We celebrate Orthodox Christmas on January 6th,' he says. 'December 25th is a regular day for us.'

'I don't have anyone to celebrate with,' I say. 'I don't suppose you'd like some champagne?' Although I dislike Evgenii, I dislike being alone with my bottles even more.

'I never refuse champagne.'

Two hours later the champagne is gone and the brandy bottle is almost empty. Evgenii is seated at Vladimir's desk with his feet on the table. I am sprawled in the chair across from him.

'I'm sitting like an American,' he says. 'Russians never put their feet on the table.'

'Can you keep a secret?' I ask.

'Russians are good at keeping secrets,' he replies.

What the hell are you doing, Katey? You don't even like this guy.

Good God, don't tell him that.

But after so much alcohol, I can't stop the words from escaping my mouth. 'I'm involved with your boss.'

'I'm not surprised,' he says, not sounding the least bit shocked.

'I think I love him.'

'Katey, Katey, Katey! He's found a weak spot beneath your skirt and now you love him.'

'Don't be crude.'

Evgenii pours the last of the brandy into our two glasses. 'This is going to cause one hell of a hangover,' he says.

'I'm not doing anything tomorrow,' I say. 'I might as well have a hangover.'

'Then maybe we should get some vodka,' he says. 'If you mix all that together, you'll be in bed all weekend.'

'I'm supposed to offer Miasnikov three thousand dollars on Monday,' I say.

'Of course,' Evgenii says, again not surprised. 'How else do you expect to get the contract?'

'Anis will fire me if he finds out I'm giving bribes.'

'Then you better not drink any vodka with him. In vino veritas.'

'I guess I'm spilling my secrets,' I say.

'A sober man's thoughts are a drunkard's words,' Evgenii says. 'A Russian saying.'

With the bottle empty, we have no reason to stay in the office. Evgenii turns out the lights and locks up. Although I couldn't stand him three hours ago, he has now become my closest friend.

'Let's walk to the metro,' I suggest.

'Whatever you say, Katey. But let's stop at a kiosk and get some vodka. It'll keep us warm.'

Even though it is bitter cold, the fresh air feels good on my face. Not for long, however, and I pull up my furry hood and zip it tight. Clothed in nothing but stockings, my legs become numb with cold in minutes and I feel my toes starting to freeze. Evgenii buys a half-liter bottle at the first kiosk and an opaque plastic bag to carry it in. We pass it back and forth as we trudge along the dark sidewalk. Although it is only half a mile to the metro, it takes us forty minutes to get there. Slipping on patches of snow, I fall on my ass several times. One time I grab Evgenii's arm for support, but end up pulling him down with me. As we struggle to get up, several people pass, staring down at us as if we have a disease.

'Disgraceful,' I hear a woman say.

Evgenii and I both look at each other, wondering who or what she is talking about but then realizing she means us, we both laugh and then hurry on before someone calls the cops.

We descend the crowded steps to the metro in rush hour, everyone moving like snails. The platform is filled with tired bodies waiting for the next train. When it arrives, crammed so full that the door is blocked, Evgenii sits down on a bench.

'Let's wait for the next one,' he says.

'It's not going to get any better,' I say.

Two minutes later another train arrives, just as full as the previous one. This time we bulldoze the bodies blocking the door with our shoulders. The people crowd in a little tighter without complaining and we squeeze in as the door closes. The air smells of sweat, urine, tobacco, and alcohol, and we add to the alcohol stench.

Pressed against the door, we fall out at the next stop, but quickly push our way back on. Before the doors close, a stocky young man charges at us like a football player, and as he rams against me, I fall against the crowd behind, almost losing my balance. His effort pays off as he takes my place near the door, leaving me squeezed against bodies from all four sides, barely able to breathe.

Nobody tries to get on at the next two stops. We push our way free at the third stop to transfer to a different line. We have a similar experience on the next train and by the time we finally reach the station near my hotel, my head is throbbing and I'm feeling nauseous. It then occurs to me that I haven't eaten since breakfast.

'Should we have a meal at company cost?' I ask. 'I'll add it to the expense report as a business meeting with a potential customer.'

'Yes, I'll be your customer for tonight,' Evgenii says.

In the restaurant we order more champagne. If the waiter notices how drunk we are, he doesn't let on. We eat black caviar, house salads, and Chicken Kiev. After the meal, I sign the check for $168.

Evgenii follows me to my room. Although I have no intention of sleeping with him, I let him come inside. I get two plastic cups from the bathroom and we stretch our legs out on the bed to finish the vodka. By this point our conversation has deteriorated to giggles and sleepy murmurs. At some point I close my eyes and when I open them Evgenii is on his back, snoring like a suckling pig. Although the alcohol hasn't completely worn off, I am thinking almost clearly and feel my headache returning.

Suddenly Evgenii repulses me and I want him out of the room. I'm relieved that we are both completely dressed. I vaguely remember telling him secrets and the thought horrifies me. I hope he was too drunk to remember.

'Evgenii,' I say, shaking him as hard as I can manage. He rolls over and continues snoring. Although I want to lie down, I can't bear the thought of sleeping next to him and turn on the light.

'Get up!' I roar, hitting him on the shoulder.

This time he rolls back over and opens his eyes. 'What...where?' he murmurs.

'Time to go!'

Gradually Evgenii realizes where he is. He sits up slowly. 'Oh, yeah,' he says. 'I should be going.'

I pick up his coat, open the door, and he leaves without a word. I don't say goodbye, as if by not acknowledging his departure, I can deny that he was here.

After he's gone, I go into the bathroom and vomit. Then I remove my clothes, brush my teeth, and crawl under the covers. Merry Christmas!

SIXTEEN

By Monday morning I've recovered from my hangover. True to Evgenii's promise, I was sick the whole weekend, ordering room service Saturday night, and venturing out only briefly on Sunday to buy bread, cheese and bananas at a nearby market.

On Monday I get up early enough to jog before breakfast. Not knowing where else to go, I run down the snow-covered sidewalk of Leningrad Prospect, passing two metro stations before turning around at the third. The crisp winter air in my lungs and against my face brings me quickly back to life.

Dressed only in a silk camisole with no bra, I stare into the mirror, pleased to see a natural redness on my cheeks instead of the corpselike pallor I'd been facing for the past two days. After applying makeup, I put on a chestnut-colored suit with a short pleated skirt and a double-breasted blazer. Then I go to the restaurant for the breakfast buffet, where I eat a bowl of muesli with a banana and drink three cups of strong black coffee. It is actually a lavish spread with everything from pastries to sausages, but I don't feel like gorging myself. I'm just reaching my room when I meet Vladimir in the hallway.

'You're early,' I say as I unlock my door.

'I know,' he says, pushing the door open and going inside. Tossing his briefcase on the chair, he places his hand on the back up my thigh, letting it slide up under my skirt. We undress without talking and make love without kissing. He acts almost like a stranger. After he climaxes much too quickly, Vladimir gets up and starts to dress.

Putting on my clothes, I remember Evgenii's words: 'A weak spot under your skirt'. I can't believe I told him all my secrets. Now I'll have to constantly worry that he'll repeat them to somebody. Maybe I should have him killed. I've heard it's not that hard to do in Russia. The Russians have a saying—*a secret is only safe if two people know it and one of them is dead.*

When we reach the office, I don't say hello to Evgenii. I don't even look at him. I'd like to talk to Sasha, but he is on the phone. Instead, I go into Vladimir's office and sit in the chair across from his desk.

'Have you read the contract?' he asks.

'Yes, on Friday,' I lie. In truth, I barely glanced at the first page.

'I spoke to Miasnikov before picking you up. He was just leaving Tula and should be here in an hour.'

I spend the next hour watching Vladimir work. Every few minutes, one of his workers comes in with a question. His secretary, Olga, a plump woman with too much eye makeup, brings us coffee with little cookies. Although she smiles at Vladimir with a face like the sugar plum fairy, she glares at me like a gorgon ready to turn me into stone.

At ten o'clock, Miasnikov appears in the doorway, dressed in a fur-lined leather jacket over a dark grey suit and red tie.

Vladimir stands quickly and walks toward him, extending his hand. I remain seated.

'You got here quickly,' Vladimir says.

'The roads were clear and free,' Miasnikov says, looking directly at me.

I stand up and extend my hand. Miasnikov takes it and raises it to his lips.

'Let's go into the meeting room,' Vladimir says, taking Miasnikov's coat and handing it to Olga, who has appeared in the doorway as if on cue.

The windowless meeting room has a table with six chairs. There is a bottle of Tula vodka, three shot glasses, a bowl of crackers and two expensive looking fountain pens. Obviously Olga knew about this visit.

Vladimir picks up the bottle and fills the glasses. After handing one to our guest and one to me, he raises the third.

'To your arrival in Moscow,' he says.

We down the drinks quickly. After small talk, Vladimir says, 'I'll leave you two alone to discuss the details.'

A few minutes later Olga returns with two copies of the contract. I have a power of attorney, signed by our general manager, which allows me to sign legal documents.

'I'm happy to see you again, Katey,' Miasnikov says, motioning for me to sit.

I'm surprised when he sits across from me instead of beside me. Perhaps he takes contract negotiations more seriously than business lunches. Or perhaps he hasn't had enough vodka yet.

'I have the contract here,' I say, passing him a copy. 'Would you like to check it.'

'I don't have to read it,' he says. 'I trust you.'

'I can guarantee you everything is in order,' I say. Thinking a drink would be appropriate to accompany my next proposal, I pick up the bottle of vodka and refill our glasses. 'To friendship and trust,' I say, clinking my glass against his.

'To friendship and trust,' he repeats, winking.

'We have a policy,' I begin, carefully selecting my words. 'The person who brings us the contract receives a bonus.'

'Yes,' he says, not looking surprised. 'I've heard that's

typical in western companies.'

I'm relieved to hear his reaction. Maybe this won't be as hard as I thought. 'I receive one, too,' I lie. 'We each get an unofficial three thousand dollars, but it's not written in the contract.'

'Of course not,' he says. 'We won't tell anyone.'

'And we included a plant visit for three people in the contract.'

'Will you be there?'

'Of course,' I say. 'I'll be your guide and chauffeur.'

'Then I think we should definitely sign,' he says.

We start by initialing each page, finally signing our names at the end. Then we exchange the contracts and repeat the process.

'Now we have to toast the contract,' he says, picking up the bottle and refilling the glasses.

'To the contract,' I say.

'To a pleasant future of mutual cooperation and profitability,' he adds.

After emptying the glass, he stands up and walks around the table. 'And now we have to seal it with a kiss,' he says. He comes around to my side of the table, puts his hands on my waist and kisses my mouth briefly. I'm surprised when he doesn't grope me. We probably haven't drunk enough.

'I have other business in Moscow,' he says. 'So unfortunately I can't stay.'

Although relieved that he's leaving, I say, 'That's a shame. I was hoping to spend the day together.'

'I'll be looking forward to our visit, Katey,' he says.

After he's gone, I return to Vladimir's office.

'I offered him three thousand dollars,' I say. 'I just have one question. Where are you going to get the money?'

'I'm not going to get it, Katey. You are.'

I feel my heart racing. 'I can't do that,' I say.

'Don't worry. We have a plan. I told Anis that you have to pay for the plane tickets for the plant visit. But Tula's copy of the contract states that Tulenergo has to buy its own plane tickets. Your copy of the contract says you have to reimburse the tickets with three thousand dollars cash. We took care of this little discrepancy, but even if we hadn't, nobody but you can read the Russian anyways. Then you give Miasnikov the money when he comes to America.'

'I'll need receipts.'

'Sasha can print them for you. His girlfriend owns a travel agency. He'll make each ticket for $1100. You give $3000 to Miasnikov and $300 to Sasha. You can even add another chunk for yourself if you want. Just tell Sasha the amount.'

'You're kidding,' I say. Then after a pause, I say, 'Aren't you?'

Vladimir responds with a wink.

Although the plan sounds easy and flawless, I can't help feeling nervous. But having made the offer to Miasnikov, I also know that I am trapped. In a way, I even find the plan exciting. I feel like a member of the Russian mafia and I am starting to understand, even enjoy, the game.

SEVENTEEN

Four months later I'm sitting in the Pittsburgh Airport drinking a Bloody Mary, garnished with a celery stalk. The plane from Frankfurt, where Miasnikov and his two colleagues transferred from Aeroflot to US Air, has been delayed an hour.

I'm driving a rental car, a 1995 Ford Scorpio. Since Anis considers my car, a 1986 Chevy Nova, to be a disgrace to the company, he suggested I use the rental. With student loan payments of over $300 a month, I can't really afford a decent car; but even if I could, I prefer to spend my money on other things. Just last week I bought diamond earrings for $300 on sale. Although I couldn't afford them, they make me feel like a princess. I have four credit cards that I got in college when I had no income, each with a limit of $5000.

Finishing the drink, I decide against a second one because the plane is arriving in fifteen minutes and I don't like to drink fast. I roam the airport, stopping at a necktie boutique where I find an attractive designer tie in shades of blue and grey and buy it for Vladimir. It costs eighty-eight dollars and I know he'll appreciate it. It's made of high quality silk and imported from Italy. I charge it to my corporate American Express Card. It will go on my expense report as a customer gift.

I haven't returned to Moscow since December. I've spent the last few months trying to get Anis's St. Petersburg customers to pay for their contract and have phoned Valentine Andreevich almost daily to discuss the problem. First, they didn't approve of the bank in Moscow which was issuing the guarantee. Although I explained several times that it is a branch office of a prominent bank in New York City, they refused to recognize it as a first-class bank, as required by the contract. I finally suggested to Valentine Andreevich that he specify an acceptable bank. After absorbing the costs of switching to his bank of choice, we reissued the guarantee and waited for payment. When no money arrived after three weeks, I was on the phone again.

This time, Valentine Andreevich aired several complaints about the wording of the letter of credit. A letter of credit is a document issued by a bank to assure that the customer receives his goods and that the supplier receives payment. The bank holds the advance payment until the seller presents documents proving that the goods have been delivered.

After making the trivial changes required by Valentine Andreevich, the bank reissued the letter of credit and we again waited for payment. When none came, I asked Vladimir to meet with the customer.

Several days later, Vladimir called me with the expected news—the customer is having financial difficulties and cannot pay the contract price. Since the four circuit breakers have already been manufactured, we risk absorbing a substantial loss. This development is sure to upset and embarrass Anis who agreed to the terms of the contract and gave the approval to start production. Although we didn't dare discuss it on the phone, Vladimir hinted that Valentine

Andreevich is expecting a bribe.

I explained the delicate situation to Anis. Since Americans aren't allowed to offer bribes, we had to disguise the action, so I arranged for Vladimir to send us a bill for $5000 for his own company's marketing services. We were able to transfer the money to Vladmir's corporate account, which he then paid Valentine Andreevich. Three weeks later, we received the advance payment and shipped the equipment. There were no more complaints about the documents.

I immediately recognize Miasnikov, carrying a leather briefcase and dressed like an American businessman—neat, but casual attire, his short-sleeve polo shirt unbuttoned far enough to reveal the first grey hairs of his chest. I notice that despite a stocky stature, he has a firm stomach. I also notice how thick his grey hair is, and think about running my fingers through it. When he sees me, his eyes light up like sparklers and his whole face smiles.

He is followed by a younger man with an adolescent body, who looks like he drinks vodka for breakfast. He is dressed in jeans, tennis shoes, and a T-shirt with the inscription 'Sport' in English, typical of Russian-made clothing designed to copy western styles.

The third man is wearing heavy-rimmed glasses and an inexpensive suit in a drab grey color over a blue and white checked shirt, topped with a brown and black striped polyester necktie. His hair is greasy with white flecks. He looks like an underpaid technical expert with no fashion sense or means to achieve it, who could easily play the role of a nice guy who never gets the girl.

Miasnikov kisses the back of my hand.

'Dmitri Sergeevich, welcome,' I say.

'Katey,' he says, pointing towards the others. 'Meet Vanya and Kolya.'

'Hello, Vanya and Kolya,' I say, pleased that I don't have

to remember long first names and patronymics. Vanya is the skinny alcoholic and Kolya is the brainy looking technician.

I get a cart and we wait for the luggage. I'm not really surprised when Vanya retrieves a box containing twelve bottles of Tula vodka.

Vanya removes a bottle before lifting the case of vodka into the trunk of my car. 'To drink on the way,' he says, his eyes red and glassy from jetlag and alcohol. I suspect they enjoyed many drinks on the airplane.

I know they shouldn't have an open bottle in a car, especially since I have also been drinking. Still, I don't object. The customer is always right.

Driving through the airport parking lot, Vanya and Kolya in the back and Miasnikov beside me, I reach down to pick up my cigarettes, which have fallen to the floor near Miasnikov's feet. I look up again just in time to crash against the rear of the car in front of me which has braked at a stop sign.

'Hide the bottle,' I say before getting out. I hope the driver is in a good mood.

Fortunately the other driver doesn't want to call the police. Since the accident occurred in a parking lot, the police aren't necessary. He is with an attractive woman and probably doesn't want to make a scene or delay his date. I give him the name and number of the rental agency, my contact information, and the name of the insurer. I'm not sure why he bothers because I can't see any damage to his car. Perhaps he has previous damage and wants to use this accident as an excuse to get it fixed at my expense.

In contrast, the front of my rental Scorpio is smashed. Fortunately I remembered to take out insurance when I rented the car. Otherwise, my company would be stuck with the damages. In any case, they won't be pleased, because the rates will probably go up.

After the other driver leaves, all three Russians get out

of the car to assess the damage. They naturally blame the other driver for stopping so suddenly, even saying they will explain it to Anis, a difficult challenge since they don't speak English.

As we drive to the hotel, they continue discussing the accident and passing the bottle of vodka around. I'm careful not to break the speed limit, well aware of the impression I would make if I got pulled over with a smashed-up car, three drunken Russians, and an open bottle of vodka.

Reaching our destination without further incident, I check them into their rooms. Miasnikov looks at me as if he expects me to come inside, but I promise to return soon for dinner. Although Anis has criticized it as a 'fast food restaurant,' I plan to take them to Red Lobster. It's likely they've never eaten this type of seafood before, especially in such generous portions.

When I pick them up at seven p.m., Miasnikov is freshly shaved and showered, dressed in slacks and an attractive blue and green print sweater. Vanya and Kolya are wearing their travel clothes and both have five o'clock shadows. Vanya's jeans are buckled tight around his waist, his legs and butt so skinny that the pants appear empty. Kolya's suit barely fits him, as if he has recently put on weight. Both men are shorter than Miasnikov, who isn't particularly tall.

At the restaurant I order a jumbo Bloody Mary. My three guests ask me what it is and then order the same, but with extra shots of vodka on the side. Like the elderly man I met on the airplane months ago, they find it strange to mix the vodka, but decide to try it anyway. And they are thrilled by the large colorful photographs on the menu. As they are admiring the pictures, I tell the waitress they are from Russia and request three souvenir menus, which she gladly provides.

I recommend mixed platters with generous portions of fried shrimp, scampi, crab legs, lobster tail, and flounder filet stuffed with crabmeat. The meals come with hushpuppies, French fries and salads. I'm curious to see how much the skinny Vanya will eat.

The jumbo Bloody Marys each contain three shots of vodka. We make a toast with the extra shot and chase it with the cocktail. They immediately want more vodka, but I refrain, remembering that a smashed car will act like a magnet for passing policemen.

When the food arrives, Vanya shovels it in as if he's just been released from a Siberian prison. I suspect that drunkenness and jetlag have increased his hunger, but I still wonder how he can eat so much and remain so thin. Miasnikov and Kolya eat politely, cutting their food slowly and chewing it thoroughly. Noticing that they keep the forks in their left hand—the European style—I feel awkward shifting mine between right and left.

They don't want dessert, but decide to have an Irish coffee. I drink a plain coffee. Because the total bill is much less than those I paid at the restaurants in Washington, I hope Anis will be pleased. I could have easily taken them to a ritzy place at twice the cost with portions half the size, but I don't think they would have appreciated it as much.

Vanya is swaying back and forth as we leave the restaurant and I hope he doesn't pass out in the back seat. Before getting into the car, he throws up in the bushes. Maybe that's how he stays thin. Fortunately, it's a short drive.

Returning to the hotel, I arrange to meet them at nine a.m. for breakfast in the hotel restaurant. Miasnikov waits while the others go into their rooms. Seeming to know that their boss wants to be alone with me, they vanish quickly.

'Would you like to come in, Katey?' he asks hopefully.

I can't refuse him. He has given me my first and only contract, my trump card against Anis. Since Vladimir believes there could be more contracts coming, I want to keep this customer happy. Besides, I need to give him the money which I have been carrying around in my purse. But before entering his room, I make up my mind not to sleep with him. Although the idea doesn't repulse me—it's not like it's Vanya or Kolya—and I'm quite sure no one would ever learn of it, a little angel with pink wings tells me not to do it. I'm in love with Vladimir, but I'm still sure he cheats on me. 'Vladimir loves the women,' Sergey said. And aren't all the best business deals made between the sheets?

I accept a glass of wine from the mini-bar and sit down on an armchair in the corner. Miasnikov sits on the bed facing me, not drinking anything. For a moment I wonder what I'll do if he forces me onto the bed. Probably I'll just shut my eyes and think about the next contract.

But we only make small talk. Several times he tells me how pretty I am, how much he desires me, and puts his hand on my knee. This seems like a good time to offer the envelope.

'Your commission,' I say, handing it to him.

'Don't you get one too?' he asks.

'Yes, of course,' I lie with a sly smile. Getting the money from my company, even with the three airline ticket receipts furnished by Sasha, hadn't been easy. Even though Anis was nervous about dealing in cash, I convinced him that we had agreed to reimburse the guests for their plane tickets. I still have $300 to give to Sasha on my next trip to Russia.

Now seems a good time to leave, but before I can stand, Miasnikov springs up and pushes my shoulders down.

'You can't go,' he says, 'without drinking a vodka toast to our mutual success.'

I notice for the first time the sexy glare of his eyes.

I remain seated as he takes the carry-on bag and pulls out an unopened bottle of vodka.

'And it's customary to use a new bottle,' he says. I've never heard that before, but assume it's true.

He gets two glasses from the mini-bar and sloshes an ample amount of vodka into each of them. Then he sits back down on the bed, close enough so that his knees touch mine.

'To our successful partnership,' he says. After we clink our glasses, I attempt to swallow the entire shot in one gulp, at least a triple, and barely get it down without gagging.

As warmth rises in my cheeks, I realize that I want Miasnikov to kiss me. He is staring and holding a partially filled glass. When he reaches for the bottle, I don't refuse a refill. We clink our glasses together and this time I take only a sip. He leans over and cups my face in his hands. His first kiss is like a feather brushing across my lips. When I don't resist, he presses his lips gently against mine, opening his mouth only slightly.

Perched on my right shoulder, the little angel is telling me to go home. But a spunky devil on my left shoulder is blowing fire into my ear. The angel tells me I'm drunk and will regret it in the morning. The devil says I'm too drunk to drive and have no option but to share this man's bed.

I'm not wearing a bra. Miasnikov reaches both hands under the tank top beneath my sweater and pulls them both over my head. When he leans over and kisses my breasts, I imagine the little angel flying away in distress and the devil cheering. After pulling his own sweater and undershirt over his head, he pushes me gently back onto the bed and lies on top of me. Brushing my lips across his neck, I am startled to smell Vladimir's cologne. I suspect Vladimir gave it to him as a gift.

Suddenly I'm unsure about continuing. But the angel is gone and my head is spinning like a Ferris wheel, so I allow this man to undress me and watch as he undresses himself. As he penetrates me, I'm aware that it is eight hours later in Moscow and Vladimir is eating breakfast with his wife and son. I wonder if they had morning sex.

Although Miasnikov is a good lover, I don't really achieve any pleasure. Afraid that he might not give up until I do, I groan and whimper when he comes (I'm remembering the famous 'When Harry Met Sally' restaurant scene) and apparently satisfy him.

When he gets up and walks naked to his suitcase, I again notice the solid body of a man who has done much physical work. He takes out a pack of cigarettes, which surprises me because I've never seen him smoke, and I accept one.

'You can't drive home, Katey,' he says.

Like Hell I can't. 'I can't leave my guinea pig alone,' I say. This weak excuse is the only one I can think of without offending him.

'What happens if you get pulled over?'

I recall that famous creek one must face without a paddle. 'I won't,' I say. 'It's only a short drive.'

I'm aware of his eyes as I dress quickly. As the vodka wears off, I ask myself what I'm doing in the room of a man almost as old as my father.

Wishing I'd obeyed the angel, I wave as I leave without offering a kiss. Although he stands up, I am out the door before he can get near enough to touch me.

I walk through the darkness to my car, which is parked in the far corner of the lot. I have trouble finding the keyhole, and when I finally get the door open, the ground is circling beneath my feet. Falling into the driver's seat, I count how many shots I drank and in how many hours. Guessing the number of shots to be at least ten and the number of hours less than six, I lean back to rest awhile before trying to drive. Before closing my eyes, I lock the door.

It is still dark when I awake. Tired, but reasonably sober, I leave the parking lot and creep along the lonely highway. In ten minutes I pull into the driveway, enter my apartment, and notice my answering machine blinking.

Pushing the play button, I am not surprised to hear Vladimir's voice. 'I just got into the office and wanted to see if the customers arrived okay. I guess you're with Miasnikov if you're not home yet. That's one way to get another contract. Keep up the good work, Katey.'

I try to detect a note of jealousy or sarcasm in his voice, but fail. Realizing that I will never become Mrs. Vladimir Kashirnikov, I give Homer a carrot stick before peeling off my clothes and climbing into bed.

EIGHTEEN

I get out of bed and brew a double espresso. Then I call Vladimir. The phone rings four times before he answers.

'Kashirnikov.'

'Hello,' I say, knowing he'll recognize my voice.

'Is everything in order over there?' he asks.

'I smashed up the rental car. I hit the car in front of me at a stop sign in the airport parking lot.'

'Weren't you watching where you were going?' I recognize the unspoken question in his tone—how could you be so stupid?

'The customers were distracting me with their constant chatter.'

'You probably dropped your cigarettes and were reaching down to get them,' he taunts.

'I confess.'

'You were out late,' he says.

'I was already in bed. I didn't hear the phone.'

The long pause indicates that he doesn't believe me. 'I thought you might have been improving customer relations with Miasnikov.'

'At four a.m?' I say. 'You have a dirty mind.'

'So do you,' he says. 'That's my point.'

'He's not my type.'

'What is your type?'

'Tall, arrogant, and sexy, with eyes the color of a mountain lake and perfect teeth.'

Vladimir chuckles and then tells me to call him back when I get to the office. He expects to be working late.

Surprised that I'm not suffering from a hangover, I realize there must be residual alcohol in my system. After finishing my coffee, I change into jogging clothes and head out the door. After running for ten minutes, I lean over and throw up the coffee on the side of the road.

Determined to replace my impending hangover with an adrenaline high, I force myself to run further, increasing my speed, and feel my sleepless body fighting the caffeine jolt which drives me forward. By the time I get home forty minutes later, sweating and breathless, most of the symptoms have vanished. And vodka doesn't have any smell—at least I hope it doesn't.

I leave the apartment shortly before eight o'clock, needing to stop at the rental agency to replace my car. When I tell about the accident, the agent reacts as if crashes are an everyday occurrence.

'Did you damage the other car?' she asks.

'I don't think so. I don't really know. There was no police report.'

'Then I guess it doesn't matter,' she says, and fifteen minutes later I drive away in a shiny new teal-green Saturn.

My three customers are already seated at a table in the hotel restaurant, drinking coffee. When I checked them into the hotel yesterday, I explained to the manager that they can't speak English and I would be meeting them for breakfast to translate. Since most Americans start their breakfasts with coffee, the waitress probably brought it automatically.

Looking spiffy in pleated wool slacks and a grey sweater, Miasnikov winks at me, making sure the others don't notice. Somehow he seemed more attractive last night. I flash him a smile. Maybe I can pretend last night was a dream.

Kolya is wearing the same outfit he had on yesterday and looks like he slept in his clothes. Although he hasn't mentioned it, I assume he isn't married. No woman could possibly have such terrible taste in attire.

Vanya is dressed in stiff-looking Levis, probably a boy's slim size because they are so tight his legs look like stilts. His red and green plaid flannel shirt is buttoned all the way to the top. He looks well rested, but nervous—he probably needs   a   drink.

Afraid I may vomit again if I eat anything, I order the big breakfast with eggs, bacon, and pancakes for everyone but myself.

'I've heard that Americans don't have anything but coffee for breakfast,' Miasnikov says.

'I even drink my coffee black,' I say.

I expect Vanya to request a beer, but he doesn't. Instead he puts five spoonfuls of sugar and three creamers into his second cup of coffee. When the food arrives, he devours it like a hungry horse, not speaking a word and not looking up until the plate is empty.

Again, I am surprised at how voraciously they eat, leaving their plates almost spotless. I'm guessing that either jet lag has increased their appetites, or they've fallen in love with American food.

It's a short drive to the office where Anis is waiting. They all shake hands and I translate an exchange of niceties, which become even triter in the translation. Their expressions indicate that they don't understand the purpose of this meeting.

'Who is he?' Miasnikov asks.

'The director of international sales,' I say.

'I thought you were,' he says.

'Not yet,' I say, and we both laugh.

'What is it?' Anis asks with a curious expression. 'What's so funny?'

'They were just wondering if we had any beer here,' I say.

'It's ten a.m.!' Anis exclaims.

'It's six p.m. in Tula and they have jet lag,' I say, suddenly realizing that a beer would taste pretty good.

'Let's at least wait until lunch time,' Anis says with an awkward smile.

Afterwards I take them in to see Jack, explaining beforehand that he is our general manager. A golf ball sails past the open doorway as we approach.

'Damn,' a voice says from inside the office. Even though I've seen executives playing office golf in movies, I didn't know they do it in real life.

The ivory-colored walls of Jack's roomy office are decorated with original oil landscapes. Light blue carpet as smooth as a golf-course green stretches from wall to wall, and a massive walnut table centers the room. The desk on the left side of the room, also walnut, is twice as large as mine. Unlike Anis, Jack has a mess of papers.

Jack is still holding the golf club when we enter the room. 'I missed a six foot putt at the golf course yesterday,' he says. 'It cost me the game and I had to buy all the drinks. I don't want it to happen again.'

The Russians laugh when I translate. Then we all watch silently, barely breathing, as Jack repeats the putt. This time the ball disappears into the cup. The three Russians applaud with the fervor of fans at a soccer game.

Miasnikov takes a bottle of vodka out of his leather briefcase and presents it to Jack like a trophy. As Jack thanks him, shaking hands with all three, I tell him the vodka is a homegrown product from Tula.

'Then we definitely need to try it,' Jack says, going to a

cabinet near his desk and returning with five shot glasses. He must have bought them after the visit of the first Russian delegation. As he starts to open the bottle, Miasnikov holds up his hand to stop him.

'That bottle is for you,' he says as I translate. He then pulls out a second bottle. 'This one is for now.'

Jack smiles and takes the second bottle. He opens it, fills the glasses with the savvy of a bartender, and then passes them around.

'A welcome toast,' he says, raising his glass.

We clink our glasses together before downing them. Since my stomach is empty, I struggle not to gag. Just as I'm about to run to the bathroom, my stomach settles and I feel better. Although Vanya is staring wistfully at the bottle, Jack doesn't offer a refill. He probably liked it and wants to save the rest for himself.

I then take the Russians on a tour of the plant. They look at everything with feigned interest, asking few questions until I show them their own six circuit breakers, which are finished and almost ready to ship.

'We just need some final testing and then we'll be shipping them,' I say. 'They should arrive in six weeks.'

I can tell they're impressed by the compact design of the breakers with their three cast aluminum tanks and six porcelain bushings. They are less than half the size of the ones they are replacing. My guests circle the equipment like children in a toy store. Miasnikov pats one of the tanks as if it were a horse and smiles. I show them the hydraulic spring mechanism which is used to separate the contacts and break the current. While Kolya examines the electrical control components with interest, the others only glance.

Soon they have seen enough and welcome my suggestion to visit the mall. I'm surprised when Vanya, who doesn't look a day over forty, wants to buy baby clothes for his granddaughter. The others want to buy athletic apparel. Jogging and golf have both recently become the rage in

Russia and so much so that even those who don't jog or play golf still want to wear the proper clothes.

After about an hour of skimming through various boutiques with few purchases—they aren't big spenders like my other customers—we walk across the parking lot to Hooters, a bar where the waitresses all wear short shorts and T-shirts stretched over big breasts. Although Anis would disapprove of such a casual eating establishment, I am quite sure the customers will enjoy it.

We order beer and Buffalo wings, served by a short waitress with a bubble butt and tits like cantaloupes. Her hair is the color of beach sand, and she is wearing enough makeup to open a cosmetic factory.

'Is she a prostitute?' Miasnikov whispers, as the waitress distributes four mugs of beer.

'No, that's her uniform,' I say. 'It's an unwritten condition of employment that you have to have big tits. I could never work here.'

They all look at my tits, but nobody says anything.

After we finish eating, I offer to take them back to the mall.

'We don't want to take up all your time, Katey,' Miasnikov says.

'It's a pleasure,' I say, meaning it. I do enjoy this part of my job; I get paid to eat, drink, and speak Russian. It's definitely more fun than sitting behind a computer calculating the price of 'high-creep' bushings.

'Can we go to a grocery store?' Miasnikov asks. 'We need to get a few things. Then you can take us back to the hotel.'

Since we just ate, his request surprises me; and seeing my puzzled look, Miasnikov says, 'We need *Zakuska*.'

Suddenly understanding that they intend to drink some of the vodka they brought, I take them to a large grocery store and get a small shopping basket, assuming they won't be buying a lot. Although they must be impressed by the vast quantities and assortments—what other country in the world has a dozen brands of toilet paper and twenty types of spaghetti sauce?—they react casually, too proud to admit that the same bounty and assortment, however unnecessary, doesn't exist in Russia.

We spend close to an hour in the grocery store. We walk down every aisle and they examine many items before making their selections. When we get to the checkout, the basket contains a jar of dill pickles, hard salami, several kinds of cheese, a can of sardines, a jar of green olives, a loaf of cocktail rye, trout caviar, and butter, essentially the same things they would buy in Russia. I pay the bill, keeping the receipt, which I will put on my expense report.

I return to the office after dropping them at the hotel. Anis is surprised to see me.

'Where are the customers?' he asks, as if assuming I've done something sinister.

'They wanted to return to the hotel,' I say. 'We stopped at the grocery store first for snacks. I think they want to drink some of the vodka they brought. I'm meeting them at six.'

'Where did you eat lunch?'

'I took them to Hooters.'

'You're kidding.' He really believes I'm kidding.

'They loved it,' I say.

'You're serious.'

'Of course I'm serious. These are simple people who feel uncomfortable in fancy restaurants. They'd rather sit in their hotel rooms, eating snacks from a grocery store and drinking vodka out of toothbrush cups.'

'Well, I guess we'll save some money. Where are you taking them tonight? Not McDonald's, I hope.'

'No, they have that in Russia. I'll take them to a Steakhouse.'

'And tomorrow?'

'A tour of Pittsburgh in the morning.' I don't tell him

about my plan to park at a shopping mall in the suburbs and take a taxi into the city. I don't want to drive in downtown traffic and I don't know how to parallel park. Besides, I'll probably end up drinking.

'And in the afternoon?'

'I suspect they'll want to finish their vodka, which is good because I'm running short on ideas. I thought I'd move them to a hotel at the shopping mall near Pittsburgh on their last day. They need to get to the airport early, so I'll spend the night there too and drive them in the morning. That way, I can entertain them in the evening.'

'Sounds like a plan,' Anis says, approving.

I use the rest of the afternoon to prepare a bid for a Canadian customer. The specification is fifty pages long, so I need several hours to read through it and identify all the requirements. I finish the bid by five-thirty and drop it off in the secretary's in-box.

Arriving at the hotel, I knock on Miasnikov's door, but get no answer. I find Vanya's door ajar. Knocking, I push it open and walk inside. They have three chairs—two from the other rooms—around the nightstand in a circle beside the bed. The table is covered with food from the grocery store. The salami and cheese have been sliced with a pocket knife. As I suspected, they are drinking from toothbrush cups. Although the vodka bottle on the table is almost empty, none of them appears drunk. I'm starting to think that vodka flows from the water faucets in Tula.

'Katey, join us,' Miasnikov says, patting his knee. Not wanting to offend him and also because there aren't any more chairs, I sit on his lap, wishing I was wearing pants instead of a short skirt. When he caresses my stockinged thigh I resist the urge to move his hand away. Instead, I stay seated reluctantly and accept vodka from Miasnikov's half-full cup. After taking a swig, I bite the end off of a pickle and relax a bit. Then remembering I have to drive, I hand the cup back.

'Are you hungry?' I ask, noticing that they've eaten most of the salami and cheese. 'I've come to take you to dinner.'

'Katey,' Vanya says. 'We're always hungry. All this drinking works up an appetite.'

NINETEEN

On Friday morning I move the Tula delegation to a hotel near a shopping mall outside of Pittsburgh. Since I have to take them to the airport at six a.m., I've also checked into a room, allowing me to spend the evening with them and get a decent night's sleep.

Although we spend most of the day roaming from store to store, they buy only a couple of small items: perfume for their wives, baby clothes for the grandchildren, and T-shirts for the rest of the family. I sneak away to buy two suits—a silk combination in eggplant and a trendy brown suit with a short pleated skirt in dark walnut. Because of my warm complexion, I look good in unusual colors.

Passing a necktie boutique, Miasnikov asks me to select a tie for him. Flattered by his confidence in my taste, I seek out the designer silks, finding a grey Hermes tie with random maroon lines and solid blue circles to match Miasnikov's eyes. It looks like modern art. Holding the tie by his neck, I am pleased how his hair blends with the grey background. Before handing it to him for approval, I discreetly check the price—seventy-eight dollars.

'Do you like it?' I ask.

'The important question is, 'Do you like it?''

'I think it's elegant,' I say. 'And a youthful style.'

'In that case, I better buy it,' he decides. 'I need all the youthfulness I can get. And the next time you come to Tula, I'll be sure to wear it.'

'Then I'll be sure to come soon,' I say, thinking only about future contracts. If I continue to keep Miasnikov happy, and he realizes that the only way to see me is to buy our equipment, then the arrangement should please us both.

'Let me see,' Vanya says, taking the tie from Miasnikov. Turning it over to see the price, he whistles a 'Whew.' It probably costs more than he paid for his entire wardrobe.

As Vanya and Kolya roam around, examining flamboyant ties with Popeye and Marilyn Monroe motifs, I take the tie from Miasnikov's hand.

'This is a present from Ampere Power Company,' I say.

'You mean the company is paying for it?' he asks.

'Yes, of course,' I say. 'It's customary.' I don't really know how Anis will react to such an extravagant gift and I know there is a risk that I will have to pay for the tie myself; but Vladimir has told me several times that my German and Swiss colleagues shower their customers with expensive gifts, unlike the stingy Americans who hand out cheap pens and bottle openers.

Miasnikov seems pleased by my gesture. Although apparently well off by Russian standards, he probably wouldn't have been eager to spend so much on a necktie. As chief engineer of Tulenergo, his salary is still much lower than mine. And although he certainly collects his share of slush money, the amounts are probably not extravagant.

We eat lunch in a rotunda bordered by fast food restaurants, the middle filled with tables. Besides the usual McDonald's, Burger King and Wendy's, there are two Chinese restaurants, a Polish deli with dill pickles the size of large potatoes, a cafe serving nothing but baked potatoes topped with everything from cheddar cheese to creamed crab meat, and another place specializing in hot, juicy cinnamon rolls. There is also an Indian restaurant, a Japanese sushi bar, a Mexican cafe and several pizza stands. There is even a breakfast café that serves pecan waffles and blueberry pancakes at all hours of the day. But the restaurant we desperately need—one serving alcohol—is missing.

When I tell them we'll have to go elsewhere for alcohol, Miasnikov insists on remaining, but I can't miss the disappointment bordering on panic in Vanya's eyes. We'll have to eat quickly and then find a nearby bar.

But instead of going to a bar after the meal, Vanya suggests we return to the hotel for a siesta. Without needing to ask, I know they are planning another vodka soirée in his room. Knowing they'll want food for the party, I take them back to the Polish deli, where they select several kinds of salami, bread, and the mammoth dill pickles.

After dropping them off at Vanya's, I politely refuse an offer to join them and go to my own room. Although I should return to the office to work on the Canadian bids, I decide to rest for the evening and watch a rerun of *Little House on the Prairie*, the episode where ten-year-old Laura puts apples under her dress to try and impress a boy at school.

Afterwards I watch Oprah. There is a woman who looks like a sumo wrestler, dressed in a bikini top and a grass skirt to demonstrate the beauty of obesity. Her boobs hang to her waist, her butt and belly jiggle as if made of jelly, loads of jelly. A man as skinny as Olive Oyl sits in a chair watching the woman perform a hula dance. He is confessing to Oprah a fetish for *voluptuous* women.

Several hours later I return to Vanya's room to witness the same scene I have viewed for the past couple of days: empty bottles, tousled hair, untucked shirts and laughter.

Again I drink a few toasts on Miasnikov's lap before taking them to dinner. Not wanting to drive, I deliberately choose a restaurant near the mall - TGI Fridays. Although I'm sure Anis won't approve of my choice—he's criticized every restaurant so far—I'm certain the customers will enjoy the lively atmosphere and friendly waitresses.

I order an appetizer of shrimp stuffed with crab meat. At my suggestion, Miasnikov orders a rare steak topped with mushrooms, tomatoes and mozzarella. He is quickly becoming an expert on American food—a cuisine which many Europeans deny the existence of. Probably feeling thirsty from so much vodka in the hotel room, everybody chooses beer. I drink three Bloody Marys.

When we get back to the hotel, they invite me to celebrate their last night by helping to finish the vodka. Feeling high from the cocktails and having no excuse to refuse, I agree to join them.

Determined to empty the last two bottles, they pour one shot after another. I make a toast to Tula, which they appreciate. Then I make a toast to Tula vodka, which pleases them even more. After a while, Vanya starts telling Russian jokes.

Three men are stranded on an island—an American, a Frenchman, and a Russian. Suddenly a mermaid appears and says she can grant each of them two wishes. The American goes first. He says, 'I want a million dollars and to go home.' The mermaid produces a million dollars and the man vanishes. Next the Frenchman says, 'I'd like a beautiful woman and to go home.' A beautiful woman appears, the Frenchman takes her in his arms and they both vanish. Only the Russian remains. He says, 'It was such a nice group. I want a bottle of vodka and both of them back.'

I begin to laugh, softly at first, but gradually louder until my whole body is shaking. Miasnikov hands me another shot and I drink it down, almost choking. Before I have recovered, Vanya starts again.

A woman comes into the apartment and says to her husband: 'I was raped in the stairwell.' He says to her, 'Go into the kitchen and eat a slice of lemon.' She goes into the kitchen, eats a slice of lemon and returns. She says again: 'I was raped in the stairwell.' 'Go and eat a slice of lemon,' he repeats. 'Why do you want me to eat a lemon?' she asks. 'Because I don't like that smile you have on your face,' he replies.

Vanya is on a roll:

A husband and wife are lying in bed,' 'The wife thinks to herself, 'Tomorrow is our fifteenth wedding anniversary. I bet he got me a nice present.' The husband thinks, 'If I had killed her fifteen years ago, I would be a free man tomorrow.'

'What's better, a beer or your mother-in-law?' Vanya asks, looking at me.

Instead of answering, I simply laugh, anticipating a good punch line.

'Both are good—cold and on the table.'

Even though I should probably be offended by all these sexist jokes, I start to guffaw. Already giddy from the vodka, I am unable to stop laughing. It doesn't take long before I am too drunk follow the jokes, but still roar at each one, leaning my head on Miasnikov's shoulder.

After a while they tire of the jokes and the atmosphere softens. Miasnikov is suddenly pensive. 'Katey, we want to help you.'

'You want to help me?' I ask. Although nothing is funny, I start to laugh again. I laugh and laugh, falling back onto the bed.

When I finally calm down, Miasnikov continues, 'The problem is that the Russians aren't aware of your company and its products. We need to inform them.'

'That's what I do—hic—when I travel around,' I say.

'I'm thinking of something bigger,' he says.

'Bigger?' I ask.

'Tula is getting the first circuit breakers to come to Russia from your company. We could invite representatives from other towns to visit and see them.'

'You mean all at once?' I ask. 'Like a big party?'

Eyes growing larger, Miasnikov says, 'Yes. We could have a seminar. You can send some of your engineers to give technical presentations. And in the evening we can have a fancy dinner. We can host the whole event at Tulenergo.'

In my state of inebriation, it sounds like a good idea. 'Do you really think anyone would come?'

'Of course they'll come,' Miasnikov says. 'Russians love a good business trip.'

Or a good party, I think.

Miasnikov says, 'Anything to get out of work.'

'Like you're doing now?' I ask. 'With lots of vodka?'

'Exactly,' Miasnikov says. 'It's the best way to establish good customer relations'.

I say, 'We can pass around the contracts with the vodka.'

And of course, Ampere Power Company will pay for it all. 'I'll have to discuss it with my boss,' I say.

'Don't bring him,' Miasnikov says. 'Bring your general manager. The Russians will like him.'

The thought of Jack drinking vodka with a bunch of Russian alcoholics in Tula sends me into another fit of laughter. Miasnikov drops the subject and Vanya tells another joke. Kolya, who has barely spoken, is now snoring softly in his chair.

Realizing I should be getting back to my room, I try to stand, but the room spins and the floor moves. Miasnikov catches me before I fall into a world of fog.

Lying under a sheet in a strange bed, I feel chills moving

through my body. Someone is snoring softly beside me. Like a bowling ball on the pillow, my head doesn't want to move. My contacts have dried out in my sleep and are sticking to my eyes like pieces of sandpaper. Although naked, I don't remember having sex. I don't remember anything after losing my balance in Vanya's room. Now I vaguely recall Miasnikov leading me out of the room and realize I am in his bed. Although not ideal, my situation could have been worse. I could have been lying next to Vanya.

The vodka hasn't worn off because I feel wide awake and giddy but without any signs of a hangover. Perhaps Tula vodka really is good. Finding my clothes on a chair, I dress quickly and quietly, wanting to leave without waking my host. I am relieved to find my keys and wallet in the pockets, although I can't imagine anyone taking them.

When I get to my room, I turn on the light and see that it is five a.m. We need to leave for the airport at six. Since I forgot to arrange a wake-up call, it's lucky I'm awake. Even though I don't have a headache, my mouth still feels like the Sahara desert and my stomach, the rolling sand. I go into the bathroom and gulp water, refilling the glass several times. Then I undress and hop into a cold shower. The jolt of icy water almost sends me into shock. I call room service afterwards and order a pot of coffee.

At five-thirty I call each of the three rooms. Only Vanya sounds like I disturbed him from a deep sleep. The other two sound well rested.

'Can I get a beer?' Vanya asks when we meet in the lobby at six a.m.

'Are you serious?' I ask.

'I am.'

'Bring four,' Miasnikov says.

I go into the kitchen and ask a waiter for three bottles of beer and a cup of coffee. With residual alcohol still in my system, I'm afraid that a beer would make me too drunk to drive.

In the midst of breakfast preparations, he is surprised by such an odd request. 'We really can't serve alcohol until noon.'

Explaining that my guests are Russian, I press a twenty into his hand and promise not to tell anyone. He returns three minutes later with a cup of coffee and a paper bag filled with three cold bottles.

'You're very kind,' I say.

'This could cost me my job.'

'It won't,' I promise. 'You will never see or hear from us again.'

They drink the beer in the parking garage. At this early hour I'm not worried about being seen. Afraid they might request a refill, I herd my customers into the car.

The freeway to the airport is almost deserted. Although the chances of a patrol car at this hour are remote, I stay just below the speed limit in the right lane, not wanting to attract attention. We reach our destination without incident.

'We'll be in touch about the seminar,' Miasnikov says.

'Seminar?' I ask. I don't remember this conversation.

'We'll get people from all the energos,' Miasnikov promises. 'It will be a great event.'

Oh God! What did I agree to last night?

We part like old friends, Vanya and Kolya kissing my hand and thanking me, Miasnikov kissing my cheek. I promise to visit them soon.

Before leaving the airport I drink a double espresso and then drive home at a leisurely pace, grateful that it is Saturday.

TWENTY

'Your hair is dry and brittle,' says the male beautician, using various hand gestures to show off his limp wrists. His own hair is pink and purple spikes. Dressed in a pink T-shirt and tight black cargo pants, he reminds me of the sweet transvestite in the *Rocky Horror Picture Show.* 'You have so many dreadful split ends,' he scolds, massaging a lock with his fingers. 'Just dreadful. Too much bleaching. It strips the hair of all luster.'

'What do you suggest?' I ask, not wanting to hear the answer. 'I wanted you to bleach the roots today.'

'No, no, no,' he says. 'You need to cut this unhealthy hair off and let the healthy hair grow out. You bleached it yourself didn't you?'

'Yes,' I confess.

'How many times?'

'I tried to do the roots each time,' I say. 'But I always ended up bleaching all of it.'

'How many times?' he repeats.

'Three or four.'

'That stuff in the drugstore is bad for your hair. Very

bad.' I notice he is wearing blue eye shadow.

Staring into the mirror, I realize that my hair does look scruffy, like pieces of straw. 'What should I do?' I ask.

'Cut it off,' he says. 'All of it. Then we can start over.'

The last time I had really short hair, I was twelve. I hesitate, breathe deeply, and then say, 'Okay, whatever you think is best.'

Once he starts to work, he stops talking. After pinning the outer locks to the top of my head, he begins snipping away at the lower layers. As he cuts the top layers, I watch my blonde locks falling like autumn leaves. Only when he trims around my ears do I realize I've made a terrible mistake. This short brown hair has transformed me into a school teacher or a dike. I look like somebody's grandmother.

'So,' the beautician says. 'Now we have nice virgin hair. How do you like it?'

'I hate it,' I say. 'I look like a librarian. Can you dye it light blonde?'

'Of course. But you need another appointment.'

'No, I mean right now,' I insist. 'I can't go out like this in public.'

'We can't possibly fit you in today,' my limp-wristed beautician says, 'You'll just have to make an appointment.' He is practically floating out of his loafers.

'I'm leaving for Russia in two days,' I say. 'I won't have time.'

'Then we'll do it when you get back. But don't dye it yourself.'

Strolling through the mall, I look for other women with short haircuts, trying to convince myself that I'm stylish, but I don't spot a single woman under sixty with short hair. And I'll be seeing Vladimir in three days!

Avoiding mirrors, I go into a jewelry store and pick out a pair of gold dangling earrings with little brown stones, hoping they will add femininity. I buy several other pairs, all gaudy and expensive.

Arriving at work the next day, I sneak into my office and sink into the chair. Before long, Diego, a sales engineer from Columbia, enters to say good morning.

'You cut your hair,' he says. It sounds like an accusation.

'Yeah, I guess I got it too short,' I say, trying to sound nonchalant.

'Short hair is no longer stylish,' he says.

'It'll grow,' I say. *Thanks for your tact.*

On the way home that evening, I buy a bottle of bleaching agent and a package of light gold blonde hair color to apply after.

I mix the blue formula and distribute it onto my hair. After forty-five minutes, my brown stubble has been transformed into the fluorescent yellow of a hundred watt bulb. Fortunately the gold blond hair color tones down the brilliance.

The next morning, I massage mousse through my freshly washed hair. Then I blow-dry it upwards, trying to create the illusion of fullness. It works fairly well and by the time I add gel to make spikes, put on the dangling earrings and apply makeup, I almost look like a rock star. Almost.

TWENTY-ONE

I'm back in Moscow at the Aerostar Hotel, wearing nothing but a sheer leopard print negligee, dangling gold earrings and high-heeled shoes. My blonde stubble has been spiked with gel. Having arrived last night at midnight and still suffering from jetlag, I am jolted from a deep sleep by the ringing telephone. It is Vladimir, welcoming me back to Moscow and calling from his cell phone on the way to my hotel.

Sipping black coffee from a tiny cup, I eagerly await his arrival. After six months, I can barely remember what he looks like. I do, however, remember what he feels like, and tremble at the thought of his hands on my body.

The phone rings again.

'Hello?'

'Hello. I'm in the lobby.'

'Can you come up? Room 322. I'm not ready.'

'Why aren't you ready?'

'I'm naked.'

'I'll be right up.'

He hangs up without another word.

Not wanting to appear a liar, I discard the negligee, but leave on my shoes and unlock the door. Then I dart into the bathroom to glance at my face and hair. When he opens the door and steps inside, I slither out of the bathroom like a mermaid appearing from the water. For a moment we stare motionless. I can tell that although he didn't believe me when I said I was naked, he's unable to hide the excitement in his eyes. His look of surprise becomes a smile, showing all his perfect teeth.

Approaching like a deer at a saltlick, I put my hands on his shoulders and brush my lips against his. Grabbing my butt with both hands, he pulls me close and drills his tongue into my mouth. With our lips locked, he presses his crotch against mine, letting me feel his arousal. Releasing my lips, he removes his blazer and sets it over a chair. I reach for the knot of his tie and loosen it. Then I unbutton his shirt and kiss his chest.

He moves his hands to my shoulders and pushes me down to a kneeling position. We still haven't spoken a word as I unbuckle his pants, pull them down to his knees, and suck the tip of his penis.

We make love on the bed with Vladimir on top, my legs wrapped around his waist. His body moves like a cowboy riding a wild stallion, fast and hard, almost violent. His torso tenses like a rope being pulled taut as he climaxes, before collapsing on top of me, our sweaty bodies sticking together.

After resting for several minutes, his breaths gradually slowing like a sprinter's after a race, he pushes his head up with his hands and looks at me. 'What did you do to your hair?' he asks.

'I missed you too,' I reply. 'Don't you like it?'

'Short hair isn't in style,' he says.

'So I've heard. But it didn't turn you off.'

'I wasn't looking at your hair,' he says. Then he says, 'I need a shower.'

We get into the shower together. Using the gel, I lather his entire body, making him hard again. As he picks me up I straddle him, and we make love under the rushing water.

'That was the last time,' Vladimir says, as he adjusts his tie.

'What are you talking about?' I ask.

'No more sex with my business associates.'

'Why the hell not?'

He stops dressing and looks at me. 'I'm a married man, Katey.'

'Did you find religion or something?' I ask, stunned.

'One of my subordinates knows I'm sleeping with you.'

'I didn't tell anyone,' I say.

'Well, I certainly didn't,' Vladimir says.

Suddenly I remember. Evgenii. In my hotel room on Christmas. There's no point in denying it. 'I'm sorry. The words just slipped out. We were drinking and...'

'I figured that. Why were you drinking with Evgenii?'

'Because you went home to your family. And it was Christmas. And I was lonely. Hell, I don't even like the guy. Can't you fire him?'

'He's my technical expert. I have no reason to fire him.'

'It won't happen again. I promise.'

'You need to be careful who you drink with. A Russian only gets drunk with trusted friends. Do you know why?'

'Why?'

'Because everyone becomes your trusted friend when you're drunk. What will happen if you get drunk in Tula and tell somebody you paid Miasnikov three-thousand dollars? You could never do business in Russia again. Never. Remember that.'

I don't believe he is giving up our relationship, but only warning me to be more careful. If he intended to end our affair, he would have said so before sleeping with me. Wouldn't he have?

'Have you spoken to Miasnikov lately?' I ask.

'Yes. He called and was all excited about a seminar in Tula. What have you two planned?'

'I'm not really sure,' I say. 'I was…'

'Drunk,' Vladimir finishes.

After I try to explain to the best of my memory, he asks, 'What does Anis have to say about this?'

'I haven't told him yet. I was hoping you would.'

'No way, darling. It's your project. But I would suggest you talk to Sergey Kushkov about the planning. He is friends with Miasnikov and I'm sure he'll be willing to help. He's quite fond of you, you know. You can call him from the office. Now let's get going. You've already made me late.'

'Hello?'

'Sergey Davidovich? It's Katey.'

Although I haven't seen or spoken to him since our dinner date last October, he recognizes my name instantly. 'Katey! What a nice surprise.'

'I need your help to plan a seminar in Tula,' I say.

'I'd love to help.' I'm surprised that he agrees without asking for any details.

'Can you come to Vladimir's office?' I ask.

'I get off work at six, and can get there by six-thirty. Is that too late?'

I look up at Vladimir who is studying a report on his desk. 'Is six-thirty too late?' I ask.

'That's fine,' Vladimir says, without looking up. 'You can take us out to dinner.'

'Okay,' I say into the phone. 'We'll be waiting.'

By the time Sergey gets to the office, only Vladimir and I are still there. Sergey and I sit, facing Vladimir behind his desk. Reaching into a drawer, Vladimir pulls out a bottle of cognac, then goes to a glass cupboard to get three snifters.

'Apparently Katey got drunk with Miasnikov and promised to put on a seminar,' Vladimir says. 'We're lucky she didn't promise to send a free circuit breaker.' Then he looks at me. 'You didn't, did you, Katey?'

I simply shake my head. *God, I hope not!*

'I think it's a good idea,' Sergey says. 'You know how much Russians love to take business trips. They get expenses paid by their company and essentially enjoy a free vacation. Now what did you and Miasnikov have in mind, Katey?'

Since I don't remember what I discussed with Miasnikov, I tell them my own ideas. 'I'd like to bring our chief engineer and our general manager. The chief engineer can give technical presentations during the morning and afternoon. During the breaks, I'll meet as many people as possible to drum up some business. Miasnikov can help me identify the key people and tell them about our successful partnership.'

'We'll need to send printed invitations to all the energos in the surrounding area. I can also call a number of people and urge them to come,' Sergey says.

'We're only interested in people at the higher levels. If they don't have influence, they can't help us. We need at least the chief engineer, and if possible, even the general managers,' I say. 'People like Miasnikov.'

'Don't worry, Katey,' Sergey says. 'I know a few of those types as well.'

'So what's the next step?' I ask.

'I'll take the train to Tula to meet with Miasnikov,' Sergey says. 'Then we can arrange the details and figure out the costs.'

'The costs?' I ask. Up to this point I hadn't really considered the costs. Actually, I haven't thought about them at all.

'You have the cost of the dinner,' Vladimir says. 'Which should be quite an extravagance if you want people to come. Vodka, champagne, caviar, sturgeon, enough to last the entire evening. And don't think Miasnikov is working for free. You'll need to pay him too. And I'm sure there will be a few more pockets to line, if you don't want trouble.'

I realize that I will also have to pay Sergey, but don't say anything.

'So how much are we talking here?' I ask. I don't have the slightest idea how much such an event can cost, but am guessing blindly at $10,000.

'I can't give you the exact amount until I meet with Miasnikov,' Sergey says.

'Miasnikov will send invitations to the general managers of all the Energos within 1000 kilometers of Tula,' Sergey says after returning from his trip. 'They may come themselves or send their chief engineers, many of whom will also bring project engineers, so he expects around 200 people. Most will come the night before and stay in Tulenergo's dormitory, a simple hotel on the premises.'

'Will we be staying there too?' I ask.

'They have a section with nice rooms where you can stay,' Sergey says.

Although I'm anxious to find out the total cost, I let Sergey continue.

'We'll start with an aperitif at nine a.m., followed by the first presentations. At noon, we'll break for lunch and continue in the afternoon, including a tour of the substation to inspect the new circuit breakers. People might be feeling tired in the afternoon...'

Or drunk, I think, remembering the Tula engineers.

'...So we'll include a coffee break.'

'It doesn't sound expensive so far,' I say.

'I haven't gotten to the main event,' Sergey says.

Vladimir, who has been listening silently, says, 'Nobody will come to the presentation unless you offer them something, Katey. We talked about that yesterday.'

'The highlight of the seminar is the banquet,' Sergey says. 'They'll be plenty of good food and drink. It will cost at least a hundred dollars per person.'

'Will a restaurant cater it?' I ask, remembering the exorbitant prices in Moscow.

'No,' Sergey says. 'Tulenergo has its own kitchen staff. And there will be plenty of nice ladies to help out.'

'So that comes to $20,000 just for the banquet,' I say. 'Wow.' Although I'm sure the banquet won't cost as much as Sergey is saying, I accept the figure, knowing the money will actually be used for other purposes.

'Then we'll need another ten grand for the other meals, the hotel, and the slush fund,' Sergey says.

'That's a lot of money,' I say. I know the slush fund is a lot bigger than he is admitting. I'm guessing that the attendees will pay for their own rooms, the banquet will probably cost half what he has quoted, and the other meals will probably be cheap cafeteria food.

'Welcome to New Russia, Katey.' Vladimir says with a smirk, taking a sip of wine.

'Anis is just going to love this,' I say. 'He'll never agree.'

'You need to convince him,' says Vladimir. 'I know you can be persuasive.'

'The one I'll really need to convince is Jack,' I say. 'Thirty grand is a lot of money. And then I have to convince both Dave and Jack to come to Tula. And God help us if Anis wants to come. All I need is to have him critiquing my every move and counting my drinks.'

'It wouldn't hurt to have someone counting your drinks,' Vladimir says, 'but I agree, we don't need him in Tula.' Then he says, 'So what are the pros and cons? You can practice on me.'

'First, it's an excellent opportunity to reach many potential customers in a short time,' I say. 'Instead of multiple trips, which are also expensive, we'll gather everyone at one location.'

'Very impressive,' Vladimir says. 'What else?'

'Jack and Dave can meet many customers on one trip. It's good for public relations to show my support from the important guys. It gives me legitimacy. I'm sure that most Russian men don't take a woman too seriously.'

'Especially one who looks like you,' Vladimir says and Sergey chuckles.

'And what's wrong with the way I look?' I ask.

'You look beautiful,' Sergey says.

'It's just hard to imagine you with that tight little ass of yours assembling a circuit breaker,' Vladimir adds.

Although I should be offended, I can't stop a smile from escaping my lips. It's nice to have your ass complimented, no matter what the context. I say, 'I don't have to touch the things, just sell them.' Then I continue, 'The very first dead tank circuit breakers will be installed in Tula. The customers will be able to inspect the actual equipment.'

'Another good point,' Vladimir says. 'Keep going.'

'Miasnikov and I have become such pals I think he'll do anything to help me and may personally convince some customers to do business with us.' Although recalling the three-thousand dollars I paid to Miasnikov, I don't want to mention the money in front of Sergey.

'Well, you've convinced me,' Sergey says.

'What are the cons?' Vladimir asks.

'There's only one,' I say. 'Thirty-thousand dollars.'

'That's a big con,' Vladimir says.

The next afternoon, I compose an e-mail to Anis, Jack and Dave, explaining our plans for the seminar. I approach the subject of money cautiously, carefully laying out all the reasons for holding the event. Emphasizing the number of trips we can avoid by one large gathering, I try to make my proposal sound as if we'll be saving money. Finally I warn against offending Miasnikov because he has expressed interest in future business with us.

Knowing that Anis will call as soon as he reads my email in the morning, I wait nervously in Vladimir's office. The phone rings promptly at five p.m.

'Hello, Anis,' Vladimir says, picking up the phone and clicking on the loud speaker.

'How did you know it was me?' he asks.

'Katey told me.'

'Is she there?' he asks.

'Hi Anis,' I say.

'So what is this seminar you want to have? I have Jack and Dave both here and we're all curious.'

'Just as I explained,' I say, wondering if he is going to make me repeat it.

'We're curious why it's so expensive.'

'I can't easily explain that over the telephone,' I say, hoping he'll understand.

'Oh,' he says. Then after a pause, he repeats, 'Oh.'

'And where do we transfer the money?' I recognize Jack's British accent.

'We don't have banks like that,' Vladimir says, enjoying himself. 'You'll have to bring cash.'

'How do we do that? Do we each stick ten grand in our socks?' I can tell by Jack's tone that he is amused by the prospect. Knowing our phones could be tapped, I'm worried about the conversation continuing.

'That's as good a place as any,' Vladimir says.

'Okay, Katey,' Jack says. 'It's a lot of money, but if you think it's a good investment, we'll trust you. Still, I want to ask one more time. What's your gut feeling? Are you absolutely sure about this?'

I look at Vladimir, trying to read an answer in his face. 'It's your call,' he says.

I take a deep breath. 'As sure as I can be,' I say.

During a long pause, I assume they have a hand over the receiver and are trying to reach a decision.

'Katey,' Anis says finally, 'we've decided to go with it. We'll discuss the details when you get home.'

Hanging up, I say to Vladimir, 'What if someone was tapping our phone and knows we'll be traveling to Russia with thirty-thousand dollars in our socks?'

'Anyone who is smart enough to tap international phone lines won't want to dig petty cash out of your socks. But I would suggest a better hiding place.'

'I don't wear bras,' I say.

'That's the first place they'd look.'

'They wouldn't find much.'

'You said it, not me.'

'Do you want me to stuff the money up my cunt?'

'Don't be crude, Katey.'

TWENTY-TWO

I'm waiting in the line at customs with two stacks of one hundred dollar bills in plastic baggies hidden in the soles of my shoes. Dave and I flew British Air to London where we met Jack, who had so many frequent flyer miles that he earned a free flight on the Condor. During our flight together from London to Moscow, he boasted about the Condor lounge, the thirty-year-old single malt scotch, the filet mignon, and the caviar. Even with jetlag, he was in such a cheery mood I thought perhaps the stewardess had left the entire bottle of scotch on his tray.

We sail through customs without being searched. It surprised me when Jack agreed to smuggle his share of the money into Russia. Lord knows what would have happened if we'd been caught. But the Russian government has become much more tolerant of foreigners in the past several years, particularly those bringing money into the country. We probably could have declared it on our custom's forms without any difficulties, but didn't want to take that chance. While ten years ago we might have been risking a one-way ticket to Siberia, now I suspect we might have only had to pay a fine and get our wrists slapped. And that just for show. It doesn't matter how or what for – Russia wants money to come into their country. But a lack of certainty still makes it difficult to breathe until the young man in uniform stamps my passport and visa, allowing me to pass through.

Vladimir is waiting for us when we leave the baggage claim. Although he has never met me at the airport, I'm not surprised that he is there for Jack. After his flight on the Condor, Jack can't be expected to hail a taxi like a simple tourist.

Since my last trip to Moscow, Vladimir's office has been moved to the southwest side of the city, occupying an entire floor of a modern ten-story building. Since the Aerostar Hotel is too far away from the new office, he brings us to a cozy German joint-venture called the Art Hotel.

The Art Hotel is a quaint little establishment with twelve rooms hidden among high-rise apartment buildings and costing much less than the Aerostar. Original oil paintings, true to the name 'Art Hotel', decorate the walls. There is a small restaurant and bar behind the lobby.

'Let's meet in the bar,' Jack says, as we depart to our individual rooms.

'I need to go back to the office for an hour,' says Vladimir. 'Then I'll return for dinner.'

'We'll be drunk by then,' Jack says.

Suppressing a laugh, I notice for the first time how attractive Jack is.

'Should we eat here?' Dave asks.

'They've got a decent menu,' Vladimir says, 'German food.'

'I need to shave and take a shower,' Dave says.

'I need a beer,' Jack says.

Although I feel tired and as grubby as a pig in a mud puddle, I can't resist the opportunity to drink a beer alone with our general manager.

'Sounds like a good idea,' I say, following him to the bar.

Without asking me, Jack orders two beers and two shots of Johnny Walker.

'I bet you're glad Anis didn't come,' he says.

Surprised by his remark, I hesitate before answering. 'Russia's not really the best place for a vegetarian,' I say. 'I mean you *can* chase vodka with bananas, but—'

'You heard about that too, huh?' Jack picks up his whiskey and I grab mine. 'To Anis,' he says. After downing the glass in one gulp, Jack looks thoughtful. 'Anis has his uses,' he says.

'I suspect he's very good with the Arabs,' I say, setting down my empty glass and picking up my beer. I can't believe I'm sitting here with the general manager discussing my boss in such a degrading manner.

'Well, who the hell else would want to go to Saudi Arabia?' Jack says. After a pause, he says, 'But the Arabs send us a lot of business.'

'I don't think Anis likes coming to Russia,' I say. I'm being careful not to say anything directly critical. Let Jack do it. I'll just listen.

'Too cold for him,' Jack says. 'I'm hungry. Where the fuck is Dave?'

As if on cue, Dave comes out of the stairwell. His freshly washed hair is still damp.

'Let's move to a table,' Jack says.

A waiter gives us a menu in German and Russian, but not in English. Then I discover that Jack can read a few words of German.

'Schnitzel,' he says. 'I know what that is. Let's get that.'

'What is schnitzel,' Dave asks.

'It's a breaded pork filet,' Jack explains.

'It sounds fattening,' Dave says.

'I'm sure they'll bring you carrot sticks if you prefer,' Jack says.

I can tell by Dave's expression that he's annoyed. He

starts to open his mouth and then closes it again. Jack is, after all, Dave's boss. 'Okay, let's get schnitzel,' Dave relents.

Jack orders three beers while we're waiting. After about twenty minutes, three plates arrive with thickly breaded pork loin and French fries. There are no salads.

'I can see my cholesterol climbing,' Dave says.

'Forget your damned cholesterol,' Jack says. 'You're in Russia, for God's sake. Be lucky you're not eating black bread and cabbage.'

'It would certainly be healthier,' Dave retorts.

Vladimir shows up during our meal. He takes the empty seat next to Dave, who is across from Jack and me, and orders a beer.

'I'm busy tomorrow morning,' Vladimir says. 'Katey can take you on a tour of Moscow. She knows all the attractions.'

'When do we leave for Tula?' Jack asks.

'I'll pick you up here at the hotel at four o'clock,' Vladimir says.

'Ein Bier,' Jack says to the waiter as he clears the empty plates.

Since neither Jack nor Dave has ever been to Moscow, the first place I take them is Red Square. We ride the metro to Revolution Square and get out on Tverskaya Street, formerly known as Gorky Street. We enter Red Square from the Northwest, passing the State Historical Museum, a red brick building covered in ornate turrets, pinnacles and decorative saw-tooth cornices.

'So they still call it Red Square?' Jack asks.

'It was called Red Square long before the Communist Era,' I explain. 'The Russian word for red, which is *krasnyi*, also means beautiful.'

As we walk across the vast cobbled expanse of the square, I point out the various attractions. The ornate facade of GUM, Moscow's 'State Department Store', takes up almost the entire eastern side of Red Square. The building combines elements of Russian medieval architecture with an elegant steel framework and glass roof. It looks more like a palace than a shopping mall.

'Would you like to see the inside of GUM,' I ask, using the correct Russian pronunciation of *GOOM*. 'It's Moscow's most famous department store.' I'm curious to see how the interior has changed since the fall of Communism. In the late eighties, when I was a student, the shops were littered with low-quality Soviet-made merchandise, like a massive garage sale. Roaming through the stores at that time, I could only describe it as a whole lot of nothing.

As we enter the building, I can tell that Jack and Dave are impressed by the elegantly decorated interior, comprised of three parallel arcades, centered around a fountain and roofed by a glass ceiling. The shabby shops of the Communist era have been replaced by designer boutiques similar to those seen in European airports: Christian Dior, Hugo Boss, Hermes, Versace, and Armani. There are also numerous electronics shops featuring video cameras, televisions, laptop computers, and digital cameras. Checking the price of a laptop computer and mentally converting it into dollars, I understand why my customers prefer to do their shopping in Washington.

'It didn't take long for them to become capitalists,' Jack says.

'Only the very rich can afford to shop here,' I say. 'After capitalism moved in, an elite group arose called the New Russians. They wear Rolexes, drive foreign cars, and build big houses in the suburbs.'

'Is Vladimir one of them?' Jack asks.

'He's working on it,' I say, remembering his pricey wardrobe.

After ten minutes, Jack has seen enough and we return

to the square.

We approach St. Basil's Cathedral. Built in the sixteenth century, it is one of Russia's most famous landmarks, a beautiful array of swirling colors and red brick towers, comprised of nine chapels, each topped with a unique onion dome.

'After the cathedral was built, Ivan the Terrible ordered that the architect be blinded to prevent him from ever building another cathedral so beautiful,' I say, remembering the blurb from a guided tour I took as a student.

'I should do that to my design engineers,' Jack says, smirking at Dave before snapping a picture of the cathedral.

'So where's Lenin's tomb?' Dave asks.

I point to a structure faced with red granite and black labradorite. The name 'Lenin' is inscribed over its bronze doors, which were originally flanked by two uniformed guards who changed every hour on the hour with an impressive ritual.

'He's still in there?' Jack asks. 'I thought they were going to bury him.'

'He's still there,' I say. 'And people still come to gawk at him.'

'Poor guy,' Jack says.

'I'm getting hungry,' Dave says.

'Let's go to Arbat,' I say. 'There are a lot of good restaurants there.'

The Arbat is Moscow's most famous pedestrian street, the favorite spot for the city's intellectual elite and also one of the city's most popular tourist attractions. The street is littered with artists selling original work, musicians with guitar cases full of foreign coins, and souvenir shops, restaurants, and cafes. There is even a 1950's American-style diner. As we walk the street, I hear people speaking English and other foreign languages which I don't recognize. Japanese tourists with video cameras scurry around like kids at the zoo.

We stop at an outdoor Italian café which accepts American Express. The Italian waiter speaks to us in broken English. I'm surprised to see calamari on the menu, and wonder where they shipped it from. I decide to take a chance and order it, while Dave selects pasta with cheese sauce, and Jack orders a steak.

'The Italians usually make a good steak,' Jack says.

'Don't forget you're in Moscow,' Dave warns. 'You don't know where the meat comes from.'

'When in Rome,' Jack says and orders a bottle of red wine for us to split three ways.

The calamari is exquisitely prepared, hand dipped with a thin batter. For thirty-two dollars, one definitely expects quality. Jack has no complaints about his steak, prepared medium rare and topped with onions. It costs even more than my meal. Fiddling with his pasta, Dave seems disappointed that he hadn't been more daring. The wine is also quite tasty, although Jack complains that it isn't dry enough. When I praise it, he empties the remainder of the bottle into my glass and orders a beer.

After the meal, we stroll the length of Arbat until reaching a metro station. We need to get back to the hotel where Vladimir is meeting us to drive to Tula. We checked out of two of the three rooms in the morning, only keeping Jack's to store our luggage and use the bathroom. When we get back to the hotel, Jack immediately heads for the bar and I join him while Dave returns to the room for some reason unknown to us.

Jack and I are drinking our second beer when Vladimir arrives at 4:15 and Dave hasn't returned from the room.

'Why don't you go get Dave,' Jack says to me. 'He's been gone a long time.'

When I get to the room, I knock before entering. Dave is seated at a desk, studying the overheads for tomorrow's presentation. Before coming to Moscow, I translated them all into Russian, emailing copies to Vladimir for corrections.

'I hope I remember what they are in English,' he says, half joking. He knows the information so well he could speak for hours without any overheads at all.

'That shouldn't be a problem,' I say. 'We have a set in English as well. I even arranged the slides for you in the same order.'

'Are you sure you'll be able to translate everything I say?'

I'm quite sure I won't be able to. Dave's level of speaking can often only be understood by fellow physicists. 'I can certainly try,' I say. 'But Vladimir will also be there to help me. I asked him to do the whole thing, but he didn't want to.'

'Why not?'

'He says it's my job.' Even though Dave thinks the customers will be deeply interested in the technical details of his presentation, Vladimir knows they will mainly be watching my legs dance around the stage. 'Don't worry, Dave,' I say. 'I can handle it.'

Vladimir's Volva whisks us to Tula as if we are being chased. Jack sits in the front beside Vladimir, Dave and me in the back. As we race along the highway, I notice that Dave has his eyes closed, as if in prayer, and is gripping his seat with both hands. He looks like someone on an airplane expecting it to crash, which surprises me, since he drives a sports car and should be accustomed to high speeds. Perhaps he only feels comfortable behind the wheel.

Since the road is straight and clear, and by Russian standards a good one, we reach Tula quickly. Since Vladimir called him from the road on his cell phone, Miasnikov is waiting and takes us to the hotel, where he presents our rooms, simply furnished with single beds, sinks, and a communal bathroom in the hallway. After showing us a modest dining room where breakfast will be served, he leads us to a small lounge where a low table between two couches is set with a variety of delicacies.

A pygmy-like woman with puffy pink cheeks, fluorescent- blue eye shadow, and lipstick the color of fresh blood, is putting the finishing touches on the table. Her blonde hair is piled high like a turban and gaudy silver earrings dangle almost to her shoulders. Butterball hips are stuffed into a gray skirt so tightly fitted the seams look ready to explode. A loose fitting blouse with two open buttons shows the ample cleavage of heavy breasts reminding me of a milk cow. Her plump feet swell at the ankles, visibly uncomfortable in high-heel shoes. The pretty Russian face hidden under the layers of make-up reminds me of a matryoshka doll.

A second woman is tall and slender, dressed in a spiffy blue pants suit with low-heeled shoes. Miasnikov introduces her as Nadezhda Simonovna, one of the project engineers for our circuit breakers. With short dark hair and a face void of makeup, she is practically the first woman I've met in Russia, me included, who doesn't look like she is going out on a hot date.

We are just getting seated when Vanya storms in, a bottle of Tula vodka in each hand. I'm starting to think it is impossible to spend a day in Russia without getting drunk and am wondering how Dave is going to give his presentation and how I am going to translate it when we both have hangovers.

Before I have time to contemplate the idea of just drinking water, a shot glass appears in my hand, accompanied by a toast.

'A warm welcome to our American partners,' Miasnikov says. I translate the toast for Jack and Dave.

After downing the vodka, which Vladimir only sips, we sample the treats on the table. There are platters of tiny open-faced sandwiches topped with salami, cheese, and smoked fish. There are little pancakes referred to as *blini*, boiled new potatoes tossed in dill, black and red caviar in chilled silver dishes, marinated mushrooms, olives, pickled beets, sliced tomatoes and cucumbers, little sausages and meat-filled pastries called *piroshki*. There is a traditional Russian salad made with mayonnaise, herring, beets, potatoes, hard-boiled eggs, peas, chopped pickles and onions. And also plenty of butter and fresh dark Russian bread.

As Vanya refills our glasses, Sergey arrives, dressed as usual in a mismatched Russian-made suit. As Sergey reaches around the table, shaking hands, I introduce him to Jack and Dave, explaining that he is a member of the inspection team.

'He's also the one we give the money to,' I say to Jack, knowing nobody will understand my English. 'He'll distribute it where it needs to go.'

'I was starting to think they'd forgotten about the money,' Jack says. 'I'm getting used to having it in my shoes.'

'Maybe we should take care of it now before we drink too much vodka,' I say.

'Are you planning to drink too much vodka?' Jack asks.

'I never plan to,' I say. 'But we're in Russia—take a look at how many bottles are on the table and at how many of us there are—and I'd rather not be holding ten thousand dollars any longer than necessary.'

'Then it's time to empty your shoes,' Jack says to Dave, who is sitting on the other side of the table.

'Let's go back to one of the rooms,' I say, standing up. 'We'll return in a minute,' I say to Miasnikov.

'First a toast,' he says, raising his glass.

Without sitting back down, I pick up my glass and hold it in the air. Jack and Dave follow my lead. 'To Katey, our beautiful partner who made this all possible.'

When I translate the toast, Jack chuckles. 'You sure you didn't make that up?' he asks.

When we get to Jack's room, he says, 'I can't believe you're going to hand this guy thirty thousand dollars.'

'Sergey made all the arrangements,' I explain. 'He knows what to do with the money.'

'Why can't Vladimir handle it?' Dave asks.

I didn't want to tell them about the nagging feeling I have that Vladimir doesn't approve of the whole affair. Perhaps he thinks we are wasting our money. Perhaps it is just going to be an expensive vodka orgy which won't accomplish anything at all. Instead I say, 'He thought Sergey would be a better choice. He and Miasnikov are old friends.'

They hand me stacks of hundreds that I put into a money bag. I've never seen so much money in my life and my heart races as if I am committing a crime. And maybe I am. I don't know how the money is going to be used.

We return to the party and I hand the pouch to Sergey, who nods silently. We are welcomed back to the table with fresh shots of vodka. This time I stand up to make the toast.

'To Dmitri Sergeevich,' I say, smiling at Miasnikov. 'Our first and favorite customer.'

'Katey, come sit by me,' Miasnikov says, patting the empty space on the couch beside him. Stumbling over knees, I go around the table to the empty spot directly across from Vladimir, who is trying not to look bored.

I feel funny staring into Vladimir's eyes as Miasnikov clutches my knee. When he caresses the inside of my thigh, I look away from Vladimir and spear a marinated mushroom with my fork. I am glad when another round of vodka is poured.

'To our distinguished American guests,' Miasnikov says, turning towards Jack and Dave. 'We are so happy to have you here in Tula.'

When I translate the toast, Jack responds, 'Thank you for inviting us. We are very happy to visit the city which is getting our first order of circuit breakers to Russia.'

When the matryoshka doll reappears to clear empty

dishes from the table, Miasnikov says, 'Verenka, why don't you join us?' He gestures toward the empty spot which I left between Jack and Dave. Unable to hide her pleasure, she squeezes in between the two men.

'Vera is my new secretary,' Miasnikov says. 'She takes care of everything for me.'

I wonder when he replaced the old secretary. I also wonder what *everything* includes, although with Miasnikov's hand inching up my thigh, I have no right to judge her or anyone else.

'What is the schedule for tomorrow,' Dave suddenly asks me, deliberately ignoring Vera, who is already helping herself to the caviar..

I translate the question for Miasnikov.

'The seminar starts at nine o'clock with an aperitif,' he says.

As I translate, Dave rolls his eyes at the mention of aperitif, well aware that it will include strong alcoholic beverages.

'At ten o'clock, we'll start the presentation,' Miasnikov says.

'Ask him if they have an overhead projector,' Dave says. 'It's very important.'

'Of course they do,' Vladimir answers before I can translate. 'Don't offend them. We're not in Africa, you know.'

Miasnikov continues. 'Lunch is at noon. After lunch, we'll walk out to look at the new installation and then return to finish the presentation.'

'When can I meet with customers?' I ask.

'There will be plenty of time in the afternoon before the banquet. The banquet starts at seven.'

I translate the bit about the banquet for Dave and Jack.

'Ah hah, the real reason they're all coming,' Jack says. 'I hope our money will be well spent.'

Vanya is pouring another round of vodka. The first

bottle is empty and he has opened the second one. I notice that Vladimir's glass is still full from the last round.

Miasnikov picks up a bottle of red wine from the table. 'Would you like to try some Georgian wine, Katey?'

Although mixing drinks is unwise, I've already consumed enough vodka to prevent rational thinking. Besides, I remember drinking Georgian wine in Tbilisi when I was a student, and it was quite tasty, fruity and sweet.

'I love Georgian wine,' I say.

After struggling with a poorly designed cork screw, Miasnikov pours me a glass. 'Vera?' he asks, holding up the bottle to his secretary.

She nods and smiles. I notice her knee pressed against Dave's leg. He doesn't have enough room to move it away.

After drinking the wine, the evening flies past me in a haze, conversations getting louder, jokes being told, and even a few Russian folk songs being sung in booming voices. At some point, I see Vladimir stand up and head out the door. Excusing myself from Miasnikov, who has his arm around my shoulder, I follow Vladimir into the hallway.

'I'm going back to Moscow,' he says. 'I have an important meeting tomorrow.'

'What?' I say in a loud voice. 'You're not staying? What about the presentation?'

'You can do it,' he says.

'I can't translate all that technical shit. I need you there to help me when I get stuck.'

'Do the best you can and nobody will know the difference. Certainly not Dave. I'll be back in time for the banquet.'

'Are you leaving because of Miasnikov? Are you jealous?'

'Don't flatter yourself, Katey.'

'Do you think I like him mauling me? I'd much rather

have you mauling me.' Wanting to prove to him that I am sober, I walk in a straight line—well, almost a straight line—and touch my finger to my nose with my eyes closed (Actually, I poke my cheek).

But without noticing, he is out the door, leaving me staring after him like an abandoned puppy. There is nothing to do but return to the party where I sit down next to Miasnikov, who places another glass of wine in my hand.

TWENTY-THREE

Soaked with sweat, I awake naked in darkness under a heavy down comforter. Even in summer, the Russians generally equip the beds as if you were in the middle of a Siberian winter without central heating. The comforter is nestled inside the double-layered bed sheet like a pillow in a pillow case with no other sheets or lighter weight blankets to use instead.

Tossing the comforter to the floor, I get up and go to the sink. Although it is always risky to drink tap water in Russia, I fill a plastic cup and drink it down in one prolonged gulp, glad that I can't see the water's color in the moonlight. My thirst is so great that I am not bothered by the rusty flavor. I refill and empty the cup twice before quenching my thirst.

Since there is no toilet in the room, and I am too tired to get dressed and go into the hall, I sit on the sink and pee, hoping it won't collapse under my weight. Then I go back to the bed, lie uncovered on my back, and close my eyes. Only then do I notice the first traces of a headache and nausea, worsened by the large quantity of impure water.

After about ten minutes I start to feel cold. Not wanting to use the comforter again, but needing some warmth, I remove the thin cotton cover from the down blanket and toss it over me, letting the blanket fall to the floor.

I awake to the sound of knocking and somebody calling my name.

'Katey? Are you awake? It's Sergey.' His words stab my forehead like a knife.

'Is it late?' I ask, holding onto my head in the spinning room.

'Everyone is at breakfast,' he says. 'Are you okay?'

'I have a head as big as Texas,' I say through the door.

'Do you want me to bring you something?'

In my current state, I am willing to accept any help which may be offered. 'That would be great,' I say, expecting aspirin.

'I'll be right back. Try to get yourself ready.'

After slipping on jeans and a T-shirt, I take a towel and venture into the hall towards a unisex shower which appears empty. Even though I can't lock the door, I go to the last shower stall and quickly undress. Expecting cold water, I am surprised when the spray almost scalds me. After washing my hair and body, I turn off the water and listen to make sure I am still alone. Then I step out of the shower and pull on my clothes, head pounding and stomach heaving.

When I get back to my room, Sergey is waiting at the door with a bottle of dark colored liquor and a glass.

'What is that?' I ask. I should have known he wouldn't bring aspirin.

'It's a drink made from a wide variety of herbs,' he says. 'It will soothe your stomach and make you feel better. Just don't drink too much.'

'Do you want some too?' I ask.

'Well, maybe just one.'

We drink two as he tells me how the evening ended. I'm

glad to know that I didn't do anything stupid. According to Sergey, I actually left the party early and returned quietly to my room. I can only hope he is telling the truth because I don't remember a thing after Vladimir left.

After he leaves, I drink another shot and then swallow two ibuprofen tablets with water. I put on a khaki-colored suit with an obscenely short pleated skirt and a double-breasted jacket over a thin silk shell. Feeling unsteady on my high heels, I head down the hall to Jack's room to see if he is still there. Just as I'm arriving, he opens the door, neatly dressed in cotton slacks and a tweed jacket.

'Did you eat breakfast?' I ask.

'Good morning to you too, Katey. Yes, I ate breakfast and yes, I slept quite nicely, thank you, except for that dreadfully heavy blanket.'

'I don't even know what time we went to bed,' I say. 'Did you happen to notice?'

'Right after you danced naked on the table,' Jack says.

For a split second I wonder if he is serious, but then I see him wink. 'I guess I shouldn't have done that,' I say.

'Is that how you get your contracts?' Jack asks.

'It seems to work,' I say. 'Isn't Dave up?'

'He was coming to the shower just as I was leaving.'

'Then I guess we all missed each other.'

'It wouldn't matter anyway. We already saw you dancing naked last night.'

Although it should feel strange having this conversation with the general manager of our company, when you're in a strange town in the heart of Russia, formalities fade away. I even wonder if I should try to seduce him. He looks exactly like Richard Burton did in the late 70's and seems to share the legendary actor's passion for the bottle. I wonder if he also exhibits the same passion for women. *Why are you even thinking about that? Can't you even look at an attractive man without seeing a challenge?*

Before long, Dave appears in the hallway.

'We better hurry,' Jack says. 'We wouldn't want to miss the aperitif.'

'I thought an aperitif is served before a meal,' Dave says.

'I guess they think they need one before your presentation,' Jack says. 'And knowing the way your presentations are, they're probably right.'

'What's that supposed to mean?' Dave asks.

'Oh, nothing,' Jack says. 'Only that you need a Ph.D. in physics to understand them.'

'Or to translate them,' I add.

'Good luck,' Jack says to me.

Dave looks at Jack as if trying to decide if he has just been complimented or insulted, and is about to say something when Miasnikov charges in from the end of the hallway.

'Good morning, good morning!' he cries in English with such a heavy Russian accent that I suspect someone just taught him the two words for the sole purpose of impressing us.

'Good morning,' we reply, almost in unison.

'How did you sleep?' he asks, switching to Russian.

'Like babies,' I lie. 'The beds were very comfortable.'

'Follow me to the aperitif,' he says. 'Everyone is waiting for the guests of honor.'

We follow him out the door and across a courtyard to the main building of Tulenergo. He leads us into a room with a wooden floor and ceiling, centered with a large oblong table covered with many of the same delicacies we had the night before. There are close to a hundred people crowded into the room, sampling tiny open-faced sandwiches with various toppings and hard boiled eggs smeared with black and red caviar. And of course vodka. There are enough bottles on the table to create a room of staggering drunks.

Miasnikov picks up a little bell from the end of the table and rings it like a school teacher. The conversation dies out like someone extinguishing a candle, and a hundred pairs of eyes turn towards us.

'I'd like to introduce and drink a toast to our guests who have made this seminar possible,' Miasnikov says. 'Fill your glasses, everyone.'

Arms reach out to the table, picking up bottles and filling shot glasses. Miasnikov hands each of us a glass and fills it with vodka.

'Please meet Mister Jack Penhaligon and Mister Dave Richardson,' Miasnikov says in Russian, pronouncing the names with such a heavy accent that they are barely recognizable. I'm surprised he even remembers 'Penhaligon', an unusual Cornish name, and wonder if he stayed up late practicing it.

'The president and chief engineer of Ampere Power Company,' he continues. Then he drapes his arm over my shoulder, making me wonder how much of the aperitif he has already indulged in. 'And of course, Katey O'Hara, who has such beautiful eyes that I couldn't resist buying equipment from her. I'm sure you will all feel the same way.'

Now I'm sure he's been imbibing. I can't resist translating the entire speech for Jack and Dave, who both laugh.

'Now let us drink to our new friends and partners,' Miasnikov says. A hundred glasses meet a hundred sets of lips in unison. Then hands reach out to the table for some morsel to chase down the vodka, and a buzz of conversation once again fills the room.

Not wanting to be totally trashed during Dave's presentation, I am relieved to see a samovar and a jar of instant coffee at the other end of the table. Although I can barely tolerate the taste of instant coffee, I'm highly addicted to caffeine, and have gotten used to choking it down in any form since traveling in Russia. After mixing the coffee so strongly it resembles a quadruple espresso, I take little repulsive sips as if drinking tar.

As I'm stuffing a caviar egg into my mouth, a friendly looking man in his early sixties with a face like an aging fox appears at my side.

'Zamirov', he says. 'Igor Antonovich.'

Shaking his hand, I say, 'O'Hara. But just call me Katey.'

'I'm from Belgorod, Katey,' he says. 'South of here. Have you ever heard of it?'

'I've heard of it,' I say, 'but I've never been there.' I am wondering who this guy is and politely wait for him to tell me.

'What in heaven's name are you drinking?' he asks instead, dangling an empty shot glass between his fingers and staring into my cup.

'Black coffee,' I say. 'I need to be awake to translate the presentation.'

'I never touch the stuff,' he says, stepping back from the table and pulling a pack of cigarettes from his pocket. 'Russians prefer tea.' After a pause, he adds 'Or vodka.' As if to prove his point, he reaches for a bottle on the table.

'May I drink a toast to you?' he asks, pouring vodka. 'Do you have a glass?'

'I set it down somewhere,' I say. 'I wasn't planning to drink anymore.'

'Oh,' he says, visibly disappointed.

'But I'll be glad to drink a toast with you,' I say quickly, realizing the importance of not offending my customers at any cost, even if it means falling on my ass during Dave's presentation. But I hope this guy is important.

Before I finish my sentence, he has a fresh shot glass and is filling it with vodka.

'To future business with the beautiful Katey,' he says.

'Thank you,' I say. 'You flatter me.'

We clink our glasses together and drink the vodka down quickly, its taste much more pleasant than my muddy coffee.

At that moment, someone grabs Zamirov's arm and pulls him away. 'Igor Antonovich, do you have a minute?'

Not trying to hide his disappointment at being yanked away from me, Zamirov nods and turns towards the man. I am disappointed myself, but for a different reason. I was hoping to find out more about him and to discuss business. For all I know, he could be another Miasnikov

Left alone, I scan the crowd and am pleased to spot Sergey at the other side of the table. Pushing through the crowd, he arrives at my side.

'Who was I just talking to?' I ask him. 'Do you know him?'

'That's the chief engineer of Belgorodenergo,' he says. 'Be nice to him. They have a lot of money.'

Now I am definitely glad I drank that vodka. Before I can ask more questions, I see Dave and Jack standing awkwardly in a corner, drinking coffee and talking among themselves. 'I better check with my bosses,' I say. 'They can't talk to anyone without my help.'

'It's almost time for the presentation,' Sergey says. 'The auditorium is in the next room if you want to set up.'

'Yes, I'm sure Dave will want to,' I say, remembering how nervous he was at the hotel. 'We'll talk later.'

'I could really get used to these aperitifs.' Jack says. 'Do you have them often in Russia?'

'Just every day,' I say, and Jack raises a single eyebrow. I ask Dave, 'Should we go set up? I need to run back to my room and get the overheads.'

Before leaving, I bring them to the auditorium. Then I hurry back to my room where I promptly go into the bathroom and toss my cookies, the acidy black coffee burning my throat as it races up like an erupting volcano. Before returning to the auditorium, overheads in hand, I rinse my face with icy water, brush my teeth, reapply my make-up, and take a long pee.

I spot Vanya setting up an outdated overhead projector

on the stage. Dave is inspecting the screen, shuffling his feet nervously—like a doctoral student preparing to defend his dissertation—while Jack relaxes in the first row of seats. When Vanya turns on the projector, I position an overhead on the glass and am relieved to see it displayed sharply on the screen. At least that's one problem we won't have.

Gradually the guests parade into the room, some still chewing a last bite of food, others looking around for an ashtray to extinguish their cigarettes. Even though the auditorium could accommodate at least 500 people, the men crowd together in the middle section, sitting side by side as if in an airplane, quite a contrast to Americans who typically stagger among the seats, feet up on the chairs in front of them. Even though Sergey promised me a crowd of 200, I estimate the group at half that and wonder where the others are. Maybe they are just late.

Entering last, Miasnikov approaches the stage. As the conversation dies, he begins to speak.

'I want to welcome you to the informational portion of our seminar. I'm sure you are eager to learn about these new products. This afternoon, we will be able to see the actual circuit breakers installed in Tula, the first western dead tank circuit breakers in all of Russia.'

I don't know if this statement is true. There are at least six other global manufacturers of dead tank circuit breakers who might very well have beaten us to this goal, but I don't object to his assertion.

'Now I'll give the floor to Mr. Richardson and Miss O'hara,' he says, pronouncing the titles as 'Meester' and 'Meess'.

Hearing his name amidst the Russian words, Dave springs to action like a mechanical toy which has just been wound, and places the first slide on the projector. It says 'Ampere Power Company' in Cyrillic letters with an aerial photograph of our plant.

'Ampere Power Company is located in a small town in

Pennsylvania,' he begins. 'We have 150 employees and produce around 250 circuit breakers annually, ranging from 38 to 550 kilovolts, which we ship worldwide.' He doesn't bother to add that only 10% of our production goes to international markets.

I translate the beginning easily, smiling at the audience, who is listening as if we are planning to give a post-seminar test and award a free circuit breaker to the highest scorer.

'All of our circuit breakers have a dead tank design.' Dave says.

I also have no trouble translating 'dead tank,' which simply means the tanks are grounded.

Switching slides to a large outdoor photo of an installed circuit breaker, Dave says, 'Our 121 kilovolt dead tank circuit breaker consists of three cast-aluminum tanks, each housing an interrupter unit. The three tanks are mounted on a single support frame.'

I translate these first statements easily, fairly certain I haven't made any mistakes.

Switching slides again to a photo of an open control cabinet, Dave says, 'Each circuit breaker contains a control cabinet with a hydraulic spring-operating mechanism.'

I manage that as well.

'When actuated, the spring energy is released, opening the contacts of the interrupter and breaking the circuit,' Dave says, using his hands to demonstrate the action of the mechanism—He makes two fists, places them together and then pulls them apart quickly, releasing his fingers like two birds taking wing.

Since the Russians probably already know how the mechanism works, I don't translate this last comment. Dave stares at me, expecting me to say something.

I say in Russian, 'He was just explaining how the mechanism operates. I assumed you already know that so I didn't translate it.'

When the room ripples with laughter, Dave glares at me,

his eyes demanding an explanation. 'They're laughing because they already knew that,' I say. 'Or maybe they're just happy.'

As if to punish me, Dave makes the next statement more technical. 'The breakers may also be designed with independent pole operating capability.'

Not remembering the Russian term for *independent pole operating capability* (or maybe I never knew it at all), which allows each phase of the circuit to be broken separately, I simply say, 'The mechanism is very compact and lightweight.'

Since the Russians' main concern is low prices, I am not pleased that Dave has mentioned a costly option neither needed nor desired. But Dave is first and foremost a scientist who would consider it a sin to withhold technical information. As a less-than-perfect translator interested only in making a sale, I can easily leave things out, especially since Dave will never know the difference.

Waving his hands around as if conducting an orchestra, Dave continues, 'There is a separate aluminum tank per phase, each filled with SF6 gas and containing its own interrupter. Because of its high density'—suddenly Dave's glasses fly from his face into the audience and he reaches out blindly as if trying to catch them.

I hear Jack's high-pitched chuckle and turn away from Dave to hide my smile—not that he'd see it anyway without his glasses.

One of the men is holding up the glasses as if he's just caught a World Series baseball. He passes the glasses to the front row where another man hands them to me. After inspecting the glasses thoroughly for damage, Dave returns them to his face and continues:

'Because of its high density, SF6 gas has superior circuit breaking qualities.'

Not remembering the word for 'density', I simply say, 'The circuit breakers contain SF6 gas.' Since Russian is a wordier language, Dave is unable to judge my translation.

His next slide is a drawing of an SF6 gas molecule and a list of it properties. 'Sulfur hexafluoride's excellent physical properties and dielectric capabilities have made it the single choice for the electrical utility industry worldwide.' Dave says.

Since *dielectric capabilities* is written in Russian on the slide, I breeze through the translation, simply reading the Russian words.

An urgent need to pee distracts me from Dave's next statement. It always happens after drinking strong coffee or alcohol on an empty stomach. My bladder feels like someone has plunged a knife into it and is twisting the blade.

'The circuit breakers contain porcelain or composite bushings which meet or exceed all ANSI and NEMA specifications. High-creep bushings are also available as an option.'

Since composite bushings, which are made of lightweight synthetic materials, are more expensive, I ignore them in my translation. And since ANSI and NEMA are probably unfamiliar to 99% of the audience, I simply say 'international standards.' High-creep bushings, which are longer than standard bushings, are recommended for high pollution areas, definitely an issue in Russia's cities. But since they are also more expensive, and I don't know the Russian term for 'high-creep', and also have to pee so badly my teeth are floating, I don't translate that part either.

Dave then switches slides to the 242 kilovolt circuit breaker, essentially the same design as the previous model, except that everything is bigger and more expensive. As he describes the equipment features, I translate sporadically, improvising what I don't know and deleting the pricey options.

If the Russians know about the expensive options, they will assume they are necessary and want to have them. Then they will complain about the high prices of our circuit breakers, comparing them to their own Russian-made versions, even though they don't contain any of these modern features, and I'll end up selling nothing. I purposely deleted the slides with such options as the computerized monitoring unit (CMU) and synchronous switching device (SSD) from the presentation, figuring if Dave can't show them, he won't be able to talk about them. The CMU, which automatically monitors the functionality of the circuit breaker, would have to be reprogrammed in the Russian language. And the SSD, which controls where on the voltage wave the circuit breaker actually closes, is still in the developmental stages, meaning it could malfunction—we already had this experience with the Canadians—and hurt our reputation in a new market.

As if reading my thoughts, Dave says, 'We have a special option called the computerized monitoring unit, available for the 242 kV breaker.' He begins shuffling nervously through the slides. After reaching the bottom of the pile, he looks up at me as if I have just stolen his blueberry ice cream cone.

I give him a *Don't-glare-at-me* look. Then I say to him in English, 'I don't think we should be trying to sell them that anyway. It's much too expensive.'

'But they should still know about it,' Dave says with obvious irritation. 'And also the SSD. Where's that slide?'

'They can't afford that either,' I say. 'And if it malfunctions, not only will we need to send a costly service engineer to Russia, we'll ruin our reputation before we even establish it.'

'I'm with Katey,' Jack says from his seat in the first row. 'If it ain't broke, don't fix it. They're perfectly happy without these options. Don't make them unhappy by making them think they need them.'

'Are you sure you didn't leave some of the slides back in the room?' Dave asks. He is obviously determined to discuss these two expensive options.

'I can check,' I say, jumping at the chance to relieve myself. 'It will take two minutes.' Then I say in Russian, 'Five-minute break.'

Since I know there aren't any slides in the room—I left the CMU and SSD slides at home—I go straight to the john. A few minutes later I return relaxed and empty-handed to the auditorium. 'You have them all, Dave,' I say. 'Don't know what happened to the other ones.'

Half of the audience has left the room. The rest are clustered in little groups talking among themselves. I have a feeling they aren't discussing Dave's presentation. Walking past a trio deep in conversation, I overhear, 'She has a nice set of tits!' and 'I was looking at her ass.' It takes another fifteen minutes for the last smokers to return to their seats.

Dave continues with slides of the 362 and 550 kilovolt circuit breakers. Assembled in the field, they look like three horses in size and general shape, but still compact by Russian standards.

Because of Russia's enormous territorial expanse, electricity must be transported over vast distances, therefore requiring 800 kilovolt power lines. I imagine their massive oil tanks, the size of three eighteen-wheelers parked in a field in Siberia waiting to explode. The Russian circuit breakers are filled with oil instead of SF_6 gas.

Despite my returning headache, the translation has been progressing well. As if sensing my success and wanting to spoil it, Dave launches a new topic: *first pole to clear factor.*

'When clearing a three-phase fault,' he begins, 'one phase is always interrupted first since all breakers always clear at current zero.'

Although I translate the sentence somewhat awkwardly, members of the audience nod in understanding.

'And in a three-phase circuit, the current zeroes occur at three different points in time.'

I manage this sentence pretty well also, and once again

the audience nods. I learned about current flow in my electrical engineering courses. Current flows through the circuit breaker like a sine wave, passing through a zero value at regular intervals. It is precisely at this zero value that the current can be easily broken.

'Once the first pole clears, the other two current-carrying phases influence the recovery voltage of the first pole. That voltage-multiplying factor is called the first-pole-to-clear factor and will vary depending on the type of fault and type of circuit.'

God help me. Not even knowing how to begin translating this technical babble, I can only stare blankly at Dave.

'This is important,' he says. 'Do you understand it?'

No. Do I look like Albert Einstein? 'I understand it. I'm just trying figure out how to say it in Russian.'

Typical of people with no foreign language background, Dave doesn't appreciate the difficulty of spontaneously translating technical information into another language. He only glares at me, waiting.

'He's explaining something highly technical and theoretical which I don't know how to translate,' I say to the audience in Russian. 'Please don't laugh or he'll know something's wrong. Just nod in agreement and he'll think I've actually done it correctly.'

Everybody in the audience nods. Although nobody laughs, I notice a few smirks.

'Are you sure you got it right?' Dave asks.

'They seem to have understood,' I say.

Dave's presentation continues in this fashion. Whenever he gets too abstract or technical, I apologize to the audience and they pretend I am actually translating. Since they've really just come for the banquet and are probably already familiar with the content of Dave's spiel anyway, nobody seems bothered by my incompetence. We finish shortly before noon.

TWENTY-FOUR

'When can I meet some potential customers?' I ask Sergey during lunch. 'Where are they all from?'

Sergey and Miasnikov look at each other. Then Miasnikov says, 'The chief engineer from Kursk is here. And the chief engineer from Kaluga. I'll introduce them to you this afternoon.'

Are those all? I fight off an urge to complain, not wanting to offend Miasnikov. When he gets up later to make some announcements, I turn to Sergey. 'I thought 200 people were expected. I haven't actually counted, but the number seems much smaller. And I thought you were going to invite all the *energos* within 800 kilometers?'

Sergey shrugs. 'We did. Most of them replied that they didn't have any money for western circuit breakers. Others said they would only buy Russian equipment. Still others had different projects which have higher priority and the rest were on vacation. It's summer, you know.'

'So only three came?' I ask, counting these two plus Zamirov. 'Who are the rest of these people?'

'Many of them work for Tulenergo,' he says. 'And they

all brought friends. Then we have some project engineers from the surrounding areas.'

They brought friends? Tula drinking buddies looking for a free party? 'Jack will have a fit when he finds out about this,' I say. 'They paid thirty grand for this seminar, not to mention our personal travel costs. I could lose my job!'

'They won't find out anything unless you tell them, Katey,' Sergey says. 'Nobody else here speaks English.'

Suddenly I understand why Vladimir was reluctant to get involved with the seminar. He must have known it would turn out like this. Why the hell didn't he warn me? 'Now I can use a shot of vodka,' I say. Before I finish the sentence, Sergey grabs the bottle and begins filling glasses.

'You want one, Jack?' I ask, knowing he would if he knew his company had just wasted thirty-thousand dollars.

'When in Rome,' Jack says. 'You too, Dave?'

'Oh, why not?' he says. 'Maybe it will improve my afternoon presentation.'

'Afternoon presentation?' I ask. 'Aren't you finished?'

'I've given the matter some thought,' he says. 'I really think we should tell them about the Intelligent Circuit Breaker. I know you don't think they can afford it or need it, but they should still know about it.'

Intelligent Circuit Breaker is the term used to describe breakers equipped with pricey computerized devices such as the CMU and the SSU, exactly the topics I have been hoping to avoid.

'But we don't have the slides,' I say.

'Yes, but they have a chalkboard. I can draw sketches. The CMU and SSU are just black boxes anyway, not really much to look at.'

'What do you think, Jack?' I say, hoping for support.

'It's Dave's presentation,' Jack says. 'If he thinks we should mention it, then I won't oppose him.'

'I'd also like to expand on some of the theoretical issues I touched on this morning,' Dave says. Looking at me, he says, 'I want to go over the dependence of transient recovery voltage on the type of circuit, whether it is resistive, capacitive, or inductive. Are you familiar with that, Katey?'

'Sorry, Dave, but I don't have a clue,' I say and instantly recognize the error of my honesty when Dave begins to explain.

'During interruption, the arc quickly loses conductivity as the sinusoidal wave of current passes through zero.'

'That I understand,' I say. 'You mentioned it this morning.'

'The interruption process generates a transient recovery voltage, which is the difference of the response voltage on the source and load sides of the contacts,' Dave says. 'Are you following me?'

'I'm trying.'

'You're giving the poor girl a headache,' Jack says. 'At least you're giving me one. We don't need a goddamn physics lesson.'

Ignoring Jack's comment, Dave says, 'It's very important that you understand this.' He then continues like a wound-up toy. 'This transient recovery voltage can cause re-ignition. Do you follow me?'

Before responding, I see a familiar face in the doorway. It's Evgenii. And he just happens to be fluent in English. Although I want to kill him for blabbing to Vladimir about our little drinking binge, at this moment I also want to kiss him.

As Evgenii approaches, I say to Dave. 'This is Evgenii. He speaks English and is brilliant about technical details. I'm sure he can translate the rest of the presentation better than I can. Besides, I need to talk to some of the guests.'

Visibly disappointed that he won't be able to continue the physics lesson, Dave turns to Evgenii. 'What do you know about transient recovery voltages?' he asks.

'It is one of the parameters tested on circuit breakers,'

Evgenii responds in perfect English. 'It varies, depending on whether you have a resistive, capacitive, or inductive circuit. Without damping, the highest peak circuit response would be twice the driving voltage, or a TRV of two. Typical TRV values for dead tank circuit breakers range from 1.2 – 1.4.'

Soul mates! I think I am going to enjoy my afternoon.

I sit beside Jack during the presentation. Evgenii doesn't miss a beat, and I can tell Dave is pleased.

After the presentation we take a short walk to the substation where our breakers are installed. Dave gives an onsite talk, opening the control cabinet and identifying all the parts. As best as I can judge, Evgenii flawlessly translates every word.

I'm not really listening to him, but rather holding a private meeting with Sergey at the back of the group.

'I need to talk to the chief engineers from Kursk and Kaluga,' I said. 'My boss is going to expect me to get some substantial business as a result of this seminar.'

'I can arrange for you to talk to them. I know these men personally, which is probably why they came,' Sergey says. 'They're standing near the front.' Then he adds, 'Don't forget Zamirov from Belgorod. He might be a serious customer and one serious customer can make this whole seminar worth the cost.'

'What do you know about the other two?' I ask. 'Do they have a price?'

'Do you mean, can you offer them a bribe?' Sergey asks. 'You can offer anyone a bribe if you do it correctly.'

'What do you mean?' I ask.

'Well, if you simply blurt out an offer of money, some might be offended.'

'My blurting it out didn't bother Miasnikov.'

'He's an exception. Although almost everyone in Russia will accept a payoff, most won't admit it,' Sergey says, 'especially to a lovely lady.'

'So how do I bribe them?' I ask.

'Tell them you are sure the partnership will be beneficial for both sides,' he says.

'And they'll understand I'm offering a bribe?'

'Bribes are a standard practice in Russia. They'll understand.'

'Should I wink or anything?'

'They might like it if you take their hand and squeeze it,' Sergey says. 'But don't wink. That's too obvious.'

When the onsite presentation finally ends, the crowd heads back down the path in a buzz of conversation. Sergey stops a gray-haired bespectacled man in his mid-fifties.

'Yakov Polonovich,' he says. 'I'd like you to meet Katey. She's in charge of sales to Russia.'

His sweaty hand dampens my palm when I shake it. 'Nak. Yakov Polonovich'

'Katey, Yakov Polonovich is the chief engineer of Kurskenergo.'

'Are you interested in dead tank circuit breakers?' I ask, wondering about his unusual surname. *Yak?*

'We have plenty of interest,' he says. 'But no money.'

Remembering what Vladimir said about all customers having no money at the beginning, I persist as if I hadn't heard him. 'Could I possibly come to Kursk for a presentation? I'll be back in Russia next month.'

'You're welcome to visit us,' he says. 'But like I said, we don't have any money.'

'I'll have our Moscow office contact you about my visit,' I say, again ignoring his confession of corporate poverty. 'I'm sure we can work something out.' I reach out and squeeze Mr. Nak's sweaty hand.

He smiles at me awkwardly before rejoining the crowd. I have a similar experience with the engineer from Kaluga, who also says he has interest, but no money. Once again I suggest a visit to his power company and again, he agrees.

I decide to use my charms on Zamirov, who seemed

very friendly and easy to talk to. Knowing Belgorod must have money, I intend to get my hands on it, and make plans to lead Zamirov into a dark corner where we can talk privately. Now that Evgenii is here, I won't need to constantly translate for Jack and Dave. Even now, I notice Evgenii walking between the two Americans.

Miasnikov catches up to us and takes my arm. 'How's everything going, Katey?' he asks.

'I don't know,' I say. 'Do you think they enjoyed the presentation?'

'We're already familiar with most of what he talked about,' Miasnikov says. 'It was a nice review, but we enjoyed it more when you were translating, especially your ad libs.' He winks.

'She's much nicer to look at,' Sergey says.

'Perhaps,' I say. 'But I'm glad I didn't have to translate all that technical shit.'

'I think your translations would have been more interesting,' Sergey says.

'More humorous in any case,' I say. Then I ask, 'Do you think I could get a cup of coffee?'

'The ladies are setting everything up in the little room where we met last night,' Miasnikov says. 'I've only invited some key people.'

These key people are few in number: Nak from Kursk, the Chief engineer from Kaluga, whose name I've already forgotten, along with Zamirov, Dave, Jack, Evgenii, Sergey and myself. Nadezhda Simonovna is also there, probably to balance out the male-female ratio. Letting Evgenii take the seat between Dave and Jack, I squeeze in between Zamirov and Nak.

This time the table is decorated with a steaming silver samovar, an elegant china coffee service, bottles of cognac and liqueur, and prianiki—spicy honey cakes filled with jam and decorated with a glazed topping.

'Tula is famous for its prianiki,' Miasnikov says. 'These

came from our finest bakeries.'

Nadezhda Simonovna slices one of the flat cakes into generous pieces and places them on little plates which she passes around to each of us, starting with Jack.

Vera enters the room carrying two coffee pots. Today she is wearing a tight neon fuchsia sweater, her watermelon breasts aimed like missiles. Stretchy back slacks emphasize her basketball butt, jiggling as she wobbles on four inch open-toed fuchsia heels. Fingernails, toenails, cheeks, and lips are all painted the color of her shoes and sweater.

She hurriedly takes the seat beside Dave, visibly disappointed that she can't sit between the two Americans. Although Dave moves away as her soft body presses against his, she responds by nonchalantly moving closer and extending her foot to touch his shoe.

'I enjoyed your presentation, Katey,' Zamirov says.

'I was just the translator,' I say. 'And I'm afraid I didn't do a very good job.'

'It doesn't matter,' he says. 'We already knew that stuff anyway. It was you we enjoyed looking at.'

'I'd like to meet with you tonight,' I say. 'We can discuss the possibility of a partnership.'

'I'm sure we can sneak away during the banquet,' Zamirov says. 'Especially now that you have an assistant translator.'

'Hello, everyone!'

I look up to see Vladimir standing in the doorway dressed casually in slacks and a tweed jacket. Without even looking at me, he sits next to Nadezhda. Even though she is older, probably married, and not particularly attractive, I can't stop myself from feeling jealous. If only I hadn't been such a drunken idiot last night. All the same, I find myself staring at the cognac bottle.

'Would you like a drink?' Zamirov asks, as if reading my thoughts.

'That would be lovely,' I say.

Zamirov pours two cognacs. I look at Vladimir to see if he is watching, but he is absorbed in conversation with Jack and Dave.

'To our friendship,' Zamirov says, clinking his glass against mine.

'And to our partnership,' I say.

Just as I set the empty glass on the table, Zamirov is already refilling it.

The banquet begins at six p.m. in the same room where lunch was served. A group of heavily made-up women, all dressed in tight-fitting skirts and high heels, scurry in and out, bringing trays of various hors d'oeuvres to the lavish table with 150 place settings. There are pickled eggs, black and red caviar, Russian-style coleslaw, herring-beet salad, plates of sweet pickles and olives, eggplant caviar, dark red salami with large flecks of fat, lox, smoked sturgeon, and various types of cheese. There is enough bread to fill a bakery and enough champagne and vodka for each guest to consume an entire bottle.

Disappointed when Vladimir sits on the other side of the table across from Jack, who has taken the seat on my left, I look around for Miasnikov and Zamirov, hoping one of them will sit on my other side. When both men arrive together, Zamirov takes the seat next to me and Miasnikov sits down opposite me. Since Evgenii is seated between Jack and Dave, and Vladimir is also present, I assume I won't be needing to translate and can spend my time with the customers.

'Hello again, Katey' Zamirov says.

'Igor Antonovich,' I say. I've made a point of remembering his first name and patronymic, which is the polite form of address in Russia. 'How nice of you to join me.'

'Dmitri Sergeevich was telling me about how impressed he was by your factory,' he says.

Did he also tell you about Hooters? 'We want our customers to see how we operate,' I say. 'Every contract includes a trip to our factory in Pennsylvania.'

'It's time to start the party,' Miasnikov says, standing up. 'Ladies and Gentlemen, I want to welcome you all to our first circuit breaker seminar banquet. I'd like to start with a toast.'

All along the table, which is shaped like a digital C, hands reach out to grab vodka bottles. Miasnikov and Vladimir fill the glasses for our little group.

'I'd like to drink a toast to our friends who came all the way from America to teach us about their wonderful circuit breakers.'

Amidst conversation and laughter, glasses clink together, vodka vanishes, and hands reach out for a tasty appetizer.

Remembering my drunken confrontation with Vladimir the night before and not wanting a repeat performance, I raise my glass to my lips, stick my tongue in, but leave it full. I notice Vladimir has drunk his 'bottom down'.

'Don't you like the vodka, Katey?' Zamirov asks.

'I drank too much last night,' I say.

'Katey, you don't want to offend your host,' Vladimir says. 'This is Tula vodka. Drink it down. We know you want to.'

I obey—I don't need much coaxing—and its pleasant warmth instantly relaxes me.

The evening starts out with many toasts. As vodka disappears, the attentive ladies bring new bottles. They also bring out little metal goblets filled with creamed wild mushrooms—Russians love them and are avid mushroom pickers. Then they bring the main course, Russian style sturgeon, which is served in a cream sauce with potatoes, topped with a layer of broiled cheese. It is amazing how many different ways they can prepare this type of fish. The toasts continue throughout the meal, becoming sillier as the vodka bottles become emptier.

'A toast to Tula vodka,' I say, standing and smiling at the

crowd. The Tula natives cheer.

Then Vladimir gets up. 'I'd like to propose a toast to the most beautiful woman in America.'

'Why are they toasting my wife?' Jack asks innocently after Evgenii translates, keeping a serious expression. But when his eyes meet mine, he can't resist a chuckle.

The men all stand, extending their glasses towards me. Zamirov puts his arm around my shoulder and kisses my cheek. Then he says. 'Now would be a good time to sneak away. Have you had enough to eat?'

'Oh God, yes,' I say. 'I can't possibly eat another bite.'

Before leaving, I glance at Vladimir, but he is absorbed in conversation with Jack.

It's almost dark as we go outside into the cool evening air. As we wander down the dirt road behind Tulenergo, Zamirov lights a cigarette and offers it to me. When I turn him down, he sticks it into his mouth.

I'm drunk enough not to object when Zamirov takes my hand.

'So, you have a need for dead tank circuit breakers?' I ask. 'What voltage level?'

'You want to talk business?' he asks, visibly surprised.

'Of course. Always.'

'Such a lovely lady shouldn't have to worry her pretty little head about such things.'

I've been around sexist Russian men enough to not be bothered by his remark. Instead, I say, 'It's my plan to sell more circuit breakers in Russia than anyone else in the whole world.'

'Keep it up and I'm sure you will,' he says.

'So, what can I sell to Belgorodenergo?' I ask.

'Okay. If you insist, we have a 110 kV substation with some ancient oil breakers I'd love to replace.'

'If you tell me the details, I can come to Belgorod on my next trip with an offer and a contract.'

'Whoa,' Zamirov says. 'I said I'd like to replace them. I

didn't say we have the money.'

I ignore his statement. 'I can make the deal quite profitable for you.' As soon as the words leave my mouth, I realize I was too direct. The vodka has removed not only my inhibitions, but also my common sense.

'I know what you're getting at, Katey,' he says. 'But I'm not interested. If Belgorod can come up with the financing, we can talk business, but you don't need to offer me anything.'

'Are you sure?'

'I've had this conversation many times in my life and my answer has always been no.'

Without a personal incentive for Zamirov, I probably won't get a contract. Deciding on a different approach, I turn toward him, place my hands on his shoulders lean forward and kiss his lips. He kisses me back before pulling away.

'I know why you're doing this,' he says. 'And it won't work with me, either.'

'Don't be silly,' I say. 'I like you.'

'Is that why you were staring at Kashirnikov all evening?'

'Was I that obvious?'

'I'm afraid so,' he says. 'Your eyes barely left him for a minute. Not to mention that toast he made. And I bet the real reason you came out here with me is to make him jealous. That's a dangerous game, Katey. I think we should go back to the party before you do something you'll regret.'

'I came out here to talk business,' I say.

'Do you know what I think?' he says. 'I think the only reason you care about getting contracts is to impress Vladimir, to force him to spend more time with you.'

I don't deny it.

'Maybe we should pretend this whole conversation never occurred,' I say.

'What conversation? I don't recall any conversation.'

When we return to the banquet hall, Vladimir's eyes meet mine and hold my gaze.

Making a commitment to stop drinking, I pour myself a glass of mineral water. Fortunately the toasts have subsided and the guests are clustered into little conversation groups.

Shortly before midnight the ladies serve coffee and ice cream. I am surprised at how quickly the evening has passed. Hoping to sober up, and because I am so tired I want to lay my head on the table, I drink two cups of coffee.

Gradually the guests depart in little groups, many walking unsteadily, most of them shaking our hands and thanking us. Looking tired, the Russian women begin clearing the rest of the dishes.

Leaving my door unlocked, I crawl naked under the heavy comforter and wait for Vladimir. Ten minutes later I hear my door open.

'You should really lock this,' he says. 'Somebody might come in and rape you.'

'That's what I'm hoping for,' I say.

'Then don't let me disappoint you.'

After we make love silently in the darkness, Vladimir gets out of bed and grabs his clothes.

'Aren't you staying?' I ask.

'Don't be ridiculous, Katey. We both need a good night's sleep. It's close to two a.m. already.'

'Damn you,' I say. 'Why do you always run away? Why can't it be like it was in Washington?'

'That was long ago and far away,' he says. 'It was a vacation from my life in Russia. Here I have a business to run and a reputation to uphold. A son.' *And a wife.*

'Now get some sleep,' he says, slipping out the door.

What am I to you? Do you love me? Do you care about me at all? The bottle Sergey brought that morning is standing on the table. I pour myself a double shot and sit back onto the bed, tears streaking my cheeks.

TWENTY-FIVE

Back in Moscow, I meet Sergey for lunch before flying back to the states. Jack and Dave flew home a few days earlier, leaving me to try and follow up on a few contacts. Before making a toast, Sergey pulls out a white envelope and hands it to me.

'What's that?' I ask.

'That's your share of the Tula money. Two-thousand dollars.'

'I can't take this,' I say. 'It was paid out by my own company and certainly wasn't intended for me.'

'You have to take it. It's for you and only you. We can't really give it back. Besides, you earned it.'

When I get back to Vladimir's office, I tell him about the money.

'What am I supposed to do with it?' I ask.

'Buy a new car. Even for two thousand, it will be better than that piece of shit you drive now.'

'Don't you think I should give it back?'

'What are you going to do? Walk up to Jack and say

here's my share of the slush money we paid?'

I look into the envelope and see the stack of crisp hundreds, the same ones which had been in my shoe several months ago. 'What the hell,' I say and put the money into my purse.

TWENTY-SIX

I have a 3:30 p.m. flight on US Air to Moscow via Frankfurt. I head out the door at 2:30 with a small suitcase and a purse. I've learned to travel light, no longer hauling the big bags I took on my first trip.

I am flying business class with Dave to Moscow and then on to Ufa east of the Ural Mountains on the edge of Siberia. The only reason we are flying business class is because Jack was supposed to accompany us and he never flies coach. For some unknown reason, however, the Russian Embassy delayed his visa and he didn't get it on time to join us. With a ticket price of over 4000 dollars each, this flight is a luxury I may never experience again. Luckily, Jack decided not to be anal and he let us keep the high-priced tickets.

When I arrive at the tiny airport, I am surprised to see nobody checking in passengers and the lobby empty. Seeing a lone man sitting at a desk behind the counter, I lean towards him.

'Isn't there a flight to Pittsburgh?' I ask. 'I have a ticket.'

The man slowly approaches the counter. 'It left at three-thirty, ten minutes ago.'

Suddenly realizing that my watch must have stopped, I freeze in panic. 'I'll have to drive there,' I say. 'I have to catch a flight at five-fifteen.'

'You better hurry,' he calls after me as I bolt out the door.

I break the speed limit heading for the highway. Since Pittsburgh is an hour away under the best conditions, I pray there won't be road construction or heavy traffic.

Once I hit the freeway I cruise along at 80 in the left lane, watching for cops. Every time I approach a slower car I weave into the middle lane and step on the gas, feeling like James Bond. My car clock says four-forty as I pass the city and the first airport signs appear. By four-fifty I'm pulling into the long term parking lot. A commuter bus pulls up near my car, as if sent by God, and gets me to the terminal at four fifty-five.

The line at security reaches to the door. Knowing I'll never make my flight if I wait, I wade past the people to the front and approach a pudgy middle-aged man who is about to place his bags on the x-ray belt.

'My flight leaves in ten minutes,' I say, flashing him a desperate smile. 'Do you think I could—'

'Sure. Be my guest,' he says, smiling back. I'm so glad he's at the front of the line instead of some fat bitchy woman with an attitude.

'Thank you,' I say, touching his hand. 'You're a life-saver.'

With no luggage to check—a trick I learned from Anis—I go straight to the people mover and wedge my way in between closing doors. When I get off thirty seconds later, I tear through the airport, as if being chased by a naked axe murderer, waving my ticket in my hand and searching frantically for my gate.

Reaching the check-in desk, I'm relieved to see passengers still boarding the plane. Catching my breath, I thrust my ticket at the man behind the counter, explain that I didn't have time to check in, and wait while he punches keys on the computer. He is very skinny with glasses and a pointy nose, reminding me of a mosquito.

'Your reservation has been cancelled,' he says as calmly as if telling me the time of day.

'It can't be cancelled,' I say, feeling my heartbeat quicken again.

'Since you didn't take the first leg of the flight, it was cancelled automatically,' the mosquito explains.

'Well, can't you uncancel it?' I ask.

'We gave your seat away,' he says. 'But maybe I can put you in coach class.'

'That's ridiculous. I told the guy at the other airport I was driving here. Didn't he let you know?' I can't believe I'm about to miss my only chance to fly business class.

'What's up?' I look to my right and see Dave standing beside me. He has apparently arrived even later than me, living up to his reputation for just barely making flights.

'I don't have a seat,' I say.

'Wait, I have one for you,' the mosquito says without looking up from the screen. 'It looks like we had another last-minute cancellation.'

'I hope it's not yours,' I say, looking at Dave.

Fortunately it isn't Dave's and three minutes later, we are boarding the plane. I sink into a roomy window seat beside a middle-aged man, dressed in a suit, with his nose in the Wall Street Journal, sipping a glass of red wine. I feel out of place in my comfortable airplane clothes—leggings, a baggy sweater, and short leather boots.

Minutes after I'm seated, the plane is ready for takeoff. I fasten my seatbelt and lean back, feeling like a celebrity. As the plane creeps towards the runway, another stewardess stands at the front of the cabin, demonstrating the use of the gas mask and life preserver. Since nobody ever survives a crash, I never pay attention to this ritual. With my luck the plane will make a once-in-a-hundred-years emergency landing in the middle of the Atlantic and I won't know how to use my life preserver. But since it's the middle of winter, I'd get hypothermia in the frigid water and freeze to death anyway before a rescue mission could arrive.

The Wall Street Journal man isn't paying attention either. Looking around the cabin, I become convinced that the stewardess might as well have been speaking Urdu. Everyone is either reading or chatting with their seat mate.

Finally she sits down and the plane accelerates. Through my window, I see the terminal zoom past, then only grass and other runways before the plane lifts into the air. My stomach dips as we soar upward. Remembering a plane that crashed on takeoff due to wind shear in Detroit in the 1980's, killing everyone on board, I am always relieved when the fasten seatbelts sign goes out and the stewardesses resume serving drinks.

This time I don't drink vodka with my seat mate. He barely talks to me. After dinner, when the lights dim, I put on my headset to watch the movie and am pleased when the cult film *When Harry Met Sally* appears on the screen. I've seen it so often I can watch it without thinking.

After the movie, I'm still wide awake and decide to track down a stewardess to give me a bottle of wine. Although I could just push a button, I feel like stretching my legs. Just as I enter the little vestibule, I bump into Dave, coming in from the other side.

'Not asleep either, huh,' he says.

'I never sleep on planes.' I say. 'I usually buy a trashy novel at the airport, but today I was so late I didn't have time.'

'I always catch my flights at the last minute,' Dave says. 'No matter how hard I try to get there on time, something always delays me. But the funny thing is I've never missed a flight. Want to drink some vodka?' he asks suddenly.

'Sure, why not?' I say. 'It's appropriate, you know,

considering our destination.'

The drink cart is parked conveniently in the vestibule. The stewardesses must be resting. Dave fishes out two little bottles of vodka. Then he fishes out two more.

I take two glasses from the shelf and pour two bottles into each of them.

'We need something to munch on,' Dave says.

'They must have some more of those fancy nuts around here somewhere,' I say, opening a cabinet door. After opening three, I find the stash.

'To Russia,' I say, raising my glass.

'That's not very original.'

'It's three a.m. and you want original?'

After swigging the vodka in two gulps, we dive into the mixed nuts, mostly cashews—we're in business class after all.

'So how's Vladimir?' Dave asks.

'How the hell should I know?'

Dave starts to chuckle. 'I can't believe you did that last year.'

'Are you talking about that dinner when I invited Vladimir to come home with me? Anis said you complained.'

Dave gives me a confused look. 'Me? Why would I complain? I thought it was hilarious. In fact, we all did, except for Anis.'

'That's what Vladimir thought, but Anis made it sound like it was the other way around,' I say.

'We were actually a bit afraid of a sexual harassment suit,' Dave says. 'But then we got to know you better and realized it wouldn't be a problem. And we also thought if you were sleeping with Vladimir, he might be more eager to help you get business. It could work to our advantage.'

It is certainly working to mine. I start to laugh so loudly and suddenly that I almost choke on a Brazil nut. 'You want some more vodka?' I ask.

Just as I realize there is no more vodka in the cart, a

pretty stewardess appears in the entrance. I wonder how she could look so good at three a.m. She must have just reapplied her make-up and used half a bottle of hairspray.

'I see you're having a party,' she says with a forced smile.

'We helped ourselves to the vodka,' Dave says.

'I see you found it okay,' she says, smiling again at the empty bottles on the counter.

'We didn't want to bother you,' I say.

'That's my job,' she says. 'Our first-class passengers certainly don't need to wait on themselves.'

She rummages through the cart, looking for vodka bottles. Since we've already taken them all, she doesn't find any. Opening a top cupboard, she pulls out a large bottle of Stolichnaya.

'This should keep you happy,' she says. 'It's our emergency bottle. Lately we've been getting a lot of Russians in business class.'

Dave presses a crisp twenty into her hand as she walks away.

'Can you keep a secret?' he says after we finish another shot.

'Sure.'

'I have a job offer from International Electric.'

'You want to leave Ampere Power?' I ask. It's a stupid question, but he has caught me completely by surprise.

'They want me to be the general manager of their dead tank plant.'

'And you're going to take it?'

'It's not like I'll ever get Jack's job. He's only 53 and isn't going anywhere. But it's not official, so don't tell anyone.'

'I'm a black body,' I say, remembering Sergey's words. 'Information enters, but doesn't come out.' Then I say, 'I'll miss you.'

'So now it's your turn to tell me a secret,' he says.

'What do you want to hear?' I ask.

'Are you still involved with Vladimir?'

Although I know I should deny it, I say, 'Sure as hell am.' Since Dave is leaving the company, he probably couldn't care less how I spend my time.

'Are you going to share a hotel room?' Dave asks.

'Not officially,' I say. 'That would screw up our expense reports. It might cause gossip if one of us doesn't have a receipt.'

'Good point,' Dave says. Then he asks, 'So do you have plans to steal Vladimir away from his wife and marry him?'

Yes. 'No, of course not,' I say. 'I don't want to marry him.' *Liar!*

It's dark and quiet when we return to our seats. I close my eyes and doze, suspended between sleeping and waking, and am surprised by how quickly the night has passed when the lights come on and I hear the clatter of breakfast dishes.

At the Frankfurt Airport, the first thing I do is find a restroom where I can wash my face, brush my teeth, apply make-up, and take a pee. After a night of drinking vodka and barely sleeping, my hair is stringy and flat, my eyes bloodshot, the Irish bags underneath them even darker than usual, my nose as shiny as Rudolph's and my face has a gray tint.

Dave is waiting for me when I come out of the bathroom.

'We have three hours,' I say. 'How about a beer?'

'It's seven a.m.' Dave says.

'It's ten a.m. in Moscow and that's where we're headed. Just in time for their morning aperitif. And it's one a.m. back home. Just the time for a good party to really get going. We aren't really here at all. It's kind of like the twilight zone.'

'Okay,' Dave says. 'You've convinced me.'

We pay four dollars each at a kiosk for twelve ounce bottles of Heineken and drink standing up. After finishing them, we buy two more before heading to our gate.

The guard at the passport check takes a long time examining my visa. 'This isn't valid until tomorrow,' he says in Russian.

'What are you talking about?'

'Today is December 5th. Your visa says December 6th.'

'That's not my fault.'

'I don't know whose fault it is, but you can't enter Russia until midnight.'

'I have to catch a flight to Ufa,' I say. Our plane is set to land at five p.m. at the Sheremetyevo airport. Vladimir will be waiting to drive us to the Domodedovo airport at the other end of the city, where we have to catch a seven-thirty flight to Ufa. Even without a visa problem, the schedule is tight.

'Unfortunately, that's not my problem.'

'Can't I just pay a fine or something?'

'Russia is strict about visas,' he says. 'You can take the flight, but it's not my problem after you get there'.

Of course I take the flight and four hours later, hand my passport and visa to a Russian customs official, pretending I'm unaware of the date problem and hoping he won't notice.

But naturally he does. 'This isn't valid until tomorrow,' he says.

'They made a mistake at the consulate,' I say. 'But please don't make me wait. I have to catch another flight.'

'I'm sorry. I can't do anything. You will need to wait outside until midnight.'

I reach casually into my purse, pull out a crisp hundred, brush it across my cheek and wink so subtly that he barely notices.

But he does notice. 'For a visa violation, the fine is 100 U.S. dollars,' he suddenly says.

I want to kiss him. I want to ask for a receipt. But I

don't do either, knowing I won't get a receipt no matter what I do and will just have to eat this expense or explain it to Anis, which would actually be worse. *You bribed him? That's illegal.* But I sure as hell don't want to sit 'outside' until midnight. I place the hundred-dollar bill on the counter, he stamps my visa, and I pass quickly through.

Since we don't have checked luggage, we are quickly outside where Vladimir is standing on the sidewalk, waiting.

'Yuri will bring the car around in a minute,' he says. 'We should have plenty of time.'

Although it is rush hour, we are driving into the city instead of out, so we cruise along at a steady speed. When we reach the city center and head towards the south end, traffic has gotten heavier and we drive more slowly. Just when I think we'll be late, we leave the city traffic and I see airport signs. We cruise the rest of the way, making it to Domodedevo twenty minutes before our flight.

The Domodedevo airport lacks the modern flair of Sheremetyevo. Instead of glimmering duty-free shops selling Versace and Hermes, there are only a few kiosks with cheap Russian goods and imported German beer. The lobby and hallways are colorless and dimly lit.

Vladimir presents our business-class tickets at the check-in counter. Then we head down a long hallway with a concrete floor and wooden walls. Seeing a ladies room, I realize that I need to pee, but Vladimir is flying so fast ahead of me that I don't dare stop him.

We reach security, a moving platform for our luggage, which looks like it hasn't been modernized in twenty years. Nobody seems interested in the contents of our bags—I don't think the woman even looked at the X-ray—and we get through quickly.

Aboard the plane, I'm not surprised to find the business section fuller than the economy section. The new Russians are always seeking a status symbol, whether it be a Rolex, a Versace necktie, or a ticket in business class.

We sit on the runway for forty-five minutes and receive no explanation. Unlike the Americans, who get fidgety and bombard the stewardesses with questions during an unexplained delay, the Russians calmly read newspapers and fiddle with their cell phones.

From my window seat beside Vladimir, I watch the last passengers wade past—a tall dark-haired man with blue eyes and perfect skin dressed like Prince Charles, followed by a tank with a bull-dog face in a black turtle neck and matching jacket.

'That was one of Ufa's wealthiest men,' Vladimir whispers after they pass.

'The big one?' I ask, surprised.

'No, the other one. The big guy is his bodyguard.'

'How do you know him?'

'I don't. I can just tell.'

'Why don't you travel with a bodyguard?' I ask.

'Because I'm not important enough…yet.'

'Was the plane waiting for him?'

As if to answer my question, the fasten-seatbelt signs illuminate and the plane starts to move.

'It looks that way.' Vladimir says. 'Someday they'll wait for me.'

TWENTY-SEVEN

Seventy minutes later after a mediocre meal, the fasten seat belt signs reappear and I feel the plane descending. Dave, who has been dozing in the seat across the aisle, opens his eyes and looks at me.

'Are we there already?' he asks.

'It sure looks that way,' I say. 'And fast, too. We must have had a good headwind?'

'It's called a tailwind, Katey,' Dave says, chuckling. 'Are you sure you're really an engineer?'

'I'm just tired, Dave,' I say. 'Of course I know the difference. I wrote my damned bachelor's thesis on airplanes and vortices, for God's sake.'

'What was your topic?'

Oh great. A quiz. 'I honestly don't remember anymore, Dave.'

'It was less than two years ago. You can't forget it that quickly.'

Yes, I really am an engineer, you asshole. 'Just let it drop, Dave.'

Dave starts to respond, but then heeds my request as the

plane hits the runway. I can tell, however, that he doesn't want to.

The people rise from their seats before the plane stops moving and start rummaging around in the overhead compartments. The cold winter air slaps my face as we descend the steps into darkness. A black BMW drives up and parks several yards from the stairwell. The same man the plane waited for climbs into the backseat, followed by his bodyguard. The car zooms away, disappearing into the darkness and leaving us like stranded peasants.

Without even a bus to meet us, we walk in a cluster across the Tarmac toward the dim lights of the terminal. Entering through a metal door, we go down a dark hallway leading to a spacious lobby with high ceilings. People bundled in winter clothing are sprawled on the seats, some sleeping, some drunk, and the rest staring into space, looking bored. There is little conversation. Several small kiosks display newspapers, German beer, vodka, and electrical appliances such as curling irons and voltage converters. They are all closed for the night.

'This isn't Ufa,' Vladimir says, like Dorothy arriving in Oz.

'Where the hell are we then?' Dave asks.

'We're definitely not in Kansas,' I say.

Vladimir gives me a strange look. I'm sure he's never seen the Wizard of Oz. 'I'll try to find out,' he says, walking towards the rows of seats. He returns after chatting with another man from our flight. 'We're in Yezhevsky,' he says.

'Where the fuck is Yezhevsky?' Dave asks.

'They made an emergency landing because of heavy fog,' Vladimir says. 'We're stuck here.'

'Stuck?' Dave says. 'In the middle of Siberia?'

'We're in the Ural mountain region,' Vladimir says. 'On the edge of Siberia…but not quite in it.'

We might as well be.

Nobody says anything for a few moments. Then Dave

starts to chuckle. In a few seconds he is guffawing like a madman ready to be clothed in a strait jacket. His laughter infects us like a disease, and soon we're all hee-hawing like pot-smoking hyenas.

'How long is the delay?' I ask.

'We aren't going anywhere tonight,' Vladimir says.

'Wait,' Dave says. 'Why does that guy you talked to know so much when nobody told us anything?'

'He's a frequent flyer on this route,' Vladimir says. 'Apparently fog and storm delays happen often.'

'Is there a return flight to Moscow?' Dave asks.

'There aren't any more flights tonight,' Vladimir says. 'I'll try to get us a room. They must have an airport hotel.'

'Oh, great,' Dave says. 'A hotel with four minus stars.'

Ten minutes later we enter our room. Although the hotel had been saving the rooms for families with children, Vladimir convinced them, probably with money, to show kindness to the poor suffering Americans.

To the left of the entrance is a small bathroom. It has a toilet with no seat and a rusted bathtub on legs. When I turn on the water in the sink, the mere sight of the brownish trickle—and it is really only a trickle—quenches my thirst.

The main room has two single beds and a chair.

I sink into the chair, motioning for the men to take the beds. 'I can't sleep anyway,' I say. 'I'm too wired.'

Not objecting, Dave removes his shoes and stretches out on the bed furthest away from me. In five minutes he is snoring. Vladimir hangs his jacket over a chair and lies facing me on his back on the other bed.

'There's room for both of us,' he says, patting the space beside him.

He doesn't need to ask twice. After turning off the light and removing my shoes, I lie down in the space under Vladimir's shoulder. It doesn't take long before my hand wanders over to his crotch. As I start to unzip his pants,

Vladimir's grips my hand.

'What about him?' he says, looking over at Dave.

'He hasn't slept in over twenty-four hours. He won't wake up.'

'But what if he does?'

'Then we'll ask him to join us,' I say.

Three hours later, I'm wide awake, wishing I had a joint, a valium, or a bottle of vodka. My bladder is as wired as the rest of me and I pee at least eight times, releasing nothing but tiny trickles. I don't think I've slept at all when dawn finally approaches. Now all I want is a strong cup of coffee.

Before the men awaken, I go into the bathroom and remove my clothes. Turning the water on in the bathtub, I am surprised by a warm gush, brown but not ice-cold like I expected it to be. After thirty seconds, the color changes to beige, somewhat more appealing. Without a plug for the bathtub I crouch naked and use my hands to splash the water. I lather my entire body, face included, with a tiny bar of soap I had in my cosmetic bag. I then kneel and stick my head under the faucet to wash my hair, working up a thick lather and massaging my scalp for a long time. Feeling as clean as I can possibly get in this dreadful little room, I use one of the tiny hotel towels, which resembles a dish cloth.

Then I take my dual-voltage hair dryer out of my suitcase and blow-dry my hair, fluffing it up and turning it under with a round brush, grateful that the fuse doesn't blow. Once my hair is dry, I apply make-up, trying to hide the Irish bags under my eyes, and cover myself with perfumed bath powder before dressing in the same clothes I slept in. I would prefer to wear something clean, but I have packed only suits, which I will need for the business meetings, and I still don't know where today's adventure is going to take us.

When I leave the bathroom, both Dave and Vladimir are sitting on the edge of their beds, putting on shoes.

'Did you have a good sleep, Katey?' Dave asks.

'I was awake all night,' I say. 'What about you? I heard you snoring.'

'I woke up a couple times, but I slept pretty well.'

'And you, Vladimir?' I ask, knowing he slept like a baby after the lullaby I sang on his penis.

'Never slept better,' he says, grinning.

'I can never sleep in strange places,' I say.

'Then you must not sleep much in Russia,' Dave says. 'What do we do now?'

'Let's have breakfast and then find out when the plane is taking off.' Vladimir suggests.

'More like if,' I add.

All we find to eat are some stale white rolls called *boolochki*, some dubious cold meat patties, called *kotleti*, and plates of eggs, sunny side up, which were probably fried yesterday. There is instant coffee, served in tiny cups with plenty of sugar, but no milk.

'You expect me to eat those?' Dave says, eying the *kotleti* as though they were cowpies.

'Just pretend you're a dog,' I say, taking a bite of the meat or whatever the hell it is. 'It doesn't taste bad with a good dose of salt'.

'The eggs are cold,' Dave says. 'And they don't look fresh.'

'They were probably delivered from a restaurant,' I say. 'It's not like she can cook in that tiny kiosk.'

'I'm going to see what I can find out,' Vladimir says, downing the last of his coffee and standing up. 'Wait here.'

'Where do you think we're gonna go?' Dave asks, picking at the gummy yolk of his egg.

'There's still fog in Ufa,' Vladimir says, returning ten minutes later. 'Nobody knows how long the delay will last.'

'Is there a flight back to Moscow?' Dave asks.

'Dave, we came all this way. We're not going back to Moscow,' I say. 'It's a five-million-dollar contract. We can't expect it to be easy.'

'What are we supposed to do?' Dave asks. 'Walk to Ufa?'

'There is no flight back to Moscow,' Vladimir says. 'But there are private taxis outside. I already talked to one of them. He is willing to drive us to Ufa.'

'A taxi to Siberia?' Dave says. 'In the middle of winter?'

'How far is it?' I ask and then add, 'Dave, it's not Siberia, it's the Urals.'

'At least 200 miles,' Vladimir says. 'And in Russia, there are no roads, just directions. So it might be a long trip.'

'No way!' Dave almost shouts. 'No fucking way!'

'Do you want to spend another night in that hotel?' I ask. 'Because it might be that long before our flight leaves. Hell, it could take a week.'

'I can't believe this is happening,' Dave says, resting his face on his hands.

'What are we going to do?' I ask Vladimir in Russian.

'Take the taxi.' He's obviously already decided.

'How do we convince Dave?' I ask. Then a thought occurs to me. 'Why don't we drink some vodka?' I say in English.

'Why the hell not?' Dave says. 'We're stranded in Siberia. We might as well do what the locals do.'

'It's not really Siberia,' I say again. 'It's the Ur—'

'Who the fuck cares?' Dave interrupts. 'It might as well be Antarctica'.

Vladimir buys a half-liter bottle of vodka and brings it to the table with three glasses.

An hour later, we crowd into a small junkyard-ripe Lada, Dave in the front seat, Vladimir and I squeezed into the back. I look for a seatbelt, but don't find one. Oh well. The driver probably wouldn't have let me wear it anyway. Russian taxi drivers get offended if you wear a seatbelt. They view it as an affront to their driving ability.

After revving up the engine for almost a minute, the driver pulls out of the airport and heads toward the city's multi-colored high-rise apartment buildings. They are designed like a patchwork quilt—random sections of orange, blue, pink and light green bricks. Although it could be a form of Soviet architecture from the past, the builders probably used whatever materials and colors they could find. And when one ran out, they simply continued with another.

Zooming past the outskirts of Yezhevsky, I notice simple undecorated shops with generic names—*Bulochnaya* (bakery), *Apteka* (pharmacy), and *Kulinaria* (delicatessen)— reminding me of my student days in Moscow before western influences led to colorful Russian chains with serial names like *Irina* and *Maxim*, as well as foreign labels such as Baskin Robbins, Hermes, and Starbucks. The Russian grocery chain *Seventh Continent* and other large foreign food retailers have replaced many of the small generic bakeries, confectionaries, and produce shops. The latter sold almost nothing, except for potatoes, cabbage, and onions and used to be found on every street corner.

'The road looks pretty good,' Dave says from the front.

'Roads are always better near the cities,' Vladimir says. 'Wait awhile.'

Like a heavy wool blanket, the sky promises snow. In early December the days are short, and by three o'clock dusk is approaching. An hour later we are travelling in darkness except for dim headlights on the road ahead.

True to Vladimir's promise, we leave the main highway and turn onto a snow-covered road.

'This way is shorter,' the man says to Vladimir. 'We'll get there more quickly.'

'What did he say? What did he say?' Dave asks nervously.

'He said it's not much farther,' Vladimir says.

I suddenly have to pee. I wish I had the bladder of a

man or at least a penis I could stick into a bottle. I decide to hold it awhile, for at least another hour. The last thing I want is to have to pee twice before we get there.

After a while, though, I *really* have to pee. 'Vladimir, I have to pee,' I whisper.

'Why didn't you go before we left?' he says. Then he says to the driver, 'We need to stop.'

'Why didn't you take care of that before we left?' the driver snarls.

The snow is piled high on both sides of the road. With no place to hide, I squat behind the car, hoping that no other vehicles drive by, which isn't likely since we haven't seen any in the past hour. But—true to Murphy's law—I notice headlights approaching just as my urine stream is reaching its maximum flow. After pushing with my pelvis to force the pee out more quickly, I am pulling up my leggings when a white car pulls up beside us and crawls to a stop.

TWENTY-EIGHT

Assuming the driver just wants to ask directions or inquire if we have any problems, I don't worry when a husky man, hidden beneath a heavy overcoat, a monstrous fur hat, and lumberjack boots, jumps out of the passenger side and approaches me.

Without a word, I try to squeeze past him, pressing my back against the side of the car, but before I make it to the door, the glimmer of metal in his right hand makes me freeze like a frightened deer. Before I can even breathe, he snatches me like a rag doll, choking me with his left hand and holding the knife at my throat with his right. He smells of alcohol and stale cigarettes.

Within seconds, the taxi driver is out of the car. He stands behind the open door, silently assessing the situation.

'Get everyone out of the car,' the burly man says. I feel the cold metal quivering against my neck. 'And give me all your money and your car keys.'

He's going to kill me. He's going to kill us all. He's going to leave our corpses lying on the road to become buried under snow until spring. Or he's going to take our car and leave us here to freeze to death. Either way, I am going to die.

A gunshot interrupts my thoughts. I don't understand what is happening until the grip on my neck loosens, and my captor falls into the snow, blood gushing from his forehead. In an instant, Dave and Vladimir are out of the car.

The other car takes off like a scared rabbit, going much too fast for the road conditions. Although I expect our driver to shoot out the tires, he lets the car go.

'My God!' Dave screams, tearing around to the back of the car. Seeing the body, he lets out a screech which sounds like a pig being slaughtered. Then he looks up to see the taxi driver standing calmly with a handgun dangling from his right index finger. 'This can't be happening! This is unreal! What are we going to do? Our driver is a murderer! He could have killed Katey!. He's going to kill us all!'

Still trembling from my close encounter with a slit throat, I listen to Dave rant without saying a word. Both Vladimir and the driver also watch him silently. I'm glad the driver doesn't understand English.

Finally Vladimir speaks. 'Dave,' he says. Then louder, 'Dave! Calm down!'

'He'll shoot us, too. We're witnesses. He'll shoot us, take our money, and drive away!'

'Dave,' Vladimir says. 'Listen. Nobody is going to shoot anyone. At least twenty people saw us get into the car with him. And you are Americans. They aren't going to forget and the driver knows that.'

'He saved my life, Dave,' I say, trying not to think about how close his bullet had come to hitting me.

'But he killed someone!' Dave continues, almost shouting. 'This is absolutely unbelievable! Like some crazy movie or something!'

The driver, who has been standing silently, finally speaks, looking at Vladimir. 'Let's get him off the road,' he says as calmly as if he were discussing an old tire. 'And wear gloves.'

'What are you doing?' Dave asks, not having understood the driver's words. 'You can't just hide the body!' He grabs Vladimir's arm.

'Get in the car, Dave,' Vladimir says, jerking away. 'And take some deep breaths.'

Dave doesn't get in the car and we stand watching as they hoist the body over the snow bank, letting it sink into a soft drift. My fear has subsided and I feel like I really am watching a movie.

'Now, let's get out of here,' the driver says.

'I'm not sitting next to him,' Dave says, climbing into the back seat. Vladimir gets in the front and I slide in next to Dave.

'We have to go to the police, Katey,' Dave says as the car rattles along the road. 'We'll tell them it was self defense, but we have to go to them.'

'The driver saved my life, Dave,' I say again. 'That bastard was ready to slit my throat. Why should we make trouble for him?'

'Nobody is going to the police,' Vladimir says, turning around. 'And Katey,' he adds, 'it might be best if you don't include this little adventure in your trip report.'

As the car bumps along, I stare glassy-eyed at heavy snowflakes swarming against the windshield like white hornets. I don't know how the driver can see. Since Dave hasn't said a word in over an hour, I'm guessing he's either asleep or in shock. The car stops suddenly, jerking me awake. Looking ahead, I see lights and cars crowded together among the snow banks.

'We have to take the ferry,' the driver says, opening the car door. 'Wait here.'

He returns several minutes later and starts the engine. 'We can just catch the last ferry,' he says.

'The last ferry of the night?' I ask.

'The last ferry of the year', he says. 'They're closing tomorrow for the winter. We're very lucky.'

The driver turns the car around and backs too quickly down a slope toward the ferry ramp, crashing into a semi approaching from the other side. Oh no, I think, expecting a shouting match between the two drivers. We're going to miss the ferry.

But not wanting to miss the last ferry of the year, neither driver gets out of his vehicle. We simply pull forward, allowing the semi to board and then back slowly onto the ferry.

We cross the river in ten minutes. I don't know what river it is and don't bother to ask. I'm glad when we are again cruising at forty miles an hour on the snow-packed road. Although I don't know how, I must have slept, because suddenly we are parked near a high rise building.

'We're here, Katey,' Vladimir says. Then he whispers, 'Give me three-hundred dollars. That's the price we agreed on.'

I pull three hundred-dollar bills out of the pouch around my neck and hand them to Vladimir, knowing he will manufacture me a false receipt when we return to Moscow, probably for even more than three hundred and then suggest we split the difference. He reaches forward and gives the money to the driver before we get out of the car and enter a winter wonderland, illuminated by hotel lights. Snow banks climb six feet high around the small parking lot. Conversing quietly with Vladimir, the driver opens the trunk, hands us our three travel bags, and zooms away.

'He's going back to Yezhevsky tonight,' Vladimir says. 'They still have fog, so he's hoping to get more passengers. That three hundred was more than he earns in a month at his regular job. He'll have to take another route because there are no more ferries. He's taking sick time so he can work these couple of days. He probably paid off his doctor to fabricate some illness.'

We enter the hotel into an empty lobby, push a small bell on the unoccupied desk, and wait. Just when I think we'll have to sleep on the couches, a tired woman appears from a closed door behind the desk.

'These are the Americans,' Vladimir tells her. 'Savochenko made a reservation.'

'That was for yesterday,' she says. 'You never showed up.'

Vladimir quickly explains about the fog, the night in Yezhevsky, and the miserable taxi ride, emphasizing how tired we are.

'I cancelled the reservations,' she says.

I take another look at the couch.

'But we still have three rooms available,' she continues, 'although they're our most expensive. I have two executive suites and a honeymoon suite. Everything else is fully booked.' (I'm pretty sure they aren't.)

'How much are the rooms?' I ask.

'$250 each for the executive suites,' she replies, which is even more than I pay in Moscow. 'And the honeymoon suite costs $300.'

'They have a honeymoon suite,' I say to Dave. 'Can you imagine going on your honeymoon in Ufa?'

Although we all know she can't possibly be overbooked in this godforsaken town in December, we're in no position to argue. We all hand her American Express cards.

'Do you want to stay in the honeymoon suite with me?' I ask Vladimir once the woman is out of hearing range. 'It will save you $250.'

'I need my own room bill for my expense report,' he says.

'You can still stay in my room,' I say. 'I bet it's a wonderful bed, maybe shaped like a heart.'

'Katey, my love, we haven't had a decent night's sleep in two days. If I have to lie next to your naked body, it will be still another sleepless night.'

'I'll wear pajamas. Heavy flannel. It's cold. We're practically in fucking Siberia.'

'Not tonight, Katey,' he says. 'I'm just too tired.'

'I'm really hungry,' I say, giving up. 'Do you think it's possible to get food here this late?'

'There's a restaurant up the road called *Russky Medved*,' the woman suggests. 'I don't know if they're still serving at this hour.'

The name of the restaurant, Russian Bear, seems appropriate. I am so hungry I could eat one.

'You might also be able to find a kiosk open,' she adds. 'But it's really late.'

'Let's skip it, Katey,' Dave says. 'I don't want to venture out into the cold. Besides, I'm tired.'

'Let's just go to bed,' Vladimir says.

'Anyone got anything to munch on?' I ask.

'Nothing of nutritional value, Katey.'

Oh well. You can never be too rich or too thin. I say, 'I've got two jumbo cans of beer and the rest of the vodka I saved from the airport.'

'Beer is taxed as food in Bavaria,' Dave says.

'So, do you want some Bavarian food, Vladimir?'

'No, I'll let you two enjoy it.'

Dave and Vladimir both vote to give me the honeymoon suite. Dave follows me into a gaudy room with a lacy canopy bed covered with a red bedspread and a collection of lacy heart-shaped pillows. The curtains are white with little Cupids printed in shades of pink. It could have easily been called the Valentine suite. I am relieved not to find a heart-shaped toilet seat in the bathroom.

'This room belongs in a dollhouse,' Dave says. 'I can't believe it's real.'

I get a plastic cup from the bathroom and fill it half-full with vodka. Then I hand Dave the bottle and a can of beer. 'You want some melatonin?' I ask.

'No, I've heard that stuff can kill you,' Dave says. 'And you want to mix it with alcohol? I don't think I'll have any trouble sleeping.'

'I can never sleep when I'm really tired,' I say.

'That doesn't make any sense.'

'I think the pressure of knowing I have to fall asleep keeps me awake.'

'You sound like Harry,' Dave says.

'Harry?'

'In the film *When Harry Met Sally*. That's exactly the kind of thing he'd say.'

'Good night, Dave.'

I gulp the triple shot of vodka. I've gotten so used to this ritual I don't even flinch as warm spirits coat my mouth, throat, digestive tract and stomach. Combined with my hunger and lack of sleep, the alcohol takes immediate effect, making my head float away from my body. Then I swallow two melatonin tablets with a swig of beer. Melatonin is supposed to combat jetlag, but so far I've never found it effective. Maybe it will work tonight.

I get undressed and slip into a brown silk camisole with no panties, in the hope that Vladimir will decide to join me. Leaving my door unlocked, I turn off the lights and crawl under the heavy down comforter. I contemplate calling Vladimir, but then realize he didn't tell me his room number.

Listening to the tomblike stillness, I lie awake for what seems hours. Although the pills and alcohol make my head feel like a boulder, I'm unable to cross over into dreamland.

But then I am dreaming.

Vladimir is walking down the streets of Moscow, holding a little boy's hand. A thin woman in her thirties with thick blond hair, perfect tits, and ivory skin approaches him. Embracing her with his free hand, he kisses her lips. I'm standing several yards away watching them. When he looks up and sees me, Vladimir simply says, 'Katey, I'm busy.'

At least I know I'm asleep.

And since dreams are an indication of deep slumber, I wake up convinced that I've rested. Not ready to leave the warmth of my blanket, I'm still dozing when the door opens.

'You forgot to lock it,' Vladimir says, shutting the door behind him.

'I didn't forget,' I say.

'We have to wake Dave,' he says, sitting down on the bed and removing his clothes. When he crawls naked under the covers and kisses me, I can't help remembering the woman in my dream. Instead of succumbing to the pleasure of him inside of me, I keep wondering how many other lovers Vladimir must have in Moscow.

Twenty minutes later we knock on Dave's door. He opens it so quickly he must have been waiting for us. We go into the restaurant for a breakfast included in the room price. As soon as we sit down, a plump waitress brings out a tray with three glasses of juice, which turn out to be a sugary fruit drink. Then she brings three flat bowls of oatmeal with a pool of butter in the center of each.

Dave laughs. He says, 'Something as healthy as oatmeal and they load it up with butter.'

'And it's probably cooked in whole milk,' I tell him. 'Nobody counts calories in Siberia. And butter is much healthier than all that margarine and other processed shit the Americans eat.'

Dave starts to say something, but instead looks at his bowl and picks up a spoon.

Since we haven't eaten since yesterday at the airport, we devour the porridge and drink the juice like medicine.

The meal concludes with little cups of instant coffee. Although I could easily have used four, I don't ask for a refill.

'So what are our plans?' Dave asks.

'A car from Bashkirenergo will be picking us up at nine o'clock,' Vladimir says. 'I called Savochenko yesterday from Yezhevsky on my cell phone and told him we'd be a day late.'

At ten past nine, a minivan pulls into the parking lot. A man with a face like a raccoon gets out from the passenger side.

Vladimir shakes his hand like an old friend and turns to Dave, introducing the man as Igor Savochenko, Chief Engineer of Bashkirenergo. He then introduces Dave as the designer of the circuit breakers, and me, only as Katey.

'This is a lovely city, Igor Yakovlevich,' I say. 'Like a Christmas card.'

As we drive along dirty snow-covered roads, our host gives us an overview of the city, which I only partially translate for Dave. Ufa, the capital of the Russian Republic of Bashkortostan, has a population of slightly over one million. Founded in 1574 as a fortress and then becoming the town of Bashkiria in 1586, Ufa is now one of the industrial centers of the Urals.

Arriving at Bashkirenergo, we enter a conference room where a large table is set with coffee service, little chocolates, water bottles, and an overhead projector. I am surprised (and maybe even a little disappointed) that there is no vodka.

We chat for ten minutes, Vladimir recounting our experience in Yezhevsky, while leaving out the most negative details. I tell him I come from northern Michigan, which has a lot of snow like Ufa, and that I find it homey here.

'Maybe we could open a sales office here in Ufa,' I say smiling at Savochenko. 'I'd be happy to run it.'

'That's a wonderful idea, Katey,' Vladimir says. 'I'm sure they would treat you well here.'

'Let's see how much business I get,' I say. 'And speaking

of business—'

'Katey is a tough negotiator,' Vladimir says. 'Always wants to talk business.'

'We would like to replace forty 110-kilovolt oil and vacuum breakers with SF6 dead tank breakers,' Savochenko says.

'They'll probably need tank heaters,' Dave says after I translate.

'How cold does it get here?' I ask. 'Does it ever get colder than minus fifty?'

'No, it rarely drops below minus forty,' Savochenko says.

'At least we won't have to worry about heaters malfunctioning,' Dave says when I tell him.

Better to keep the design simple and the prices low, I think.

A knock on the door brings three men into the room. Savochenko introduces two of them as project engineers and the other as the chief service engineer.

I start with my marketing presentation, which I've given so often I am no longer nervous. I show color slides of each class of circuit breakers, giving an overview and listing the main features, while avoiding technical details—that's Dave's job—and leaving out the expensive options. Emphasizing the compactness, reliability, innovative technology, and simplicity of maintenance, I present our products with the savvy of a door-to-door vacuum cleaner salesman. Although the customers appear attentive, their eyes remain focused on my legs and derrière.

I'm dressed in a poppy-colored suit with a skirt to mid-thigh and a trendy short blazer over a matching knit silk shell. Even my shoes and lipstick are poppy. Several years ago a beautician said that with my coloring, I should wear poppy and teal to really make a statement. I don't look good in red or black, but I can sure wear poppy!

At the end of my talk, I wait for the most popular

question. It's inevitable.

'How much do they cost?'

'It depends on which one you're talking about,' I say.

'The 110 kV.'

'I can't give you a price without seeing your specifications. Then we have transport and installation costs,' I say.

'Can't you even give a rough estimate?' Savochenko asks.

Being the boss, he expects an answer. Remembering Vladimir's advice to leave room to negotiate, I jack up the price.

'With transport and installation, about $165,000,' I say, leaving room for at least a ten-percent discount. We've sold the same breakers to the Canadians for less than $90,000. Since Dave might not understand our business strategy, I'm glad Vladimir isn't translating my presentation.

I sit at the table beside Savochenko and let him pour me a cup of coffee. He offers me sugar, milk, and chocolate, all of which I refuse.

In Dave's presentation, he uses the same materials as in Tula. I'm relieved to have Vladimir as a translator, who also omits numerous details, either because he doesn't consider them relevant or doesn't understand all of Dave's speech either.

Dave talks for over an hour, during which time I develop a growing urge to pee. When he finally stops, I excuse myself, hoping no one will think the presentation has made me nauseous.

I find a door in the hall with a drawing of a woman in a skirt and the Russian letter ж which resembles a spider. There are no doors on the stalls and no toilet bowls, just holes in the floor designed like distorted funnels upon platforms resembling thrones. Placing my feet on the two metal planks, I squat like a female dog, hoping my thighs are strong enough to hold me above the commode. No matter how I aim my pee, it ricochets and sprays my inner thighs. Instead of toilet paper, there are squares of non-absorbent newspaper. I make a mental note to carry tissues with me in the future.

That evening we invite Savochenko to dinner in the hotel restaurant. I sit beside him on one side of the table, Vladimir and Dave opposite us. Vladimir orders a bottle of vodka and a bottle of French rosé. As he fills the shot glasses, I turn mine over.

'I think I'll stick to wine,' I say.

'A lady's drink,' Savochenko says, filling my glass. He says, 'I'd like to drink to a successful business partnership.'

'*Do dnya!*' Vladimir says, the Russian words for 'bottoms up'.

'You too, Katey,' Savochenko says, pointing at my full wine glass.

'The customer is always right, Katey,' Vladimir says in English.

I chug it down in three gulps. Since I haven't eaten anything, I start to feel giddy. Savochenko immediately refills my glass. So much for controlling my alcohol consumption by skipping the vodka!

An hour later both bottles are empty, our stomachs full with Chicken Kiev, and Savochenko and I, the best of friends. Vladimir takes a picture of us kissing. Although I'd rather be kissing Vladimir, this sacrifice seems small for a five-million dollar contract.

After ice cream and coffee, we part for the night, planning to take the morning flight back to Moscow. Savochenko's driver has been waiting the entire evening in the parking lot to bring him home.

After Savochenko leaves we get our keys from the front desk and take the stairs to our rooms. Planning to sneak back to Vladimir's room, I say goodnight to him in the stairwell and walk with Dave down the dimly lit hallway. He waits while I unlock my door, push it open, say goodnight, and enter the room.

I see a firefly floating in the darkness. *Oh my God, it's the tip of a cigarette! Somebody is in my room!*

TWENTY-NINE

As my eyes adjust to the darkness, I make out a shadowy figure seated at a room-service table. I switch on the light, revealing a man dressed like midnight in a black suit over a black T-shirt which also matches his hair. He has a deep scar on the left side of his face which looks like a knife wound. Although I wonder briefly if he put it there deliberately to make himself look scary, I somehow know the history is much more sinister. He is leaning back in the chair, long legs stretched under the table and crossed at the ankles. I notice he is wearing black shoes and black socks.

A stainless steel bowl of black caviar on ice, a basket of white bread, butter, and open bottles of champagne and vodka are arranged on the table. Without a word, he fills two glasses with champagne, picks one up, and hands it to me.

'I took the liberty of calling room service,' he says. 'I've heard you like caviar.'

Who the hell is this guy? And since when do we have room service here? Trying to hide my fright, I sip the champagne, my hand shaking so hard I almost spill it. I don't ask who he is or how he got in. I assume he made an agreement with the hotel manager and paid to enter my room.

'I also heard you're working on a five-million-dollar contract with Bashkirenergo.' He gives me a nod of approval. 'That's a lot of money.'

I don't say anything.

'And with a 30% profit margin, that's a big profit.'

'We don't have that high a profit,' I finally say.

'Don't lie to me, Katey,' he says. 'I have my informants.'

Nobody in Russia should have known the size of our profit margin. I haven't even told Vladimir. Yet, this guy knows. The thought that he must have an informant right inside my company in the United States sends a chill through my spine.

'I'll be direct,' he says, taking a gun out of the inside of his jacket and placing it on the table. 'We expect 10% of your profits. That's $150,000. We usually expect 20%, but since you're just getting started in Russia, we'll give you a break. We don't want to chase you away before you even really get here.' He takes a slice of bread and spreads it with butter. Then he spoons a thick helping of caviar on top and takes a large bite. 'Sit down, Katey. Have some caviar.'

I remember when I was a student in Russia in the 1980's. I felt as if I were on a movie set where nothing bad could happen to me. I used to ride the subway alone at all hours. I even got into strange cars late at night, paying the drivers to take me back to my dormitory. In retrospect, I could have been raped, robbed or murdered, but as an arrogant American, I was sure I'd always be safe.

Ten years later, although I still feel like I'm on a movie set, I now know this fashion model could easily put a bullet through my head, finish his caviar, smoke a cigarette, and waltz out of the room as casually as if he'd just taken a long relaxing shit. He'd go home to his family—he probably has a gorgeous young wife and adorable little girls in pink dresses and pony tails with faces like china dolls—and say grace before eating supper.

In a hopeless attempt at defiance, I say, 'You don't know as much about me as you think you do. You got it wrong. I don't eat white bread.'

The man simply chuckles. 'No, I got it right. The white bread is symbolic. You love caviar and you can have all you want, but you have to eat it with our white bread.'

It isn't hard to decipher the symbolism. Not knowing what else to do, I sit down at the table and spread butter on a slice of bread. Then I top it with a large spoonful of caviar.

'The money will be due in full as soon as the contract is paid. You'll be given the number of a Swiss bank account.'

By the time my guest leaves, it is after midnight. Although I want to run to Vladimir, I am afraid to leave my room and lie stiffly in bed, unable to fall asleep. By morning, I'm feeling calmer and decide not to tell Vladimir the news until we return to Moscow. I don't want Dave to get wind of it.

'If I don't produce a hundred and fifty grand, my brains will become modern art on the walls of the Moscow Subway.' We're sitting in Vladimir's office drinking strong coffee. Evgenii has taken Dave souvenir shopping.

'I've seen worse modern art.'

'I'm serious, Vladimir. There's no way in hell Jack will let me pay them off. If he and Anis find out I've even been talking to the mafia, they'll pull me out of Russia so fast I won't even have time to blow you a good-bye kiss.'

'It's so difficult to work with the Americans,' he says with feigned contempt. 'I never should have bothered with you.'

'It's not my fault,' I protest.

'I don't think you're really an American,' he says.

'Should I show you my passport?'

'But in your soul, you're a Russian,' he says. 'You think

like us, you drink like us, you understand our jokes…' He pauses for a few moments and then adds, 'There's only one solution to this problem.'

'What's that?'

'Switzerland.'

'You want me to move to Switzerland?'

'Yes, it's much easier to work with the Swiss. You'd fit right in.'

'How do you plan to get me there?'

'Actually, they're looking for someone. They're trying to get a twenty-million-dollar contract to build several substations for Mosenergo. They need a project manager.'

'What makes you think they'll want me?'

'They've heard about you. And I've also recommended you. They want you to come and work for them.'

'You mean to say you've already been planning this without even asking me?'

'I'm asking you now.'

'But they've never even met me.'

'They trust my judgment.'

'But I can't speak German, and certainly not Swiss German.'

'You don't have to. The official language of the company there is English. The marketing manager is from Australia. You'll like him. His name's Conrad Lambeer.'

'What about the contract with Ufa? What's going to happen to that?'

'It's very simple. The Americans make a contract with the Swiss and the Swiss make a contract with Ufa. You'll be acting as a middleman.'

'And what about the $150,000?'

'That's simple, too. The Swiss will simply add an extra $150,000 to the contract price.'

'So Ufa will actually be paying the mafia?'

'Indirectly, yes. But it will look like you are paying them.'

'But if we raise the contract price, we'll have to pay even

more to the mafia.'

'Another ten thousand." Vladimir shrugs and then continues, "Okay, so we raise the contract price by 160 thousand or so. Ufa can pay that too. And it's no big deal anyways. I think it's even tax deductible in Switzerland.'

'So Ufa pays the mafia and the Swiss deduct it from their taxes.'

'Yeah. The Swiss are cool.'

'Anis will never agree,' I say. 'He won't share his profits with the Swiss.'

'He'll agree to it.'

'How can you be sure?'

'Because after you're in Switzerland, I'll tell him about your midnight visitor. Then he'll be happy to let the Swiss do his dirty work.'

'Then he probably won't want to do business with the Russians or the Swiss.'

'Yes, he will. He's much too greedy to turn down a five-million-dollar contract.'

'Switzerland,' I say. 'Why the hell not?'

Zurich, Switzerland
February, 1997 – February, 1998

THIRTY

Switzerland—The land of precision, order and punctuality. If a train is late in Switzerland, it's either not a Swiss train or not a Swiss clock. Switzerland—the country every American dreams of until they actually try living there.

Zurich—the city of watches, chocolate and secret bank accounts. Zurich—one of the top five most expensive cities in the world. Almost every store on its famous *Bahnhof Strasse*, the city's main boulevard, has Rolexes in the windows or designer clothing such as Bally, Chanel, Armani and Versace with neckties costing over two-hundred dollars. Tired looking pedestrians, dressed like royalty and speaking Swiss German, don't return your smile as they pass. Zurich—considered by many to have the highest quality of life in the world—definitely has the most banks.

What's the difference between Arlington Cemetery and the *Bahnhof Strasse* in Zurich? Arlington sees more action.

Conrad Lambeer, a native Australian and my new boss, is so anxious to get the twenty-million-dollar contract with Mosenergo that he offers me a job without even meeting me. When I spring the news on Jack and Anis, they threaten to call Lambeer and block the transfer, arguing that Lambeer had violated company policy by *stealing me away* without getting Jack's permission. Jack gets over it though, and his parting question to me is 'Who's going to play the elf at our next Christmas party?'

"I'll miss you, Jack."

He smiles.

In any case, I'm flying business class to Switzerland, feeling like a movie star amid fat-cat businessmen with their martini's and Wall Street Journals. I'm dressed in jeans, reading a chick-lit novel, and drinking champagne. Sometimes I think my life is a chick-lit novel.

My flight stops over in Zurich for two days so that I can meet Lambeer and learn about the project for Mosenergo. Then I'll be flying on to Moscow to meet our new customers. Vladimir has promised to introduce me to the president of Mosenergo, who just happens to be his long-time friend. Then if we can convince him to sign a contract with us, I will become the manager of a twenty-million-dollar project. According to Vladimir, the president has already decided in our favor.

Arriving at the Zurich airport, I marvel at its glamorous design and neat appearance. But since at seven a.m., I am tired from the flight and want nothing more than a hot shower, I take a taxi to the Swissôtel in Oerlikon where Lambeer has reserved me a room. Since he is picking me up in the lobby at nine o'clock, I'll just have time to shower, change into a suit, and grab a cup of coffee.

It takes less than ten minutes to reach Oerlikon. When I give my name at the hotel desk, a woman with thick dark hair and heavy eye makeup hands me a key, explaining in excellent English that Ampere Power–Switzerland is paying my bill. I ask for coffee to be sent to my room.

My tenth-floor room has a European double bed—two

mattresses placed side by side in a single frame, much lower to the floor than an American bed. Each side is covered with a folded comforter and a large feather pillow. I collapse onto the bed and lay back on the pillow. Although I am dead tired, I've never managed to sleep during the day and don't have time anyway. Whenever I've been up all night partying, typing a term paper, or flying across the continents, I spend the next day like a space cadet, watching television, drinking, and waiting for darkness.

My coffee arrives in five minutes. The Swiss really are punctual. Not having any Swiss francs, I tip the young bellboy five dollars, too much for coffee, but everything is more expensive in Switzerland. Maybe it isn't even enough.

At five minutes to nine I'm standing in the lobby still exhausted from the flight and strung out from the coffee. Even with my carefully applied make-up, I'm convinced I look like a walking corpse. My taupe suit, which the sales girl said would accentuate my face, only adds to my drabness.

'Ms. O'Hara?'

Hearing my name, I turn to face an attractive man of average build with curly black hair and a mustache.

'Conrad Lambeer,' he says, extending his hand. 'Did you have a nice flight?'

His Australian accent is so heavy that I have trouble understanding him.

'Yes,' I say after a few seconds hesitation. 'Very comfortable.'

'It's a five-minute walk to the office. Did you get some breakfast?'

'I had coffee. It was enough.'

When we get outside, I'm not surprised by the dismally cold weather, the sky heavy with gray clouds. While studying Swiss German with a set of language tapes, one of the first phrases I learned was *S'Wahter ist schlacht!*, meaning *the weather is bad.* Apparently the Swiss love to bitch about the weather, and if today is any indication, they do so with good reason.

As we walk through the railroad underpass, Lambeer says, 'This is the Oerlikon train station. It's less than ten minutes to downtown Zurich. Do you plan to buy a car?'

'No, I don't think I'll need one,' I say, not adding my terror of driving in a foreign country.

'This is the kiosk,' he says, pointing to a small glass-walled structure. 'It's the only store open from Saturday afternoon until Monday morning. It's expensive—well everything's expensive here—but at least you won't starve if you forget to buy groceries.'

We approach a fenced-in compound, guarded by a gatekeeper in a booth, who checks Lambeer's ID and makes me fill out a guest pass. When we get inside, I notice a monstrous barn-shaped building to the right, which must be the factory, and a drab flat structure to the left, which must be the offices.

'We'll be moving to a new modern building in September,' he says as we approach the offices. 'It will even have air conditioning,' he adds as if this is a novelty.

'Does it ever get hot here?' I ask, shivering. Hoping to impress him, I say 'I've read that *S'Wahter ist schlacht*.'

'I see you've been practicing your Swiss German,' he says, chuckling. '*The weather is bad*. Unfortunately, you'll really be able to use that expression here.'

'I don't really think it's possible to master Swiss German unless you're born here,' I say. 'But I tried to learn a few phrases.'

'*Grüezi*,' he says. 'That's the only Swiss German word I ever use. It means hello, good morning, good afternoon and good evening. In other words, you can always use it. Just don't try to say kitchen cupboard'

'How do you say it?'

'*Khukhikaeskhtli*,' he says, making the *kh* sounds particularly guttural.

'It sounds like a bulldog choking on a chicken bone,' I say. 'How on earth did you learn it?'

'With a great deal of practice. When I butcher it, it always gets a few laughs.'

Soon we arrive at Lambeer's office, a spacious room with a luxuriant desk, complete with a designer pen and inkwell. Sitting in a plush chair behind the desk, he motions to an empty seat in front of it, grabs the receiver of a simple-looking phone, and punches two numbers.

'Adriana,' he says. 'Could you bring coffee for two?' Then he looks at me. 'You did want coffee?'

'Yes, please.'

'So what do you know about the Mosenergo project?' he asks.

'I know it is for two gas insulated substations, costs nearly twenty-million dollars and that we are competing with several Russian companies for the contract, companies which offer inferior quality but at a much lower price. Vladimir thinks we have the project in the bag—he has a good relationship with the company president. Mosenergo has plenty of money and they don't want to sacrifice quality for something this important.'

'You've heard correctly,' he says. 'Vladimir told me we needed to get a project manager over to Moscow right away to handle the negotiations. He knows which people you need to speak with.'

'What about slush money?' I ask.

'I've included an extra 1.5 million in the cost estimate.'

'What's your profit margin? There's a good chance the mafia will want 20% of our profits.'

'Our real profit is 30%, but I've added some phantom costs to make the margin look like 20% on paper.'

'So we pay the mafia $800,000,' I say, after doing a mental calculation. 'That leaves another $700,000 for the Mosenergo team. This is really the big leagues.'

'Do you think you're up to the challenge?' he asks.

'Just call me J.R. Ewing.'

Two days later I'm in Moscow, seated in front of Vladimir's desk.

'We lost the project,' he says. He doesn't sound surprised or even seem to care.

'What? How could we lose the project? I've got 1.5 million in slush money to pay out.'

'You have to understand. The Russian economy isn't doing too well and there was a lot of political pressure to give the contract to a Russian company. You can't bribe the government.'

'I thought everyone had a price,' I say, really feeling like J.R. Ewing.

'You learn fast, Katey. But this time the pressure was just too great.'

'But what am I supposed to do now? The only reason Lambeer hired me was because of this project.'

'Be happy. You're in Switzerland. I got you what you wanted.'

Suddenly it dawns on me. 'You knew.'

'Lambeer has been talking to me about hiring you since last summer. I knew he would never get his ass in gear unless I put some pressure on him. So I told him if he wanted this contract, he better get himself a Russian-speaking project manager, preferably a pretty one.'

'But you already knew the contract was lost.'

'I suspected.' He shrugs. 'Yes, I knew.'

'And now what?'

'Tomorrow we're flying to Ufa. You've got a good chance at the dead tank breaker contract. Bashkirenergo has plenty of money and they're not concerned with politics.'

At that moment Vladimir's phone rings. Picking up the receiver, he says in a deep voice, 'Kashirnikov.'

I use this interruption to sneak into the bathroom. I'm wearing thigh high stockings under a sleeveless silk dress, with a matching jacket and high-heeled boots. On impulse, I remove my skimpy silk panties and stuff them into my purse. Vladimir is just hanging up the phone as I return to his office.

'I have one more phone call to make,' he says, punching in a number.

Sitting back in my chair, I hike the skirt of my dress up above the tops of my stockings. When I see Vladimir staring at me, I quickly pull the skirt up to my hips and cross and uncross my legs, revealing my secret. Just like Sharon Stone did for Michael Douglas in *Basic Instinct*.

Surprise scurries across his face, then he smiles and hangs up the phone. 'No answer,' he says, still staring at my crotch.

I slide my skirt back down just as Olga barges into the room. 'I need your signature on these expense reports,' she says, placing several papers on his desk.

He signs them hurriedly and hands them back to her, his eyes focusing on my crotch. Once she is gone, he gestures for me to spread my legs, and as I comply, my skirt rises again.

'Lovely,' he says, staring under my taut skirt. Then he stands up and says, 'Let's go to lunch.' He doesn't usually invite me to lunch.

In the privacy of the elevator, he pulls me to him, kissing first my nose and then my lips. As his tongue explores my mouth, his hand reaches under my dress and finds my little secret, giving me a mini-orgasm before we reach the ground floor. Fortunately, nobody else gets on the elevator.

Once outside, Vladimir takes my arm, holding me protectively close to him as we walk through the slushy snow.

An attractive man passes us, staring into my eyes.

'He knows,' Vladimir says.

'How does he know?' I ask coquettishly.

'By the expression on your face. You look sexually excited.'

'The cold wind blowing under my skirt is quite stimulating,' I say, huddling closer.

We enter a café with bar stools and a counter, Vladimir pulling his stool close to mine, letting our knees touch.

'Everybody knows,' he says, teasing me.

'How do they know?' I ask.

'Men are like dogs,' he says. Then he asks, 'Are you going to keep your panties off all day?'

'Do you want me to?'

'I won't be able to get any work done.'

Back at the office, Vladimir keeps finding excuses to keep me near him. When I'm out among the others, conversing with Sasha, he calls me back into his office.

'You can't just walk around with a bare pussy,' he says.

'Why not? Nobody knows but you.' I feel like he is under my power. It may not get him to marry me, but I am enjoying the moment.

'Sit down.'

I spend most of the afternoon in Vladimir's office, watching him read through contracts and listening to his phone conversations. Every time I go out to the main office to chat with Sasha or Evgenii, or even just to go to the bathroom, he comes looking for me with some excuse or another to summon me back to my chair. After six o'clock, when the last of his employees have gone home, he drives me to my hotel where we make love for the first time in months, just as passionately as the first time I met him.

I fall asleep that night feeling sexy, loved, and excited about the trip to Ufa. Maybe Vladimir is falling in love with me. Maybe he just can't resist me sexually. I wonder if he knows the difference.

THIRTY-ONE

I have a wake-up call and a room-service order for coffee at seven-thirty the next morning. Dressing quickly in skintight spandex shorts and a tight-fitting tank top, both in shades of navy and turquoise, I take the elevator to the ground floor and waltz across the lobby in my running shoes to a staircase in the front corner of the hotel leading to a fitness room and sauna.

American music blares in a room containing two treadmills, steppers, and weight machines, all of exceptional western quality. I start one of the treadmills and raise the speed to six miles an hour. I keep raising the speed at two-minute intervals until I am sprinting at ten miles an hour. Just as my heart seems to be beating out of my chest and my leg muscles are screaming for relief, I decelerate and allow my pulse to return to normal, sweat dripping from all parts of my body.

Back in my room, I take a cold shower, water gushing with the intensity of a fire hose. After rubbing my skin pink with a towel and blotting my hair, I pull on thigh-high stockings and step into high heels. Without dressing further,

I style my now-golden blond hair with a blow-dryer and round brush, turning the ends under and fluffing my bangs. After the fiasco haircut I had a year before, I am pleased with the results of the expensive Swiss beauty salon.

I put on the gold earrings which I bought before leaving for Switzerland and apply Chanel make-up—shades of brown eye shadow, coral rouge, matching lipstick, and loose translucent powder. Then I dab Opium from Yves Saint Laurent onto my neck, breasts, and the inside of my upper thighs. I leave the door unlocked.

Ten minutes later Vladimir barges into my room without knocking, dressed in a light grey Armani suit, accentuated by a necktie resembling a Picasso painting from the Blue Period. I can tell by his smile that he is pleased to find me naked.

'I'll be ready in just a minute,' I say, going to the closet to get my suit.

'We've got time,' Vladimir says, removing his blazer. 'Plenty of time.'

'I thought you were always in such a hurry in Russia,' I say, wondering if he knows I am teasing him. I take a sleeveless silk top from a hanger and start to dress.

Before I can get the top over my head, Vladimir is taking it out of my hands and kissing me deeply, pressing the bulge of his erect penis against my stomach, his hands caressing my butt and sliding between my legs.

Make him beg for it. Although wanting desperately to let my body melt into his, I pull away.

'Do you have a plan for this Ufa contract?' I ask. 'We haven't really talked about it.'

'Later,' Vladimir says, moving closer.

'Large sums of money make me really hot,' I continue.

'You make me hot,' Vladimir says. 'And when I'm horny, I'm a great negotiator.'

'Then I'll have to keep you horny for a while,' I say, grabbing my shirt from his hand.

'Are you going to wear panties today?' he asks.

'Should I?'

'As far as I'm concerned, you can throw them all away,' he says. 'I like you much better without them.'

'I'll just put on this little bitty thing,' I say, holding up a skimpy lace thong.

'I'll have to get my scissors to keep you from wearing it.'

'Are you crazy? It cost me twenty bucks.'

Vladimir and I arrive in Ufa with a prepared contract exceeding five million dollars. Conrad Lambeer and I redid my initial cost estimate to include mafia money, bribes, perks and gifts. Since we obviously couldn't list these expenses in the estimate, we simply increased the number of labor hours by twenty-five percent and the material costs by thirty percent, giving us the sum we needed. Since the mafia already knows about the thirty percent profit margin, we didn't make any effort to disguise it. Any mole they might have in Switzerland with access to our computers will find nothing suspicious in our data.

'We've gotten offers from Ernst Werner AG and International Electric. Representatives from both countries are here today,' Savochenko says after completing the initial small talk. 'Your bid is the most expensive.'

'We've also got the best quality,' I say. 'I can arrange for you and your top engineers to visit our plant and see for yourselves. At our expense, of course.' *At your expense, of course. It's hidden in the contract.*

'And why is the contract coming from Switzerland?' he asks.

'Ampere Power is an international company,' Vladimir says. 'Everybody works for the same pot. When Katey got transferred to Zurich, she continued with the contract negotiations. It's her project, and we wouldn't want anyone else here.'

'Convincing our general manager to pay your prices will be difficult,' Savochenko says.

'Let me talk to him,' I say. 'I'm very persuasive.' I don't mention that I'm planning to offer him a $50,000 incentive. Since Savochenko already seems to be on our side, I'm assuming that Vladimir has also offered him something.

'We're all meeting in the conference room for the presentations,' Savochenko says. 'I know you already gave yours, Katey, but some people missed it.'

The big table in the conference room is almost full when we arrive. I shake hands with the sales engineer from Ernst Werner AG, a skinny Russian kid in his twenties with silver rimmed glasses and acne scars. I don't think I'll have to worry about him.

The sales manager from International Electric is a paunchy, balding American in his forties who can't speak a word of Russian. He's dressed in a cheap suit, probably from Sears, and a polyester tie with diagonal stripes in pink and burgundy. We shake hands like two fighters before a boxing match, smiling politely, but coldly.

The International Electric representative gives the first presentation. Although his overheads are in Russian, they are filled with laughable mistakes, probably translated by an American with limited language training and no engineering knowledge. His interpreter, a plump Russian woman with henna hair and orange lipstick, struggles with the technical terms. The American speaks much too fast, leaving her several paragraphs behind.

Next, the Ernst Werner AG representative mumbles through a dry-and-detailed presentation, listing all the equipment's technical data and practically putting his audience to sleep.

In comparison to my predecessors, my performance is like a cabaret. Dressed in a dark teal suit with a short pleated skirt and trendy jacket, I prance around on high heels like a show girl, a song I sang in the seventh grade girls' chorus popping into my head.

I'm a girl and by me that's only great
I am proud that my silhouette is curvy.
That I walk with a sweet and girlish gait
With my hips kind of swively and swervy.

I begin by describing our plant, showing vibrant color pictures of smiling workers and shiny circuit breakers. Avoiding boring technical details, I concentrate on the quality and compactness of the product. Lastly, I mention that a plant visit to inspect the equipment is offered free of charge to a three-man delegation.

Knowing the American won't have the balls to offer a bribe, especially since he would need his translator, and knowing that the young Russian has neither the authority nor the credibility to offer one, I am convinced the contract will be mine.

Lunch is served in a cozy room with a long table lavishly set with appetizers, vodka, and beer. Curious to learn more about the American, I sit down next to him. He seems pleased by the chance to speak English.

'Your first trip to Ufa?' I ask.

'Actually, yes,' he says. 'We're just getting started in Russia.'

'It's a tough market,' I say, hoping to discourage him. 'Nobody has any money and a lot of businesses have been scared away by corruption and the mafia.'

'Do you have problems with the mafia?' he asks, suddenly sounding concerned.

I did until I transferred to Switzerland. The mafia is threatening me and it's illegal to pay out bribes or protection money in the United States. I didn't want to get shot by the mafia, so I went to Switzerland. The Swiss are a lot more relaxed about these things. But it's still illegal in Russia. According to their penal code, you can be sent to Siberia for up to seven years or even be shot in the back of the head if the amount of the bribe is high enough.

I imagine him jumping on the next plane back to Atlanta.

But of course, I simply say, 'I've got it under control.'

'Do you pay them?' he asks.

'Do you?' I reply.

'Touché,' he says. He pours two shots of vodka and hands me one. We clink our glasses together and drink it down. I chase mine with a swig of beer.

The first entrée is *shchi*, a soup made with cabbage and chunks of beef, topped off with a dollop of sour cream. Preferring to sip a beer, I simply watch while the others slurp their soup.

I pour us another shot of vodka. 'You can't do business in Russia if you don't drink vodka,' I say.

His face is already flushed, ears like a stove unit set at high. But he accepts the glass and makes a toast. 'To fair competition,' he says.

'May the best man win,' I say.

'You mean the best man or woman,' he says.

'I've always hated being politically correct,' I say. 'Besides, I'm man enough to work in Russia.'

'I'll drink to that,' he says, emptying his shot glass.

Having eaten only a few hors d'oeuvres to absorb the alcohol, I'm starting to feel giddy. I notice Vladimir on the other side of the table, absorbed in conversation with Savochenko.

The main course is beef stroganoff with noodles. Although I accept a plate, I only pick at the chunks of meat and mushrooms.

The clinking of knives and forks on the plates dominates the room for the next five minutes. Then Savochenko pours himself a shot of vodka and rises.

'I'd like to drink a welcome toast to our guests,' he says in Russian. He waits while everyone fills their glasses.

'Katey O'Hara from Ampere Power-Switzerland, Barry Watters from International Electric in America, and Yuri Ivanov from Moscow, representing Ernst Werner AG.' He gestures with his glass at each person as he says their name.

After the meal Vladimir and I return to Savochenko's office where he offers us coffee and cognac. I accept both, alternating sips.

'It was a very nice performance, Katey,' Savochenko says. 'But unfortunately, one that didn't eliminate the problem of your higher prices.'

I want to say that those higher prices include mafia money and bribes, his own as well, which neither of my competitors has considered in his price. If Barry gets the contract, he'll also get a midnight visit like I did, one that will send him running like a scared jackrabbit. And Ernst Werner AG isn't taking the job seriously. Otherwise they would have sent a more experienced and charismatic negotiator rather than a Russian kid with a technical degree.

'Can I meet the general director now,' I ask.

'Let me call,' Savochenko says. He picks up the phone and punches three keys. 'Vasilii Ivanovich,' he says. 'I have an American lady here from Ampere Power who would like to speak with you. In ten minutes? Great.' He hangs up the phone.

'He'll be happy to meet with you,' he says.

A knock interrupts us. I recognize the face as one of the engineers at the presentation.

'Excuse me a moment,' Savochenko says, rising and leaving the office.

'What should I say to the general manager?' I ask Vladimir. 'Should I offer him $50,000 for the contract?'

He pauses before saying. 'Yeah, go ahead.' Perhaps if I hadn't drunk so much vodka and wasn't so hot for this contract, I would have noticed the hesitancy in his voice and expression. Instead, I take him at his word.

Ten minutes later I'm seated across from the general manager in his office, his round face reminding me of a lion.

'What can I do for you, Miss O'Hara?' he asks.

Leaning back, I cross my legs, letting my skirt sneak up to mid-thigh and trying to appear cool. 'I have a proposition for you,' I say. Then much too quickly I continue. 'If we get this contract, you get fifty-thousand dollars in cash.'

As soon as the words escape my mouth, I realize my mistake. He looks as if I've just told him I shot his wife. The five-second silence seems like an hour and my J.R. Ewing confidence starts to slip away.

'Igor Yakovovich is handling the contract negotiations,' he finally says in a voice as cold as an iceberg. 'You need to discuss the details with him.'

Not sure if he has accepted my bribe or refused it, I stare blankly. Then I simply say the only thing I can, 'Well, I just wanted to say hello.'

'Thank you for stopping by,' he says as if the previous conversation didn't take place. 'And I hope you enjoy your stay in Ufa.'

'I think we made a mistake,' I tell Vladimir as soon as I catch him alone.

'What happened?' he asks.

'I offered him fifty-thousand, just like we talked about.'

'You mean you just outright offered it?'

'Isn't that what you wanted me to do?' Suddenly I'm feeling sober.

'I expected you to be more subtle, Katey. Give him a nice smile, show him your legs—'

'I did that.'

'Invite him to America—'

'You didn't tell me to do that.'

'So how did he react?' Vladimir asks, looking like he's dreading the answer.

'As if I'd just drawn a weapon.'

'In a way, that's exactly what you did. He has a very high position and definitely wasn't expecting a pretty young American lady to come into his office and act like a mobster.' Then Vladimir chuckles. 'I wish I had seen his face.'

'Should I offer something to Savochenko?'

'Do you enjoy playing Santa Claus?' Vladimir asks. 'I've known Savochenko for a long time. He expects one percent of the contract price. Don't worry about him.'

'What do we do now?' I ask.

'Don't worry, be happy,' he says in a singsong voice.

'I hate that song,' I say.

Vladimir, Savochenko, and I climb into a minivan, complete with a chauffeur, who I assume is taking us back to the hotel. Instead, we drive only a short distance, stopping in front of a rustic building that needs a paint job. We enter a small room where four men, whom I recognize from the morning presentations, are already seated around a table, laden with vodka and simple hors d'eourves: marinated vegetables, sliced cheese, salami, fish conserves in oval tins, and dark Russian bread. The raspy voice of the Russian bard Vladimir Vysotsky growls out a drinking song from a CD player.

'Have you ever been to a genuine Russian *banya*?' Savochenko asks.

'I can't say I have,' I answer, realizing where we are. I notice a glass door behind the table, clouded with steam.

'Did he invite International Electric and Ernst Werner AG as well?' I ask Vladimir in English.

'Nope, we're the guests of honor,' he says.

Still worried about my performance with the general manager, I drown my fears in several shots of vodka. Since someone is always waiting with a tilted bottle to refill my jigger, before long I'm feeling like the Godfather of high voltage switchgear.

Turning to the man on my left, I say much too loudly, 'If you help me get this contract, I'll pay you five-thousand dollars.' As I'm turning to Savochenko on my right, ready to raise his bonus to two percent, my eyes catch Vladimir's and I see him shaking his head. Obviously he heard my first offer, meaning everyone else in the room probably did too. Suddenly I feel an urgent need to divert their attention.

Standing up and removing my jacket, I say, 'Time to go into the *banya*,' and drink another shot, before unlacing my boots, stepping out of my skirt and slipping off my silk top. As I'm unhooking my garter belt, Vladimir's eyes meet mine and I notice he is not smiling.

Standing there in nothing but a lacy-blue push-up bra— I don't usually wear them, but this one actually gives me cleavage—and a matching thong, I drink the vodka refill which has magically appeared in my glass. 'Who's coming with me?' I ask.

The man to whom I offered the five grand rises. Although stocky, he has a clean-cut appearance and a friendly face. I notice that his left hand is missing several fingers.

'Valery Antonovich is Bashkirenergo's most sought-after bachelor,' Savochenko says.

'Maybe Katey can marry him and live in Ufa,' Vladimir says, with a trace of sarcasm that only I detect.

Valery Antonovich, who has also been slugging the vodka, removes all his clothing and drapes everything carefully over a chair. Completely naked, he heads into the sauna. 'Are you coming?' he asks, turning around. I notice he has a hard-on.

Trying to follow him, I lose my balance and grab a chair for support. The chair tips backwards and I fall on my ass, the chair landing on my stomach. Savochenko helps me up.

Then he opens a cupboard and pulls out two fluffy

white towels. Tossing one to the naked man, he says, 'Cover yourself, Valera. You're among ladies.'

'Where? I don't see any,' Vladimir says in English.

'Fuck you,' I answer back, too drunk to care if anyone understands.

The *banya* contains a five-foot deep pool of clear water with a tint of rust. A wood-paneled alcove houses two levels of benches encircling a pile of hot rocks, heated by an electrical unit. A bucket of water with a ladle stands beside the rocks, and leafy tree branches resembling fans are scattered on the floor, reminding me of Biblical paintings of Palm Sunday.

With the towel wrapped securely around his waist, Valery enters the alcove. He picks up the ladle and scoops water onto the rocks, causing a cloud of sizzling steam to fill the tiny space. Then he leans back on a bench and closes his eyes, seeming to have forgotten about me.

Not wanting to be too close to this naked stranger, I sit across from him, wondering if I can sweat the alcohol out of my system. Before long I'm roasting like a pig on a skewer.

Picking up a tree branch, I ask, 'What are these for?'

'Those are birch branches,' he says, sitting up and staring at me. 'You use them to open up your pores.'

'What do we do?' I ask. 'Beat each other with them?'

'Exactly,' he says. 'Want to try it?'

Letting the vodka speak for me, I say, 'Yeah, sure. Why the hell not? When in Rome…'

'Lie on your stomach.'

I stretch out on the bench, expecting the branch to come lashing down like a buggy whip. Instead he taps my back like a Priest dispensing holy water, producing a pleasant sting.

'It looks like Katey is really getting into it.'

Recognizing Vladimir's bass voice, I jump from the bench and cover myself with the towel. He is standing there with Savochenko, both with towels around their waists, as if awaiting their turns.

Not knowing what else to do, I plunge headfirst into the pool and icy water attacks my body like a thousand knives. Surfacing, I see the three men seated on the sauna benches, Valery leaning over to add more water to the hot stones.

I cover myself with my towel, fastening it around my armpits, and return to the room where the other four men are sitting, still completely dressed. One of them has already filled my jigger with vodka.

After drinking it, I'm suddenly as hungry as a bear in springtime. Grabbing a fork, I spear a marinated mushroom and pick up a slice of bread which I cover with cheese and salami. After eating that, I grab a fish tin and shovel the entire contents into my mouth. Shortly later, the urge hits me.

'I need to go to the little girl's room.' I slur my words as I stand up and grab the table.

'It's down the hall to your right,' says one of the men.

Dressed only in my towel and underclothes, I locate the bathroom, which smells fouler than the worst outhouse I ever encountered in northern Michigan campgrounds. There is no toilet paper whatsoever, not even newspaper. Trying to position my feet on the platform, I tumble onto my butt like a baby learning to walk.

When I return, Vladimir, Savochenko and Valery have not yet reappeared from the *banya*. The other three men are busy imbibing and stuffing themselves with food. Two empty vodka bottles are flanked by two full ones. In line with the Russian tradition not to leave the table until all bottles are empty, I assume they intend to drink it all.

A shimmer of sobriety convinces me to get dressed. Too wasted to get the stockings on without tearing them, I wad them up with my garter belt and bra and stuff the bundle into my briefcase. I pull on the skirt and slip the silk shell over my head without tucking it in and pop my bare feet into the boots.

But the fleeting sobriety vanishes like a cat in headlights, and soon I'm downing another shot of vodka. Shortly the others return from the *banya*, and at some point in the evening, I remove all my clothes again and head back towards the pool with nothing but a towel which I'm holding loosely against my chest. This time Vladimir follows me. I vaguely hear him telling the others he wants to make sure I don't hurt myself or drown.

'Are we going to fuck?' I ask as we sit down on the bench.

'Katey, you are so shit-faced, I'd be surprised if you still remember your name.'

'So, are we?' I repeat.

'My only concern is to get you back to the hotel. There is a meeting tomorrow at nine a.m. and if you want this contract, you better be ready to negotiate.'

'Can't you negotiate for me?' I ask.

'I'm taking the first plane back to Moscow. I've got a meeting of my own.' He stands up and walks out of the banya. Apparently he no longer cares if I drown.

Trying to become sober, I jump into the pool and emerge as a shivering drunk.

When I return to the room, wrapped only in a towel, the men are still seated around the table. As I rejoin them, Savochenko refills the glasses with vodka.

'I'd like to make a toast,' I say, standing and letting the towel fall as I pick up my vodka. I almost lose my balance as the floor seems to move beneath my feet. Completely naked, I say 'To Vladimir Kashirnikov, the only man I've ever loved. One way or another, he is going to marry me.' I catch a glimpse of Vladimir's horrified expression before blacking out.

THIRTY-TWO

Without knowing how I got there I'm back at the hotel, bare-legged and barefoot, pounding on Vladimir's door.

When he doesn't answer, I bang harder, using the side of my fist and making such a racket that the neighboring door opens to reveal a plump woman with baggy cheeks and a flowered bathrobe.

'Can't you tell he's not at home?' she says.

Still plenty drunk and pissed off that Vladimir won't open the door, I scream in English. 'Go fuck a two-headed wolverine with herpes, you Communist bitch!'

Withering under my rage, she disappears back into the room and closes the door.

After giving the wood several more whacks, I give up and return to my room. Either he isn't home or doesn't want to see me; I suspect the latter. In any case, I'm determined to reach him, so I call his room. After the tenth ring, someone picks up the phone and hangs it up again without saying a word. Repeating the phone call, I get a busy signal.

Although I don't remember sleeping, my bed is rumpled and the clock reads four a.m. No wonder the woman was bitching and Vladimir didn't want to be bothered. I must have returned to my room from the *banya*, fallen asleep fully clothed on the bed, woken up several hours later, and wandered into the hallway.

I step out of my skirt, remove my wrinkled blazer, and crawl under the covers. At some point everything goes black again.

And when you wake up in the morning
With your head on fire
And your eyes too bloody to see
You can cry in your coffee
But don't come bitchin' to me
Because you had to be a big shot,
Didn't you
You had to open up your mouth
You had to be a big shot,
Didn't you
All your friends were so knocked out
You had to have the last word, last night
You know what everything's about
You had to have a white hot spotlight
You had to be a big shot last night
But now you just can't remember
All the things you said
And you're not sure you want to know
I'll give you one hint, honey
You sure did put on a show
                              (Billy Joel, 1978)

An impatient knock on my door awakens me from a sound sleep. Sitting up, I feel an axe chopping my head in two. *Oh God. Not this.*

Pressing a palm against my forehead, I stumble towards the door and lean against it, gripping the door knob.

'Vladimir?' I say, the sound of my own voice slicing my brow.

'Katey, this is Savochenko. Vladimir left for the airport this morning. The others are already waiting in the lobby.'

I open the door a few inches. 'I need about twenty minutes to get ready,' I say. 'I just woke up.'

'It's good to know you're alive after that performance last night.'

I utter a hopeful 'Was it really that bad?'

After a pause, 'Yeah'.

'The way I feel, I'm not sure I want to be alive right now.'

'Don't be silly. It's nothing a hair of the dog won't cure. We'll be waiting downstairs.'

I quickly take four Ibuprofen tablets, hoping I won't up-chug them, and step into the shower. Afraid to worsen my headache, I avoid the cold-water shock treatment and let pounding heat massage my back.

Before dressing, I assume the yoga-corpse pose on my bed, hoping the pills kick in fast, and ten minutes later, my headache has dwindled to a minor irritant. The wonders of modern medicine!

Fortunately I have an extra suit, chocolate-colored with a short straight skirt—conservative enough for a formal negotiation, but still sufficiently sexy. After applying rouge, eye shadow, and a dark lipstick, I almost look human. But despite my best styling methods, I'm having a bad hair day—flat and fly away. I wish I had one of those trendy hats that you can wear inside.

Barry, his interpreter, and the young Russian, whose name I don't remember, are standing with Savochenko in the lobby. Barry is cleaning his glasses.

Savochenko tosses me a knowing glance, making me wonder what I did last night after the blackout. What if Vladimir left the party after I embarrassed him? What if Savochenko brought me back to my room? What if he had sex with me? What if I'm pregnant? I mentally count the days since my last period. Twenty-two. Diseases? Savochenko is in his late fifties, married, and lives on the edge of Siberia, not a likely candidate for AIDS. What if I slept with someone else? What was that guy's name with the missing fingers? I'm being ridiculous. A classic case of post-alcohol paranoia. I'm sure Vladimir wouldn't have left me passed out on the floor. Nobody would have driven him back to the hotel without me. Or would they have?—that damned paranoia again.

Savochenko takes my arm and guides me away from the group.

'Are you going to be able to handle the meeting?' he asks.

'My stomach is queasy, I'm dying of thirst, and I'm dizzy,' I say. 'But the pills got rid of my headache. Where's Vladimir?'

'He took the first flight back to Moscow,' Savochenko says. 'He has a meeting. Didn't he tell you?'

'I guess in all the excitement I forgot.' *That bastard! How does he expect me to negotiate the contract without his help? He knew I'd be death on two legs this morning. He could have called Moscow and postponed his meeting.*

Although I expect Savochenko to mention last night's events, he acts as if they only happened in my nightmare. 'Just remember, Katey,' he says. 'The general director has to make the final decision based on the recommendation of his deputy, Ivan Borisov. I've done my best to support your equipment, but if the price is too high, there won't be a whole lot I can do.'

'The others will raise their prices later,' I say. 'Our price is solid.'

'Then I suggest you lower it and also raise it later,' Savochenko says.

I'm chewing on his idea as we return to the group and climb into the waiting minivan. Conrad Lambeer was quite firm about the price and I don't think he'd approve of me lowering it. My sparse business knowledge tells me that once you lower a price, you can never raise it again. And I certainly don't want to drive down the prices in Russia. Besides, Savochenko doesn't know about the fifty grand I've offered to the general manager. Although the general manager may have been initially shocked by my offer, he is probably now making plans to buy a new dacha or a Mercedes.

A bald-headed man in his fifties with a face like Porky Pig is seated at the head of the table, all three proposals spread in front of him. I assume this is Borisov, the deputy general manager. I wish I had gotten a chance to speak to him and offer some slush money to cement the deal. I can only hope that none of my competitors has the same idea, but as I said before, that isn't likely.

Without appearing obvious, I grab a seat as near to Borisov as possible, glad to be wearing a short skirt. Savochenko sits down beside me. Barry and his interpreter find empty seats across from us, and the Ernst Werner AG geek takes a seat at the other end of the table. I recognize several tired-looking faces with bloodshot eyes from the sauna.

After a few minutes I'm feeling nauseous and thirsty again. My headache is returning. I have trouble concentrating when Borisov starts to speak.

'We've looked over all three proposals and have recommendations from our chief engineer and the chief service engineer. Before making a decision, however, I would like to pose a question to each of you.'

He pauses, allowing Barry's interpreter to translate his words.

'Ampere Power,' he continues, 'Would you be willing to lower your price?'

I breathe deeply and pause for several seconds before

diving in. I then make my argument slowly and deliberately: 'I've already made the price as low as possible. I can guarantee this price, however. We won't raise it under any circumstances. If our competitors offer you lower prices, they either have inferior equipment or are planning to raise their prices later.'

Glancing at Savochenko, I notice a concerned expression and fear I am using the wrong approach.

'Ernst Werner AG,' Borisov says, staring at the Russian kid at the far end of the table. 'Is your price fixed or negotiable?'

Looking nervous, the young Russian man avoids a direct response. 'I would have to consult my boss, but I think, yes, negotiation is always possible.'

Not exactly a yes, I think. Now I am nervous about Barry's response. Borisov poses the question one more time and I hold my breath until the interpreter finishes speaking.

'Yes, of course,' Barry answers with the confidence of a spelling-bee contestant who knows the word his competitor has just missed. 'We're always willing to negotiate.'

I wish I had been the last speaker. Then Borisov might have remembered my warnings. Instead the last idea planted into his head is Barry's offer to mark down his prices, prices already lower than mine.

Borisov stacks the three proposals in front of him and clasps his hands together. He looks at me and then at Savochenko. I think I detect a trace of guilt in his eyes.

'I am going to recommend to Vasilii Ivanovich that we proceed with International Electric.'

Oh my God! I just lost a five-million-dollar contract. Lambeer is going to fire me. Damn you, Vladimir! Why aren't you here when I need you? What kind of a fucking meeting in Moscow was so incredibly important?

Listening to his interpreter's translation, Barry smiles like a masturbating hyena.

'It's no big deal,' Savochenko says softly. 'A

recommendation is a long way from a decision.'

'Is there any way I can meet with Borisov?' *Maybe I can get him to change his mind. I'll offer him $100,000. Then he can buy a dacha AND a Mercedes.*

'Just relax, Katey,' Savochenko says, holding up his hand. 'Right now I think we should go have a beer—you look like you need one—and discuss this calmly.'

'I'm never going to drink again,' I say.

'Well, I'll have to change that attitude,' he says. 'Come on, you'll feel better. Let's go to my office.'

'You should have said you'd be willing to negotiate, Katey,' Savochenko says as we sit on the couch in his office, drinking Holstein. 'That was all Borisov wanted to hear.'

'But I already have the prices as low as possible,' I say.

'I didn't say you had to lower them,' he explains. 'Just say that you will.'

'What do we do now?' I ask.

'You fly back to Zurich—Switzerland is very beautiful—and don't worry your pretty little head. I'll try to convince the general manager of the superior quality of your equipment. I'll tell him you decided afterwards that you would also be willing to negotiate.'

'Are you sure I won't be committing myself to an offer I can't deliver on?'

'Don't worry about a thing.'

How can I not worry? True, Savochenko stands to make $50,000 from this contract. But how can I be sure that one of my competitors, despite an innocent appearance, hasn't offered him more?

THIRTY-THREE

'I guess I fucked everything up.' I'm sitting across from Vladimir in his office, waiting for the taxi to take me to the airport.

'You said it, not me,' Vladimir says.

'I didn't want to offend anyone by not drinking,' I say.

'You can also offend people by drinking too much.'

Although he could have said a lot more, he lets the subject drop.

All the customers see when they look at me are sexy legs and a pretty smile. Would they take me more seriously if I looked like a librarian? Maybe I should start wearing beige pantsuits and a pair of horn-rimmed glasses. I want to guzzle vodka without getting drunk. I want my bribes to be accepted unconditionally in exchange for million-dollar contracts. I want so desperately to be accepted on the same level as Vladimir. I want everyone to respect me. And I want Vladimir to love me.

'What's going to happen now?'

'I'll take another trip to Ufa and see if I can convince Savochenko to put some pressure on Borisov. I'll offer

Borisov an incentive. You go back to Switzerland and get settled into your new job.'

Damn it! Why are you sending me home? Why can't I go with you? Why can't I offer the bribe to Borisov myself?

'Does Lambeer know we lost the contract with Mosenergo?'

'Not exactly.'

'What do you mean?'

'I told him the Russian company would probably fail to meet the contract obligations, and that the contract would revert back to you.'

'Is that true?'

'Anything's possible, Katey. The important thing is to keep Lambeer's spirits up. You don't want an unhappy boss.'

Just then Olga walks through the open door. 'Taxi's here,' she says.

I'm surprised when Vladimir also stands, picking up a small suitcase from behind his desk.

'Are you coming too?' I ask.

'I've got my own agenda,' he says. 'But yes, I'm on the same flight. I'll explain on the way to the airport.'

'So what's up?' I ask once we are in the taxi.

'I'm flying to Zurich,' he says. 'I have a connection to Nuremberg.'

'We don't have any companies in Germany,' I say.

'I have a meeting with Ernst Werner AG,' he says as if I shouldn't be surprised.

'That's our competitor.'

'They want me to become their country manager in Russia. It's quite a step up from my current position.'

'What? You're going to leave me? I arrive in Switzerland, lose a major contract, and now you're just going to abandon me?'

'I have to. Ampere Power Russia bypassed me for country manager and gave the job to a Swiss guy who can't even speak Russian.'

'Take me with you,' I say.

'Patience, Katey. You just got to Switzerland. It wouldn't look good to pull you out now.'

'What about our contract with Ufa?' I ask. 'Ernst Werner AG also made an offer. Are you going to betray me?'

'Of course not,' he says. 'Once I leave Ampere Power Company, I can work as your personal consultant.'

'Aren't you afraid your own company will find out?' I ask.

'I'm going to be their president. They'll only find out what I want them to find out.'

'How do I know you won't return to Ufa and convince them to go with Ernst Werner AG?'

'Because I don't work for Ernst Werner AG yet, Katey. And also because Ufa wants dead tank breakers. Ernst Werner AG is proposing live tank.'

Suddenly an idea occurs to me. 'I'll pay you,' I say. 'I'll give you fifty grand if I get the Ufa contract and a hundred grand if you get me Mosenergo back.'

Instead of answering, Vladimir extends his hand and grips mine, a subtle smile forming on his lips. 'You've finally caught on,' he says. 'I'm glad I didn't have to spell it out directly. I think we can work very well together.'

Suddenly I understand why he wanted me to come to Switzerland. He is going to promote my career and I am going to fill his pockets.

Once we're in the airplane, Vladimir lays out his plans. Since the business section is almost empty, we have no fear of eavesdroppers. 'I need you to open a secret account at a Swiss bank under the name of Moscow Electrical Consulting.'

'What is Moscow Electrical Consulting?'

'MEC is the name of my new business. I'll help you with your contracts and you pay my percentage into that account. I also need you to get an official stamp made with the company name and address which I can use to stamp our consulting contracts.'

He has obviously given this plan serious consideration. 'Do you have an address?' I ask.

Vladimir laughs. 'I'll use the address of some abandoned building in a remote section of Moscow.'

We stop talking when the stewardess begins serving drinks. Vladimir gets a beer. I ask for coffee.

'What's in it all for me?' I ask after the stewardess has pushed the cart away.

'For a start, you'll make a lot of sales and be very successful. What comes next depends on you.'

'Won't this partnership conflict with your new job?' I ask. 'I'm going to be your competitor.'

'Nobody is going to know about our partnership except you and me. Just make sure you don't get drunk and start blabbing.'

'I intend to quit drinking,' I say, holding up my coffee. 'It's much too risky to drink in Russia.'

'Katey, cows will roller-skate before you quit drinking. You're Irish, for heaven's sake.'

Damn your lack of confidence! 'I bet you a thousand dollars I can go for two months without a drink,' I say, extending my hand.

Vladimir hesitates, realizes I am serious, and then grips my hand. 'I could use a little extra spending money,' he says with a smile.

'I'm not going to lose,' I say. And I mean it.

THIRTY-FOUR

The first thing I do when I get to my hotel room in Zurich is call room service and ask them to empty out the mini-bar, claiming I need the refrigerator space. Before I have time to reconsider, I grab a complimentary bottle of Swiss Rosé from the table and dump it into the bathroom sink, watching the pink river flow into the drain like diluted blood. I feel like a trusted friend is abandoning me.

Then I take a long hot shower and change into cuddly pajamas. Opening a bag of goodies I bought at the airport, I pull out a bottle of cherry juice, several bars of white chocolate, and a thick slice of cheesecake. Lastly I take out a thick adventure novel about medieval Europe by Ken Follet, *Pillars of the Earth*, and settle down into my bed for a quiet evening. The book is so absorbing that I read for almost three hours before turning off the light.

The next morning I dress in an expensive pants suit which I bought before leaving for Switzerland. It has slim-fitting slacks and an elegant double-breasted blazer, pin-striped in two subtle shades of brown. Then I step into conservative low-heeled pumps in a matching color. After drinking the room-service coffee and brushing my teeth for the second time, I head out the door for my first official workday in Zurich.

Adriana smiles as I approach her desk. 'Conrad is expecting you in his office,' she says with a British accent so heavy I barely understand her. 'But first he wanted me to show you *your* office.' She stands up and walks around to the front of her desk. She is young and willowy, moving with the grace of a ballet dancer, in a flowing lavender pantsuit which appears to be silk.

My *office* turns out to be a drab cubicle in the corner of a larger partitioned room. As we walk towards it, I notice the backs of several men, either leaned over desks, staring at computer screens, or smoking and staring into space. Other than the clicking of keyboards, the room is eerily quiet, as if it were a monastery. Although fluorescent lights cover the ceiling, they are turned off, making the atmosphere even more dreary.

At the office in Pennsylvania, there were always lively conversations accompanied by roaring laughter. We had bright lights, and someone was always running around nervously, worried about deadlines. When I ask Adriana a question, I feel like I should whisper.

'Should I see Conrad now?' I ask softly.

'Yes. Like I said, he's waiting,' she says in a voice which makes me feel like I've done something wrong.

I follow her until she slithers back into her seat, reminding me of a snake. 'Go on in,' she says, pointing to Conrad's closed door.

I knock three times before opening the door. Conrad is on the telephone.

'I know I didn't follow the procedure,' he is saying. 'But what the hell difference does that make? Either way, she's here now and you couldn't have stopped her.'

Holding the receiver a few inches from his ear, Conrad

looks up and motions for me to sit down. Obviously he is talking about me, either to Jack or, more likely, to Anis.

When Conrad starts speaking again, his tone has become almost argumentative. 'Yes, you do that,' he says and hangs up without a good-bye.

'Guess who that was?' he says, smiling.

'It could only have been Anis,' I say.

'Yes, he is threatening to report me to the executive headquarters.'

'Can he force me to come back?' I ask.

'He doesn't want you back,' Conrad says. 'He's just being anal. He's upset that you went behind his back and succeeded.' He clears his throat and changes the subject. 'So what the bloody hell happened with Mosenergo?'

'According to Vladimir, the chief engineer preferred our offer, but a manufacturer in St. Petersburg was pressuring the president of Mosenergo to use domestic production. The good news is Vladimir doesn't think the Russian company will be able to handle the job and it will eventually revert back to us.'

'What do we do in the meantime?' he asks.

'We wait,' I say. 'There's nothing else we can do.' Then I say, 'I'm a bit worried about marketing entire substations in Russia. Most of the power companies don't have that kind of money. Selling them individual pieces of equipment was hard enough.'

'Then sell individual pieces,' he says. 'Our first goal is to sell an entire substation. If that fails, we try to sell part of a substation. If that doesn't work, we try to sell a circuit breaker. And if that doesn't work, we try to sell a surge arrester.'

And if that doesn't work, I sell a bloody extension cord?

'But don't you have other departments dealing with individual equipment?' I ask.

'If you make the sale, we get the credit. And you have a good working relationship with Vladimir. He can help you.'

'Speaking of that,' I say. 'I have more news, good and bad.'

'Give me the bad news.'

'Vladimir is going to work for Ernst Werner AG.'

'Bloody hell! What's the good news?'

Even though Vladimir didn't want me to, I see no choice but to tell my boss. 'He's going to work as my personal consultant and award himself a percentage of every contract he secures for us.'

'He's going to compete against his own company?'

'He doesn't see it that way,' I say. 'Vladimir says he's committed to giving his Russian customers the best possible service, even if from a competitor. Nobody will know anyway. His name won't appear on the contracts.' Then, after a pause, I admit, 'Yes, I suppose he is going to compete against his own company.'

'Bloody hell,' he says again.

In Zurich, banks are even more plentiful than chocolate shops, their modern structures towering over the streets like gods. I find one with revolving glass doors and glass walls, eight stories high. I wonder what they do with all that office space.

Approaching one of the counters, I say slowly in English, 'I'd like to open an account.'

A young woman with short black hair, purple lipstick, and a pointed nose looks at me through tiny purple glasses. 'What kind of an account?' Considering all the foreigners with Swiss bank accounts, I am not surprised when she speaks flawless English.

'A secret account,' I say, as if it were a routine occurrence.

'Oh, I see,' she says. 'I don't handle those. You'll have to talk to one of our account managers. Should I call one?' She is already picking up the phone and punching in a number.

I don't bother to answer her question.

'Herr Meierhofer?' she says. 'Eine junge Frau möchte Ihnen sprechen.' She looks up at me and smiles, the receiver pasted against her ear. She says, 'Geheimkonto.' Then she says. 'Amerikanerin.' *Am I that obvious?*

After a short pause, she hangs up the phone. 'He'll be right down,' she says.

Herr Meierhofer looks like he spends most of his time at a computer. He is dressed in an impeccable dark grey suit, snow-white starched shirt, plain navy blue tie, and freshly polished black shoes with laces. Although he tries to give a firm handshake, I am afraid I might hurt his fragile fingers.

'Meierhofer,' he says.

I don't tell him my name.

'Let's go into my office,' he says, motioning toward an open door on the other side of the lobby.

Once we're seated—he behind a massive oak desk, I on a pricey leather office chair— he links his fingers and leans forward. 'Now how may I help you?'

'I'd like to open a secret account.'

'And for what purpose?'

I'm surprised by the question. I didn't think I would have to provide a reason and details.

When I don't answer, he continues. 'Will it be a savings account? Or will money be going in and out?'

'Money will be going in and out of it,' I say quickly, relieved that his questions aren't overly inquisitive.

'We don't usually offer this service for a normal *giro* account,' he says. Then he asks, 'How much money?'

'I'm expecting a small transfer of $50,000 to start with,' I say. 'Then larger deposits will be made on a regular basis.'

I can tell by his eyes that my announcement pleases him. He says, 'We have two options. With a numbered account, your name and address will be provided on the account opening agreement together with your signature. No personal information other than the account number will be entered in the general bank system. The account will be assigned to an individual account manager for personal handling.'

'Do I have to give you my name?' I ask.

He continues. 'The second option is a fictitiously named account. In this case, you do not have to give your name. The account opening agreement contains a fictitious name so that there is no written evidence of the account owner. The drawback is that the operating costs of such an account are quite high.'

'The operating costs are no problem,' I say, assuming Vladimir is already aware of them. 'How do I access the account without a name?'

'You have a pseudonym and an access code that only you and I know,' Meierhofer says.

'How does someone else deposit money into it?'

'He just needs the account number and the bank code,' he says.

Since I'm not providing personal information, it doesn't take long to arrange the paperwork. I open the account under the name of Moscow Electrical Consulting, using the Russian word *matryoshka* as my access code. At no point do I reveal my identity. We part with a handshake and my promise of a fat deposit in the near future.

My next stop is a print shop where I order an ink stamp with the company name and phony address, which will be used to authenticate contracts made between Ampere Power and Moscow Electrical Consulting and probably be signed with a fabricated illegible signature.

I only hope I'm not doing anything that could land me in a Siberian prison. *A knock on my hotel room door at midnight. An interrogation room in the basement of the Lubyanka. Thumb screws. One Day in the Life of Ivan Denisovich. One Day in the Life of Katey O'Hara.*

Although Vladimir told me it was legal in Switzerland to offer bribes to get foreign contracts, Russia is a different story. My feelings are a mixture of fear and excitement, like

bungee jumping or walking a tightrope over the Grand
Canyon with no net.

THIRTY-FIVE

After the embarrassing scene in the Siberian sauna, I decide to change my image from that of a blonde bimbo to that of a suave businesswoman, dying my hair a rich shade of brown and darkening my complexion with makeup in shades of brown and copper. In one of Zurich's boutiques, I buy myself a pair of matching high-heel boots and a calf-length dress in brown suede material with a plunging neckline. Finally, I select an elegant designer briefcase in leather as soft as a baby's butt. My new look is as sophisticated as a panther at midnight and cost me almost an entire paycheck.

I haven't returned to Russia in two months. In the meantime, Lambeer has given me some proposals to prepare for Great Britain and Egypt. I've been learning how to read line diagrams of power plants comprised of circuit breakers, high voltage switches, voltage transformers, and surge arresters. It's boring as hell.

My determination to abstain from drinking has kept me away from Russia. I could never win the bet under the influence of my customers. I don't care that much about the thousand dollars. I am more concerned with proving to Vladimir that I can be a serious business partner and that I won't get drunk and blab all our secrets. But when Lambeer asks me when I am finally going to return to Russia to pursue the Mosenergo and Ufa projects, I decide to book a flight.

Two days later I check into the Hotel National, not far from Red Square and a five-minute walk from Vladimir's new office. When I made the reservation two days earlier, I was told that the only available room was a special suite for $350 a night. Since the Swiss aren't as uptight about expenses as the Americans—they even let me fly business class—I accept the room, one which could have belonged to an eighteenth century czarina.

Arc-shaped windows, flanked with green velvet curtains reaching the ceiling, reveal the sweep of Tverskaya Street with the Kremlin hovering in the background. The king-size bed, not divided in the middle like most European beds, must have been imported from France. The dressing table is adorned with a dozen red roses, a plate of Russian chocolates, and a bottle of champagne on ice. There is even a whirlpool in the bathroom.

The next morning I run on the hotel treadmill, eat a breakfast of fruit and coffee, and then return to my room to create my new image, starting with a brown lace thong and dark thigh-high stockings. I fit my breasts into a brown lace push-up bra from Victoria's Secret. Then after applying brown eye shadow, copper rouge and matching lipstick, I slip the brown suede dress over my head and step into the matching boots. My brown hair, which has grown to shoulder length, frames my face like a lion's mane, the bangs almost touching my eye lashes. The blonde bimbo is history.

'Katey, you look different,' Sasha says as I enter the

office. 'So dark and mysterious—Like a fashion model for Vogue.'

Thank you!

When Vladimir left Ampere Power Company to work for Ernst Werner AG, he took Sasha with him. I'm not surprised that he's familiar with Vogue. Often the Russians know more about American culture than the Americans.

'This is actually my natural hair color,' I say. Well, almost. I'm no longer sure what my natural hair color is.

I head for Vladimir's office, coming face to face with his new secretary, a woman younger, skinnier, and more buxom than me, with natural blonde hair, jade eyes, expertly applied make-up, tight-fitting jeans, high heels, and a vibrant blue blouse with plenty of cleavage. She looks like a movie star. *Where in the fuck did she come from?*

'Is he alone?' I ask. 'Can I go in?'

'Let me check,' she says, picking up the phone. 'Vladimir Igorovich?' she asks. 'I have a…what's your name?' she asks, looking at me suspiciously. I can't find a single flaw in her fucking face. Where did Vladimir get her? A modeling agency? I bet she can't type more than ten words a minute.

Katey,' I say.

'Katey's here,' she says as if pronouncing a bad word. After a short pause, she hangs up the phone. 'Go on in.' Although she smiles, her eyes are like frozen marbles.

Vladimir's new office is luxurious with a desk almost as large as a double bed. There are two leather-upholstered chairs in front and his throne behind it. A mahogany coffee table to the left of his desk is flanked with a black leather couch and several easy chairs. A matching bar and liquor cabinet decorate the right side of the room. He is seated at his desk, dressed in a starched white shirt and an elegant tie in muted shades of blue, green, and brown.

'Nice office,' I say, walking to the back of his desk. Then I say, 'Nice tie,' and finger the material. Although I want to throw myself into his arms and kiss him, I purposely act cool. *Keep him guessing. Surprise him with unpredictable behavior.*

Looking up from a pile of papers, Vladimir lets his eyes wander from my hair to my toes. Although I wait for a comment on my new look, he says nothing. Typical man. Does he even know I look different? Maybe I should have died my hair violet blue and worn a toga.

'Did you check out of your room yet?' he asks.

'Not yet. My stuff is still in there. It's the best room in the hotel. I hate to leave it.'

Vladimir stands up and grabs his blazer from the back of his chair. 'Why don't you show it to me,' he says with a wink. Maybe he noticed my appearance after all.

We walk past the new secretary. Despite a china doll smile, her eyes have become missiles aimed at my heart.

With a temperature in the low sixties, a cloudless sky and a warm breeze, this April day is unusual. Snow often falls as late as early May in Moscow. Tverskaya Street is packed with shoppers, many looking like they escaped from People Magazine's list of worst-dressed people. A man in black slacks, white shoes, a red blazer and a cell phone practically plows me over. We pass a woman looking like an ad for the color purple—purple skirt, purple pumps, purple sweater, purple eye make-up, purple lipstick, purple fingernails and several locks of purple hair. I wonder if her pubic hair also matches. Another woman dons a teal-and-pink combination which is almost fluorescent. I even see a girl with spiky pink and blue hair, a black leather jacket studded with metal, a pair of Doc Martin boots, and black lipstick.

Still others can compete with Prince Charles, James Bond or one of his lovers, dressed like the mannequins in the windows of the many West-European designer boutiques—Versace, Hermes, Hugo Boss, Armani. In any case, the people look different from the drab Muscovites I remember from my student days just ten years before.

When we get to my hotel room, Vladimir shuts the door and pulls me to him, his hand reaching down and lifting up my dress. Before I can tell him that the check-out deadline was half an hour ago, he's pulling down my panties and drilling his tongue into my mouth. Then he picks me up and tosses me onto the massive bed, easing my panties over my boots and letting them drop to the floor.

Although I expect him to prove his manhood, he reaches down, picks up the panties and stuffs them into his jacket pocket. 'I'll hang on to these,' he says. 'You can have them back after I fuck your brains out in Ufa.'

Damn you! I haven't seen you in two months and now you want to play games. What are you going to do? Go back and fuck your secretary? She's probably waiting for you, sprawled on your desk with her legs spread, ready to take a memo. New job. New office. New lover?

Stay cool! 'Aren't you going to give me something of yours?' I ask.

'What do you want?'

'That's a nice watch,' I say. 'Is it new? Let me wear it.'

'Are you kidding? It's a Patek Phillipe. It was a present from my new company. It's worth $25,000.'

'I want to feel it against my skin,' I say. 'I've never had that much money. It's a real sexual turn on. In fact, I may just get an urge to try some new things tonight.' I reach my hand out and stroke his erection through his pants. When he looks at me, I flick my tongue like a snake.

Without another word, he removes the watch and places it in my hand.

When we return to the office, I hold up my wrist, flashing the watch in the secretary's face. If her eyes had previously been missiles, now they are nuclear bombs.

The next morning we meet with Savochenko in Ufa.

'We're having financial problems,' he says. 'We'll have to delay the project.'

I give Vladimir a pleading look, my eyes begging him to please do something.

An unsettling thought creeps into my head. Vladimir's new company represents live-tank circuit breakers. Live-tank circuit breakers are less expensive than dead-tank. Bashkirenergo is having financial difficulties. *Oh Shit! Why should Vladimir help me? He has his own company now, his own contracts to worry about. He even has a new secretary. What the hell does he need me for?*

But I have promised him fifty grand to get me the contract, not to mention the standing agreement for future contracts. It will just depend on which is more important— quick financial gain or success in his career at Ernst Werner AG. Somehow I don't think his affection for me will be a deciding factor.

'Shouldn't you be representing Ernst Werner AG?' Savochenko asks, looking at Vladimir with skepticism.

'Yes, I do work for Ernst Werner AG,' Vladimir says. 'But I started this contract negotiation while working for Ampere Power and I like to finish what I start. Besides, dead tank circuit breakers are more suitable for your needs, and I believe in giving the customer the best solution, even if a competitor gets the contract.' Then he smiles and winks at me. 'And, of course, we all want to help Katey.'

His little speech doesn't calm my worries. I suspect Savochenko knows that Vladimir is motivated by more than good will. I can only hope I promised enough money. Maybe I should have offered him $100,000.

Strangely enough, the decision made on our last visit to give the contract to International Electric seems to have been forgotten. I can only guess that Vladimir managed to sway some opinions when he was here without me. But in what direction did he sway them?

Back in Moscow, I am seated in Vladimir's office for a last meeting before my taxi takes me to the airport.

'What do I tell Lambeer?' I ask.

'Tell him that getting money from a Russian customer is a slow process. You have to woo him like a lady, send flowers, shower him with attention. Nothing happens fast. Meanwhile, we should plan another visit to Tula. You haven't talked to Miasnikov since you left Pennsylvania.'

Just then his secretary barges into the room, faded jeans hugging her body like a second skin. As she passes, I notice her tiny waist, round hips and slender legs. Her breasts, much too large for her slim build, strain against the front of a short-sleeved purple cashmere sweater.

'Thank you, Lara,' Vladimir says as she hands him several envelopes. I try to ignore the flirtatious exchange of smiles between them.

Does that fucking bitch think she can just waltz in here and snag a company president? Tramps like her are a dime a dozen in Moscow, but there is only one Katey. *He's mine, you dumb slut.*

'I heard Anis hired somebody new,' I say. 'Some older Russian immigrant. He'll probably be going to Tula as well. Plus, there's also your replacement—what's his name?'

'Radoyko. But don't worry. I'll call Miasnikov and tell him that our agreement is only valid for contracts he signs with you,' Vladimir says. 'I'll tell him you went to Switzerland because it is too dangerous to offer incentives while working for an American company. Then even if Anis's new man is clever enough to use our approach, Miasnikov will be afraid to negotiate with him.'

'What about Ernst Werner AG?' I ask. 'Your own company. Remember?'

'I'm working on several large power-generation projects,' he says. 'High voltage circuit breakers are just a tiny part of my business. I'm willing to let you have the contract. Besides, we don't even produce dead tank breakers.'

Feeling excluded to hear him say 'we' in reference to Ernst Werner AG, I say, 'Why don't you get me a job in Germany?'

'Because I need somebody in Switzerland whom I can trust to handle customer needs outside of my company's product line. And don't forget about Moscow Electrical Consulting.'

'I won't.' I haven't forgotten our bogus company. The Swiss bank is still waiting for its first deposit and will probably close the account if I don't produce something soon.

'By the way,' I say, 'I won the bet.'

'What bet?' He looks surprised.

'I didn't drink for two months.'

'Not a drop?'

'I swear it.'

'In that case…' Vladimir digs a black wallet from his back pocket and counts out ten one-hundred-dollar bills as if they were ones. 'I always pay my bets,' he says, handing me the stack.

Somehow it doesn't make me happy.

THIRTY-SIX

Back in Zurich, I struggle to keep busy in the office. Knowing I'll fail anyway without Vladimir and Moscow Electrical Consulting, I haven't bothered to meet the new director of Ampere Power Company in Russia, Radoyko Kosic. Since Kosic is supposed to approve all of my activities in Russia, he was quite incensed to hear of my continued relationship with Vladimir, especially the visit we made to Ufa—although I'm not sure how he knew about that. I wonder if Vladimir told him. Kosic called up Lambeer, ranting and raving about my 'getting into bed with the competition.' I suspect he meant it literally.

'You have to pretend to work with Radoyko, Katey,' Lambeer says as I sit in his office sipping coffee.

'It's a waste of time,' I say. 'He's Bulgarian. Russians don't trust other East Europeans; he'll never be able to win the customers' trust.'

'I said pretend, Katey. Visit his office. Give him our newest brochures. And most importantly, stay away from the Ernst Werner AG office and make your meetings with Vladimir more clandestine.'

A week later, I make my first appearance at Radoyko's office. Only a few inches taller than me, he's dressed in a cheap suit which definitely isn't Armani, and a red tie, which definitely isn't Versace. And never will be. He has thinning black hair, tiny silver-framed glasses and eyes which never seem to blink.

After a few words of small talk, he descends on me like a Tsunami.

'I must approve every business meeting, trip, or contract that you arrange in Russia. I want to know your travel plans and agenda. I want to know exactly what you are offering to whom and at what price. If you're using any third parties, I expect to know about them. If you're offering any bribes, I expect to know about them. If any contracts are signed—'

'You expect to know about them,' I say.

He starts to scowl, breathes deeply, starts to speak, and stops. After a pause he says, 'Now that we've cleared that up, what is your current agenda?'

'I was hoping your office could arrange some customer visits for me,' I say. 'I assume you know better than I do where the best prospects lie.' Brown-nosing isn't my forte, but I am determined to do my best.

'Yeah, well,' he says. 'We already have our own sales engineers in the various regions.'

'Are you saying you don't need me?' I ask.

'I'm telling you that my representatives have regular contact with the customers. If a customer expresses interest in your products, my sales engineers will contact you to prepare an offer.'

'Radoyko,' I say, looking up at the ceiling. When I was a student in the Communist era, we were convinced that the rooms were bugged through the sprinkler system. 'Let's take a walk.'

Once we are outside, I continue, 'There are certain discussions which should be held without witnesses. I don't think the customers would be happy to have another Russian listening in when I offer a bribe—especially one who is fresh out of college and earns around $200 a month. And you know damned well we won't be able to sell a coat to a naked man in a Siberian snowstorm, unless we provide incentives.'

'My representatives don't have to be present when you have these discussions. But there is no reason they shouldn't know about them.'

'There sure as hell is,' I say. 'It happens to be illegal. I'm risking my ass and I want as few people as possible to know about it.'

'Is that why you offered bribes in Ufa two months ago in front of witnesses?'

The question is like a punch in the stomach. Who in God's name told him? Vladimir? Would Vladimir have told him? Savochenko? The general manager?

'I don't know what you're talking about,' I say.

'I heard what I heard,' he says.

'Well, it isn't true,' I say, knowing that it is. 'Let's make a compromise. I'll inform you of my dealings, but not the local representatives. You don't want them involved in illegal activities anyway.' I don't really intend to inform him about anything, especially not about Moscow Electrical Consulting.

'Okay,' he says. 'We have an office in Yekaterinburg. From there, our representative can accompany you to Perm, Chelyabinsk, and of course, Ufa. I talked to your old boss Anis Nanji and he told me about your possible contract with Bashkirenergo. I want my representative involved in all of the meetings.'

Hasn't he heard anything I said? Okay, just make him happy. Maybe I can whisper into my customers' ears at dinner.

'Olga can arrange a ticket for you and let the representative know you are coming.'

Apparently he inherited Vladimir's former secretary.

A short stocky man in his early forties with a face like a baby bear meets me at the airport in Yekaterinburg, holding a sign with Ampere Power Company written on it. Although he's mild mannered, his handshake has a strong grip.

'Yuri Bortwin,' he says.

After exchanging niceties, he leads me to his Moskvich, a boxy little car from the Soviet era which looks like it has seen better days.

'Is this the company car?' I ask, trying to hide my sarcasm.

'No,' he says and laughs. 'We don't have a company car. Just a small office with me and a secretary. I'll take you there now.'

Watching cows graze would be more exciting. What does he do there all day? According to Vladimir, Yuri Bortwin has not yet made a single sale in his entire region.

'What's our schedule?' I ask.

'After you see the office, I'll take you to your hotel,' he says. 'We have a meeting tomorrow morning at Sverdlovenergo. Then we'll go by car to Chelyabinsk for a presentation at Chelyabenergo the following morning'

'In this car?' I ask. I can't imagine driving more than a few miles in this piece of junk. If it breaks down between Yekaterinburg and Chelyabinsk, we certainly won't be able to call triple A.

'Yes, why?'

'Just wondering,' I say innocently.

'After the presentation, we'll drive to Ufa, arriving in the evening. They're expecting us on Thursday.'

I hope Vladimir has contacted Savochenko. He needs to know that Yuri Bortwin is NOT to be involved in our negotiations and that the payments we agreed upon will only be valid if my signature appears on the contract.

Otherwise, Radoyko could get the idea to pursue the contract directly with Anis and cut me out of the loop. Without knowing about the incentives we've offered—and I have no intention of risking my ass by telling them—they could run into trouble. I can imagine Anis's reaction if I were to tell him the customers are expecting over a hundred grand in slush money, which he wouldn't possibly be able to pay—not only because he wouldn't have included the money in the cost estimate, but also because bribery is highly illegal for American companies, and Anis would not want to spend his retirement behind bars.

'Finally we'll drive north to Perm for a presentation at Permenergo on Friday, returning to Yekaterinburg on Friday night.'

'You're not allowing me much opportunity to get to know the customer. Usually I take them out to dinner.'

'We only have a week,' Yuri says. 'I don't want you to be stuck here over the weekend. Besides, I doubt if the customers will have time to eat with us. When I visit them, they never accept my invitations.'

Of course not. You are you and I am me. But I don't argue. I'll have plenty of opportunity to return on my own with neither Yuri nor his Moskvich.

Yuri's 'office' is one room, sharing the ground floor of an apartment building with a bakery and a butcher shop. A pale blue carpet covers the floor and the walls are white with several prints of modern art, one consisting of three overlapping triangles in various colors. A homely woman with skin like sandpaper sits in front of a computer screen. She looks up as we enter the room.

'Katey, meet Lyudmila Ivanovna,' Yuri says. 'Lyudmila Ivanovna, Katey O'Hara.'

The woman is close to fifty with heavy-framed glasses and too much rouge. She's wearing an orange and green polyester print dress which looks like it was salvaged from the Soviet era. I notice her plump finger swelling around a wide, gold wedding band.

'You came all the way here by yourself?' she asks, surprised. 'All the way from America?'

'Actually I live in Switzerland now,' I say.

'All by yourself?'

'Yes, of course,' I say, turning to Yuri, who has taken a seat at his computer and lighted a cigarette. I ask, 'Do you get much business out here? You seem to have a large region.'

'We're working on some projects,' he says.

'Have you sold anything?' I ask. I can't resist the stab.

'We haven't been open that long,' he says.

I let the subject drop. I'm here to make friends. And I don't want him to complain to Radoyko.

'You must be tired,' he says. 'As soon as I check my e-mail, I'll bring you to the hotel.'

'May I invite you both to dinner?' I ask. 'It's the least I can do to thank you for your hospitality.'

'In a restaurant?' Liudmila asks, a smile forming on her weathered face.

'Yes,' I say. 'Would you like to choose one?'

'Oh, I'd love to,' she says. I know I've scored a few brownie points.

During the dinner—by no means a good one, but possibly the best they have—Yuri gives me a boastful overview of Yekaterinburg. Known as Sverdlovsk during the Soviet Era, the city was established almost three centuries ago by Peter the Great as one of Russia's industrial and administrative centers. With a population of nearly two million, Yekaterinburg ranks as Russia's fifth largest city, boasting more than 100 research institutes, fifteen universities and academies, and fifteen stadiums. The city is also home to the Uralmash factory, the biggest producer of heavy machinery in all of Europe.

Yuri omits the one fact that makes Yekaterinburg world famous—the execution of the Tsar's family by the

Bolsheviks in 1918. In the post-Soviet era this event is no longer something to be proud of.

Our visit to Sverdlovenergo is a farce. Except for my twenty-minute presentation, Yuri does all the talking. Since the chief engineer keeps staring at my legs, which are exposed to my upper thigh, I make a mental note to visit him alone in the near future. Although he turns down Yuri's lunch invitation, I am sure he would have accepted mine.

I take Yuri to lunch at a Bistro, where we eat *pelmeni*, savory pork-filled dumplings served with melted butter and vinegar. After black caviar, they are my favorite Russian food.

We then take off in Yuri's Moskvich across the Uralian outback. As he steps on the gas pedal, I feel the little car tremble. Ominous noises are coming from the engine.

The countryside is beautiful—fields of green grasses illuminated by the summer sun, grazing cows, quaint cottages with green-painted shutters reminding me of gingerbread houses, snow-capped mountains in the distance and the roads almost deserted except for an occasional sixteen-wheeler or Russian car.

After reaching Chelyabinsk, we check into a nameless hotel which doesn't accept credit cards. Instead of a shower stall or bathtub, there is simply a drain on the floor, a handheld shower head, and no curtain. There is no telephone and no T.V. Luckily I have a good novel to read, although the low wattage on the nightstand lamp will probably make it difficult.

That night at dinner Yuri briefs me about Chelyabinsk. Once a small town, the city grew into a major industrial center during the Second World War when Stalin decided to move a large part of Soviet factory production to places far away from the advancing German armies, bringing new industries and thousands of workers to Chelyabinsk. Now with over a million people, Chelyabinsk is home to more than a dozen universities and is a center of heavy industry.

The meeting with Chelyabenergo is just as disappointing as I expected. Once again Yuri dominates the discussion, this time not even bothering to invite the chief engineer to lunch. Obviously he wants to control all business activities in his region. He is probably afraid of looking bad if I upstage him by making a sale.

From Chelyabinsk we head to Ufa, rarely speaking. I can't think of anything more to talk about.

Two hours later, smoke rises from the hood of Yuri's car. Since I had the same experience myself several years ago, I recognize the problem immediately.

'Yuri, your radiator has a leak,' I say.

Without speaking, he pulls to the side of the road, releases the hood, and gets out of the car. Since Ufa is a hundred miles away, I hope he has mechanical skills. I walk around to the front of the car where Yuri is bent over inspecting the radiator.

'All the fluid is gone,' he says without raising his head. 'I'll have to patch it and refill it. You don't have any chewing gum, do you?'

'Do you want to chew it or should I?' I ask, digging wild cherry Bubble Yum out of my purse.

'If you don't mind,' he says. 'I have false teeth.'

I pop two chunks of gum into my mouth and chew ferociously, making a soft pink glob which I spit out and hand to him.

'The patch won't hold long,' Yuri says. 'We should take the quickest route back to Yekaterinberg.'

'I need to get to Ufa,' I say.

'And I need to fix my car,' Yuri says. 'You'll have to go another time.'

As he is reaching to patch the rusty hole, I hear the sound of an engine and looking behind me, see a green tractor approaching with a hay wagon. A ruddy man with a dirty face is seated behind the wheel, accompanied by a middle-aged woman plainly dressed in a long grey skirt and dark wool sweater, contrasted by a shawl around her shoulders with colorful flowers on a black background. Her brown hair is tied back in a ponytail.

'What's the problem?' the man shouts, stopping the tractor beside us.

Yuri explains the situation.

'I need to get to Ufa,' I say. 'How far is the nearest train station?'

'There's no train station around here,' the man says. 'But we've got a car up at the house. I can take you to Ufa for a reasonable price.'

'I'll give you a hundred dollars,' I say and the man nods in agreement, unable to hide his surprise and pleasure. It's probably more money than he earns in a month.

'I can't let you go,' Yuri says.

'My company invested a lot of money for me to make this trip,' I say. 'Savochenko is expecting me in Ufa and I plan to be there.'

Before Yuri can respond, I take his keys from the ignition, open the trunk and grab my suitcase. 'Don't worry, Yuri,' I say as I climb onto the seat beside the woman. 'If you get the car fixed, you can meet me in Perm. Otherwise, I'll call you with a full report.' Considering how long it takes to get spare parts in Russia, I'm confident I'll be visiting both Ufa and Perm alone.

'It's unusual for a young lady to be traveling all alone in the Urals,' the man says. 'Your accent sounds like you're from the Baltics.'

I tell him who I am and explain my business.

'I've never met an American,' he says.

'I can't wait to tell my friend Masha,' the woman says.

In ten minutes we pull off the highway onto a dirt road in the direction of a wooden house, painted dark brown with green shutters and surrounded by wheat fields. A large, scruffy dog, which looks like a combination of at least five different breeds, approaches the wagon and barks. The small car parked near the house looks older than Yuri's, and for a moment I wonder if I've made a mistake.

'I'll drive you to Ufa tomorrow morning,' he says. 'You can sleep in our spare room.'

His announcement surprises me. I was expecting him to drive me there immediately.

'I'll call Masha and Oleshka,' the woman says. 'Mashka plays the balalaika. Have you ever heard real Russian folk music?'

'Never a live performance,' I say. Maybe this will be fun. Certainly more enjoyable than driving back to Yekaterinburg with Yuri.

When we enter the house, my eyes focus on the *pechka*, a traditional Russian stove made of ceramic tile, which stands against the back wall of the room with wood piled beside it. Red Persian-style carpets decorate the wood-paneled walls and wooden floors. The house smells of cooked cabbage and greasy meat.

An ancient woman with a face like an apple-head doll, dressed in ragged clothes and felt slippers, emerges from an adjoining room. She speaks to the man with such a heavy accent that I don't understand her.

'You can sleep in here,' the younger woman says, opening a door.

I enter a small room with dark wooden walls and a single window. The bed is small and covered with a heavy comforter. Although I suspect it's been slept in, I'm not in a position to complain. Hopefully, I won't be attacked by bedbugs and can take a nice shower in the morning.

'Where's the bathroom?' I ask.

The woman shows me another door. When I open it, expecting to see a complete bathroom, I enter the backyard of the house and face an outhouse sixty feet away. Suddenly I know I won't be taking a shower.

When I return to the house, the man is gone.

'Grigorii is fetching our neighbors,' the woman says. 'We've never had an American visitor before.'

Thinking I should offer her an American gift, I go into the bedroom and open my suitcase. My company souvenirs, Swiss army knives, pens, and little flashlights, seem inadequate for a woman. I pull out one of each trinket for Grigorii and select an unopened pair of spandex pantyhose from Victoria's Secret. Since I'm constantly snagging my stockings, I always bring enough extras.

The old woman is fiddling around in the kitchen, the food smells becoming stronger. The younger woman is sitting in front of the *pechka* in a rocking chair.

'I have a few gifts for you and your husband,' I say. 'As a thank you for your hospitality.'

'That isn't necessary,' she says, but I can tell by her expression she is pleased by the gesture.

'My name is Katey,' I say. I wait for her to tell me her name, but she doesn't. I sense that she distrusts me and is only tolerating my presence because of the hundred dollars we agreed on.

'Have you always lived here?' I ask.

'I was born a few miles up the road, but Grigorii was born in this house.'

'Do you have children?'

'We have a ten-year-old girl, but she is accompanying my parents to Moscow. They like to take the train several times a year.'

'Do you ever go there?' I ask.

'I've never been farther than Ufa.'

'Is the other woman Grigorii's mother?' I ask.

'No, she's his grandmother. She's 92 years old.'

We make small talk for another ten minutes, until being interrupted by voices from outside. Grigorii enters, accompanied by another man and a woman, whom I assume to be Masha and Oleg, also in their thirties and plainly dressed. Oleg is carrying bottles of vodka and champagne, one in each hand. Masha holds a guitar-like instrument with a triangular base, which I recognize as a balalaika.

'Irina!' comes a voice from the kitchen. Now I know the name of my host.

'I'll help,' Masha says and the two women disappear into the kitchen, leaving me alone with Grigorii and Oleg.

'Irina, bring some glasses!' Grigorii calls after his wife.

She reappears with shot glasses in both hands.

'Do you drink vodka?' Grigorii asks me.

Do tigers live in Africa? 'Not very often,' I say.

'Oleshka's father made this vodka,' Grigorii says. 'The best stuff far and wide.'

During Gorbachev's war on alcoholism ten years earlier, a lot of Russians died of alcohol poisoning. They were forced to distill their own vodka because it was so difficult to buy. Some even drank rubbing alcohol and cheap cologne. I push these thoughts out of my mind.

Grigorii pours six glasses. 'Irina, Mashka, *Babushka!*'— the Russian word for grandmother— 'Come and drink a toast to our guest.'

I am amused to learn that the withered woman enjoys vodka. I guess if the moonshine hasn't killed her yet, it won't kill me either.

The *Babushka* comes out carrying plates of pickles and salami. Irina brings a tray of marinated vegetables and a basket of dark bread. Grigorii passes the glasses around. 'A toast to our American guest,' he says.

Although it's better than some of the vodka I've tasted, I'm not eager for more. But Grigorii is already refilling the glasses.

The women return to the kitchen to bring more appetizers and a big bowl of *piroshky*, little meat-filled pastries. Although bathed in grease, the pastries are delicious.

As we drink champagne, finish the vodka—the men have been drinking most of it—and start on another bottle, I start to feel tired. Just as I am preparing to excuse myself and go to bed, Marina strums the balalaika.

Like a shot being fired, the Babushka starts to sing—or should I say yodel—in a shouty voice which reminds me of symbols clanging. She sings so fast and with such a strange intonation that I don't understand the words.

Everyone starts clapping to the rhythm. Although I'm too tired to enjoy the festivities, and the singing is also giving me a headache, I clap along with them, not wanting to offend my hosts. Like the Energizer Bunny, the Babushka keeps going and going and going. When she finally stops, Grigorii begins singing a Russian ballad, Moscow Evenings, which soothes like a lullaby. At the song's conclusion, the other guests rise, say their goodnights with hugs and kisses, and go out into the night.

After venturing to the outhouse with only the dim lights of the main house to guide me, I go into my room, get undressed, and crawl into bed. I'm almost asleep when I hear the door open. Expecting it to be Irina or the grandmother needing something from the room, I am surprised to see a man's shadow. Before I can utter a word, Grigorii pulls off the blanket and crawls on top of me, covering my mouth with one hand and groping at my panties with the other.

I jerk my knee against his groin. Groaning in pain, he releases my mouth and slaps me, causing my eyes to water. Before he can cover my mouth again, I let out a scream.

'Grisha.'

Recognizing Irina's voice, I lift my head to see her shadow in the doorway.

Grigorii crawls off of me and slithers past his wife. She stands for a few seconds, staring at me without speaking. If I could see her eyes in the darkness, they would probably kill me or at least turn me into stone or something. Then she closes the door behind her.

Feeling like an unwelcome stranger, I want to pack my suitcase and escape into the night. Instead, I close my eyes and try to sleep.

I awake to the sound of voices and the clatter of dishes. Knowing it would be pointless to ask for a shower, I dress quickly in a pants suit and flat shoes. If Grigorii is driving me to Ufa, I don't want to appear seductive.

I notice a water pitcher, cup, bowl and towel on the dresser near the door. Someone must have brought them in while I was sleeping. After washing my hands and face, I pour water into a cup and attempt to brush my teeth. With no place to spit, I open the window and lean my head out. After applying makeup with only the tiny mirror from my compact, I take a deep breath and enter the main room.

Irina and the grandmother are eating at the table. Irina stands up and scoops a bowl of porridge from a large pot, pours water from a teapot and points to a can of instant coffee. Without speaking, she motions for me to sit. The two women ignore me, conversing in soft tones, while I concentrate on my food, creamy oatmeal lavishly sweetened. Then I mix a cup of coffee.

Finally, Irina speaks. 'As soon as you're ready, I'll drive you to Ufa. Grisha is busy.'

'Thank you,' I say. Somehow I'm not surprised to hear the news. She doesn't want her husband anywhere near this American slut. 'I need to use the outhouse and then we can go.'

After I return, we go out to the car. Irina says, 'I'd like to see your money before we leave.' Her unspoken words— *I don't trust a bitch who would seduce my poor husband*—don't escape me.

Accepting my hundred-dollar-bill without thanks, she starts the engine.

We drive to Ufa in silence. I could use a hacksaw to cut through the tension between us. It's not my fault, I want to cry out. That drunken bastard of yours tried to rape me. But I know it won't do any good. Instead, I stare out the window, enjoying the pleasant view of a cloudless sky, wheat fields, farmhouses, and grazing cows and horses. And At least I am going to Ufa without Yuri.

When I arrive at Savochenko's office shortly before noon, Yuri is already there. Apparently he made it back to Yekaterinburg in his own car and then borrowed his brother's car and drove half the night to get here fast. Although Yuri greets me coldly, Savochenko seems pleased to see me, offering cognac and chocolates. Since he doesn't mention our pending contract, I assume Vladimir told him not to include Yuri in the negotiations. Ignoring Yuri's efforts to dominate the discussion, Savochenko addresses his questions to me, sticking to the subject of Swiss substations. Then he gathers several engineers together, most of whom I recognize from the sauna, and I give my presentation.

Savochenko and I share a half liter of vodka at lunch, Yuri sipping a coke because he has to drive. While Savochenko questions me about life in Switzerland, Yuri constantly interrupts, trying to divert attention to himself and the business. When Savochenko brushes him off, Yuri scowls and stares into his coke.

After drinking so much vodka, I fall asleep in the car on the way to Perm, which is good since I'm tired of talking to Yuri. It takes us four hours to cover the 180 miles and we arrive in the evening.

After I awake and shortly before our arrival, Yuri gives me the run-down on Perm, an ancient city dating back to at least the ninth century with fifteen-hundred archeological monuments. It has a current population of a million people. Although I'm tired of his geography lessons, when he mentions timber, mining and petroleum production, I become hopeful that barter may be a possibility. If the customer doesn't have cash, we may be able to accept natural resources in lieu of payment, using a middleman to sell them on the open market.

The next day I repeat my presentation one more time, afterwards letting Yuri speak to the customers, and again missing out on a chance to invite them to lunch.

We drive the 180 miles back to Yekaterinburg, and I fly to Moscow the next day, satisfied that I've performed my duty of kissing ass to the local representatives.

THIRTY-SEVEN

It's one of those days in Zurich when you expect it to never stop raining, when the clouds are so grey and heavy you can't imagine that anything blue could possibly be hiding above them. Following my typical rainy Sunday routine, I've just returned from pumping iron for two hours at the health club, my muscles limp with fatigue. It's actually the second health club I joined since moving here, the first having gone bankrupt one week after I paid the yearly fee of 800 Swiss Francs, money that will probably never be refunded.

I'm eating fresh rye bread with lox, butter and onions while watching a rerun of Dallas dubbed into German. Although I only understand a fraction of the dialog, I am familiar enough with the series to know what is happening—J.R. is secretly trying to instigate a revolution in some unnamed Arab oil state.

I've just taken a full bite of food when the phone rings. Nobody ever calls me except my parents, and they called yesterday. I let it ring several times while I finish chewing, then pick up the receiver with a simple hello. Although most Swiss say their last name when they answer the telephone, I have no desire to reveal my identity to a stranger.

'Hello. How are you doing?' My heart races as I recognize Vladimir's voice.

'That's funny,' I say. 'I was just thinking about you. What's up?'

He pauses for a few seconds and then says, 'I'm getting a divorce.'

'Oh, I'm sorry,' I say. *Hallelujah!*

'My son is kind of upset,' he says. 'I just spent the whole afternoon talking to him about it.'

'Why are you getting divorced at this particular time?' I ask. 'Is there a certain reason?' *And why are you calling me?*

This time he pauses even longer, as if he doesn't know what to say. 'I've been planning it for a while,' he finally says. 'I wanted to wait until my son was older, but I can't live with her any more. I've purchased a condo in the center of Moscow.'

I didn't realize he had so much money. Housing is exorbitant in Moscow and you can't really get mortgages, so he must have paid in cash.

'Can I stay there when I come to Moscow?' I ask flirtatiously.

'Listen, I have to get going,' he says, ignoring my question.

'Vladimir,' I say. 'Now that you're about to become one of Moscow's most eligible bachelors, watch out for gold digging blonde bitches.'

'Yeah,' he says.

After he hangs up, I go to the refrigerator and take out a bottle of champagne. 'To me,' I say, toasting the empty room. 'To the future Mrs. Kashirnikova.' Why else would he call me on a Sunday to tell me about his divorce? But he sounded a bit sad, even regretful. I am suddenly unnerved. What is he hiding?

My new job in Zurich is frustrating. Our factory produces gas insulated substations, GIS, which are compact and completely sealed, making them ideal for urban areas with space restrictions and high pollution. But they are also much too expensive for most Russian budgets and usually not even necessary. Why would anybody pay an exorbitant price for a space-saving solution in Siberia where space is their largest asset?

My product is simply unsuitable for the Russian market, with the exception of the big cities like Moscow and St. Petersburg. But Moscow already turned us down in favor of a Russian producer of GIS. And even though Vladimir has left me hoping that the contract will revert back to us, I've recently found out from Radoyko that the Russian competitor has already started production. And since this producer is located in St. Petersburg, I probably won't be able to compete there either.

Although I could probably sell some dead tank circuit breakers, Anis is refusing to do business with me, claiming his own representative can handle the customers just as well. My only consolation is that he hasn't had any success. I call Vladimir every week to ask about the pending contract with Bashkirenergo in Ufa, but he simply tells me to have patience. And I can tell Lambeer is becoming impatient and questioning my ability to finalize a sale.

I take a trip to Tula without informing Radoyko, afraid he would insist that one of his engineers accompany me. Instead I convince Vladimir to let me use his car and his chauffeur. Miasnikov assembles a group of his engineers, including Vanya with his blood-shot eyes and rose-colored nose, and Kolya.

Although two years earlier, I exulted dead tank circuit breakers as the best solution for Tula's substations, I now sing the praises of GIS. Showing colorful slides—A GIS assembly with its pipes of yellow, green, red, and blue could be a work of modern art—I emphasize the high reliability of the maintenance-free equipment, the compact design, and the short lead times—The Rolls Royce of high voltage switchgear. Miasnikov nods and smiles during my presentation.

Afterwards, I invite Miasnikov to lunch, where he tells me that Anis's representative, someone named Oleg Fischer, has already visited him together with Radoyko, trying to get another contract for dead tank circuit breakers. Radoyko has also called him several times.

'I think we have a good partnership,' I say. 'and should continue our little agreement.'

'What should I tell Radoyko Kosic?' Miasnikov asks.

'Tell him you're only interested in doing business with me,' I say, imagining Radoyko's reaction. 'In the meantime, maybe I can convince you of the advantages of GIS over dead tank breakers.'

'GIS is impressive,' he says, 'but expensive, I'm sure.'

I don't know whether he is only humoring me, but we look over a line diagram of a substation where the oil breakers could be replaced with GIS. Desperate to spark his interest, I raise my offer to 2% of any contract we sign, due on receipt of payment. I also subtly point out that 2% of GIS is a lot more than 2% of a few dead tank circuit breakers. After drinking half a bottle of vodka and having sex on his couch, we part with his promise not to do business with Oleg Fischer or Radoyko and to contact Vladimir concerning possible contract negotiations for GIS. It's amazing what 2% and a blowjob can accomplish.

Back in Zurich, I haven't been able to reach Vladimir for several days, getting his mailbox every time I call his cell phone. Finally it rings on a Friday afternoon.

'Hallo?' says a female voice which I don't recognize.

A woman? Why is a woman answering Vladimir's cell phone?

Panicking, I hang up the phone without speaking. Then I dial the number again, this time hearing Vladimir's husky voice. 'Kashirnikov.'

'Vladimir, where are you?' *Who answered your phone?*

'I'm on my way to Astrakhan,' he says.

Who was that woman? No. Don't ask. Don't appear jealous. 'Why?'

'I was invited for the weekend,' he says as if the news shouldn't surprise me.

By this woman?

Before I can say anything, he says, 'Listen, I'll call you on Tuesday.'

'Why not Monday?' I ask. But he has already hung up the phone.

Tuesday? What are you doing on Monday? For the first time, I realize that Vladimir has a private life which involves neither me nor his company.

All I can do is wait until Tuesday.

As promised, the phone rings on Tuesday morning before I leave for the office.

'Katey, there's something I need to tell you,' he says in English. He doesn't usually speak English to me.

'Go ahead,' I say, somehow sensing that the news will not be good.

He pauses so long I almost think the connection has broken.

Finally he says, 'The reason I'm getting divorced is because I'm getting married.'

Oh my God! That bitch who answered his telephone! 'Who?'

'Lara.'

I picture the little blonde bitch wiggling her ass in Vladimir's face the last time I was in his office. 'She's your goddamned secretary,' I say.

'Bill Gates married his secretary,' he says.

'You're not Bill Gates.

'Not yet,' he says.

'Bill Gates is a geek,' I say.

'He's a rich geek.'

'He's the richest geek in the world,' I say.

'My point exactly.'

Suddenly it occurs to me. 'What did you do? Knock her up?'

'What do you mean?' he asks, not understanding my slang.

'Did you get her pregnant?'

'Yes, she's pregnant,' he says.

I can't believe this is happening. 'You just got rid of one Russian bitch,' I say. 'What do you want another one for?'

'I love her,' he says rather hesitantly, as if trying to convince himself.

I'm sure she knew exactly what she was doing when she got herself knocked up and now he wants me to believe he loves her. Several weeks ago, I was sucking his cock. 'Yeah, and I'm the Tsarina of Russia,' I say. If he understands my sarcasm, he chooses to ignore it.

'I thought you were getting divorced to marry me,' I say. 'I thought you wanted to live in the United States.'

'Don't be silly, Katey,' he says. 'I'll never leave Russia.'

After he hangs up, I stare at the receiver for several minutes before placing it in the cradle. After calling Adriana to tell her I have the flu, I go to the kitchen and take a bottle of chardonnay from the refrigerator. Unable to stop the tears, I sink into the couch, slugging the wine like a thirsty mule.

When the bottle's empty, I get another one. After drinking half of it, I call Vladimir's cell phone. 'You can't marry her,' I say when he answers. 'I love you.'

'I can't talk about this now,' he says.

'Why?' I ask. 'Are you with Lara?' I say her name as if it were a dirty word.

'I can't talk now,' he says again, breaking the connection.

I finish the second bottle of wine before redialing his number. I'm frantic, all of my dreams shattered by two words—*she's pregnant*.

'How do you know it's yours?' I ask when he picks up the phone.

'I'm in a meeting,' he says with the iciness of a Siberian winter. 'I can't talk now.' He hangs up.

I hit the redial button and wait, this time getting his mailbox.

Too drunk to do anything else, I lie on the couch, watching German talk shows which I don't understand.

Then I leave the apartment and go to the train station, where I buy another bottle of wine and a pound of Swiss chocolate. *Who cares if I get fat?* After drinking wine and devouring chocolate all afternoon, I finally pass out on the couch towards evening.

The next morning, I take four Ibuprofen and my last two Prozac tablets, and then jog six miles. Feeling better, I go into work and tell Lambeer I'm booking a flight to Moscow.

'How may I help you, Frau O'Hara?' The Swiss psychiatrist is bald on top with grey locks reaching to his shoulders. He stares at me through tiny glasses.

I always feel old when they call me 'Frau'. 'I need a prescription,' I say, as casually as I can manage.

'And what are we taking?' he asks.

I don't know what you're taking, but I need... 'Prozac', I say.

'I see...fluoxetine. And why do we take fluoxetine?'

'I suffer from chronic depression.'

'How long have we had this problem?'

Since coming to Switzerland. 'For a while,' I say. 'I don't really know".

'How long have we been taking fluoxetine?'

He must be confusing the formal usage of you in

German with the English we. 'Three years.'

'And how high of a dosage do we require?'

Sixty to eighty milligrams. 'Forty milligrams,' I tell him.

'I think we can arrange that,' he says. 'Have you tried psychotherapy?'

Uh oh, here we go. I try to imagine myself with a Swiss psychotherapist.

'Why you are depressed?' he would ask.

'Because the Swiss are so damned arrogant and unfriendly. Because I can't get a single contract with Russia. Because the love of my life knocked up his secretary.'

'Knocked up?' he would ask, not understanding.

'No,' I say. 'I don't think it would help.'

'No?'

'My problem is hereditary.'

'I see...your Mother?'

'My whole family,' I lie. My family is full of smiling optimists. I'm sure everything will work out, they always say. If only they could see how things are working out now.

'I see,' he says. But of course, he doesn't. Instead he starts writing the prescription.

THIRTY-EIGHT

Before leaving for Moscow I go on a spending spree, starting with a stylish haircut at an elite salon in the *Bahnhof Strasse*, which includes a dye job back to my former blonde color, but this time even lighter. In an exclusive boutique, I pay 600 Swiss francs for an elegant Chanel suit in a rich shade of violet blue. The skirt hugs my hips, barely reaching to mid-thigh, the jacket short and fitted with a plunging neckline. A lacy silk camisole in a lighter shade of the same color and a chic pair of matching shoes with three inch heels complete my external look.

I buy Chanel Number 5.

Then I find an exquisite lingerie shop where I buy several pair of ultra-sheer thigh-high stockings with black lace bands. I don't buy any panties.

I buy a pair of 18-carat gold earrings which dangle like little wind chimes.

In a cosmetic shop, a salesgirl helps me select the best shades for my coloring, and I conclude my shopping spree with a collection of designer makeup.

I pay for everything with my corporate American

Express card.

I don't inform Vladimir of my travel plans.

Two days later, I'm once again in the presidential suite of the Hotel National. I don't believe it's a coincidence that it's the only available room when I make my reservation. Knowing I'm willing to pay, the director has probably put me on a special list of people who receive only the most expensive rooms.

In the morning I run five miles on the treadmill, increasing the speed until my heart seems to beat right out of my chest. The adrenaline rush gives me the confidence to face Vladimir.

After applying my makeup with such finesse that my eyes look like works of art, I slip into my thigh-highs and don my camisole. When I put on the skirt, it barely covers the black lace of my stockings, and the plunging collar of my jacket reveals the lace of my camisole. Standing before the mirror, I admire the bulge of my calf muscles, the fluffiness of my hair, and the curve of my derrière under the closely fitted skirt. I raise my skirt slowly as if performing a modern dance, exposing first the lace of my stockings and then my naked mound of pubic hair. *Perfect.*

When I call Vladimir's direct number, I am surprised to hear a woman's voice which sounds much older than Lara's.

'I'd like to speak to Vladimir Kashirnikov,' I say.

'I'm sorry,' the voice says. 'He's gone to Astrakhan with his fiancée to visit her parents and won't be returning until Monday.'

Today is Tuesday.

I debate my next action and finally call Sasha. We meet in a café not far from my hotel where I order two beers.

'I need your help,' I say. 'I need airline receipts for my expense report. I was hoping you could help me again.'

Without questioning my motives, Sasha simply asks, 'And where would you like to pretend to go?'

'Make one to Ufa, leaving this afternoon. Then I'll need one from there to Novosibirsk, returning to Moscow on Saturday.'

'No problem,' he says.

'Can you also make me some hotel receipts that look official? One should be for a hotel in Ufa, and the other for a hotel in Novosibirsk.'

'How much would you like to pay for these hotels?' Sasha asks.

'Upward of 200 dollars,' I say.

'And what are you going to be doing in the meantime?' he asks.

'First I'll move to the Art Hotel—it's quite a bit cheaper—and then hang around here until Monday,' I say. Then I ask, 'How much will all these receipts cost me?'

'Nothing,' he says. 'But don't forget the words of Marlon Brando. *Someday—and that day may never come— I'll call upon you to do a service for me. But until that day, accept this justice as a gift on my daughter's wedding day.*'

'You don't have a daughter.'

'I'm also not Don Corleone.'

'You're a great guy, Sasha.'

'I know.'

'Sasha, will you take me to a genuine Russian night club? I'll pay for everything,' I say. 'I'll put it on my expense report.'

'What kind of club are you looking for?' he asks.

'Some place where I can meet rich men. And they shouldn't be too young.'

'Do you like to dance,' he asks.

'I can't dance worth shit,' I say. 'I like to drink.'

'I know a place you'll like,' he says. 'It's called *Rusalka*.'

Rusalka means mermaid. 'Oh great,' I say. 'Do the waitresses dress in scales and fins?'

'No, they wear a lot less,' Sasha says.

Sasha meets me at the Art Hotel at nine p.m. I'm dressed in the same outfit that I chose to seduce Vladimir except that now I'm wearing panties. We take a taxi to *Rusalka*. The entrance shimmers with neon arcs in a rainbow of colors above a black door. Several men in dark clothing are hanging around the entrance.

After I pay the ten-dollar cover charge for each of us, we enter a dark lobby with a coatroom. The attendant takes our coats and hands each of us a numbered token.

We enter a smoky dance hall with a black floor and colored lights. There is a band playing Anita Ward's 'Ring My Bell', a number-one disco hit from the late seventies which I hated then and still hate today. A man is singing the lyrics in a convincing falsetto, and a handful of people are dancing. I notice a woman dressed in a red sheath with a plunging neckline and plenty of cleavage. Another one has a tight black knit tube dress with no shoulder straps. The men are dressed in brightly colored sport coats, and most seem to be over thirty.

'It's still early,' Sasha says. 'The real crowd won't come for another couple hours.'

'Do you come here often?' I ask.

'Not on Tuesday. It's oldies night. But you said you wanted to meet old men.'

'Not *old* men,' I say. '*Older* men.'

He shrugs. 'Do you want to dance?' he asks.

'No,' I say. 'I already said I don't know how. I'd like a drink.'

I use my corporate credit card to run a tab, starting with thirty dollars for a glass of white wine for myself and a tequila sunrise for Sasha. Apparently American cocktails have become the latest rage. In any case, it's going to be an expensive evening. I'll have to tell Lambeer I brought Miasnikov here to discuss a substation project.

I'm drinking my third glass of wine. It's still early—not

yet eleven—and the first crowds are drifting in.

'You were fucking Kashirnikov, weren't you?' Sasha says, much to my surprise.

'I wouldn't put it quite so crudely,' I say, 'but yes, we were having an affair.'

'You're in love with him, aren't you?' he says. It isn't really a question.

Instead of answering, I say, 'I can't believe he knocked up his secretary.'

'Katey, you have a lot to learn about Russian women. They can be quite devious. Once Lara decided to sink her claws into Vladimir, he didn't stand a chance. He could have fucked her in the ass and she still would have figured out a way to get pregnant.'

'So why is he making it so easy for her?' I ask.

'Because a scandal could hurt his career. Instead, he announces their engagement and everyone thinks he planned it.'

'Even if he doesn't love her?'

'I'm quite sure he doesn't give a shit about her. Why do you want to see him so badly that you're willing to hang out in Moscow for a week? I hope you don't think you can win him back. It's a done deal, Katey.'

Before I can answer, a tall, attractive man with dark bushy hair and eyes like sapphires presses his shoulder against mine. 'Hey beautiful,' he says. 'Do you want to dance?' Then he looks at Sasha. 'Do you mind,' he asks.

Sasha shakes his head.

'I'm Anton,' the man says, extending his hand. He's dressed in a black sport coat over a black t-shirt. I notice he is wearing a Rolex.

'Zelda,' I say.

The band is starting a slow dance—Dr. Hook's *Sharing the Night Together*. It was one of my favorite songs in the eighth grade and the first slow song I ever danced to with a boy. When Anton pulls my body to his, I rest my head on his shoulder, close my eyes, and return to that night on the dimly lit floor of the junior high gymnasium, where I danced with a boy who was several inches shorter than me. His body had been hot and had smelled faintly of sweat. I remember wishing the song would never end.

Although the singer is doing his best to pronounce the English lyrics, I would never have understood the words if I didn't already know them:

> *You're looking kind of lonely, girl.*
> *Would you like someone new to talk to?*
> *Oh yeah? All right.*
> *I'm feeling kind of lonely too.*
> *If you don't mind,*
> *can I sit down here beside you?*
> *Oh yeah? All right.*

Anton is wearing cologne which reminds me of a forest after a spring rain. His body is warm, but not sweaty. Although I know nothing about him except his name—if it's even his real name—he makes me feel safe. I would be happy to dance all night.

When the song ends, instead of releasing me, Anton pulls me closer and kisses me lightly on the lips.

As if catering to us personally, the band starts another slow song, 'We've got tonight' by Bob Seger. This time Anton pulls me tightly against him and I lose myself in the music.

> *I know it's late,*
> *I know you're weary.*
> *I know your plans don't include me.*
> *Still here we are,*
> *both of us lonely.*
> *I know it's late, girl.*
> *Why don't you stay?*

I'm disappointed when the soothing lyrics end and the band strikes up 'I Want to Hold Your Hand' by the Beatles. Pressing his hand against my butt, Anton guides me to a round ebony table in a dark corner. We sit with our knees touching, his hand fiddling with the top of my thigh-high stocking.

Glancing back at the bar, I see Sasha talking to an attractive young woman who doesn't look like a prostitute. He appears to have forgotten about me.

Anton orders me another glass of wine and a martini for himself. After the drinks arrive, he makes a toast.

'To my newly found beauty,' he says. We clink our glasses together, take a sip, and I wait for his kiss. Instead he says, 'Whatever that other guy is paying you, I'll double it.'

'What the hell are you talking about?' I ask, sitting back in my seat. 'What other guy?'

'Your sponsor,' he says. 'Isn't that guy at the bar your sponsor?'

'My sponsor for what?' I ask.

'I run a high-class escort service. I can make you one of my top ladies.'

Suddenly I know where the conversation is going. This new love of my life is a pimp. Appropriately, the band starts another disco song, Donna Summer's 'Bad Girls.' Anton must be paying them to perform on cue.

'Listen,' I say. 'I'm sorry to disappoint you, but I'm not a call girl. I'm an American businesswoman. I live in Switzerland.'

His eyes declare his disbelief. 'That's a great line,' he says. 'Our clients will love it. An American businesswoman! Super!'

'I'm not kidding,' I say.

'You *are* very convincing.'

Even though I shouldn't be showing a stranger my documents, pride forces me to prove I am not a prostitute. 'Do you want to see my passport?' I ask. Reaching into the purse which has been hanging from my shoulder all evening, I pull out the blue booklet and hand it to him.

He opens it and glances at the photo. For a moment, I fear he is going to steal it. U.S. passports get a good price in Russia. Instead he hands it back and says, 'You are Katherine O'Hara. I was in New York once.'

'I've never been to New York,' I say.

'Maybe we could do business together,' he says. 'You can help me get American clients. I even have a few hot numbers who speak a little English.'

'I'm not in Moscow that often,' I say. 'Like I said, I live in Switzerland.'

'I'll double your salary, get you a nice flat,' he says. 'All you have to do is frequent the hotel bars in the evening and offer our services to the American and European businessmen. They'll trust you. You're an American with an innocent face.'

'Sure,' I say. 'I've heard Siberian prisons are quite luxurious.'

'Don't be silly,' he says. 'The police commissioner and the mayor are two of my best clients. Like I said, I have really high-class ladies.'

The offer sounds tempting, even exciting. More money. More time in Russia. *Katey the Madam.* My job isn't going too well in Zurich. I wish I could trust the guy, but my instincts tell me he has other plans for me than to procure clients. Suddenly I find him creepy. 'I'm flying back to Switzerland tomorrow,' I say. 'Why don't I give you my phone number in Zurich and you can call me next week.' I take out a sheet of paper and write down my number, replacing a four with a seven and reversing the last two digits. 'Your offer is enticing,' I say, handing him the paper.

'I'll be sure to call,' he says.

Standing up, I say, 'I have an early flight tomorrow. I need to get back to my hotel.'

'Who's the guy?' he asks. 'If he's not your sponsor?'

'Just a coworker,' I say truthfully.

Anton kisses my cheek as we part. Then he approaches

a scantily dressed girl at the bar wearing fire-engine-red lipstick and starts talking to her. So much for high-class ladies!

'I'm going home,' I say to Sasha. 'I'll sign the bill first, but after that, you're on your own.'

'Do you want me to get you a taxi?' he asks, making it clear that he plans to stay.

'No, I'll manage.'

'Enjoy your flight to Siberia,' he says with a wink. 'See you Monday?'

'Looking forward to it,' I say, wondering what I am really going to do until then.

When I get outside, a man asks if I need a taxi. When I nod, he leads me to a shiny new Ford Taurus without a taxi sign. Since Moscow has a lot of businesses called 'Rent-A-Car' where you can order a car and driver, I'm not worried about getting into this unmarked car. I don't think a serial killer would show his face so openly in a public place.

All the same, I'm relieved to see the lights of Art Hotel thirty minutes later.

THIRTY-NINE

I waltz into Vladimir's office, unannounced, on Monday morning. Lara's desk is empty; she's probably adjusting to her future role of full-time housewife. Vladimir, who is on the telephone, grins when he sees me. I'm once again dressed in my Chanel outfit. It cost me twenty-five dollars to get it dry-cleaned. I shouldn't have worn it to that smoky nightclub.

I sit down in front of his desk and cross my legs, letting my skirt ride up to expose the lacy tops of my stockings, and run my fingers seductively through my hair, exposing a dangling earring of eighteen-carat gold.

'I didn't expect to see you here,' he says when he hangs up the phone.

I get right to the point. 'I don't want to stay in Switzerland. I want a job with Ernst Werner AG in Germany.'

Vladimir hesitates. 'The time isn't right,' he says.

'I don't have a single contract, not even a possibility for a contract.'

'What about Miasnikov?'

'He means well,' I say. 'But GIS is just too expensive.'

'What about the dead tank breaker contract in Ufa?'

'What about it? You tell me? I don't think I'll ever get a contract with Ufa. That meeting was months ago. And remember, they decided to go with our competitor.'

'Damn it, Katey. I told you to be patient.'

'My own contract expires in January. If I don't bring in some business—which I won't—Lambeer won't renew it, and then I'll be stuck in Zurich with no work permit, no residence permit, and not even enough money for a plane ticket back to America.'

'He'll renew your contract,' Vladimir says. 'You haven't done anything wrong. And I can always talk to him. He'll listen to me.'

'I don't want to take that chance. You work for his competitor now. He may not trust you as completely as he used to. Use your damned connections and your influence. Get me a job in Germany. You owe me.'

'Why do I owe you?'

'Because you're marrying *her* instead of me. I always assumed you would marry me. Couldn't you have at least worn a fucking rubber?'

Vladimir sits back in his chair and clasps his hands together. 'Katey, Katey, Katey, won't you ever understand. Personal relationships come and go. Friendship and business relationships are all that really matter. I love you and I'll always love you. It doesn't matter who I marry.'

'Then prove it,' I say. 'Get me out of Switzerland.'

Four weeks later, I have an interview in Erlangen, Germany, in the medium-voltage department of Ernst Werner AG. The marketing manager, Heinz Mueller, has a starchy demeanor and the personality of a test pattern. Dressed in a navy blue suit, a pressed white shirt, a maroon tie, black-lace shoes, and glasses, he is the prototype of an upright and humorless German businessman. His handshake is weak, his skin soft, and clammy.

'We have a medium-voltage plant in St Petersburg,' he says in slow, careful English. 'They are ready to start production and we need someone with connections to the regional customers, who can travel around Russia and promote our product.'

'Promotion is my strength,' I say. 'I have good relations with a large number of Russian customers. Up to now, the main problem I've had is a resistance to buy equipment from western companies. But since this equipment will be produced in Russia by Russian workers, it should be much easier to sell.'

'Do you have any experience with medium-voltage equipment?' he asks.

'No,' I say. 'But I just have to sell it, not understand it.'

When he doesn't respond to my feeble attempt at a joke with even the hint of a smile, I know I've made a mistake. I quickly say, 'I'm a fast learner. As a mechanical-engineering student, I had several courses in circuitry, so I have a basic knowledge of how everything works.'

'We have a six-month training program,' he says. 'Including four weeks of intensive German study.'

'I'm really excited about this opportunity,' I say. 'I promise I won't disappoint you.'

'Herr Kashirnikov highly recommended you. Don't prove him wrong.' It almost sounds like a threat.

Two weeks later, I receive a job offer to start in February, after my contract in Zurich expires. When I inform Conrad Lambeer of my plans, he tells me he is also resigning and returning to Australia. I don't ask him why. In any case, he isn't upset to see me go.

Part 3
Germany, February 1998

FORTY

My new city of employment in Germany's Central Franconia has 100,000 residents and is known for two things: a major university and Ernst Werner AG, the city's largest employer. The city is also home to 400 bars and restaurants and more bike routes than any other German metropolis. Every morning, thousands of bicyclists give motorists migraines as Ernst Werner engineers, dressed in white shirts and ties with briefcases strapped on back fenders, and students touting backpacks maneuver through the streets to offices and classrooms.

While making arrangements to move to Erlangen, I start up a telephone friendship with Monika, Heinz Mueller's bilingual secretary. She arranges for a moving company to drive from Erlangen to Zurich to pick up my belongings and then comes up with a 'brilliant idea' to have me ride in the moving van with the truckers. Although I'm wondering why my new employer is too cheap to buy me a plane ticket, I accept Monika's plan, not wanting to appear uncooperative before I even start working.

The cabin of the moving van is wide enough for me to

sit comfortably between the two drivers, who switch places every two hours. Other than to offer me an occasional cigarette, they pretty much ignore me, which is okay because my German isn't good enough to carry on a conversation.

When I arrived in Switzerland one year earlier, I was required to register at the *Anmeldeamt*. What I didn't know is that I needed to deregister at the same place when leaving the country.

Without my deregistration, bringing my cargo into Germany proves difficult and we are required to take an alternate route, entering Germany at the customs bureau in Baden Baden. It takes the driver an hour to get through the long line of cars and finish the paperwork, although not understanding much German, I can't identify the problem.

When I reach my destination, the drivers take me to an apartment building belonging to Ernst Werner AG, first stopping at one of the company's security offices to pick up my key. I move into a furnished studio apartment with a telephone, but no television. My furniture is being stored by the moving company until I find a permanent place.

The next morning I go jogging, being careful not to get lost. At the intersection, I notice a tired, but attractive taxi driver staring at me. He drives away when the light turns green.

I then dress conservatively in a brown designer suit with a matching short-sleeve turtleneck under the blazer. Since it's February and quite cold, I put on a pair of high-heeled boots. Although the mile walk to the office is uncomfortable in high heels, I have no idea which bus to take.

Heinz Mueller is waiting for me and greets me in German. While in Switzerland, I studied German at home with a ninety-lesson set of tapes and can respond to his simple questions.

Copying the modern American business style, the office

is one large room filled with workstations consisting of a desk with a computer, a telephone, and a storage cabinet. Even Heinz Mueller doesn't have a private office, just a workstation near the door. My desk is directly in front of his, beside the man who has been handling the Russian market up to now. In his early fifties, Peter speaks a Bavarian dialect, and looks like he should be wearing Lederhosen and drinking a liter mug of dark beer. He has rosy cheeks, a pot belly and a hooked nose, typical of the Franconian folk.

Before long, I realize that Peter detests Russia and everything associated with it. My German is just good enough to understand his gripes about the country: it is too cold, the water contains parasites, the airplanes fly like they are going to crash, and even though everything in Russia costs a fortune, the customers never have any money. I also learn about his disadvantageous divorce settlement, his affinity for good beer, and his distaste for vodka ('tastes like cheap motor oil').

Heinz Mueller has informed me that I will be starting my training plan with a four-week intensive German course in the small Bavarian town of Prien am Chiemsee, located between Munich and Salzburg. I am scheduled to leave in five days, meaning I'll be moving out of my furnished apartment and moving into another apartment in Prien.

Since I'll be needing an apartment when I return, Monika gets a list of two-room units from a rental agent. The first one we look at has a bedroom smaller than my king-size bed, definitely a student dive. The next one is in a basement and smells like a sewer. Finally I find a flat above a family-owned butcher's shop. The butcher and his wife seem friendly and the apartment is modern and clean with a balcony looking out onto the street. And if I get hungry, I'll only need to go downstairs.

What the secretary neglects to tell me is that the agent collects a finder's fee equivalent to three months' rent, and the landlord typically requires a security deposit of another three-month's rent. The rent is 650 marks a month plus utilities. That means 1950 marks for the agent and another 1950 marks for the security deposit plus the first month's rent. It will cost me more than four thousand marks—slightly more than two thousand dollars—just to move into my apartment, due when I return from Prien am Chiemsee one month later. So much for my first paycheck.

The train ride with a transfer in Munich takes four hours. Absorbed in a trashy novel, I barely notice the passing time or the countryside and before long I am dragging my suitcase across the Munich Station looking for platform 21. Not wanting to miss my stop, I now stay alert, reading the names of the train stations, constantly on the lookout for Prien.

On arriving, I find several taxis waiting at the station and grab the first one. Since Prien is a small town, we quickly arrive at the Rothkirch Institute of German Language, a massive 19th century house surrounded by a low wooden fence with a gate.

A friendly woman, speaking English with a heavy accent, welcomes me. 'You have an apartment with Frau Schmidt,' she says. 'I will take you there.'

As we're walking along the sidewalk of a narrow street, I notice a large number of 'Rooms to Rent' signs on the large three-story houses. Since Chiemsee is one of Germany's largest lakes, Prien is a popular resort town. At the end of February, however, with temperatures in the forties, the town seems deserted.

My apartment is on the third floor of a stucco house with wood trim and balconies. There is a tiny bedroom with a double bed under a slanted roof. The other room is a combination kitchen-living room with a television getting only two stations. I notice two puzzles on the shelf under the television—a cathedral with a thousand pieces and a baby giraffe with five hundred.

Without a bite of food in the apartment, I decide to find a restaurant or grocery store. Worried about getting lost, I write my new address on a small sheet of paper before venturing out into the dusky street. An icy rain is glazing the sidewalks with a shiny wetness, starting to form a glassy surface as the temperature drops. Since the weather is perfect for roasting a chicken, I decide to hunt for one.

After walking two blocks, I see a grocery store called Norma. Going inside, I discover nothing but packaged and frozen foods. Determined to find a fresh chicken, I leave the store empty-handed and continue toward the downtown area, eventually finding another grocery store called Comet. Here, I spot fresh chickens and select the fattest one. Then I buy garlic and a bottle of imported Italian Rosé.

With the smell of garlic-roasted chicken filling the apartment, I pour myself a glass of wine and spread the giraffe puzzle onto the dining room table. I finish the entire border before the chicken is ready.

I'm looking forward to gorging myself with poultry when the phone rings. Who the hell knows my number?

'I'm a father!' Vladimir says. 'It's a boy.'

'Congratulations.' *What else am I supposed to say?* 'How did you know my number?' I ask.

'I called your office earlier and asked for it,' he says. 'I wanted to tell you that I called Miasnikov and he is interested in medium-voltage equipment. Then Lara went into labor and I had to leave the office urgently.'

'When will you be back to work?' I ask.

'Tomorrow. I have too many big projects to take time off.'

I wonder what big projects he has. Certainly none involving me. I say, 'Tell Miasnikov I'll plan a trip to Tula as soon as I finish my training program.'

'I'll call you tomorrow,' he says. After a short pause, he says, 'I love you.'

I am too shocked to answer and finally whisper *I love you* to a dial tone.

Eating the chicken without tasting it, I drink a third glass of wine. Then I get into bed, planning to read my novel, but am too tired, upset, and drunk to concentrate. After reading the same paragraph four times without understanding it, I set my alarm for seven and turn out the light. The German classes start at eight. Lying in darkness, I imagine Vladimir at his wife's hospital bed, a cuddly baby at her breast. He's holding her hand and they are both smiling. He says, 'I love you.' I can't stop the silent tears from staining my cheeks and lie awake for a long time.

The next morning at Rothkirch, I meet a group of young professionals from all over the world, mostly in their twenties, all employed by Ernst Werner AG. The first thing we do is take a placement test, which will be graded during the coffee break, and then we'll be divided into groups.

During the break, one of the young American men says to the entire group, 'So I guess our common language is English.'

There are people from all over the world here—South America, Eastern Europe, China, Japan, Turkey, and Greece. 'Es ist Deutsch,' I say.

I'm not surprised when I test into the most-advanced group and my fellow American into the beginners.

The course is taught entirely in German, four hours in the morning and two hours in the afternoon with a two-hour break in between. I use the free hours to lift weights at a local health club, which allows me to pay on a weekly basis. Several hours every evening I study the lessons, ignoring invitations from my classmates to go to the bar. I am determined to speak fluent German by the end of the course.

The director calls me into her office at the end of the third week.

'Herr Mueller called us to see how you're doing,' she

says in German. 'We told him you are our best student.'

'That's very kind,' I reply, also in German.

'He wants you to end the course early,' she says. 'Apparently he needs you in the office.'

FORTY-ONE

When I return to work, expecting Heinz Mueller to praise my excellent progress in the German language, I hear only criticism.

'You should have told me you can already speak German,' he says, 'instead of wasting company time and money.'

'I couldn't already speak German,' I protest in the best German I can manage. 'I'm just able to learn languages fast and I studied very hard.'

I can tell he doesn't believe me, choosing to think I was enjoying a vacation in Prien while pretending I couldn't speak German.

'In any case,' he says. 'I need you to start selling in Russia. Immediately. I want you to fly to Moscow and get in touch with our country manager.'

'What about my training program?' I ask.

'It will have to wait,' he says. 'Vladimir Kashirnikov convinced me you were the best in the business, and now I need you to prove it.'

Without any training? I'd made it clear at the job interview that I didn't know much about medium-voltage equipment. Although it hadn't seemed to bother Herr Mueller at the time, now his tone is accusatory. I wonder who he's been talking to.

'What would you like me to do?' I ask, still struggling to speak German and wishing he would switch to English. He doesn't.

'It's your market,' he says. 'You tell me.'

I pause for a moment. Then I recover quickly and say, 'First, I should visit all of my former customers and tell them about my new product. I can plan a trip to Moscow, Tula, Ufa, and Tiumen to start with.'

'You have to clear all trips with our plant manager in Yekaterinburg,' he says. 'Dieter Fickstein expects to know your plans.'

Here we go again. Another stone in my path. 'Does he speak Russian?' I ask, hoping I won't have to talk to him in German.

'Yes, of course,' Herr Mueller says. 'He's from the former GDR. They all studied Russian in school.'

A former Communist. 'Should I call him?' I ask.

'You should call him and have him arrange your trip. He will want to send someone with you or even accompany you himself.'

Oh God, a watchdog! And the Russians will just love to have some East German poking his nose into their somewhat shady business.

'I've been working very closely with Vladimir Kashirnikov,' I say. 'We have some projects already started.'

'Katey,' he says. 'Herr Kashirnikov is now the president of Ernst Werner AG in Russia and has other responsibilities. We have a strict hierarchy that you need to follow. Your contact person is Herr Fickstein.'

'Then I guess I better get a ticket to Yekaterinburg,' I say.

'Katey, one more thing,' he adds. 'I don't expect you to

wear a suit every day. Try to relax a bit. We have a casual dress code.'

The one thing I never expected in Germany was to be told I dress too well. Copying Vladimir's taste for fashion, and the general tendency of Russians to dress formally, I've purchased a dozen suits over the past year. Other than suits, I have jeans, leggings, and trendy mini-skirts, nothing appropriate for the sexless polo-shirt and chinos dress code he is suggesting. And after the money I just paid for my apartment, I am close to broke.

'The Russians dress more formally,' I say. 'I try to dress appropriately for the customer.'

'But there are no Russians here,' he says.

I guess I'll have to go shopping again and use my Corporate American Express card.

After talking to Mueller, I call Vladimir.

'Mueller wants me to work with Fickstein,' I say. 'I'm supposed to tell him all my plans.'

I expect Vladimir to be incensed. I expect him to call Mueller and explain that I need to work alone. What I don't expect is Vladimir's reply.

'Fickstein's a good guy,' he says. 'You need to go out and meet him.'

'You can't mean that,' I say. 'What about us? What about Moscow Electrical Consulting?'

'Be patient, Katey,' he says.

'I'm tired of being patient. I want to make a sale.'

'Listen, Katey, I have a meeting in five minutes. I need to get ready for it. Take your trip to Yekaterinburg. Let Fickstein help you.'

'How can someone from East Germany named Fickstein possibly help me? His name means fuck stone.'

'Get your mind out of the gutter, Katey.'

Dieter Fickstein is even more irritating than Radoyko.

With the business mentality of a communist and the pettiness of a German, he places procedure above success, planning each of my trips according to specific guidelines.

'We have a business office in Ufa,' Fickstein says. 'You can go there first and introduce yourself to the local representative. If you want to visit any customers, my representatives will make all the arrangements and accompany you at all times. You're to have no secrets from them. Or from me.'

He's obviously heard things about me already and as he speaks, I realize I'll never make another sale. The only hope for success is to sneak behind Fickstein's back. But if I do that, Mueller will fire me.

And then another thought occurs to me. Mueller won't authorize any payment to Moscow Electrical Consulting unless Fickstein knows about it. And I'm certain Vladimir won't want Fickstein to know about our little deal. I might as well pack my bags and polish my résumé.

When I get to Ufa, I'm not surprised to be met by the same skinny kid who had been competing for the dead tank breaker contract a year ago. Since we didn't talk to each other during our last encounter, I learn now that his name is Vadim Palkin. When we visit Savochenko, I feel like I have a pet dog.

'The dead tank breaker contract is still pending,' Savochenko says as we're seated in his office.

'I don't represent them anymore,' I say. 'I work for Ernst Werner AG now. We have a plant in Yekaterinburg that produces medium-voltage equipment.'

'There are many Russian companies producing good medium-voltage circuit breakers,' he says. 'We have standing orders with several of them.'

I bet they won't give you a five percent bonus, I think. But with the local representative sitting next to me, I can't possibly offer a bribe. I can only hope to convince Vladimir to visit Savochenko himself.

Probably not wanting to share a meal with my escort, Savochenko turns down my lunch invitation. I'll need to figure out a way to come here alone. I'll have to have a serious talk with Mueller, but only after I get the contracts. Surely he'll forget procedure if I'm successful. Or will he?

Two weeks later, I'm on a plane to Yekaterinburg. Although my final destination is Ufa, I have to make Herr Mueller believe I am visiting Fickstein. I actually plan to take a taxi from the airport directly to the train station—there are no timely flights from Yekaterinburg to Ufa—and continue on my journey without stopping at the local office. I can only hope that Mueller doesn't call Fickstein during my absence. Can I really be so stupid to believe he won't call?

Since I had a flight change in Moscow, I stayed overnight in the National, hoping to see Vladimir. But when I called his office from the hotel, dressed in a sexy negligee, a secretary—not Lara—told me he had flown to Germany unexpectedly on urgent business. Since he knew I was coming to Moscow, I can't help wondering if his sudden change of plans was deliberate. I even considered dropping by office to see if he was really gone.

When I reach the train station at seven p.m., I am relieved to see that a train is departing for Ufa in less than an hour. Having made my plans without checking the train schedule, I'm relieved I won't have to wait long.

I pay for the first class ticket in rubles, the equivalent of fifty dollars. The train is leaving at ten minutes to eight, arriving in Ufa five hours later. I had called Savochenko from Moscow, telling him of my visit, and he had promised to reserve me a room in the same hotel where I always stay. Hopefully, I'll be able to wake the night manager.

Before getting on the train, I buy four half-liter cans of German beer at the kiosk. It's going to be a long ride.

It turns out to be a sleeper train with coupes. Apparently the train is continuing to some further destination after stopping in Ufa. My first-class car has two beds, the other still unoccupied. I set my suitcase and backpack on the bed, plop myself down, lean back against the wall, and snap open a beer.

A few minutes later, a tall man in his late fifties enters the coupe. Dressed in a high quality dark suit with a classy tie, he's either a businessman or a mobster. He has bushy eyebrows and grey wavy hair, a weather-beaten face, and kind eyes. Perhaps the ride won't be so boring after all.

'Beer isn't a lady's drink,' he says.

'I live in Germany now,' I say. 'Beer is everybody's drink in Bavaria.'

'May I offer you Armenian brandy?' he asks, producing a bottle of amber liquid. 'It's the very best.'

Why the hell not! 'Sure,' I say, expecting him to hand me the bottle.

Instead, he pulls two snifters from his bag, sloshes some brandy into one of them and hands it to me. I wait while he pours his own. Then we raise our glasses and he gives a toast.

'To new friendships,' he says, clinking his glass against mine.

It's the best brandy I've ever tasted, even smoother than the cognac I drank with Andrei at Aerostar. Drinking it is like swallowing pure silk.

'What's your name?' he asks.

'Scarlet,' I say. 'And yours?'

'Albért,' he says.

Two hours later, I'm sprawled naked on top of Albert on his skinny bed. The brandy bottle is almost empty.

'Do you always sleep with strangers?' he asks.

'Only when I drink Armenian brandy on Russian trains,' I say. 'Besides, you're not a stranger. You're Albért.'

'I think I can help you with your little problem,' he says.

I've spent the last hour pouring my heart out to him

about Vladimir and his marriage to Lara, making her sound like Medusa with snakes swirling around her head and fingernails like talons.

'What do you mean?' I ask.

'We can get rid of the girl.'

'Get rid of—' Suddenly it dawns on me. 'That's crazy. I don't want to kill her.' *Do I?*

'*Kill* is such a nasty word,' he says. 'We prefer to say *disappear.*'

'As if Vladimir would ever marry me knowing I arranged to knock off his wife.' *Would he?*

'Maybe he would thank you,' Albért says as if reading my thoughts. 'Besides, he doesn't need to know you were involved. We'll make it look like an accident.'

'You're just kidding, aren't you?' I ask. 'I mean this is all a joke, isn't it?' I can't believe I am even contemplating this. *Katey O'Hara sentenced to Siberia for murdering the wife of the Ernst Werner AG country manager in Russia.*

'Think whatever you want, Scarlet.'

We make love again and finish the brandy, our conversation becoming choppy and hazy. Barely aware of my actions, I give him my real name and phone number. Then I tell him where Lara works. He says he'll call me in Germany and tell me where to transfer the money and how much.

I doze off and when Albért wakes me, we are almost in Ufa, our last conversation seeming like a dream. When he doesn't mention it again, I start to believe it was. In any case, I certainly hope it was. We part like strangers, knowing we'll never meet again. Or will we?

FORTY-TWO

'Do you remember Igor Zamirov?' Vladimir asks when I return to Moscow. Apparently his trip to Germany was a short one. I bet he didn't go there at all and has just been avoiding me. 'From the Tula seminar? Remember? The chief engineer from Belgorod?'

'How was Germany?' I ask. 'Did you see my boss?'

'Huh?'

I rest my case.

'Belgorodenergo is giving Zamirov a sixtieth birthday party. There will be a lot of people there from other energos. It's a good chance to establish contacts. Achim Zapp is coming with me.'

Achim Zapp is an East German in Ernst Werner AG's power-generation department. He speaks fluent Russian, enjoys vodka and seems be one of Vladimir's closest friends. Before the wall collapsed, he must have had a cohort of Soviet drinking buddies who helped him refine his skills.

I wonder if he also shares a secret Swiss bank account with Vladimir. It's probably seeing more action than mine.

Surprisingly the bank hasn't closed my account, even though I still have a zero balance after promising regular deposits in six-digit figures. Then it occurs to me that they don't even know my name. They probably closed the account and were unable to notify me.

Not wanting to be left out, and thinking I might be able to seduce Vladimir on the sleeper train, I say, 'I definitely want to come. But I want my own coupe. I don't like to sleep with strangers.'

'Then you'll have to buy two first-class tickets. I'll be sharing a coupe with Achim.'

That's what you think!

'By the way, did you have any luck with Savochenko?' Vladimir asks.

'He was vague, as usual, but said he would look for a project.'

'Don't get your hopes up, Katey. There are a lot of medium-voltage producers in Russia. And their equipment isn't all that bad.'

'This is getting frustrating,' I say. 'I'm starting to think I'll never make another sale.' The one contract I signed with Miasnikov at the beginning of my career seems like a hundred years ago.

'I've got even more bad news,' he says. 'Your boss called Fickstein to see if you arrived okay in Yekaterinburg. Fickstein says he never saw you and was furious to learn you were in Russia without telling him. And your boss isn't too happy either.'

'Can you call them both?' I plead. 'Can you explain that the trip was your idea? After all, you're Fickstein's boss.'

'I'll see what I can do. But remember, Fickstein's a German and I'm a Russian. I'm not really his boss. He's getting paid by Ernst Werner AG in Germany.'

I suspect something brown and stinky is going to hit the fan when I get back to Erlangen.

'Werner AG is a massive organization, Frau O'Hara. It can only function if everyone follows the procedures.'

I'm sitting at a table in a windowless room with Heinz Mueller. Apparently he's been on the telephone all week with Fickstein, listening to him rant and rave about vigilante business practices. He's even banned me from visiting Savochenko, claiming his acne-scarred little Russian can do the job better himself. Apparently Vladimir neglected to call my boss.

I try to explain that I can't do business successfully unless I can meet the customers alone. They have to trust me personally. I can't very well offer a bribe with a pubescent weed sitting next to me taking notes.

'Then you have to explain that to Herr Fickstein,' Mueller insists. 'If you're making deals with customers, I expect you to give him a full report. You can trust him.'

I can trust him? Every time I offer a bribe, I run the risk of getting sent to Siberia. And I'm supposed to trust him? If the shit comes down, it won't be his neck on the chopping block!

'There's a problem,' I say. I don't know if I should tell him this, but what the hell! 'I'm using a Russian agent called Moscow Electrical Consulting. They are helping me to negotiate with Savochenko and specifically said they didn't want anyone else in Russia to know about it.'

Surely he'll understand. All I'm trying to do is be successful. You can't apply German business practices to the Russian market. You can't tame a rabid lion or open a petting zoo in the jungle.

'Either you find a way to do business in Russia without keeping secrets from your superiors or we'll find someone who can.'

He has to be bluffing. He better be bluffing. What if he's not? All I know is I need a substantial contract and I need it quick.

The first thing I do is call Vladimir, partly out of habit and partly because I desperately need his help.

'Mueller threatened to fire me,' I say as soon as Vladimir picks up the phone. 'Why didn't you call him?'

'I did call him.'

Liar! 'What do I do now?'

'He won't fire you.' Vladimir says.

'He's asking me to do the impossible,' I say. 'I have to follow his rules and still be successful. I can do one or the other. I can't do both.'

'Then I would suggest you follow his rules. At least for a while.'

FORTY-THREE

Trip Report
To: Heinz Mueller, Dieter Fickstein
From: Katey O'Hara
Destination: Belgorod
Dates: June 16 – 18, 1998

I accompanied Vladimir Kashirnikov, President of Ernst Werner AG - Russia, and Achim Zapp, Sales Director of Power Generation, to Belgorod to celebrate the sixtieth birthday of Igor Zamirov, Chief Engineer of Belgorodenergo. It was a good opportunity to strengthen my relationship with Zamirov and to meet many potential customers. There was a great deal of eating, drinking, singing, dancing and toasting late into the night.

While we were dancing, I had a brief opportunity to inform Zamirov of my new role as sales engineer for medium voltage equipment and we agreed I would return to Belgorod in the near future to discuss possible projects.

'Frau O'Hara, this is not a trip report,' Mueller says. 'Nobody is interested in how much drinking and dancing you did.'

I am so sick of this man. He is never going to get with the program. 'I didn't drink,' I say truthfully. After that notorious incident in the sauna which sent Vladimir into the arms of

Lara, I've become very careful about drinking with customers.

'That's not my point,' he says. 'We send you to Russia for business meetings, not for parties.'

'It's very important in Russia to attend parties and establish contacts,' I say. 'If you don't drink with the Russians, they won't trust you.'

'I thought you said you didn't drink.'

'I've drunk with most of them often enough in the past that they'll trust me with their deepest secrets.'

'I don't want them to trust you with their deepest secrets,' he says. 'I want them to buy our equipment.'

'The two actions go hand in hand,' I say.

'That's not how we operate,' he says. 'We're a serious company with a solid image.'

I don't say a word. How do I explain to him that you can't force German values on Russian customers. How do I make him understand that the Russians aren't interested in our solid image, but rather in the little favors we can do for them?

When I don't speak, he continues.

'We have a good product, made in Russia, that the customers desperately need,' he says. 'I don't see how you can fail.'

'They need a reason to buy it from us and not from somebody else,' I say. 'Savochenko told me there are plenty of good Russian companies producing medium-voltage equipment. He's bought from them in the past. I need to give him a reason to buy from me.'

'You have to convince him of our superior quality,' he says. 'That should be enough.'

'That isn't enough,' I argue. 'Russian business practices are very personal. First you need to forge a friendship with the customer, get him to trust you. I can't do that if I always have a local representative tagging along.'

'Why not? Why can't the customer trust the local

representative?'

'Because the local representatives are Russians. Russians don't trust each other as easily. And the rep in Ufa is just a kid.'

'And what about Fickstein? He's not a Russian.'

'He's an East German. For the Russians, that is almost the same thing.' *And he's a complete asshole as well.*

'Then you need to introduce him to your contacts. You need to explain that you are working through Fickstein and his team.'

I'm starting to think my boss has a learning disability. 'Do you want procedure or do you want success?' I ask.

'I want both,' he says.

FORTY-FOUR

I'm already in bed on a Sunday night when the phone rings. Stumbling in the dark, I pick up the receiver on the fourth ring.

'Katey,' says a voice that I don't recognize.

'Who is this?' I ask, slightly nervous that a male voice late at night knows my name.

'Albért.'

'I don't know anyone named Albért,' I say.

'We met on the train to Ufa,' he says. 'I wanted to give you the number of a Swiss bank account where you can transfer the money. Remember?'

Suddenly I remember. Armenian brandy, making love, making plans...*oh God! The hit! He's calling about the hit!*

'No,' I say. 'Call it off. I wasn't serious.'

'I can't call it off, Katey. These contracts go through so many channels I don't even know who to contact. They're expecting $5000.'

'What if I just don't pay?' I ask.

'I wouldn't advise that,' he says. 'There's a man out there expecting payment. He may have already spent the money.'

'Listen, Albért,' I say. 'I'm not a murderess. I can't let this happen.'

'If you don't pay, they may come after you as well,' Albert says with the warmth of an icicle.

'There must be something I can do,' I plead.

'Okay, Katey,' he says. 'You're a nice lady, so I'll try to help you. First, you pay the money, then I'll try to stop the hit. But I can't guarantee anything.'

'That's not good enough,' I say. 'You have to stop the hit.'

'That's the best I can do, Katey.'

'I don't have $5000,' I say.

'I suggest you find it. Do you have something to write with?'

He gives me the account number in Switzerland. Not knowing what else to do, I promise to transfer the money the next day. Albért assures me he will try to stop the hit.

After he hangs up, I pour myself a double whisky and sit on the couch, wondering if I should warn Vladimir. But what if I tell him and Lara ends up dead? He'll know I did it. No. I'll just have to trust Albért. Maybe he is just trying to scare me. Maybe the money is really for him and he hasn't even arranged a hit. No. I can't take that chance.

The next day, I use my credit card to transfer $5000 to Switzerland.

A week later when I ask Vladimir how Lara is doing, he gives me a strange look and says she is fine.

FORTY-FIVE

Two weeks later, I'm facing Heinz Mueller and his own boss in the executive office with the door closed.

'Your probationary period ends next month,' Mueller says. 'We have to decide what to do. So far, the only feedback we've gotten about you has been negative. Herr Fickstein has requested that you don't come to Russia anymore.'

'How can he do that?' I ask. 'How much has he sold?'

'As much as you have, Katey,' Mueller says. "And to answer your first question, we have a very strict hierarchy here. Herr Fickstein is in charge of Russia. You are not important enough for us to go over his head."

That's where you'll wrong. The Russians love me. Or do they really? 'I've only been here five months,' I say. 'I didn't even get to complete my training program.'

'You should be working together with Herr Fickstein, not competing with him,' Mueller says. 'Your business style doesn't fit with our organization. We're a big company and expect all of our employees to follow our procedures.'

Since Mueller's boss hasn't spoken, I assume he is there

as a witness.

'I've decided to terminate your employment,' Mueller says. 'I can give you two weeks.'

His words are like a shotgun blast. 'I have a contract until January,' I say. 'I just moved here. I don't even have enough money to fly home.'

'I'm sorry,' he says. 'We can keep you employed until the end of your probation period. Peter will find some tasks for you.' He closes his folder, or should I say, my dossier. The meeting is over.

Determined to show no emotion at all, and certainly not my impending tears, I get up and leave the room. When I get to my desk, I grab my purse and head for the door, not even bothering to say good-bye to Peter, who gives me a knowing look. He was probably part of the lynch mob.

I exit the building, already deciding never to return. *Until the end of my probation period, my ass. Fuck you, Mueller. Fuck you, Fickstein. And fuck you as well Vladimir! Fuck Russia!*

Not wanting to wait for the bus, I tramp home on high heels. I'll probably never need to wear them again anyway, so who cares if I ruin them. When I get to my apartment, I throw my blazer into a corner like an old rag. Then I step out of my shoes, skirt, and pantyhose and toss them after the blazer, not intending to ever wear them again.

I find a pair of faded brown Levis and an army green tee-shirt. I put on a brown jeans jacket and step into comfortable shoes with laces: my drinking attire. I'm going into town. And I'm going to get drunk.

I take bus number 294 to the central post office. There's an Irish pub on the other side of the street and I go inside, not surprised to find it empty at the early hour of five p.m. I order a Guinness and drink it in a dark corner. Then I order a second one and drink that also.

Bored, I leave the bar and look for another one. I find a Mexican place called Sausilitos near the train station. Taking a seat at the bar, I order a margarita. It doesn't take long before a bespectacled man with bad breath sits down and starts talking at me. Although my German isn't good enough to understand his regional dialect, I don't let on. I simply finish my drink, pay the bartender, and leave quietly, as if I were just going to the john.

I explore an unfamiliar street—*Hell! They're all unfamiliar*—and look for a decent bar. It shouldn't be hard to find one since Erlangen has over 300 of them. After about ten minutes, I enter a district far away from the Ernst Werner AG conglomerate with many apartment buildings and several drinking establishments. A few minutes later, I'm standing in front of *Murphy's Law*, another Irish bar decorated with shamrocks and leprechauns.

Going inside, I focus on a white-bearded man seated at the bar. Although he looks familiar, I can't place the man's face. Suddenly it hits me—my first business trip to Russia almost three years ago. We drank vodka on the airplane while discussing his unsatisfactory sex life. I never learned his name.

Seating myself on the empty stool beside him, I order another Guinness. At first he only stares blankly, but then smiles in recognition and shakes my hand.

'I got fired today,' I say. Small talk doesn't seem necessary.

'So you're out celebrating?' he asks.

'What else am I supposed to do? I'm broke, unemployed, and living in a foreign country. I don't even have enough money to fly home.'

As I'm speaking, my eyes suddenly focus on Clint Eastwood. Okay, it isn't really Clint Eastwood, but the likeness is uncanny. He has rugged features, strong forearms, large hands and an expression that says 'Make my day'. He's playing backgammon with an Arab and drinking beer in a tall glass. He's probably a truck driver or an undercover cop.

'That one,' I say. 'The one who looks like Dirty Harry. I

want him.'

My companion looks over at the man in question. After a few seconds, he says, 'He's wearing cowboy boots. He certainly doesn't have much fashion sense.'

All the better. 'I don't care. I want him.'

'He's probably from East Germany,' he says.

'I like his face.'

'He does have an interesting face,' the man admits. 'It has character.'

'He's gorgeous. I have to find a way to meet him.'

'If you keep staring at him like that, he's sure to notice.'

'Then I'll have to keep staring at him,' I say.

'I wish you'd stare at me like that.'

We continue drinking beer and I continue to stare. I watch as my new dream man takes out a pouch of tobacco and rolls a perfectly shaped cigarette. After a few minutes, he looks up and sees me watching him. After he takes a drag of his cigarette and slowly blows out the smoke, I notice the hint of a smile.

'I have to get closer,' I say. I'm drinking at least my fourth Guinness of the night, not to mention the margaritas, and am feeling bold. 'There are some Americans at that table next to them. Let's go over there.'

'You go ahead,' the man says. 'I don't like Americans.'

The Americans are friendly enough, all in their late twenties and working for Adidas. Since we're all intoxicated, it doesn't really matter that we have nothing to talk about. Every remark seems funny and we do a lot of laughing.

Just as I'm getting another beer, I see Dirty Harry close the backgammon set and look up at me. He raises his glass in a toast. It's now or never.

I don't really know how I got there, but suddenly I'm sitting next to him. He signals a waitress and within minutes, two tall glasses appear before us.

'Hefeweizen,' he says, pointing to the beer.

We clink our glasses together and I bring mine to my

lips. I've never tasted such a mild and refreshing beer.

'Es ist gut,' I say. *It's good.*

Apparently I've said the right thing because he leans over—he has to lean over because he is much taller than me—and kisses my lips.

'Es ist sehr gut,' I say, hoping he'll kiss me again. *It's very good.*

He does kiss me again and it lasts a bit longer this time. The feel of his lips on mine sends a pleasant jolt through my body.

'I'm a taxi driver,' he says in German, 'from Transylvania'.

Dracula! 'That's perfect,' I say, meaning it.

'Will you marry me?' he asks. 'Will you grow old with me?'

I wonder if he still would have asked me if he knew I was unemployed with twelve thousand dollars in credit card debts, and somehow I think he would have.

Because I'm pleasantly inebriated, because he resembles my all-time favorite actor, because he definitely doesn't own a designer tie, because he probably thinks Armani is a type of race car, because he drinks the best beer I've ever tasted, because he's not married—otherwise he wouldn't have proposed, would he?—and because he's nothing that Vladimir is and everything Vladimir isn't, I say in the best German I can manage, 'Yes, I'll marry you.'

And I mean it.

Katherine Kelly-Bruss

AFTERWARD

The story you have just read is based on my actual experiences. Since real life is rarely as exciting as our own fantasies, however, I did embellish and even invent enough scenes to classify my work as fiction. From 1995 – 1998, I was indeed employed by two major European companies in the high voltage equipment industry and actually travelled to all of the locations described in my book. Most of the characters are based on real people and I portrayed them almost exactly as I experienced them, or at least as I remember them. Whether those who are still alive will ever read this book and how they would react to it, I do not know. In any case, I would like to thank them for accompanying me on my Russian adventures, which became the subject of this book.

I would also like to thank my father for his helpful and honest criticism as he carefully edited my entire work and also my mother for her insightful and valuable advice. I also want to thank Rich and Jess for ensuring that I got the engineering details right. I hope that I did not disappoint them. And a special thanks to Katharina Hubner for her beautiful photography and her ability to make me look young again.

'Taxi to Siberia' is a humorous portrayal of a unique time period in both Russia's history and in my own life. I have not been back to Russia since my last business trip in 1998. I do not know what became of the various people I encountered or even if they are still living. But if they ever come across my writings, I hope they will have a good laugh or at least forgive me.

Photoshoot for cover design, June, 2015

57981974R00226

Made in the USA
Charleston, SC
28 June 2016